ALSO BY LAURIE FRANKEL

The Atlas of Love
Goodbye for Now
This Is How It Always Is
One Two Three

FAMILY
FAMILY

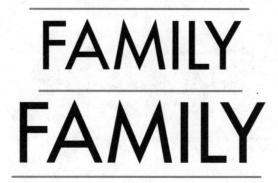

FAMILY
FAMILY

A Novel

LAURIE FRANKEL

 HENRY HOLT AND COMPANY   NEW YORK

Henry Holt and Company
Publishers since 1866
120 Broadway
New York, New York 10271
www.henryholt.com

Henry Holt® and ⒽÒ° are registered trademarks of Macmillan Publishing Group, LLC.

Distributed in Canada by Raincoast Book Distribution Limited

Library of Congress Cataloging-in-Publication Data

Names: Frankel, Laurie, author.
Title: Family family : a novel / Laurie Frankel.
Description: First edition. | New York : Henry Holt and Company, 2024.
Identifiers: LCCN 2023017078 (print) | LCCN 2023017079 (ebook) |
    ISBN 9781250236807 (hardcover) | ISBN 9781250236814 (ebook)
Subjects: LCSH: Actresses—Fiction. | Adoption—Fiction. | Family secrets—
    Fiction. | LCGFT: Novels.
Classification: LCC PS3606.R389 F36 2024 (print) | LCC PS3606.R389
    (ebook) | DDC 813/.6—dc23/eng/20230414
LC record available at https://lccn.loc.gov/2023017078
LC ebook record available at https://lccn.loc.gov/2023017079

Our books may be purchased in bulk for promotional, educational, or business use. Please
contact your local bookseller or the Macmillan Corporate and Premium Sales Department at
(800) 221-7945, extension 5442, or by e-mail at MacmillanSpecialMarkets@macmillan.com.

First Edition 2024

Designed by Steven Seighman

Printed in the United States of America

1   3   5   7   9   10   8   6   4   2

For my daughter,
her birth mother,
her foster mother,
and every other member of an adoptive family
all over the whole entire damn wide world.
We are multitudes.

"Happy are they that hear their detractions and can put them to mending."

—Benedick, *Much Ado About Nothing*

FAMILY
FAMILY

MONDAY

It all started the way *it all* started. There was a tiny matter. And then it exploded.

Fig had gotten an A on her Big Bang diorama, so even though her fifth-grade science unit had been vague on a lot of details, she knew enough to know they were in really deep trouble.

Right before what happened happened, back when they were a hot, tiny ball of dense singularity, Fig's family was just a family. Maybe people would guess that Fig and Jack left school in a limousine to eat lunch at a fancy restaurant every day and rode horses in their backyard and lived in a giant mansion, but really they went to school in a normal car and ate lunch in the cafeteria and lived in a regular-sized house.

Fig had never ridden a horse.

Fig's mother was famous, but she wasn't horses-in-your-backyard famous. And Fig and Jack didn't go to summer camp. Fig's therapist made her keep a list of things that scared her, and it included roasting marshmallows over a campfire, singing songs around a campfire, and scooting close to a campfire to avoid mosquitoes. Since most camp activities seemed to involve fire, Fig had nowhere to learn to ride a horse.

It was strange, given what had happened to them and given that they were twins, that Jack didn't mind fire. He also didn't mind other things people might not like about camp, like never taking a shower and whatever bug juice was. But Fig knew Jack wasn't sad about not going to camp and staying home with her instead. She and her brother didn't always like each other, but they did always like to be together rather than apart.

Being apart was on both of their lists of scary things.

Scientists—or at least Fig's science teacher—did not know what caused the Big Bang, but they did know that billions of trillions of unlikely factors had to be exactly right for it to occur. If it had been fall or winter or spring, Fig and Jack would probably have been at school. If Fig hadn't been afraid of fire, they would probably have been at camp. If she didn't have to share a phone with her brother or even if it had been her turn or especially if Fig had been a different kind of ten-year-old, she might not have been reading the newspaper that morning. But none of those ifs came true. So conditions were unlikely, but unfortunately perfect, for their entire lives to explode.

1998

Whereas for Fig's mother it all began, quite a bit after the birth of the universe, with *Guys and Dolls*.

India Allwood had been smart and well-read, even as a seven-year-old. Skipping second grade was fine when everyone else was eight or nine, but when middle school started she was only ten and a boy at her bus stop was already shaving. At least, he said he was. At school, girls she had once been friends with made fun of India's teeth and boobs, some of which were too prominent, others not prominent enough, and how she didn't have a father and her clothes and hair were both hopeless and her name was a country.

India's mother's teeth, hair, and boobs were fine, so India was hopeful that hers were merely still in progress. Her father hadn't left them, which would maybe have been embarrassing, but had in fact never been anything more than a first-names-only fling at a work conference. It's not like he took off because India's breasts weren't in yet. The right clothes maybe were cool but definitely were ugly, and she was willing to take a hit to her popularity to avoid a crocheted sweater vest every time.

But her name was her mother's fault, and India held it against her.

To make India feel better, her mother bought tickets for them to see *Guys and Dolls*. India's mother was named after the female lead, Sergeant Sarah Brown. The "Sergeant" part made the character sound like a badass, but she was actually a missionary with the world's most boring name. India's mother's point was that *she* had gone the creative route and ensured no daughter of hers would get stuck with a boring name, and India should be grateful. This was not the point India took, however. She started crying when the curtain went up and cried straight through until it came back down again.

"You're more congested than Miss Adelaide," her mother observed on the way home. Miss Adelaide had a song in act one where she argued that her cold was caused by her boyfriend's unwillingness to marry her.

"That was amazing!" ten-year-old India gushed. "So so soooo amazing."

"That your grandparents could have named me Adelaide—interesting!— but instead went with boring old Sarah?"

"That's what I'm going to do when I grow up," India said. "That's the only thing I want to do."

"Run a gambling ring?"

"Be onstage."

"Gambling's more lucrative," her mother warned. "And has better odds."

"I have seen the future."

"If that's what you want—" her mother began.

"Not what I want," India corrected. "When you see the future, it's not what you want to happen. It's what will happen. I am going to be a Broadway star. For sure."

"Then you should thank me." It hadn't been her mother's point, but she took it. "India Allwood is a great stage name. It's a name people will remember."

She had no idea.

MONDAY

"By the time we're adults," Fig was sorry to report from behind the unfortunate newspaper, "it's going to be like eleven white guys with all the money."

"*I'm* a guy!" Jack cheered. "I'm not white but—"

"All the natural resources will be gone. No rain forests. No trees. No clean water. Wildfires."

"This is why I said no to the paper." Their mother reached over and plucked it from her hands.

"Censorship!" Fig shrieked.

"The news is too old for you."

"I'll be circumcised."

"Circumspect. And still no."

"Just the Arts section?" Fig grabbed it from the bottom of the pile on the kitchen table without waiting for an answer. Then she read the very top headline. Then she folded up the whole section and sat on it.

"What are you doing?" Jack said out of the side of his mouth.

"Hiding the newspaper from Mom," Fig said out of the side of hers.

"I don't think it's working," Jack whispered.

Their mother stood in front of Fig with her hand out. "Give it."

"No."

"Why not?"

"I wasn't circumcised enough."

"Don't worry about it," their mother said.

Fig broke the news to Jack. "AHAM hated Mom's movie."

"A ham hated your movie?"

Fig knew a sentence teachers often began about her brother but never finished was *Jack is not unintelligent but.*

"Not a ham," she said. "AHAM. Adoptee Healing and Mediation."

Their mom's new movie was called *Flower Child.* It was about a woman who got pregnant when she was a teenager and had to give her baby up for adoption. Their mom's role was the woman twenty years later. She was still really sad about it. The baby wasn't a baby anymore, but she was also really sad about it. This caused them both to do a lot of drugs. The article said AHAM said, on various social medias Fig and Jack were not allowed to look at, that the movie was inaccurate and offensive and they hated it.

"That's mean," said Jack.

"They're angry," Mom said. "It's okay to be angry."

"They're most mad about the ending." Fig read the rest of the article. "They didn't like the big coincidence where the characters go to the same drug rehab program and get cured and live happily ever after."

"I liked the ending," Jack said. They had been to a special screening for families and VIPs a month earlier. There had been one of those hot fudge volcano machines.

"Me too," said Fig. "They figured out they were mom and baby. They got off drugs and found health and happiness together instead."

"That's the problem," their mom said.

"They overcame their problems."

"Not their problem. AHAM's problem. They wish the characters in the movie hadn't gotten over their trauma and anger so easily."

"They wanted more trauma and anger?"

"They wanted us to acknowledge that some people have good reasons to be angry. Remember how my character didn't want to place the baby for adoption, but that doctor made her? Remember how the family the baby grew up with wasn't very nice to her?"

Fig nodded. It was a sad movie.

"Real people would probably have a tough time finding their happy ending from there. AHAM wanted us to show that trauma like that is hard to move past."

"Why didn't you?" Jack said.

"One"—their mother started counting off on her fingers—"I didn't write it. Two, I didn't direct it. Three, movies are short."

"So is Fig," said Jack.

"Sometimes I wish I had an identical twin," said Fig, "instead of an infernal one."

"Fraternal," said her mother.

"I was doing wordplay."

"You only get about one hundred twenty minutes for a movie," their mother said. "Sometimes you spend too many on the juicy bits, and then there isn't enough time to fully explore the nuances of getting over them."

"So they're right?" said Fig.

"Not right. Not wrong. Mad and sad. That's okay. Sometimes people are mad and sad."

"What do we do?"

"Let them have their say, express their concerns. Listen. Learn something if possible."

"They're using capital letters." Jack was looking at the social medias, even though they weren't allowed. "That means yelling."

But their mother wasn't worried. "Ignore them and they'll go away."

That was when the tiny matter started drawing together and heating up.

It had been a long time since Fig's mother had taken fifth-grade science, though, so that was probably why she didn't notice.

2001

ndia actually worked it out during geometry her first month of high school. Seven hours a day, five days a week, four weeks a month, nine months a year for four years worked out to 5,040 hours of high school. Think of all the other things she could do with that time.

She was pleased with herself for this calculation—not the calculation itself, which was just multiplication and anyway she did it on a calculator—but for thinking to do it like that, all big and epic and sweeping in scope. Unfortunately she made the mistake of presenting it to her mother at work. This was her own fault because she knew better. At home, her mother was sometimes relaxed and laid-back and wearing sweatpants and weary of legal logic. At work was another matter entirely.

Every day after school, India walked to her mother's office because it was too far to walk home, and she was obviously not going to stay after school and do sports. Because the school year coincided with the rainy season in Seattle, because Seattleites did not believe in umbrellas despite having a nine-month rainy season, she usually arrived damp and dripping. But her mom did important lawyer work for immigrants, which meant India could not be cranky about the long, wet hours she had to wait for her and which also meant she spent a lot of time in the break room eating the snacks that were always around and revising essays and solving geometry proofs and making study cards.

Except for the snacks, this was a waste of time.

"Five thousand forty," she walked into her mother's office and announced without even saying hello first. In the elevator on the way up she'd taken all her books out of her backpack so she could drop them with a dramatic thud to the floor.

Her mother swiveled her swivel chair toward her but did not turn her eyes from her computer screen. "Five thousand forty what?"

"Hours of high school." India bent to gather up her books.

"Till what?" Her mother still wasn't looking at her.

"Not till anything. Total."

Not because she was compelled by what her daughter was saying, but only because her daughter was not making sense, her mother finally turned first her body then her face then her eyes to India. "What are you talking about, darling?"

"High school is five thousand forty hours," India said. "Think of all I could do with those hours if I didn't have to go."

Her mother took off her glasses. "What could you do with those hours, India?"

Another rookie mistake, thinking she was building an argument for her mother when what was really happening was her mother was dismantling hers.

"I could see the world. Instead of taking French, I could move to Paris, get a job in a café, learn to make pâtisserie, take a train to Saint-Tropez and sunbathe topless."

"If your argument is that you don't need to go to high school to learn how to show your tits to a beach full of tourists"—her mother put her glasses back on—"so granted."

India was undeterred. "Or it doesn't have to be France. Think how much more I would learn about ancient Greece actually *in* ancient Greece instead of in history."

"Long plane ride to ancient Greece," her mother said to her computer screen.

"You know what I mean. Greece was the birthplace of theater, so obviously I have to go there. Plus, I could do geometry at the actual pyramids instead of ones on graph paper. I could meet real people instead of high school students. I could learn life skills instead of all this crap which I am never going to use in the real world and you know it."

Her mother turned back toward her, removed her glasses again, leaned the seat of her swivel chair backward, and propped her high-heeled feet on her desk. "Let us examine the skills you'd require to move to Cairo."

"Cairo?" India said.

"You'd need some geography to help you determine where the pyramids are. Egypt is not in ancient or even present-day Greece. And Egypt is a big country. The pyramids I assume you reference are at Giza in the desert outside of Cairo, yes?"

"Yes?" India guessed.

"You'd do well to know some Arabic."

"Arabic?"

"The official language in Egypt."

"What about Egyptian?"

"Not a language," her mother said. "It would be good to have some history. Do you know any Egyptian history?"

India had been to a seder one Passover at her friend Mark's house, but that was about it.

"Or modern Middle Eastern history? Or current Middle Eastern politics?" her mother mused.

"But high school's not teaching me any of that," India cut in. "But high school's taking up valuable brain space I could be using for all those things you just said."

One of her mother's life theories was any argument had to have two buts. One objection wasn't going to convince anyone. If you were going to change your mind or someone else's, you had to have at least two, and they both had to be rebuttal-proof.

Which these two, apparently, were not. "High school teaches you skills you will later apply to, to take your example, living abroad. Critical evaluation of texts, analysis of cultural bias, negotiation of challenge, synthesis of diverse skills and knowledge sets, to name but a few."

"I'm not learning that in high school either," India said.

"Give it five thousand forty hours," said her mother.

"You don't need a high school education to become an actress." India wasn't sure if you were supposed to say "actor" instead of "actress" because of feminism, but she guessed feminism's point was something like she could do anything she believed she could, and she believed she could—in fact, had to—become whichever term she was supposed to use. "You have to learn about the world by living in it. You have to learn about other people and their lives by overlapping yours with theirs. You have to learn about the entire universe so you can convincingly portray some small corner of it on the stage."

"'The universe' seems ambitious," her mother said. "And if you don't go to high school, how will you go to college?"

"I'm not going to college," India reasoned. "I'm going to be an actor."

Her mother swiveled to her bookcase and pulled out a book that proved, when India received it, to be called *The Oresteia*, however you were supposed to pronounce that. "Are you planning to understand Aeschylus by overlapping your life with his?"

"Um. No?"

"What will you do if your agent calls to offer you Clytemnestra, and you have to decline because you don't understand the plays?"

"Will they teach me *The Oresteia* in college?" India asked.

"If you pick the right one," her mother said. "But you have to get accepted. But the best programs are naturally the most competitive and will require an excellent high school performance record."

India's guidance counselor said she was only a freshman, and it was too early to start picking colleges. He said it was premature to have settled on a major. He said she didn't need to be worrying about any of this yet and should focus instead on having fun, trying new things, and making friends. He said to come back and see him in two years.

So India had to figure out about college on her own. She only looked at schools with top-ranked theater programs. She only looked at schools with top-ranked theater programs in New York City because that's where Broadway was. She wrote each school down on its own index card. On the back she wrote down what you needed to do to get in. Then she set about getting grades to match her cards.

She bought more index cards and used them to make flash cards for French vocabulary. She used them to make study cards for history. She used them to arrange facts for her research papers. India ran the numbers on her index-card habit and concluded it would take at least two hundred dollars' worth to get into the college of her dreams.

Her guidance counselor was wrong. She did not need friends or fun or new experiences. She did not need a love life, sexual experimentation, popularity, or memories to last a lifetime. All she needed were good grades and index cards.

She proved herself right about that for three whole years.

Then she found out she was completely, exactly, entirely wrong.

MONDAY

Fig's therapist had named herself Mandela. She said it was not polite to ask what her name used to be or why she changed it, but she was big on the renaming part. For instance, she wanted Fig to rename all the items on her things-that-are-scary list so that she could make them her own.

"I don't want them to be my own," Fig said.

"You do," Mandela explained, "because if they're yours, then you're in charge."

Items that appeared on everyone's list, they had to own and rename as a family. The first one Fig and Jack and their mother did all together was Mean and Terrible People on the Internet. The problem was, that was a lot of people to own and rename.

"PEOPLE WHO YELL IN ALL CAPS," Jack demonstrated.

Fig took her hands off her ears to add, "Name-callers. Threateners. Mean-ies. Liars."

"People with an inadequate hold on rules of punctuation, laws of grammar, and the advisability of proofreading," her mother threw in.

"Those people aren't scary," said Jack.

"It is terrifying," their mother shuddered, "how people use apostrophes in this world."

"Racists, sexists, bigots, fishmongers," said Fig.

"Fearmongers," said her mother. "And the fear part is implied. That's why they're going on the list. Don't give them any more power. They're not powerful. They're dweebs. Dweebs on the web."

Therefore, an hour after their mother declared that ignoring AHAM would make the problem go away, Fig and Jack already owned the name for why it hadn't.

"The dwebs didn't go anywhere," Jack told Mom when she came downstairs from her shower.

"They might have," she said. "They might be different dwebs, and you didn't even notice."

"You're a hashtag," he said.

"*You're* a hashtag."

"Do you even know what a hashtag is?"

"I'm not eighty."

"Why would I be a hashtag then?"

"I thought we were just teasing each other."

"Why would 'You're a hashtag' be a good burn?"

"I don't know, Jack." Their mother was cranky before her second cup of coffee. "Who cares?"

"You do."

"I don't."

"You should because you're a hashtag, and ignoring the dwebs didn't make them go away."

"What now?"

"They say you're vacationing in their pain," Jack reported.

"It's been forever since we've been on vacation." Fig was not complaining. She preferred to stay home. At home, you didn't have to rename anything to own it because everything was already yours. At home, nothing was ever on fire. She didn't like vacations, but she did want to change the subject.

It didn't work, though, because Jack kept reading from their phone. "They're saying their trauma is not for you to exploit and make money off."

"I'm not exploiting anything," their mom said.

"They're saying boycott."

"Boycott what?"

"You. The movie. *Val Halla.*"

"*Val Halla* doesn't have anything to do with the movie."

"Can I tell them?" Jack's finger was hovering over the phone, ready for action.

But their mother took it out of his hands and threw it in the kitchen drawer with the rubber bands and the paper clips and the probably-but-not-definitely-dead batteries. "Let's go for a swim."

Their phone stayed in the drawer, but their mom's came outside with them and rang and rang and *ping*ed and *ping*ed. She ignored it though until Ajax called because when your agent calls you have to answer.

"You're trending" was what he said instead of hello, "and not in a good way." Ajax claimed he didn't yell, but he must. Otherwise how could Fig always hear him through the phone?

"So I'm told," her mother said.

"People—not just the AHAM people, other people—say you're being canceled."

"'Canceled' doesn't mean literally," Fig's mother informed him. "And a TV show can't be 'canceled' by 'people' anyway." An example of how good an actor Fig's mother was, was you could tell when she was making finger quotes around a word even if you were on the phone with her and couldn't see her fingers.

"Jesus, potatoes, and gravy!" Ajax liked to yell in threes. "I know what 'canceled' means."

"I'm not arguing with the dwebs, Ajax. The dwebs cannot be argued with."

"What in holy hell is a dweb?"

"Dweeb on the web," Fig's mother reminded him, or maybe reminded herself that "dweb" was a term no one used—or needed—but them. "AHAM has a fair point, but the people calling me names, threatening me, deriding my kids, saying I can't act or I'm too ugly for the big screen or no wonder I'm single? Let's not pretend this is reasonable discourse."

Aha, Fig thought. So she *had* been reading around online. She'd just been playing dumb with Jack before. She was trying to protect them. Which was worrisome, since it meant there was something they needed protecting from.

"I think you should let me issue an apology on your behalf." Ajax was loud even when he was trying to compromise.

"I can issue my own damn apology, Ajax."

"Then I think you should issue your own damn apology."

"To whom?"

"Anyone offended."

"That'll make them more offended."

"Maybe, but less righteous."

"Wanna bet?"

"Less right, then. They'll still be mad, but once you've apologized, their anger comes off as petty. You've said sorry—what else do they want? You've moved on—why haven't they?"

"Apologize for what? They're mad we told this story, and they're mad we don't tell this story often enough. They're mad I'm acting too traumatized when I don't know their trauma, and they're mad I'm not acting traumatized enough. You can't apologize for one thing and its opposite too."

"Doesn't matter what you're sorry for, just that you're generally sorry."

"I can't say, 'To anyone I might have offended, I am generally sorry.'"

"Why not?"

"Among other things, I'm not."

"Good news," said Ajax. "You don't have to be. You're an actor."

She hung up, and her lips sucked into her mouth, and her eyebrows crawled together to the top of her nose. When she made that face around Ajax, he said, "Knock that off unless you want to start playing grandmothers." Fig was thinking if threatening old-lady roles herself would help. She was thinking about asking her mother what she was lying to protect them from. She was thinking of offering her good ways to say sorry even though she wasn't (maybe her mom didn't have a lot of practice because she was an adult, but kids—especially ones with twin brothers—had to apologize without meaning it sometimes several times a day). But before Fig could decide, her mother shook her head and put her eyebrows back where they belonged and cannonballed into the deep end.

The phone rang again before the ripples even stopped rippling. She put it on speaker so she didn't have to get out of the pool. "What now?"

"India Allwood?" said the voice on the other end.

"Ajax?"

"No, this is Evelyn Esponson from *ME*."

"From you?"

"Not from me. From *ME*."

"You're just saying the same word twice," Fig's mother advised.

"*ME. Media Entertainment.* We're a synergistic conglomerate of old and new media including—"

"*Media Entertainment?*" Fig's mother said slowly so that, Fig knew, Evelyn Esponson could hear for herself how ridiculous she sounded.

"We're a—"

"Please don't say 'synergistic' again. *Media Entertainment* doesn't mean anything. Even less meaning is conveyed by that name than by your unnecessarily confusing, if probably apt, acronym."

"As long as I have you on the phone—"

"I'm sorry," their mom interrupted again. "I didn't really mean to answer. I thought you were my agent."

"But since we're talking—"

"No comment."

"I haven't even asked a question yet," Evelyn Esponson laughed. And maybe that was why. Fig's mother was in the pool with *ME* giggling on speakerphone. Maybe that made Evelyn Esponson seem sort of like a friend.

"True," Mom admitted. "What did you want to ask?"

"Well, I was going to ask for a comment about the criticism being directed at you—the calls for a boycott, the online furor you find yourself swept up in at the moment—but you've already made your position on comments clear."

"That's right," Mom said. "Thank you for calling."

She was reaching for a towel so she didn't get her phone wet when she disconnected, but Evelyn Esponson kept talking. "I wonder though if you have anything you want to say to AHAM or any of the other groups and individuals registering their concerns about your latest project?"

Maybe she was caught off guard or maybe she liked Evelyn Esponson's laugh or maybe she was listening to Ajax for once or maybe she was just wet because what she answered was "I'm sorry."

"You are?" said Evelyn Esponson.

"Yes."

"You're issuing an apology?"

"I'm not sorry *to* them." Fig's mother shook her head sideways to make water come out of her ear. "More like I'm sorry *for* them."

"You feel sorry for them?" said Evelyn Esponson.

Fig and Jack were very still in the pool.

"They've clearly had a tough time of it. They have sadness and anger and good reason for both, and I'm sorry that they do. I acknowledge their pain and wish they didn't have it. That's it."

"That's your statement?" said Evelyn Esponson. "Nothing to add?"

"Nope," their mother said cheerfully. Then she hung up.

Fig didn't know what happened at the exact moment of the Big Bang because no one did. But one trillionth of a trillionth of a trillionth of a second after it started, the small matter blew up faster than the speed of light and inflated and expanded and got hot gas all over everything.

This was a lot like that.

2004

"I *am* sorry." The drama teacher, Ms. LaRue, picked one often unlikely word to emphasize in most of her sentences. India thought it was weird and kind of pretentious, but of her objections to the woman, this was the least of them. "You cannot *sing*, my dear."

India could index-card her way out of the hardest tests, the longest essays, the most boring exercises. But there was nothing she could do about high school's biggest nightmare: the musical.

Every semester, India tried out for the musical, and every semester she did not get cast. She understood this was because she couldn't sing, a fact about which she had no illusions. But she was a good dancer and a great actor. She was a great actor who was going to be an extraordinary actor, the actor of her generation, and how could she be expected to take Broadway by storm if she couldn't even get a part in her high school show?

This was the question she put to Ms. LaRue.

"You cannot *sing*," Ms. LaRue reiterated, then added, "and I cannot *teach* you."

"Isn't that your job?" India did not say this to be rude. She was genuinely asking.

"Singing is not like algebra or *basketballs*." Ms. LaRue did not seem offended. Just certain. "If you cannot do it, you cannot learn."

"But I'm a good actor," said India.

"Then audition for a *play*," said Ms. LaRue.

"But the drama department doesn't do plays," said India. "Only musicals."

"I am in *thrall* to audience demands." Ms. LaRue brought her fingers to her lips and drew deeply on an imaginary cigarette. "No one ever went wrong by giving the people what they want."

India was pretty sure that wasn't true, but she wasn't learning anything useful in history so couldn't come up with any counterexamples off the top of her head.

"What if I wrote a play?" India offered. "Then we could put it on, and I could be in that."

"The problem is not lack of *plays*. The problem is lack of *people* who want to see them."

"Lots of the kids you cast in the musical can't act." India switched tack. "Or dance."

"Ahh, but you won't *notice*"—Ms. LaRue pointed her imaginary cigarette at India to emphasize her point—"because they can sing."

This year, this last year, her last chance, they were doing *Guys and Dolls*. After auditions, on her way out of the auditorium, India turned back to Ms. LaRue to add that the show was part of her lore, that seeing it was how she knew she would become a Broadway star one day, that her grandparents had been so moved they'd named their baby girl for it. Ms. LaRue had looked something you could interpret as impressed, which was why India got her hopes up that maybe this time would be different.

It was. It was life-changing. And not just for her.

She didn't want anyone to see her not seeing her name on the cast list. But even after she looked, something made her sit in the hallway outside the stage door anyway and watch everyone come up to check for theirs. She pressed her back to the wall and sat on the cold, no doubt filthy floor and hugged her knees into her chest and made herself watch as person after person came and checked and celebrated, jumped around or pumped their fist or hugged one another or hugged themselves. Was she the only student cut from this entire stupid show? Maybe. Was no one even slightly disappointed to be cast in the chorus when they'd had fingers crossed for the lead? Apparently the chorus line knew their limitations and were happy just to be involved, as India would have been. That she made herself sit there and watch was unlike her, but she did not cry. In fact, she made so little noise and was so pathetic no one noticed her.

Almost no one.

"Hi."

She looked up from her knees and the linoleum. "Hi."

"What's going on?"

She didn't know what he meant. "Nothing?"

"People keep coming back here."

"To check the cast list." She nodded at it with her chin.

"Cast list for what?" he said.

She tilted her head, but it still made no sense. "Who are you?" It was not a huge school. She didn't know everyone's name, but she recognized pretty much everyone's face, and she had definitely never seen this guy before. She would have remembered.

"Robbie." He said this like it answered her question.

"Who's Robbie?"

"I am."

"Robbie who?"

"Robbie Brighton."

She was still sitting on the floor, looking up at him, mostly heartbroken, slightly intrigued.

"New kid," he added, then pointed to the list. "So I probably didn't get a part."

"Me neither." India looked back at her knees. "And I'm an old kid."

"I can't believe you didn't get cast," said Robbie Brighton. "You were robbed."

She looked up again. "How would you know?"

"You have an expressive face," he said. "And look how you're sitting. Very emotive."

She was speechless for a moment. Then she admitted, "I can't sing."

He wrinkled his nose. "Me neither."

She waited for him to say something else, but when he didn't, she asked the obvious question. "What are you doing here?"

"Checking to see if I made the play."

She wasn't sure if he was making fun of her or of himself or had some other agenda, but she did notice she was much less upset.

"Wanna show me around instead?" Robbie reached a hand down to her, and hers reached up to his as if by reflex. He pulled her up from her seat. She'd thought maybe he just looked tall because she was on the floor, but even standing, she had to tip her head back to see him. Like clouds.

"Instead of what?" she managed.

"Instead of being in their stupid show."

She wanted to do both, but one was nice too, maybe. Up close, his hair was five or six different colors at once and pointing in as many directions. His mouth was how she came to understand what books meant when they described someone's smile as lopsided.

She started the tour with the theater since they were standing right outside it, opened the door and peeked inside at all the closed-up seats in the auditorium, the empty stage with its lone piano on its casters, the gently raked floor. It was quiet in there after three days of (bad) dancing and (good) (well, loud, at least) singing and teenage nerves, drama, and heartbreak. Hushed is what it was.

"It's amazing, isn't it?" she whispered.

"Absolutely," he whispered back. "How so?"

"All the magic these seats have seen. The stage longing for stories to tell. That piano holding its breath. Lights awaiting their cues. Dressing rooms awaiting their actors. It's like a fairy tale."

"I give it a C-plus," said Robbie Brighton.

Her eyes whipped from the auditorium before her to the boy at her side. This was gospel in her mind. Waxing romantic about it was de rigueur.

"They don't want us in their dumb play?" he said. "Who needs 'em."

"Who are you?" India asked again.

He'd arrived in town a few hours before, decided to bike over to take a look. "Get a feel for the place," he said.

"What does it feel like?"

"Feels like a high school."

He didn't have a schedule yet because the guidance counselors and teachers who might have helped him were gone for the day, so she couldn't show him where his classes were. They looked at the cafeteria. At the senior lockers and the gym. At the front office, where he'd start his day tomorrow. At some of India's classrooms, because maybe their schedules would overlap. A girl could hope.

"Do you want to see the track or the football field or anything?"

Robbie Brighton wrinkled his nose again. "I'm a Zen hen."

"A Zen hen?"

"I'm a lover, not a fighter."

* * *

He wasn't in her morning classes, and she sat through French, history, and calculus thinking that the hour they'd spent poking their heads in and out of empty classrooms (plus the sixteen she'd spent replaying it) was all she'd ever get. But when she went to her locker after calc to get her lunch, he was leaning against it waiting for her.

"There you are! I've been looking everywhere for you." He looked happy to see her. Maybe he was just relieved because she was the only person he knew, but she'd heard the hallway buzz all morning. He'd have his pick of tables in the cafeteria.

"Where have you been looking?" she asked.

"PE, psych, Spanish."

"I take French," she admitted.

"Ah, oui, je already parlay perfecta Frencha, so I do not need to étude it."

"I can see that."

"Why French?"

She swapped some books for some other books, retrieved her lunch, and headed for the cafeteria. He fell companionably in alongside her, as if they'd done this every day for years.

"It's dramatic," she explained. "And I might live in Paris."

"Ooh la la, I love Par-ee."

"You've been to Paris?"

"No. But I like that pointy thing."

"The Eiffel Tower?"

"That's the one."

It wasn't like a movie. It wasn't like they opened the door to the cafeteria and everyone stopped talking and froze with their sandwiches halfway to their mouths and stared at them. But she could see a dozen hands rise to cover the whispers of a dozen mouths. She could feel everyone wondering how the hell she'd pulled off being the one who won the new kid. She knew how they felt. She was also wondering how the hell she'd pulled off being the one who won the new kid.

"How do you feel about outside?" she asked.

"I love the outside," he said.

"To eat."

"Ah oui, alfresco."

"I think that's Italian."

"Ciao, bella."

It was raining, even though it was only September and the rain should have held off for a few more weeks at least, but the one eaves-covered table was blessedly empty.

"Turkey with ketchup." He peeled open his sandwich to show her. "I was feeling saucy when I made it this morning."

"Cheese with Dijon," she confessed. "I was feeling French."

"Should we meld?" he said, and she had no idea what he meant but it seemed like a great idea.

"Probably?"

He unfolded his napkin on the table, laid bare her sandwich then his, put half of each half of his on half of each half of hers, pressed them neatly back together, and held her reassembled sandwich back out to her.

"Thanks?" She did not believe ketchup belonged on a sandwich. She couldn't remember if she'd ever seen a guy pack a napkin. She imagined she could taste his fingers when she took her first bite.

"I'm an excellent cook," he said. "Just wait till I make you dinner."

So he wouldn't see her flush at that prospect, she demanded to look at his schedule, and, as if there hadn't been miracles enough already, there turned out to be more. "After lunch we have chemistry together!"

"During lunch too," he said.

"And then English after that." She couldn't stop smiling. "It's kind of boring, though. We're reading *Grapes of Wrath*."

"We'll be interesting enough on our own." He was undeterred. "We'll be way more entertaining than Ernest Hemingway."

"Steinbeck," she said.

"We'll be way more entertaining than Ernest Steinbeck."

She had his dad to thank. He was a music teacher. India thought "music teacher" like the vocal coach whose house her mother had paid for her to go to twice a week after she'd failed to make the musical her freshman year. The coach had breathed weird and made India breathe weird, but she had not really improved her singing, so maybe Ms. LaRue had been right about that. Robbie's dad was a musicology professor, though, something it was apparently harder to convince anyone to pay you for, at least for more than a semester at a time. "Visiting artist" sounded like a cool gig to India, but this was Robbie's fourth high school, and she could see how that would be hard if you were like Robbie. If he'd stayed in one place, he would be the most popular kid in school, president of the student government, captain of the sports, prom king, whatever. So India gave silent thanks for the mercurial nature of the gods of visiting professorships.

"Want to know the biggest difference between high schools?"

She'd have guessed the required courses, the individual teachers, which sport was the important one, size of the student body maybe.

"Dating," he said.

Whereas that seemed like it would be the same anywhere.

"Some places there is no dating, and everyone just goes out in a big group. Some places there's no dating because there's no place to go, and everyone just, like, makes out in someone's basement. Some places it doesn't even count as a date unless you drive there. Like the whole point is the part in the car."

"I don't have a car," said India.

"I was thinking about karaoke."

"When?"

"Just now. For our first date."

She waited a beat so she would sound as nonchalant as possible when she checked to make sure. "We're going on a date?"

"We are."

"But we can't sing." It was the first thing they'd learned about each other.

"Even the tone-deaf deserve love," he said.

India's knees and hands and everything were shaking, possibly because she was going to have to sing but also possibly because sitting next to Robbie in English was different from sitting next to Robbie on a date. The karaoke bar specialized in surprisingly good egg rolls and very bright drinks. She thought the latter might help her, but the first thing their server did was point at each of them and pronounce, "Underage. Underage," so she would have to sing sober.

When their turn came, Robbie picked a duet—"I Got You Babe," which had to be the easiest duet in the world, but India was still terrified. They got up onstage, hot and giggling and full of egg rolls, unable to hold hands (because the microphones somehow required both of them) but bumping together more often than apart.

The music began.

Robbie winked at her. "You start."

"*They say we're young and we don't know / We won't find out unti-i-i-l we grow*," she warbled. And he cracked up while she did. And it seemed so perfect—they *were* so young; they *didn't* know—and so funny that she almost, *almost* didn't want to die from being such a terrible singer in public.

Then he turned toward her and looked into her eyes and sang, "*Well, I don't know if all that's true / 'Cause you got me and, baby, I got you*," which would have been romantic if he hadn't done so in the most crystalline, sonorous, pitch-perfect voice she'd ever heard.

He went on to the chorus.

She swatted at his arm with her microphone, which screeched with feedback.

"Hey," he sang instead of "Babe."

"You said you were a terrible singer."

"I'm a great singer," he admitted, while the music played and the words scrolled by on-screen.

"So I hear."

"I just wanted to make you feel better. Did it work?"

"Briefly."

"I like singing with you," he said.

"Of course you do. It makes you look good."

"It makes me sound good," he allowed. "You're a terrible singer—"

"Hey!" she echoed.

"But you *look* great."

"If you're not going to sing, get off the stage!" People started yelling and throwing egg rolls. Which was a real waste of egg rolls.

"They're screaming for an encore," Robbie said.

"Always leave 'em wanting," said India.

They fled the bar, out into the night where the rain felt good on their hot faces, and they could not stop laughing. Then they headed toward home. He reached over and took her hand as they walked, like it was something he'd done a thousand times before.

"You were right," she said.

"Always," he agreed. Then, "About what?"

"They should have cast you in the show. You got robbed."

The following week they finished *The Grapes of Wrath*, and the next unit was *The Merchant of Venice*. Everyone had to memorize a passage and perform it in front of the class, and everyone complained about it, and everyone picked a Shylock speech, the same Shylock speech. Maybe if they'd each been assigned a different speech, the performances might have been interesting to watch, but since they all picked the same one, it was repetitive. And though India appreciated her classmates' arguments that they were never going to use memorizing-a-Shakespeare-speech nor sitting-through-the-same-Shakespeare-speech-twenty-five-times in the real world, the same, India hoped, could not be said for her.

She picked the Portia speech instead, the one where Portia's a lawyer and lecturing everyone about justice versus mercy. It was the sort of speech her mother would give, so she gave it like her mother, leaning back in a chair (she had to sub school chair for swivel) with her feet up on the desk (she had to sub sneakers for heels), using her glasses (she had to sub sun for reading) for punctuation, patient but pointedly patient like if people (she subbed her classmates for her mother's daughter) tried just a little bit harder, she wouldn't require such forbearance. At the end of the speech, no one said a word. Then everyone burst into applause.

"You're a really good actor," Robbie said. They were walking to a park to go for a walk, which India felt was the sort of absurdity that happened to teenagers when their parents wouldn't buy them a car.

"Thanks," she said.

"No." He stopped so she stopped. They were under a tree. He put his hands on her shoulders, turned her to him. "You're a really, really good actor."

She smiled, but she was puzzled, a little annoyed even. "You sound surprised."

"Well, karaoke . . ." He grinned, and she pushed him away, and he bounced right back.

"Singing has nothing to do with acting!" she said.

"That's not what I meant, actually. I thought you were good at acting like I was good at karaoke. But you're not."

She looked at him harder.

"You're good at acting like the karaoke bar is good at egg rolls."

And before she could get her breath back from that, he put his hands back on her shoulders and said, "I have to ask you a question."

"Okay."

"But I'm embarrassed."

"Okay."

"But it's important."

"You're making me nervous," she said.

"I'm thinking of kissing you," he confessed.

She actually felt this sentence in her chest. With his hands on her shoulders, she wondered if he could feel the reverb. "That's not a question," she managed.

"I'm getting there, I'm getting there. Don't rush me." He smiled his lopsided smile at her. "Will you be happy if I kiss you?"

"I don't know. You've never done it before," India answered honestly. "Is that your question?"

"No, my question is *if* you let me kiss you and *if* you then claim to be happy about it, how will I know whether you're actually happy about it or just acting?"

"Why would I act happy about it if I weren't?"

"So you didn't hurt my feelings?" he guessed.

"Why would I care about your feelings if you're a shitty kisser?"

He laughed and then he stopped laughing so he could move his hands from her shoulders to the sides of her face and gently pull her lips, and then the rest of her mouth, to his. It started raining—this was romantic in the movies but just the way first kisses were in Seattle—so they pressed up closer to the trunk of the tree they were standing under, but they did not stop kissing.

India would rather have gotten wet than stopped kissing. She would rather have gotten struck by lightning. It felt a little like that anyway, her life and her plans for it lit suddenly, electric, ablaze, so you could see the whole thing but only for a second, less than a second, half of a half, not long enough to take a breath even before being plunged into mystery again, bright then dark, bright then dark, a strobe, a pulse, over and over and over. That's what it was like: Romance and poetry and a stark, mysterious beauty. Not passion and lust and urges and appetite. Not for another week, at least.

India was not willing to give up studying for sex. But she was willing to add studying to sex. Or, really, she was willing to add sex to studying. Robbie started dropping his dad at work in the mornings so he could borrow the car for the day so he and India could go back to her house after school so she could make flash cards and snacks and then they could make out in her bedroom and have sex. Her mother was saving two Honduran families and one Haitian one from deportation that fall and often didn't get home until eight at night, by which time India was back to her flash cards and Robbie long gone.

The sex was not like it is in movies either, not that aesthetically perfect or balletically coordinated. But India felt there were only two definitions of successful sex and only one at a time. If your goal was to make a baby, having sex successfully meant you got pregnant. If your goal was absolutely, positively, most importantly not to get pregnant, having sex successfully meant only that. Robbie said what about feeling good and making someone else feel good and bringing them closer together and expressing their love and trying new ways and learning stuff? She said that was all relevant but did not figure definitionally into success.

They had sex successfully most weekdays for a month and a half.

Then they had sex unsuccessfully.

MONDAY

"Hamburger, fries, and a Coke!" The next time the phone rang, not very much later, Ajax really was yelling. "What did you do?"

"What you told me to," Fig heard her mother say. "I apologized."

"Like hell you did. Before you were just trending. Now you've taken over the internet. The entire internet is interested in one thing and one thing only, and that thing is you."

"That doesn't sound right." Fig's mother made her fingers go *blah-blah-blah*. Fig and Jack clapped their hands over their mouths so Ajax wouldn't hear them laugh.

"You feel sorry for them?"

She groaned. "That's not what I said."

"You were misquoted? Please tell me you were misquoted, India."

"Misunderstood, more like. Willfully."

"Explain. It. To. Me."

"I didn't mean *sorry for them* sorry for them, like I pity those pathetic hams. I meant—in fact I think I said—'sorry for' instead of 'sorry to.'"

"India!" The roar came over the phone, then calmed itself. "Unlike everyone else on the planet at the moment, I'm on your side, and even I don't know what you mean."

"I meant—"

"I know what you meant. It doesn't matter. Apologize for real. Broadly and vaguely. And quickly. The reporter who broke the story—Evelyn Something?—is willing to do a follow-up."

"I bet."

"Let her help you."

"She's not trying to help me."

"No, but since it's also helping her, she'll do it anyway. I'm going to hang up, and the next person who calls is going to be her. Broadly and vaguely. You misspoke. You did not mean. You intended no offense. You are sorry to anyone whose feelings might have been impacted in any way. Got it?"

"Can I remind you that I don't work for you?" Fig's mother said.

"If you don't do this right, soon you're not going to work for anyone."

Fig's mother got out of the pool and dried off.

"Are you going to get fired?" Fig tried to make this sound like a joke, no big deal, not at all something to worry about, but she was not as good an actor as her mother.

"Of course not," Mom said.

"Are you going to be in trouble?"

"Not that either." Though Fig thought she didn't look as sure.

"Are you scared?"

"I am not. Are you?"

Fig nodded so her mouth and nose dipped under the water then back out again.

"What are you afraid of?" Her mother came back and sat on the side of the pool and put her legs in.

"You getting fired and in trouble and scared," Fig said.

But before there could be comforting and reassuring, Evelyn Esponson called back. Fig's mother put her on speaker again so Fig could hear for herself there was nothing to worry about. Then her mom did what Ajax told her to. She said she misspoke. She did not mean she felt sorry for the members of AHAM. She did not mean to suggest they were pitiable or pathetic or in need of her sorries. She did not mean to offend anyone she might have offended. Or anyone else for that matter. She apologized—uniformly and unhesitatingly and unreservedly.

"I don't believe you," Evelyn Esponson replied, calmly, but Fig got worried again anyway, "which is fine because I also don't happen to think you have anything to apologize for. So why don't you say what you actually mean? You certainly have everyone's attention."

"Thanks to you."

"You can't make it worse," Evelyn said.

And what Fig's mom replied was, "You know, there are some aspects of the movie that maybe could have used some . . . finer tuning."

Which was going to make it quite a bit worse.

Fig and Jack were still in the pool, but even from there, they could hear Evelyn Esponson breathe in hard on speakerphone.

"Don't get me wrong." Their mom was making funny eyes at them to reassure them everything was fine. But it was not fine. "*Flower Child* is a good movie. We faced some unusual challenges making it, and I think we did a really good job. Not everything's great. Not everything's going to win an Oscar, and that's okay. Sometimes good's enough. Sometimes that's all you can do. I loved doing this film. I worked with some really wonderful people on it. I'm proud of it."

"But?" Evelyn prompted.

"But I don't know." It wasn't too late. She could still stop there. Fig prayed she would stop there. But she did not. "I'm a little bit sick of that story."

"The movie's story?"

"All the movies' stories. Birth mom is broken by adoption. Child feels incomplete forever. Neither time nor distance nor fate can keep them apart for the mother-child bond is universal though also irreplaceable, supernatural though also super natural. Hero is plucky and resourceful because she's an orphan, or sad and alone because her adoptive family can never really under-stand her, or lost because without her 'real parents' she has no idea who she is. Or you know how many villains' origin stories are their parents were killed or they found out their nemesis is secretly a blood relation? It's just kind of . . ." She trailed off.

"What?" You could almost hear Evelyn Esponson rubbing her hands together.

"Boring. Reductive. Repetitive. AHAM is right that people don't get over a lifetime of trauma in ten minutes, but at least the trauma part gets told. What about adoption stories that aren't tragedies? Not all stories of adoption are stories of pain and regret. Not even most of them. Why don't we ever get that movie?"

"Plot? Representation?"

But Fig's mom wasn't buying it. "There are lots of ways to make a family. Suggesting yours is tragic unless everyone's blood related isn't serving anyone."

"Some might argue happy kids don't need their stories told."

"Everyone needs their stories told, and not just told. Celebrated. Everyone needs to see themselves on-screen. Among other things, that's one of the ways they get to be happy in the first place. We keep telling kids they're incomplete just because they're adopted. Maybe that's what's making them feel sad they don't belong."

"Everyone feels sad they don't belong sometimes."

"Exactly." Fig's mom sounded weirdly happy for someone agreeing everyone was sad. "So we have to do better than telling adopted kids that they're the only ones or that being adopted is the reason why."

AHAM did get quieter, but it wasn't because they felt good about the apology or the apology for the apology.

It was because they were drowned out.

2004

India thought it happened the opening night of *Guys and Dolls*.

"Let's not go," Robbie said.

"I have to."

"Why?"

"It'll look like sour grapes otherwise. It'll look like I'm being a bad sport just because I didn't get cast."

"No, it'll look like you have better things to do than go to some crappy high school musical."

"I don't."

"Let's find something."

"What?" she said. "Plus, what about being a good theatrical citizen?"

"I don't know what that means." He wrinkled his nose in that confused-amused way he had.

"It means if I want people to come see a play I'm in, I have to go see ones they're in."

"Right, but the difference is your plays are good whereas theirs are embarrassing."

"That's nice of you to say, but I'm not in any plays yet so who knows if they're good."

"Okay, fine," he said. "Let's go and laugh at everyone. We can go out to dinner first. It'll be fun."

It was not fun. The show was really good. Like, really good. The singing was indeed incredible. The dancing was as good as she could do. And honestly, even the acting was fine. They did laugh, but only at clever comic timing.

"The acting required for *Guys and Dolls* isn't real acting," he said at intermission, "not like you can do."

But in the second half, he just sat in the dark, squeezing her hand tighter and tighter. She was grateful he could feel that a tragedy was unfolding before her, but it was still a tragedy. Here was the most important thing in her life, the theater, the only opportunity she had to actually practice it, and it was really great, and all she was allowed to do was watch it go on without her.

He drove her home. It was dark in her house. Her mother had gone to bed—it was a long show—and they let themselves in quietly.

In her bedroom, he whispered, "I'm so sorry."

"No, no." She tried to pretend it was silly of him to offer condolences on the success of a show she had nothing to do with.

"That was really good," he said.

She wiped angry tears. "It was."

"But not as good as you."

Did he mean as good a performance as she would give when she got to give performances? Or did he mean her herself in her heart, in the herness of her? She didn't know. And she didn't find she cared.

Later she thought maybe watching an excellent performance of *Guys and Dolls* had torn something inside her. She thought maybe all the protective barriers had come crumbling down.

She knew the first time she threw up. She threw up and went to school, and Robbie was sitting on the wall waiting for her like always, and she saw him see her, and she saw him look really happy to see her, even though they were spending every possible minute together already, and she felt terrible because whatever happened next, it was going to ruin everything.

"I'm pregnant," she said.

She was smiling, laughing a little, but it was nerves. Or maybe hormones. But it confused him, of course. He sat grinning back at her, waiting for the punch line.

"No, really." She tried to swallow her smile. "I'm pregnant."

It took another beat. "Oh," he said finally.

"Yes." She was worried she'd cry. She was also worried she'd barf.

"I'm . . . so sorry," he settled on.

For getting her pregnant? Or for the shit that now befell them?

"Me too," she said.

He was pale. He was so pale she was worried about him. "Maybe the test was wrong?" he said. "Or expired or a dud or something?"

"I haven't done one yet," India admitted.

Hope sparked on his face. She felt terrible for lighting it. She felt terrible for leaning over and blowing it out like birthday candles. "How do you know you're pregnant then?"

"I threw up this morning."

"Maybe you have food poisoning," he said hopefully.

"I had dinner with you last night," she pointed out. "Did you throw up?"

"Maybe you have the flu." He reached out and put a cool, dry hand against her forehead. That really did make her cry. "It's only on TV that throwing up means you're pregnant."

They cut first period, went to the drugstore and bought three tests, stopped for bagels neither of them ate.

She went into the bathroom at the bagel shop, came out four minutes later and showed him the sticks.

"On TV and in real life," she said.

They went back to school. They didn't know what else to do. It was like when she'd met him: she looked exactly the same as before, except suddenly every single thing about her and her world was completely different. For the moment, embracing that sameness seemed the way to go. Keep going to school. Maybe they'd learn something there that would help them.

She threw up in history. She wasn't even going to make it to the bathroom so she threw up in a trash can in the classroom right in front of everyone. Having apparently never seen TV, Mrs. Xavier sent her to the office with a note to go home for the rest of the day.

"No one here wants to catch whatever you have." Mrs. Xavier was not very sympathetic, but this was probably the truest thing India had ever learned in history.

Robbie called ten seconds after the last bell of the day.

"We'll do whatever you want," he said.

"I want to stop throwing up."

"About the pregnancy, I mean."

"I don't know what I want."

He was undeterred. "We'll figure it out, and then we'll do that."

"What do *you* want?" she asked.

"Whatever you do."

This was probably meant to be helpful, but it was not helpful.

"I love you," he said.

"I love you too," she said.

"No, I mean I love you so we could get married. You shouldn't get married just because you're pregnant or you got someone pregnant. But if you got someone pregnant and you love her, getting married is fine."

Got her pregnant. The verb weirded her out.

It became their mantra. "What do you want?" they asked each other; they asked constantly. When they met on the wall in the morning, at lunch in the cafeteria, in the moments they packed up after the bell rang at the end of the day, when they were lying around together after sex—which they kept having because why not?—when they were cuddled up on one couch or another eating popcorn and watching a movie, that was what they said: What do you want? What do you want? What do you want?

"First love," he answered one night.

"We already have that," India scoffed. "That's what got us into this mess. No offense."

"Not first love. First," he paused, "love. Like with a comma in between. Like that's how we should decide. That's what we should do first: love."

"We did that too."

"Do that too," he corrected.

"I don't think it's enough," she said. "What's second?"

* * *

He came into the cafeteria the next day looking triumphant and slammed a stack of index cards onto the table before her.

"What's that?"

"What comes after love," he said.

"Marriage?" A jump-rope rhyme from her childhood.

"Study cards."

They read: "abortion," "adoption," "family," "duet."

"Duet?" She thought of "I Got You Babe." An entire lifetime ago.

"Like, we have the baby, but we don't get married or anything, and we just trade it back and forth. Sometimes it's just you and the baby. Sometimes it's just me and the baby."

"So I have to have a baby *and* you're going to dump me?" she said.

"Not unless it wins," he said. "We're going to play Baby War."

"Baby War?"

"You know that game?"

"No?" She didn't mean to be so shrill, but no one knew that game.

Then it turned out she did know it after all.

He had fifteen copies per card, per choice. He dealt them out so they each had a pile. "We each flip over our top card," he explained. "Higher card takes both."

"Which card is higher?" She sounded—and felt—hysterical.

"That's what we have to find out," he said.

It was silly, but actually it was not unrevelatory because each time you had to decide which was the higher card, what you wanted most. They played for hours. They played for days. They had to go to war a lot because there were only four cards so they often came up together. Double and triple wars were common too. India thought that was apt, like her whole world had been laid to waste by marauding hordes. It was a tricky game, though, because whereas 5, say, is always higher than 4, and a queen is always higher than a 10, the stakes kept shifting here. That was the whole point of playing. "Family" always beat "duet." Everything always beat "duet." "Duet," appropriately, was a 2. It lost every time. Everything topped breaking up followed by single parenting. Honestly, India thought rabies might have topped breaking up followed by single parenting. But exactly what "family" meant wasn't clear. And "abortion" and "adoption," which were quite different from each other, nonetheless blurred. They were unseen tracks heading who knew where, and how do you make a decision to embrace or avoid something when you don't know where it's going?

"This is fun, but it isn't working," India said one day. "We're just stalling."

"Because I need a fifth card." He was getting frustrated.

"What?"

"The do-whatever-India-wants card."

"Why does this have to be my decision?"

"Because it's your body," said Robbie. "That's what they always say."

"Who?"

"I don't know. *They*." He waved around at all of them.

"That means if I want an abortion, you can't say no. It doesn't mean I have to choose by myself."

"Who said by yourself? I'm here, aren't I?"

She loved him, which made her think she would love him forever, but she couldn't work out how they would live together and have a baby and pay for stuff like rent and food if she also went to college and also went to New York and also auditioned for plays on Broadway. She could picture them all together—her and Robbie and their daughter or son—in ten years, in twenty, thirty. She could picture her and Robbie old and wrinkled and stooped and in love at their great-grandchild's production of *Guys and Dolls*. What she could not picture was nine months from now with Robbie and an infant, living in her same old bedroom, working staggered schedules at the bagel shop or the karaoke bar, and a life that was that and that and that stretching indefinitely into infinity.

They didn't know, and they didn't know, and they didn't know.

And then, one day, an envelope came in the mail.

Dear Ms. Allwood,

We are very pleased to congratulate you on your acceptance into the Lenox University School of Dramatic Arts.

More envelopes came in the days after that. She got into NYU and Columbia and Juilliard. She got in everywhere.

This was never going to happen—the very best theater programs, the very best theater city, every single dream and wish she had coming true—but this happened anyway.

And it clarified two things:

She could not not go. She could family with Robbie Brighton someday, yes, but she could not family with Robbie Brighton right now because first she had to go to New York and become an actor. Maybe he could come with her. He'd been planning a gap year after all the transferring from high school to high school, but going to New York was like going abroad—across the country if not across the world—or maybe he could go abroad, then meet her back there afterward. She would be . . . she thought the word you were supposed to use was "honored," or "blessed" maybe, to family with him someday. But not this day. And so, not this baby.

But the other thing that came clear was this: it is awesome when dreams come true. And she had growing within her the true-making of someone else's dreams.

It was even awesomer when the dreams were good ones that would only make the world better, and better for everyone, as opposed to the kind that made the world better for you but worse for someone else. Good singers got cast in *Guys and Dolls*, so India did not. India's mother stayed late to help a client, so India had to have dinner alone. Robbie's father got to teach musicology for a living, so Robbie had to spend his whole life shuttling from one place to another. Grading on a curve was not fair on exams, and it definitely was not fair in life. Everyone should get to be happy.

What she was growing inside her might make everyone happy. Not *every-one* everyone, of course, but everyone involved, and it was starting to be a lot of people. More every day. She thought this was what people meant by win-win. It might be win-win-win in this case. It might be win-win-win-win, and for something that was, the internet told her, the size of a chickpea, that was pretty impressive.

She had her two buts: But she had to go to New York. But she *got* to go to New York. And since she got to, it seemed only right that someone else get lucky too.

She was sure, but she slept on it. She woke up still sure (nauseous, but sure). He was waiting in their spot on the wall when she got to school. She held the card out to him like he was going to announce the Tony for Best Actress. He took it from her and flipped it over.

He read it out loud—"Adoption"—and raised his eyes to hers.

Later India would wonder at the look that flashed across his face, through his eyes, like the wind: fast, invisible. She would think that fleetingly, momentarily, he looked disappointed, crushed even. She reached for his hand but missed. Because he was pulling away from her? No, worse. Because he was ripping the card in half and in half and in half.

"You're angry." She felt her heart sink and her eyes fill.

"Punctuating," he corrected, then added, because her face stayed wet and bewildered, "We're done. We decided. We don't need the cards anymore."

She wasn't quite done with them, though. She took his hand and turned it so the torn-up fragments fell from his palm into hers. Then she threw them over him.

"*You're* angry," he surmised, reasonably.

But she shook her head. "Confetti. I'm celebrating."

"Celebrating what?"

She hadn't stopped crying quite, but made herself smile. "Everything."

STILL MONDAY

"Everything's fine." Fig's mother did not wish to discuss the fact that she'd just told a journalist her own movie was bad. Instead she sent Fig and Jack up to shower off the chlorine. When they got back downstairs, they discovered Ajax had moved from yelling on the phone to yelling in the kitchen.

"Sex, lies, and videotape, India! The studio's furious. The network. Haley, John, Evan, Michaela. Hi, loves." Ajax interrupted himself to hug Fig and Jack as they scooted by to get chocolate-covered bananas from the freezer. Then he went right back to being mad. "Hell, I'm furious. What were you thinking?"

"Banana?" Mom held one up for him.

"What am I, a cranky toddler?" He took two anyway. They're really good. "Answer the question."

"No, you're not a toddler."

"Not that question."

"I said what I was thinking. Was I unclear?"

"You were clear." He pointed one of his bananas at her. "You were woefully clear. You were disastrously clear. Didn't I say broadly and vaguely? Weren't those my exact words?"

Fig was starting to think everything was not fine.

"That's not what you asked. You asked what I was thinking." Her mother got out some wine and two glasses. It felt like it had been a long day already, but it was barely lunchtime.

Ajax looked at the bottle. "It's your argument that Sancerre is what goes with chocolate bananas?"

"You don't have to drink it."

"Like hell I don't."

"You'd have me lie?" Fig's mother asked. Not really asked. This was the kind of thing her mother said when she didn't want you to answer her out loud but only in your head so you could learn a lesson. "You'd have me pretend to be sorry when I have nothing to be sorry for and pretend to be stupid and opinionless when I am smart and opinionful?"

"Yes. Absolutely yes. Obviously yes. How is that not clear?" It wasn't Ajax's fault he couldn't tell the difference, though, because Fig's mother was not his mother.

"I'm not a toddler either," she said. "I'm an adult, an intelligent adult."

"You're an actor."

"They're not mutually exclusive."

Ajax raised one of his eyebrows.

"They're not always mutually exclusive."

"This is your job, India. Not just to act in the movie. To support the movie. To make public appearances which suggest that the movie is unmissable and that you, as its face, are a sane and reasonable human. If you aren't, fake it."

"My job is to act in the movie, not in real life. India Allwood isn't a role. I can't pretend to be her. I *am* her."

"Bullshit," Ajax said. "And what's more, you know it's bullshit. No one wants to hear your ideas. Your job is to say other people's ideas in a clear, convincing, compelling way. And then get *out* of the way. If you want to say your ideas, write your own damn movie."

"I'd love to!"

"Oh yes, because that's just what we need right now." Ajax's other eyebrow climbed up beside the first one. "More words from you."

"You have chocolate on your chin." Fig's mom handed him a napkin. "And if you don't want my words, don't have a reporter call me."

"Evan and Michaela are making noises about breach of contract. They're using phrases like 'compensatory damages' and 'morality clause.'"

"How have I been immoral?"

"You said their movie was bad!"

"First of all, I said no such thing. Second of all, nothing I did say was remotely—"

"They like you, India, but they won't stand by you. Studio execs don't do that. Even friends don't do that. You won't believe the list of people who will desert you if a few thousand nutcases on the internet turn against you."

"The nutcases on the internet weren't nutcases in this instance," she said.

"Not at first. Now they're saying . . ."

He glanced at Fig and Jack and trailed off, but unfortunately, her mother had a phone too.

"They're saying the reason the movie wasn't great is because I'm too ugly," she finished.

This was beyond Fig's ability to imagine. Her mother was the most beautiful person in the world. But Ajax just said, "Yes."

"They're saying I'm ungrateful, untalented, and unappealing, too fat for movies, too young for the part, too old for the flashbacks, with weird eyes, and tits that manage somehow to be both too small and too saggy, and it's fine for TV but I have no business"—she put on a funny accent—"'doing film,' and no one cares what I think, and I should just shut my mouth." Her eyes flicked over to Fig and Jack. Jack was unwrapping a third banana. Fig kept her eyes away so her mother wouldn't see if they showed she knew everything wasn't fine. "And those were the polite ones."

"Yes," Ajax agreed again.

Her mom got out her phone and started reading. "They're saying I should never have been cast because 'the only part of poor, abused, drug-addicted, white trash, dead-end, uneducated, pregnant high schooler she is is white.' I'm quoting here."

"We could tell." Ajax winked at Fig.

"They're saying I have no 'lived experience.' I do not know and cannot imagine what it feels like to 'give my baby away,' so of course my performance was 'inauthentic,' by which they seem to mean acting."

"Yes."

"Which is my job."

"Not all of it," Ajax said.

"They've made a #NotEverythingsGreat hashtag." She held out her phone to show him. "It doesn't have an apostrophe."

"That's your objection? You are not stupid, India."

"That's my point. Among all the other things I am is right."

"Who cares?" Ajax threw his head back and asked the ceiling. "No one cares if you're right. No one's listening anyway. All anyone heard—internet nutcases and internet geniuses and every single person in the benighted hellscape we call Hollywood—was you shitting on your own movie. Right has fuck all to do with it. No. One. Cares."

"I do." Jack was not afraid of yelling.

Fig was afraid of yelling, but she put up her hand to say she cared too.

"No one you're not related to." Ajax made his voice quieter. "So unless your kids have a production company I don't know about, you need to fix this."

Jack and Fig did not have a production company.

Fig was going to admit this, though she thought Ajax probably knew, but suddenly her phone started *ping ping ping*ing from the drawer where her mother had stashed it before they went swimming.

And there was only one person who *ping ping ping*ed her.

2004

The other thing deciding made possible—besides not having to think and talk and play Baby War about it anymore—was that India was finally able to tell her mother. It would have been hard and terrible and possibly impossible to have to say, "Mom. I need to tell you something. I'm pregnant." But it was not so hard, terrible, or impossible to say, "Mom. I need to tell you something. I'm pregnant, but it's okay because I got into college, and I have a plan, one that's good for everyone, so you don't have to worry."

The next morning was Saturday. When India came downstairs, her mother raised first her eyes then her eyebrows at her up-before-noon, changed-out-of-pajamas-already daughter. India pretended to ignore this. She got herself some cereal she couldn't eat. Her mother folded her newspaper and waited.

India swallowed. "I got into NYU and pregnant." Someone in her head was calling, *Line? Line?* helplessly into empty wings.

Her mother got up and traded her newspaper for a cup of coffee.

"I mean," India clarified, "I got into college—everywhere actually—and I also got pregnant."

"I understood that the first time," her mother said. "I was waiting for more information. About the latter."

"Oh. Okay. I got pregnant. A couple weeks ago. Well, I found out a couple weeks ago. I think it was actually at *Guys and Dolls*. Well, not *at Guys and Dolls*. After *Guys and Dolls*. But it's okay." She stopped talking. Her mother sipped her coffee. "Why aren't you saying anything?"

"I am waiting to hear why you believe this is okay."

Ahh, right, she'd forgotten. This was what she was supposed to lead with. This was what was going to make this conversation non-hard and non-terrible and non-impossible. "I have a plan."

"Oh good," said her mother. "What, pray tell, India, is your plan?"

"I'm going to give it up. For adoption."

"You are going to place. The baby. For adoption," her mother corrected. "You are going to make an adoption plan. For the baby. Your baby. To whom you are going to give birth in, let's see"—her mother counted the fingers of one hand with the other then the next hand with the first—"August?" She looked back from her fingers to her daughter. "Is that your plan?"

"Yes." India sat on the counter and looked at her feet swinging over the kitchen floor. This had sounded so much clearer in her head.

"And how are you going to execute this plan?" her mother wondered.

"Execute?"

"Yes, a plan suggests a detailed proposal addressing all necessary steps and eventualities between one's current state—pregnant and admitted to college—and one's goal state—childless and enrolled."

"I . . . haven't worked out the details yet," India confessed.

"I see. So you don't have a plan. You have a dream."

"A dream?"

"An outcome you are hoping for with no particular sense of what it means or entails or how to cause it to occur."

"I guess?"

"You guess?"

Her mother was maddening. "Robbie made study cards. We played Baby War."

"You played Baby War?"

"You know, abortion versus adoption, getting married versus breaking up. Single parenting. That kind of thing."

"I see." Hadn't her mother said "I see" half a million times already? "And adoption won?"

"I mean, not won," India said, "but yeah."

"You do realize what this means, India?"

"I . . . think?" India asked.

"Well, just in case," her mother offered, "let's play this out a bit, shall we?"

Her daughter nodded mutely. This wasn't really a question.

"In order to place a child for adoption, you need to grow the child. Inside your body. For the next . . . sounds like about thirty-two weeks."

"I know," said India, "I'll get more and more pregnant."

"No. You will remain exactly as pregnant as you are right now. You will get more and more large. You will get more and more bloated. You will get more and more uncomfortable. But you will not get any more pregnant. You will find it harder and harder to do many of the things you do now without thinking about them. Fitting into the chairs at school, for instance. Sitting for long hours to read, write papers, study for exams, complete homework assignments. Entering the cafeteria without everyone staring and making rude comments. Your social life in general, I imagine, will take quite a hit. May I ask how Robbie feels about all this?"

"He wants to do what I want to do," India said, and for the first time in the conversation, she saw something other than carefully corralled horror pass over her mother's face.

"Which is to say he agrees that adoption is the best path forward," her mother asked, "or that his position is one of support for whatever you decide?"

"The latter, I think?" India was glad for the opportunity to talk about this part with someone.

"You discussed"—her mother required a sip of coffee to get it out—"marriage?"

"I mean, sort of? We love each other, but—"

"Yes," her mother interrupted, "but. Tell me more about that 'but' please."

"It just seemed . . . I mean we would have to get jobs but. And then the baby. It seems like an apartment would be . . . And it would be kind of gross. I guess. You know?"

"Remarkably, I do know. I'm glad you do too. And may I ask why you— you two—decided against the obvious answer?"

"Abortion?"

"Abortion."

"Well, I got into college."

"The admissions officers won't know. And if they did know, they would still allow you to matriculate."

"Right, but see, I was never going to get into all these incredible programs." It was important she say this right. It was important her mother understand this part. "And then I did get in. And this baby, if you imagine it when it grows up, the little kid it turns into, and the big kid, and the high schooler, and the adult after that, that was probably never going to happen either. The odds of this person existing were less than the odds of me getting into NYU, but that happened, so this can too."

"Can? Yes. *Should* is my question."

"Right, yeah, no. So I mean I wasn't going to get into NYU, and then I got into NYU, and that feels good."

"Yes."

"And no one got hurt."

Her mother squeezed the bridge of her nose. "Please make sense, India."

"My dream came true. It's so amazing. It's the best thing that could have happened to me. It's the best thing that's ever happened to me. And no one suffered. No one feels sad because I feel happy. There's no downside. There's only upside. Robbie's going to come with me and get an apartment near campus. You can come out and visit and see my plays."

"What does this have to do with—"

"It sounds stupid when I say it," India admitted, "but everything's better when your dreams come true instead of not coming true."

"While I am not willing to grant you that in perpetuity, the more pressing question is this: Are you telling me it was your dream to be an uneducated, unemployed, pregnant teenager?"

India laughed out loud. "I'm saying my dream came true. Someone else's should too."

"Who?"

"Whoever really, really wants a baby."

"Ahh." Her mother said. Then she didn't say anything else.

So India kept talking. "Somewhere out there there's a person, or a couple, and maybe they can't have a baby, and all they want is a baby, and I can give them a baby. I can make their dream come true just like someone made my dream come true."

"That's very kind, India." Her mother softened and exhaled a little, like a quiche when you take it out of the oven. India could see her turn from her lawyer into her mother, and that was good because she needed a mother more than she needed a lawyer at the moment. "But first of all, someone didn't make your dream come true. You made your dream come true. You studied for all those tests. You revised all those essays. You made those audition tapes. And second of all, there are other ways to spread joy and kindness in the world than by making babies for strangers."

"But if I gave them my baby, they wouldn't be strangers. They would be family. I mean not family who you have Christmas with or really ever see again, but there are lots of different kinds of families."

Her mother inhaled, exhaled, declined, India could see, to address that for the moment. "Have you considered what this would do to your life?"

"High school is a waste of time anyway," India enthused, for this was the part she *had* thought through. "It's not like Ms. LaRue's going to cast me in the spring show. It's not like I'm learning anything practical. I already got into college."

"I don't mean just academically." India was surprised because her mother always meant just academically. "What about socially? Mentally? Emotionally?"

"Well, I'll still have Robbie. And it's not like I've ever been super popular or whatever. I've had a lot of practice not caring what anyone thinks." If she'd had social standing to lose, if she were otherwise going to be prom queen, if because she was pregnant she couldn't be top of the cheerleader pyramid or class president or yearbook editor, if because she was pregnant she couldn't be in the school play, then this would be a harder decision to make. As it was, she had none of that to lose. This was something no one ever talked about, how being socially awkward was great preparation for being knocked up at sixteen.

"Are you going to talk me out of it?" she asked when her mother had nothing to say to that. She did not ask if her mother was going to try to talk her out of it. Her mother could successfully talk anyone out of anything she chose, so the question was only whether she would.

"I would never talk anyone into or out of anything on this front," her mother said, more carefully than she usually said things. "Robbie is right. The choice is yours, and the job of the people in your life is to support you in it."

Which made India cry.

Which made her mother come over and hop up on the counter next to her, press her hip to India's, run her hand over India's hair then face.

"But it is my job to make sure this decision is not undertaken lightly."

"You want me to get married?" India wondered.

"God, no." It was also unlike her mother to answer directly, unequivocally, unsocratically. "In fact, that I might try to talk you out of."

"You don't like Robbie?" She felt wounded. And protective.

"Oh, Robbie's fine." Her mother waved her hand in front of her like Robbie was a cobweb she had to walk though. "He's a sweet boy. But good lord, if you were twice as old as you are now, I'd still think you were too young to get married. And besides, having a baby has nothing to do with having a husband."

India nodded. She knew this, of course. It was maybe the first thing she had ever learned from her mother. Then she said—barely whispered, really, "I could have an abortion."

"Yes, you could," her mother agreed. "And you are lucky that you can. Lots of people can't. Lots of people fight for you to have that right."

"I know," India said. "But that doesn't mean I have to."

"No," said her mother. "In fact, it means you don't. You having the right to an abortion means you having the right not to have an abortion."

"But?"

"But it's okay to want this to go away."

"Yeah, but then it would all have been for no reason."

"Sometimes you have to cut your losses," her mother said.

"And no one's dream would come true."

Her mother nodded. Then she put her arm around her. "Congratulations, India."

"On being pregnant?" That didn't make sense if she was giving up the baby. Placing it. "On making a decision?"

"On getting into all those drama programs."

"Oh. Yeah."

"That's really wonderful."

"Yeah. Thank you.

"I'm proud of you."

Her mother never said she was proud of you. And she especially never said it after you told her you were pregnant. It would have been a nice place to leave what had been a fairly hard and impossible conversation after all. But she still needed help.

"I don't know where to do it," India said finally.

"Where to do what?"

"Where to give the baby. Like the actual giving. The actual putting up." Like a poster on a wall, India thought, or a hat you weren't planning to wear all that often anymore but weren't ready to get rid of forever.

But that was the part where her mother could help.

India was picturing an orphanage, like the semester she failed to get a part in *Oliver!*, or like the animal shelter where her mother made her volunteer one summer in order to convince her she didn't really want a dog. She knew there wouldn't be babies in pens with cement floors and wire cages, but she was expecting something frightening, bad smelling, sad. The adoption agency, though, was cheery and bright and a suite of offices. She was welcomed like a hero, though whether that was because these people worked with her mother all the time or because she was donating the goods, she couldn't say. Everyone told her how brave she was and how strong and how impressive that she got into so many great schools and how generous of her to make a plan like this and how her child would be so loved and how she was going to make an adoptive parent or parents very happy and how she wasn't committing to anything and could change her mind at any time and would never be compelled to do anything she didn't want to do. Did she understand? She understood. Did she have questions? They had answered ones she didn't even know she had.

India had not realized that where the baby went would be her decision. She was not entirely convinced it should be. She didn't know anything about choosing parents because she had never done it before. Shouldn't someone who was an expert in parent-picking be in charge? Or maybe they could take a DNA sample from the baby—couldn't they do that while it was still inside?—and determine it would be tall and athletic and place it with basketball-loving parents, or an X-ray that showed its brain was unusually large and they could find some parents with PhDs, or maybe they could tell it was allergic to peanuts and place it with parents who were also allergic to peanuts who would for sure never have peanuts in the house and would also be great at showing a child where peanuts might accidentally or secretly be.

Instead, applicants submitted binders about themselves, which seemed like they would provide lots of information but did not. The would-be parents all looked like, well, parents. They looked like adults. So it was weird that they

When people thought of mothers, they smelled cookies baking and chocolate melting. But actual mothers got shit for giving their kids too much sugar. When people thought of mothers, they thought soft and warm and cuddly. But actual mothers went to great lengths to eradicate their soft warm cuddly bits. When people thought of mothers, they thought of mama bears and cheerleaders—fierce love and unconditional support—but actual mothers were accused of coddling and helicoptering.

Camille Eaney did not enter into scenarios where you were damned if you did and damned if you didn't. She did not play games that could not be won. She did not believe "helicopter" was a verb. And therefore, she did not want any part of this.

Except that wasn't quite true. She wanted one part.

Camille was a planner. Honestly, she couldn't understand why everyone wasn't. Making plans resulted in results. If you wanted what you wanted—and by definition, who didn't?—you had to make a plan.

At first she thought she'd just get pregnant. Martin would probably still be willing. He liked sex. He liked sex with her. He'd make her sign some forms absolving him of financial obligation in the event of reproduction in this universe or any other in perpetuity, but he'd draw up those papers himself so she wouldn't have to pay for them, and obviously she didn't want him or his money in her life or that of her child. Otherwise, she wouldn't have divorced him.

But she'd meticulously rid herself of everything Martin, so she wasn't wild about having his DNA learn to crawl in her home.

were all also kissing her ass. They all wrote letters that began, "Dear Birth Mother," or "To a special birth mother," or "Thank you, Birth Mama." She was grateful not to be abbreviated BM, but she wasn't sure the M was appropriate anyway. She wasn't a mother. Not at the moment. And the whole point of this process was so she wouldn't become one. Not at the moment.

They thanked *her* for considering *them*. They admired her courage and generosity. They hoped she knew she was so strong and what a wonderful gift she was giving the world and how much God loved her and how happy she could make them. They hoped she knew how much they would love her baby.

She didn't want anyone to love her baby because she didn't want it to be *her* baby. She wanted it to be *their* baby.

They all promised family holidays and a good education, trips to the beach, grandparents, ice cream, and fresh air. They all promised snuggles and birthday parties and bedtime stories. Some had tire swings in their backyards. Some had skis in their mudrooms. Some had secret recipes for pancakes and gardens to supply the blueberries. They told her how they met. They told her their favorite pizza topping and their favorite band and their favorite TV show and their favorite baseball team, and though she wasn't sure what criteria it did make sense to base this choice on, she couldn't figure out why it would be any of those.

Some of them told her why they couldn't have their own child, and though she saw what they meant, she didn't want them to say "own child." She wanted *this* child to be their own child.

There were so many binders filled with so many photos and so many facts and so much hope, and India felt like she needed to look at every page. It had taken her two hours last August to pick which backpack she wanted for the school year, and there had only been five or six choices, and that decision didn't matter. She considered letting Robbie pick, but none of the letters said Dear Birth Father or even Dear Birth Parents. Plus, lots of them promised to tell the child all about her, and she didn't want some kid to have to walk around with "Your birth mother didn't really give a shit what our favorite band was." Nor "Your birth mother was so overwhelmed she let her boyfriend decide even though he'd already proven himself to be completely irresponsible what with the whole you-existing thing."

And then, one afternoon, she found Camille.

She thought about going to a sperm bank—were they still even called sperm banks?—but could only picture Greek-columned buildings full of men in expensive suits whispering in expensive tones who heard a sudden noise and all turned at once to front doors flung open by a positive deluge of spunk.

But adoption? Adoption was spunk free. It was ex-husband free. It was giving an out to someone in a position she didn't want to be in and a home to a baby who needed one. It seemed like a better choice in exactly the way single was a better choice than married: not the obvious choice, not lots of people's first choice, but the best choice, at least for her.

There was a lot of paperwork. Camille was good at paperwork. She looked through scores of profiles filled out by other would-be adoptive parents and gleaned two important facts: they did not know how to use apostrophes, and they all wrote the same thing. The apostrophes would take care of themselves. (Camille had excellent grammar and usage.) But she could see that standing out was hard when that list of qualities that made someone a good mother was so fixed in people's minds.

She spent three days trying to decide what band a desperate pregnant teenager might like her to like. The latest thing would look immature or as if she was trying too hard. The honest answer would make her seem old and joyless (or wouldn't make her seem anything since no teenager would ever have heard of it). Eventually she decided anyone who picked parents on the basis of their favorite band was not someone whose genes she wanted in her house for the next two decades anyway.

Plus, she didn't want to trick anyone into picking her. It was important to be honest. If ever there were a journey to start off on the right foot, surely it was this one. Lots of people's journeys to parenthood started on the wrong one—drunken nights, regrettable hookups, poor decision-making on any number of fronts—but Camille knew she'd have to explain herself to her kid someday, and "I guessed your birth mom's favorite band" seemed a bad way to begin. It was important to be undemanding, too. Being pregnant and not wanting to be, being pregnant but not ready, growing a baby with whom you planned to part seemed stressful enough. As much as she could, Camille wanted to ease their way, these women, these birth mothers. Asking them to absorb a hundred-page scrapbook seemed like a lot.

So she settled on an easy-to-read, easy-to-use guide to herself. She made a table of contents and color-coded section tabs. She used Times New Roman 12-point font, double spacing, and numbered lists. She eschewed puns, rhymes, and imagery (in the parent profile and in life). She used not a single exclamation point.

She asked herself what a birth mother would want to know about the person who would be her baby's parent and concluded it probably had less to do with the person she was than the mother she would become. A would-be mother's favorite bands, movies, and ice cream flavors were irrelevant for lots of reasons but mostly because all her predilections were about to be usurped. Instead, Camille detailed:

TYPES OF MUSIC I WILL TOLERATE IF THE BABY GROWS UP TO LIKE IT

1. Rock
2. Rap
3. Classical
4. Jazz
5. Top 40 [Camille was not a monster. She understood that listening to shitty but trendy music was an unfortunate but unavoidable stage of adolescence, like snootiness toward your beleaguered mother, or braces.]

TYPES OF MUSIC I WILL NOT TOLERATE, EVEN IF THE BABY GROWS UP TO LIKE IT*

1. Country
2. Heavy metal
3. Musicals
4. Opera

* In these eventualities, I am, however, willing to purchase headphones and an iPod (or whatever an iPod evolves into).

ACTIVITIES A CHILD MIGHT COME TO ENJOY WHICH I WOULD BE WILLING TO INDULGE

1. Team sports
2. Board games
3. The arts
4. Skiing
5. Scouts

ACTIVITIES A CHILD MIGHT COME TO ENJOY WHICH I WILL NOT BE WILLING TO INDULGE UNDER ANY CIRCUMSTANCES

1. Anything involving horses
2. Anything involving weaponry
3. Opera

KINDS OF DESSERTS I WILL ALLOW

1. Any with three or fewer unpronounceable ingredients
2. Except licorice, which is gross

She included one photo of herself, her headshot, the one she used on her website: professional, capable. She wasn't embarrassed about how she looked in pictures and she wasn't trying to be coy, but it seemed smug to press vacation photos on someone who was unlikely ever to have been anywhere yet. It seemed unkind to show photos of her big, supportive family—Camille had six brothers—to someone who was turning over part of hers.

Whereas most parent profiles were literally bursting from their seams, Camille's was compact, easy to read, and largely monochrome, just like Camille herself.

When she submitted it, Marie, the social worker, laughed. She thought it was a joke. Camille rarely explained herself, but she made an exception for underpaid, overworked adoption social workers.

"I know the binders sometimes seem silly," Marie admitted, "but it really does help everyone get to know each other."

"It's all in there," Camille assured her. "Everything pertinent."

"I just worry you're going to take yourself out of the running with a lot of birth mothers."

"That's the plan," Camille smiled. To find someone who valued directness, honesty, and simplicity rather than someone diverted by packaging, trivialities, and shiny things. Everyone else's portfolio screamed "Pick me!" Hers whispered and did the picking for her.

Camille was not a control freak. She was a control connoisseur.

Now though, sitting at the agency, waiting, she was uncharacteristically worried. She had come fifteen minutes early. Fifteen minutes was the bare minimum of early Camille allowed herself to be. Whoever showed up second was always at a disadvantage, a disadvantage she could make sure wasn't hers without sacrifice or expense or even any hard work. All she had to do was be wherever she was going anyway. She had no idea why everyone didn't go where they were going early, but she was glad they didn't. She also felt this was exactly the sort of life hack a child would be lucky to learn.

Therefore she was watching alone when the trio bundled into the lobby, late, dripping on everything, soaked to the skin. Was it normal to want to parent your maybe-child's parent? What if this child—the child carrying her maybe-child—got sick? And what about the woman with her, clearly her own parent? Was this how what had happened happened? Was knocked-up-at-sixteen what you were when no one thought to make you put on a raincoat?

The girl and boy kept laughing together and dripping, but Camille locked eyes with the mother. The mother of the mother.

What passed there? Neither could have said, but they both felt it. Possibly it was:

MOM OF MOM: You're taking my grandbaby.

CAMILLE: I promise to be worthy.

Or maybe:

MOM OF MOM: You're helping my daughter.
CAMILLE: Yes, but also she's helping me.

Or likely:

MOM OF MOM: I forgot an umbrella. It was stupid.
CAMILLE: If you throw a couple extra in the trunk of your car, you'll never have this problem.

Everyone filed in. Camille tried to keep her eyes on India's face but they wouldn't stay and kept wandering to her stomach instead. It was wet and round. It was so wet and round it was obscene. Why round and rained on should conjure such a feeling of indecency, Camille did not know, but she really tried to keep her eyes off the stomach and on the face.

"I hope you're not cold," Camille said. Absurdly. What a time to forget how to talk like a person.

"God, no," said India. "I'm a million degrees. Just watch—I'll be steamed dry in like three minutes. I haven't been cold in months." She rubbed her round, wet belly. "It's like a furnace."

It. The baby. India's baby. Camille's baby. Camille's maybe-baby.

"I want to apologize for the brevity of my binder." Camille was surprised to hear herself say this since she did not believe in leading with an apology, especially one she didn't mean. But this was too important a thing to begin the wrong way, and she didn't want the girl to think she was being cagey or secretive.

"Oh, I loved your parent profile. That's why I picked you. Most people go on and on." India waved her hands around. "I mean, I have homework."

Camille laughed. "You can ask me anything. I don't want you to feel like you can't."

India leaned forward immediately. "Why did you say no musicals?"

"Oh, uh . . ." *Shit.* She should have anticipated the girl might be one of those high school theater geeks. "Of course, if musical theater is important to you, or important to the child, I could be flexible on that point."

"But why musicals in particular?" India pressed.

"I just"—Camille reminded herself she was aiming for honesty in this meeting—"find their unpredictability unnerving."

"Unpredictability?"

"How they might start rhyming or dancing at any moment or break into song with no warning." It sounded ridiculous when she said this out loud. "Or, I don't know, maybe I'm just jealous because I can't sing myself. I'm happy to negotiate if that's a deal breaker for you."

"No need," India smiled.

When she seemed to have no further questions, Marie jumped in. "Why doesn't India tell you a little bit about why she's making the decision she's making?"

"I got into college," said India.

"Congratulations," said Camille.

"I got in everywhere, but I decided on Lenox. At first I thought, *Duh, Juilliard*, but it's a little bit like when you order a chocolate chip cookie and it's all chip. Chocolate is good, but if that's all you wanted, you wouldn't have ordered a cookie, you know?"

"I meant the decision you're making about placing your baby for adoption," Marie said.

"That's what I'm doing. Juilliard is the obvious choice, but it's not the only choice, and when I thought about it, I realized it wasn't the right choice for me. Adoption is the same."

Camille nodded slowly. "Me too."

"Really?"

"Not the obvious choice, not the one many people would make, certainly, but a really good one and the right one for me."

India beamed. "Getting into Lenox, getting in everywhere, it was a dream come true. *Is* a dream come true. So I wanted to make someone else's dream come true too. I know that sounds cheesy."

"It doesn't sound cheesy at all," Camille allowed herself to lie. Then she turned to Robbie. "Do you have plans to go to college?"

He looked surprised to be addressed. "Maybe. I had been planning a gap year, but now I'm going to go to New York with India. Get a job. See what happens."

"It's ironic, right? We're staying together, but we don't want a baby. You're single, and you do." India waved toward Robbie to include him in her "we," but she was looking at Camille so she didn't see the wince that lightninged the space between his eyes.

Camille wished she could ignore this. She wished she could go back in time three seconds and keep her eyes on India's and miss Robbie's reaction altogether. She wished she could take a moment to explain a working definition of "ironic." But she knew she couldn't do any of these things. Instead, she reached her hand along the table in Robbie's direction and said, "Are you sure?"

He looked startled. They all looked startled. "Sure what?" he said.

"Sure this is what you want to do."

"I want to support India." He said it instantly. Reflexively. Camille knew a mantra when she heard one.

The mother shot her a look. The mother of the mother. It said, *Yes, I know, but he's not the priority.* It said, *They're children still, and they have other things they need to do.* It said, *It's better this way, and just because this boy doesn't believe it yet, doesn't mean it isn't true.* India's mother was supporting what her daughter wanted and needed. Camille supposed Robbie was right that he should do the same.

"India and Robbie have decided on a closed adoption," Marie said, even though everyone in the room knew it already. The agency encouraged open adoptions, and that was what most birth families chose, at least a little open, slightly ajar, cracked to let the light in. But India didn't want that.

"I mean, if you need a kidney, call me, obviously." India's tone suggested this was an eventuality as likely as the earth falling into the sun. She was sixteen. But Camille knew sometimes you needed a kidney.

"Or me." Robbie wrinkled his nose like his glasses were slipping, but he wasn't wearing glasses. "I have kidneys too."

India squeezed his hand. "But we want this baby to be your baby, totally, completely, in every way yours, and we just kind of thought if we had scheduled visits or check-ins or even just you have to send us pictures every few months, it'll feel more like . . . not like a loan or going halfsies or whatever. I know technically the baby will be yours but . . ." She trailed off again.

"We find that open adoptions help ease the transition"—Marie had clearly given them this speech already and had no qualms about giving it again—"and lend support going forward to everyone involved: birth parents, adoptive parents, children who often have questions about—"

But India waved her away. She'd already heard this. She'd already decided. "We don't want it to be like you and the baby owe us anything," she said to Camille. "We don't want it to be like we're this huge chunk of your family, but we're mostly totally absent all the time. We don't want . . . do you call it 'half measures'? Like we want to commit, one hundred percent, and we want you to commit, one hundred percent. We're all in." She nodded once, hard. "The baby's all in. We want you to be all in too."

Camille's ear snagged on that "we" every time it came out of India's mouth, but if Robbie disagreed, he was doing a good job of faking it. They weren't adults, but they were old enough to make a decision, and Camille thought second-guessing it or lecturing them about what the grown-ups knew best was selling them short. She also thought making them guess what a child who didn't exist yet would or wouldn't want from them was asking a lot. They had already put the baby first, in the most generous way Camille could imagine, and it was enough, more than enough.

"I'm all in too," she assured them. "The only kind of *in* I ever am is *all*."

As she got bigger and rounder, as rumors spread, as it slowly dawned on her classmates and teachers that she had not just become overly fond of cake, India braced herself for savage laughter and too-loud whispers in the cafeteria, slackened jaws and pointing fingers, appalled eyes raking all of her but her face. Instead, she became invisible. Hubbubbing classrooms fell silent when she entered. Faces turned away as she passed. Teachers would not meet her eyes. She became a ghost roaming the halls of her high school, unnoticed but implacable, a reminder to one and all about the unremittingly gossamer fragility of life-as-you've-known-it. And of condoms.

She thought Robbie would start to be grossed out by her body. It *was* kind of gross. But he didn't seem to mind. When her fingers got too swollen, they held toes instead. When her toes got too swollen, he sat at the other end of the couch and pressed the bottoms of his feet against the bottoms of hers. It was comforting but weird but sweet but skeevy all at the same time, kind of like being pregnant. Sometimes he liked to put his head on her knees where her lap used to be and talk to the baby inside. "You're such a lucky baby," he told it. "We picked you such a good mom."

Or, "My teeth hurt when I eat chocolate ice cream but not any other kind of ice cream. Just so you know what you're up against."

Or, "One of my uncles has six toes on his right foot. My dad started going bald in high school. My mom can't roll her tongue. It hasn't held her back, though."

Sometimes he made up songs to sing to it:

Little baby
Someday maybe
You will wonder
'Bout our blunder
But we're happy
That your nappy
Is the problem
Of your mo-om—

"Why are you crying?" he broke off to ask India.

"I'm not crying."

"Why are tears coming out of your eyes and running down your face?"

"You're such a good singer." She kept crying, but she was laughing too. "I was wooed under false pretenses."

"Good thing, though," Robbie said. "This baby has a fifty-fifty shot at being able to sing. Imagine if you had a baby with someone who sings like you do. Poor kid wouldn't stand a chance."

She pushed him off her tiny lap but laughed until she peed a little.

"Seriously," he said when he'd picked himself off the floor. "I think we're lucky we can share our talents with the baby."

"I'm not sure heredity works that way."

"No, like if I were a good painter, there would be no way to show it my paintings because it's still inside. If I were good at numbers, I couldn't do math for it. But it can hear me sing. And it can hear you act. Do your *Merchant of Venice* monologue for it."

"No. I'm embarrassed. Babies don't care about Shakespeare."

"Don't you want to share your gift with it? Don't you want it to know what you can do?"

"'The quality of mercy is not strained,'" she told it. She could not tip back in a chair anymore. She could not raise her feet as high as a table. "'It droppeth as the gentle rain from heaven.'"

One day while she was making peanut butter toast in the kitchen, he waited until she was done and said, "Can I ask you a question?"

"Sure."

He got down on one knee, and her heart stopped, which couldn't have been good for the baby.

"Will you go to prom with me?"

And she laughed until she cried, which was not that long.

She thought it would be impossible to find a dress that would fit her, but apparently lots of pregnant women had formal affairs to attend, and if the black off-the-shoulder dress she chose therefore looked like something her mother would wear, a little old for her, a little less sequined than everyone else's, it was classy, and for the first time in maybe ever she felt pretty. She felt beautiful, even.

The music was too loud, and there was too much jostling and nothing good to eat, and her feet hurt, but they slow-danced, very close around the baby between them, and she looked at him in his tuxedo and could not stop herself from picturing their wedding and the road she had resolutely refused to take. Under her dress, on the front of her enormous underpants, she had written "NYC" in black marker just under her popped-out belly button. She had written it backward for exactly this eventuality, and she excused herself from the table at which they were sitting and holding hands during the fast songs and went into the bathroom and hoisted her dress up so she could read it right way around in the mirror. She stared at herself, at her stomach, at her stretch marks, and those letters, "NYC," turned to face her, indelible. Two girls burst in, laughing too loudly, but stopped when they saw her like they'd been silenced by a spell. They met her eyes in the mirror. She turned her whole body toward them so they could see. They backed out of the bathroom silent and somber as stones.

There were only three more weeks of school. Of her five thousand forty hours, she was down to less than a hundred.

MONDAY
(AFTERNOON, FINALLY)

F ig didn't want to get in trouble, but she couldn't stand the *ping ping ping*ing anymore. She sneaked across the kitchen to get the phone from the probably-dead-battery drawer where her mother had sequestered it. When she looked at the screen, her face felt hot and cold at the same time, so she didn't even notice when Jack went to tattle that she'd taken their phone out of the drawer without asking. It turned out not to matter anyway because their mother said she didn't care, and when Jack said she would care if he was the one who did it, she admitted that was true, and when he said it wasn't fair, she admitted that was true too, and when he asked what was she going to do about it then, she said, "You are using all capital letters at me," and he said, "You're ass damn right I am."

Usually, their mom was not a movie star. Usually, she was a TV star. On her TV show, the only bad words she was allowed to say were "ass" and "damn," because "ass" is a homonym and might mean a donkey, and "damn" is a homophone and you can't tell how words are spelled when you say them out loud on TV.

Their mother was stricter than the FCC, though, so Jack got sent to his room for time-out.

That gave Fig enough quiet time alone to read all of her texts.

The first one said: RU seeing this?

The second one said: [emoji of two eyeballs looking]

The third one said: Where RUUUUUUU??????

The fourth one said: [snorting steam emoji, Xs for eyes emoji, soft serve of poo emoji]

The fifth one said: [eleven pressed-together hands followed by eleven phones]

The sixth one said: [five strawberries]

The seventh one said: Why isn't there a fig emoji????

Fig's hands were shaking, which made it hard to reply, but she managed: I'm here!!

Then she said: Sorry our phone got taken away

Then she said: Yes I am seeing this

Then she said: If you want a fig emoji you have to download it specially

Which of course she had so she sent a few to show what they looked like.

The reply said: It's not fair

What was happening to her mother, Fig assumed, not that fig emojis weren't standard.

The reply added: [Sad face emoji]

Fig said: What should we do?

Three dots. Three dots. Three dots. Then the reply said: Should I come out?

Fig said: To LA?

The reply said: Of the closet

Fig said: You're gay?

The reply said: [Rolling eyes emoji]

When Fig and her brother turned ten, they got a phone. The first thing Jack did was download ten games, the max he was allowed, one for each year he'd been alive. The first thing Fig did was use the internet to do some sleuthing. She thought it was probably hard to find a spy or a person in witness protection or someone who had to hide so something bad didn't happen to them. She thought it might also be hard if you were old and bad at technology. Fig was young and good at technology. Most people's usernames could be anything, but Fig had a good guess about what username you would choose if your last name was Eaney.

So she found who she was looking for almost at once.

When she did, she sent EaneyMeaney05 a DM: Hi. This is your sister

EaneyMeaney: I don't have a sister

Fig sent an emoji of a hand waving and an emoji of two girls standing really close together.

EaneyMeaney: ?

Fig: I'm your family

EaneyMeaney: Who dis?

Fig: Well not family family

EaneyMeaney: ?

Fig: My mother gave birth to you. That makes us sisters

Three dots. Three dots. Three dots. Then a thumbs-up emoji.

So Fig was used to understatement. She was used to texts she had to read and reread to get every last crumb of meaning from, like when you lick your cupcake wrapper.

She took the rolling-eye emoji to heart and tried to ask a better question: How would you come out?

EaneyMeaney: [shrugging emoji]

But then: Video?

Fig: Of what?

EaneyMeaney: The truth

Then: Might help

Fig: How?

EaneyMeaney: [six people's brains exploding]

Fig: Let me think about it

EaneyMeaney: [thumbs-up]

But an hour later, Fig and Jack's phone *ping*ed again. It wasn't a text. It was a link to a video. The video had only been posted a few minutes before, but it had already been viewed 392 times. In the three and a half minutes it took Fig to watch it, that number became 4,227. In the three and a half hours she took to decide what to do about it, it became 1.1 million.

2005

It was the middle of the night when it started, quiet pain and then louder, waves which receded but did not subside, and she sat up waiting, alone, feeling bad about waking her mom who had to be up for work in not too many hours (it did not occur to her that her mother would have to take the day off), not wanting to call and wake Robbie who, it turned out later, had been up all night as well, sympathetic wakefulness, a premonition, or just a general feeling of change, everything unsettled, everything coming, ready or not. In the morning, she came downstairs and reported to her mother, "I'm in labor."

India's mother looked up from the paper and smiled. "About time." She left the kitchen and made a phone call, then went upstairs and changed out of her work clothes.

India sat at the table and stared at the wall, concentrated on breathing.

"Early labor is best weathered at home," her mother said when she came back in the room. "I was in the hospital with you for hours and hours before anything happened, and then by the time I really was in labor, all I wanted to do was go home so we should maybe—"

"It started at like eleven thirty last night," India said, then added, "It really hurts."

Her mother paled, which was unlike her mother. "Of course it hurts, baby. It's supposed to hurt. Want to call Robbie and get going?" She was going for breezy, but India knew this was as flustered as her mother got, and she was grateful because if things were about to get worse and faster, if things were going to happen that could never unhappen, the least her mother could be was flustered about it.

They picked up Robbie on the way, like carpool, and he sat in the back, also like carpool, and her mother dropped them, then went to park the car. Marie was there, so her mother must have called her. Camille was there, and even at that moment, India felt a flash of smug gratitude to her past self for choosing someone local. The baby was having a hard day too, so would probably be glad to have its mom there when it came out. Camille looked nervous. Excited but nervous. Robbie looked more like terrified, clammy and pale.

When her mother got back, when Marie excused herself and said she'd see them soon, when they were all installed in a too-small, too-hot room, no one seemed to know quite what to do.

Camille said, "How are you feeling, India?"

And India said, "People die in childbirth."

"People die doing all sorts of things," her mother said, apparently in an attempt to be comforting. "Your body is young and strong and knows just what to do."

"You're smart to do this now," Camille added.

"'Smart' maybe isn't the word I'd use," her mother said.

"All my friends waited until they were older to have babies," Camille went on. "Sure, they had more money and more education and more stability and more life experience, but their bodies couldn't do what yours can do as smoothly and easily as yours can do it." She reached over shyly and gave India's hand a small squeeze. India squeezed back like a blood-pressure cuff. "I'm grateful to you, of course," Camille said, "but I'm also grateful to your body. Your body is amazing."

"That's what I always say," said Robbie.

Her mother gritted her teeth.

But it was true. India's body was strong. It was fast. It expanded even further and in directions she had not previously imagined. It could handle some pain. It could make a baby and then push it into the world. It could scream and sweat and breathe deep and quick and widen without tearing and widen without shutting down or out and spread to encompass basically everything.

"Breathe," Robbie said.

"Breathe," her mother said.

"Thank you," Camille said, through it all, again and again in a voice India would dream of over and over, over the years. "Thank you, thank you, thank you." Through her haze, India kept replying. She said, "You're welcome," and she said, "No problem," and she said, "Happy to do it," replies which got more and more ridiculous the more she said them through clamped-together teeth and between closer and closer contractions and while gripping the sides of the bed so hard she had visions she'd bent them.

Later, though, she thought maybe Camille wasn't thanking her. Maybe she was thanking God. Maybe she was thanking the universe. Maybe she was thanking the baby. *Thank you for coming, baby. Thank you, baby, for all the work you're doing and the journey you're undertaking and the fear you're surmounting and the pain you're undaunted by, even though you're so young, so little still, even though you haven't even met your mother yet. Thank you, baby, for coming.*

India's body became its own thing, separate from her, nothing to do with India. It was less like her body took over and more like it kicked her out. India's body forgot her. It bled and pushed and hurt and waited and pushed and pushed and bled. Another body came out of it, a whole other body, and then it was down to zero. Empty. India wondered when she would be let back inside and who would do the letting. For the moment, she could only wait and watch and be patient, like everyone else. Slowly, her body deflated, but not as much as you might have hoped. And eventually, she sort of eased back in, less a triumphant welcome through wide-flung front doors and more a weary sneak around the back, but she was home. Slowly, she was home.

And then, all India's body could do was cry. India in her body cried and cried. She cried in Robbie's arms while he sat next to her awkwardly and tried to hug her until finally he gave that up and climbed all the way into bed behind her and beneath her and around her, became her mattress and her pillow and her blanket, and she got snot all over his shirt, and he cried too then, into her hair, and they could not stop.

"Are we upset?" he asked her through tears.

"I don't know," she said.

"Are we sad? Are we happy?"

She was crying too hard to give him an answer, but she also didn't *know* the answer. He held her tighter. She held him back.

"Are we doing the right thing?" he whispered finally. "It's not . . ."

He trailed off, but she knew what he would say, and she pulled him tighter around her, not like a sweater, like a cocoon, so he would know it was okay for him to say it. "It's not too late," he whispered into her hair.

And she extricated herself the barest few inches from his chest to look up into his face, for this was the one thing, the only thing, she knew for sure. "We are doing the right thing." She kissed his cheeks and his mouth and his neck and his chest. "We are. We are. We are."

Later, who knew how much later, India heard singing. Very bad singing. It was Camille, and she was singing softly to the baby, who fit snug along her forearm.

I love you a bushel and a peck
A bushel and a peck though you make my heart a wreck

India managed to sit up. "That's *Guys and Dolls*."

"My dad used to sing it to me." Camille's eyes didn't leave the baby's face.

"But you said no musicals."

"And this is why." She was whispering so she wouldn't wake the baby. "Did you expect I would break into song?"

"You *are* a bad singer," India said.

"I told you!" Camille laughed. "I guess it's true: motherhood changes you."

India wondered if *she* could sing now. She knew she still wasn't a mother— that was the whole point—but maybe the hormones or something had changed her vocal cords during labor.

That wasn't what Camille meant, though. "Still can't sing worth a crap. But now apparently I do it anyway."

The baby was a girl. Camille had her wrapped up like a burrito. She was smaller than India had ever imagined a human could be. She was smaller than India's belly, which she supposed made sense since she hadn't been shrink-wrapped in there but swimming around. She was smaller than the idea of her, which was huge, the fact of her, which was also huge, the implications of her, even though they'd taken pains, painful pains, arduous, onerous, soul-flaming pains to keep those as small as possible.

India didn't recognize her. The baby looked different on the outside. She looked nothing, really, like the ghostly glowing lines on the ultrasound. She looked nothing like the concave inside of a ball, even if India's stomach still looked distressingly like the convex outside of one. Neither of those was a surprise, of course. India was hormonal, not delusional. But the baby also looked nothing like she'd been imagining, though India could not say how except that the baby had spent nine months literally living inside her, so she felt she should have recognized her.

She didn't quite recognize Camille, either. Like her daughter, Camille looked different. Same hair, same body—quite a bit samer than India's—same outfit even, but completely changed, and not just because she was singing show tunes. Something about her face was brighter, fuller. More aware. More alight. There was more weight behind it, maybe. And she was smiling in a way that was completely different from her pick-me smile, from her so-glad-we're-doing-this smile, from her won't-we-make-an-interesting-family smile. Different even from her supportive-during-labor smile. Camille looked quiet and whole. India felt loud and emptied.

Camille came and sat on the edge of India's bed. She kept the baby pressed into her but rocked toward India so she could see.

"Isn't she beautiful?" Camille whispered.

India nodded, too cried-out to locate her voice.

"Do you think she looks like you?" Camille asked.

India looked closely. The baby looked like a baby. Small and red and wrinkly. "I don't think so," she managed.

"Me neither," Camille said neutrally, though somehow India felt it deep below her sternum. "Do you think she looks like Robbie?" Camille wrinkled her nose as she said it, which made India laugh, which made everything below her navel shriek with pain, but it was worth it. In the last couple hours, she'd forgotten all about laughing.

"No, actually," India said, finding her voice again.

"Me neither. I mean, don't get me wrong, Robbie's cute for a teenage boy. I totally see why you're into him." Even Camille's voice had changed, her tone, her words. "But that whole lanky goofiness he's got going on would look weird on a baby."

"Probably," India giggled.

"Do you want to hold her?" Camille asked, and when India raised her eyes to see if she was serious, she found Camille gazing at her already, holding the baby out. "Go on. She won't bite." And when India still hesitated, "I mean, hell, she might. I've been a mother for like an hour and a half, so what do I know? But even if she does bite, she doesn't have any teeth."

India made her arms into a triangle, and Camille slotted the baby in. She fit perfectly. Possibly because she was perfect. India tried to look up at Camille and say something like "She's so small" or "She's so beautiful," but she could not remove her eyes from the baby's face, not even for a second.

Camille was taking pictures.

India was taking breaths, one after another, timing them to the baby's. Or maybe, from long practice, it was the other way around.

Then the door opened, and Robbie and her mother came back from wherever they'd been.

"Good news. The lobby shop had Red Vines *and* gummy bears. I got both." He held them up, one in each hand. Then he saw India and the baby. "Oh," he said.

"You could hold her too?" India half asked, half offered before remembering that offer wasn't hers to make. "Is that okay?" she asked Camille.

"Of course."

He went right to the sink and washed his hands. He grabbed a clean towel from the cabinet. And then he did the most remarkable thing: he grabbed either corner of the hem of his T-shirt and pulled it off over his head. Camille and India eyed him, then each other.

"What?" he said when his head popped out. "I've been reading up about babies. Newborns are comforted by skin-to-skin contact," and Robbie installed himself in the glider, and Camille took the baby from India and lowered her into Robbie's arms, and she snuggled up against Robbie, just like he said she would, and broke India's heart.

"What did you name her?" Robbie asked, a perfectly reasonable question, though India wanted to close her ears so she wouldn't hear the answer. It was easier—would continue to be easier, she imagined, in the years to come—to keep thinking of the baby as "the baby," not as a person, a growing-up human with a name in the world.

"Rebecca," Camille said softly anyway. "After my grandmother."

MONDAY NIGHT

When they'd switched from DMs to texts, the first thing Fig learned was Rebecca's name wasn't Rebecca.

Rebecca: Stop calling me Rebecca!!!!!!

Then: Everyone calls me Bex

Fig: Oh

Then: Why?

Bex: Because it drives my mother crazy [winking emoji]

Then: Also it sounds like sex [two winking emojis]

Then: Sorry. Are you too young? I forget 10. I'm sweeeet 16

Fig: I know

Bex: You do?

Fig: Mom told me

Three dots. Three dots. Three dots. She talks about me?

Fig: All the time

It was hard to think of Bex as Bex after so many years of thinking about her as Rebecca. It was hard to think of her as a junior in high school after so many years of thinking about her as a baby. It was hard to think about her as a sister when she wasn't really, or as a friend when they'd never met, or as her own person when Fig was used to thinking of her as Camille's, as someone her mother gave Camille. Really it was hard to think of her at all because she was a secret. Fig told her mother everything, but she didn't tell her this. It's not that she thought she would be mad, exactly, but she didn't know what she would be, and she knew if her mother told her to stop texting with Rebecca—Bex—she would have to. And she didn't want to stop. She was learning so much.

For instance, she learned maybe she could be in choir because Bex was in choir which was surprising because . . .

Fig: My mom can't sing

Bex: I know

Fig: You do? How?

Bex: [Laughing till it cried emoji]

Fig thought about how it was weird that one of the things her mother was famous for was something she couldn't do. She thought about the whole nature-versus-nurture thing and decided there needed to be a third category since she and Bex could both sing.

Besides choir, Bex's other elective was video production, so the one she'd made wasn't just a regular selfie video. It had music and good lighting and a great special effect. In the video, Bex said she couldn't be silent anymore. It was time to come forward. Someone close to the situation (it was Fig!) agreed that help was needed, and the person who could provide the help was her. She knew she had to do the right thing. She owed it to the person who needed the help. She owed it to the world. She took a deep dramatic breath and brushed her hair off her shoulders and lowered her chin so she could look up through her lashes at the camera.

Then she said, "My name is Rebecca Eaney. I'm sixteen years old, adopted, and live in Seattle, Washington. And India Allwood—yes, *the* India Allwood—is my birth mother." She waved all up and down herself and stopped with her hand near her boobs. "In case you're math addled or just generally clueless, this means India Allwood gave birth to me when she was a teenager. So if you've been acting like a total fuckwad, you can stop now." Bex was India Allwood's child only in genetics, not in real life, so Fig guessed she could say whatever bad words she wanted. "She's legit. She's authentic. She's a 'trauma local'"—Bex had the camera pull away so you could see the quotation marks she was making with her fingers—"not a 'trauma tourist,' or whatever you're calling her, and anyone who says she's inauthentic doesn't know what they're talking about because India Allwood definitely knows what it feels like to be a pregnant teenager and give a baby up for adoption."

Then she did her special effect. The camera panned to a picture in a heart-shaped frame which clearly showed a girl in a hospital gown in a hospital bed, who was obviously a teenager and also obviously Fig's mother, holding a tiny swaddled baby. "That's me," Bex's voice said while the camera zoomed in on the tiny baby. Then it moved up to Fig's mother in the picture. "And that's India Allwood." She looked different, but she didn't look that different. Fig thought anyone would recognize her. But then Bex did a thing where the sixteen-year-old images of baby Bex and Fig's mother dissolved into current Bex and a photo taken of Fig's mother on the red carpet at the Emmy Awards last year. Her head was in the same sort of position, and she had the same sort of smile on her face, so you could see that not much had changed (for her mother; Bex, of course, had become a person instead of a baby) and that it was definitely India Allwood. Then Bex's video cut to her taking the photo out of the frame and pointing with green glitter nails to the date printed right on the bottom so you could see it really had been taken sixteen years before. Then Bex replaced the photo with her face, just as close, so you could see right up her nose when she said, "India Allwood gave me life. Lots of you really need to get one too," flashed a sideways peace sign, and stopped the video.

Later, hours later, after the video got viewed a million more times, after probably half of those views were by Fig's mother herself, after the dwebs spent the whole rest of the day calling her mother horrible names the FCC definitely would not let them say on television, after Ajax came back and talked loudly in the kitchen some more, after Evelyn Esponson rang her mother's phone forty-four times and left seven voice messages, after every reporter in California came with a camera and a microphone to the end of their driveway, after Fig felt like it would probably be understandable if her mother wanted to forget she even had children, given the day she'd had, but then stuck to their bedtime routine anyway except for tucking Fig in like she was wrapping an overstuffed burrito that absolutely could not leak because she planned to put it in a really nice purse, so tightly, in fact, Fig was sweating by the time she managed to free a hand from under her sheets to grab her phone, she found another text from Bex:

Maybe you were right the first time

Fig: When?

Bex: When I said I should come out and you said to LA

2005

"How do you feel?" her mother asked when they got home the day after the baby was born.

"I'm happy for the—Rebecca." India waved her hand around her middle where Rebecca had lived for so long until so recently. "She's like an old friend. It was great when she was here, and I miss her now that she's gone, but I'm so happy for her for the wonderful life she gets now."

Her mother nodded and said nothing.

"And I'm happy for Camille. She wanted to be a mother so much and now she is."

"Yes," her mother said carefully, "but I didn't ask how Rebecca and Camille feel. I asked how you feel."

India was surprised when her eyes spilled over. She hadn't even realized they were filling up. "I feel sad and happy and tired and grateful and excited and scared and worried and weird," India admitted.

"Me too," her mother admitted back. India had had so many people to think about—including the baby—she had forgotten to think about her mother and all the people she had to think about too. Including the baby. It made sense she would also feel a lot of things. But all she added—could add, maybe—was "Give it time. It'll pass."

"How do you feel?" her mother asked a week later when she got home from work to find India in her room surrounded by every piece of clothing she owned in a giant pile on the floor.

"Fat," said India.

"Fat is not a feeling," said her mother.

"Nothing I own fits anymore."

"Give it time. It'll pass."

"That's what you said last week."

"And do you feel better than you did last week?"

"That's not the point," India insisted.

"What's the point?"

"The point is I can't pack if none of my clothes fit."

Her mother shrugged. "So we'll go shopping."

"I need a whole separate suitcase for index cards."

"They sell index cards in New York."

"I need a wide variety."

A pie place opened near Robbie's house, and every day he brought over a new flavor. They ate it sitting at opposite ends of the sofa, holding feet even though India's fingers weren't swollen anymore.

"I can't wait till we have roommates besides my mother," she said.

"I like your mother."

"Me too, but think how much more freedom we'll have when I'm living in a dorm and you have a cool apartment in the city."

"I don't think it's going to be cool."

"You're going to get an uncool apartment?"

"I think cool apartments are expensive in New York. I'm going to have to live in someone's closet in someone's bedroom in someone's crappy house in New Jersey. Except I won't be able to afford it so I'll have to get a roommate."

"Edgy," said India. "Artistic."

"I'm not going to have time to be edgy or artistic," Robbie warned. "I'm going to have to work like a thousand hours a week so I can afford half the rent for my New Jersey closet."

"Maybe you can get a job on campus and we can line up our breaks. And when you have late shifts or early shifts, you can just stay over with me in my dorm."

"I think campus jobs are probably for students."

"Maybe you could wait tables at a fancy New York restaurant and bring back gourmet leftovers."

"I'm pretty sure I'm going to be washing dishes. In New Jersey."

"At a fancy restaurant?"

"Fingers crossed."

"I can study on the train," she said.

"What train?"

"The train to New Jersey. When I come to stay for the weekend and lotion your chapped hands and help you fill out applications for colleges in the city and eat gourmet leftovers."

"Speaking of gourmet leftovers, we're practically adults, right? We can have seconds on pie?"

India went to the kitchen to fetch it. "You know what might save a lot of money?"

"What?"

"If you worked at a pie shop in New York."

And then suddenly it was time. It was good she was going into college and not fourth grade, India thought, because her "What I Did on My Summer Vacation" essay would have been seriously traumatizing for a bunch of nine-year-olds. Three days before they were scheduled to leave, Robbie came empty-handed. The pie place had closed just as abruptly as it opened. Had it failed so quickly? Had Robbie been the only one who ever went there? Did this mean India's plan for him to work at a pie shop in New York was misguided? These were questions without answers.

They quickly became the least important ones.

"Listen," Robbie said.

"Always," said India.

Then he didn't say anything. He looked at her and looked away, closed his eyes and kept them closed when he said to her, "I can't come to New York."

"What do you mean?"

"I can't come to New York."

"Of course you can. Anyone can go to New York."

"Not me."

"Why?"

"I don't know."

"What do you mean you don't know?"

"My dad got a job in Arizona."

"It's like the pie," said India.

He looked at her to see what she was talking about, but not like he was thinking of changing his mind.

"We're adults now," she explained, "so you don't have to go where your dad goes."

"No, I know, but I'm not staying here. There's nothing for me here once you're gone."

"Right! That's why you're coming with me."

"I love you, India," he said gently, so gently, "but I'm not coming with you."

"Why?" She flung her arms wide, felt desperation spread through her body like some kind of fast-acting drug. Or fast-acting poison.

"Look at you." He gestured not at her but all around her room. "You're packed. You're ready. You're starting a new life. Classes, a dorm, new friends, a whole new city to explore."

"Yes, with you. A whole new city to explore with you. New friends to make with you."

"Yeah, but I won't be in your classes. I won't be in your dorm."

"That doesn't matter. You'll be nearby and—"

"And that's not all." He didn't let her finish. "There will be plays. Finally. Auditions to go to, directors who will actually cast you, late-night rehearsals, tech weeks with eighteen-hour days."

"So I'll see you the week after."

"Standing ovations to receive."

"I want you there. Standing in the audience."

"I know you do," said Robbie, "but I don't want to be there."

She crumpled then, folded right to the floor. "Why?"

"India, I would love to see you star in a play. I would love to be there when everyone in the entire theater leaps to their feet because they can't stay seated anymore because of how great you are. You think I don't want to see that? I want to see that more than anything."

"So what's the problem?"

"Because what about me? I'm just going to wash dishes all day while you think about philosophy and modern art? I'm going to hang out at home with my closet-mate while you learn and grow and star in stuff and meet people and make friends and all your dreams come true? New York is great for you. I'm thrilled for you. But it's not great for me. You're not thrilled for me."

"I *am*." She grasped his hands. "I am because it's the best city in the country. It's the best city in the world. You're my friend. And when I make new friends, they'll be your friends. And over dinner we'll talk about what I'm learning in philosophy and the dorm and what you're learning in your closet and the real world, and it'll be amazing."

"No."

"Why not?" she demanded.

And he said, very softly, "Because I don't want to."

"You used to."

"I didn't."

"You said you did. You were lying?"

"Not lying. But wrong, maybe."

"Don't do this, Robbie," she begged.

"It's better this way. It is. You won't have to miss out on hanging out with the girls on your floor so you can come over to my closet. You won't have to miss out on talking about all the stuff you're learning to all the people you're learning it with so you can talk to me about what it's like to wash dishes."

"But I'd love to talk about washing dishes with you. I love to talk about everything with you." She could hear that her crying was starting to sound more resigned than desperate and she didn't want this, tried to change the tone of her weeping. "But you'll take classes too. But we'll talk about washing dishes. But you won't wash dishes forever. Just for a little while. That was three buts!"

He reached down and pulled his shirt up over his head, stood before her naked from the waist up. "Come here." He opened his arms to her.

"I'm not a newborn."

"I know," he said. "Come here."

And she came into his arms, and he held her there, and he was warm, and he was all around her, and the baby books were right. It was comforting. But it did not make her stop crying. It made her cry more.

"We can make this choice, and it will be okay."

"It won't," she said, her ear against his heart, knowing it.

"There's nothing tying us together anymore. That was the whole point of doing what we did."

"No." She did not want to pull her face from his chest, but she did it anyway so she could look at him. "No! That was not the whole point. That wasn't any of the point. Just because we didn't want to get married right now doesn't mean we don't want to be together. Just because we didn't want to get married right now doesn't mean we might not want to get married someday. Just because we thought the—Rebecca—would have a better life with Camille than with us doesn't mean we have to break up."

"I think it does mean that." Robbie wrinkled his nose. "I think that is exactly what it means."

"Please," she whispered finally, desperately, "please. For me."

"That's it exactly," Robbie said. He was crying too, but he would not change his mind. "For you."

He left and India could not stop crying. He left and India could not stop wondering whether she was an idiot for not marrying him and having his babies when she had the chance. She could not stop thinking of those stupid cards and how maybe she had picked the wrong one. She was sure she had chosen right for Camille. She was sure she had chosen right for Rebecca. But maybe she had chosen wrong for her and Robbie.

She didn't know if she would ever stop crying. She didn't think it was going to be great when she showed up at college with bloodshot eyes and snot waterfalling out of her nose and her face puffed like a blowfish. She refused to get out of bed for two days.

Her mother came and stood in her doorway, arms crossed, lawyerly.

"How do you feel?"

"Terrible," India said. "Like I want to die. Like I don't want to die but that's too bad because I'm going to anyway."

Her mother kicked off her heels and climbed into bed with her, unlawyerly. "Give it time." She pulled her daughter into her arms. "It will pass."

TUESDAY

When Fig woke up in the morning, she had a new text from Bex. It was a screenshot of an email.

Which was a receipt for a ticket on an airplane.

Which was landing in fifteen minutes.

Fig's mom was having a hard week already, and now she was going to find out Fig had been keeping secret a secret friendship she was secretly having with Bex. Her mother wasn't the only person who didn't know—the only person who did was Jack, and that was only because they had to share a phone—but she didn't think pointing this out was going to get her out of trouble.

Fig had that hot-and-cold feeling again. She went to wake her brother.

"Will you sneak out the back with me?"

"I'm asleep," he groaned.

"You *were* asleep," Fig corrected.

"Why do you want to sneak out the back?"

"There's smears out front."

"There's always smears out front."

This was true, but it did not make them less terrifying.

At the top of Fig's scary list—and also Jack's and also their mom's—was the paparazzi. Maybe you would think number one on Fig's list would be fire, but if you were careful—and Fig was very careful—fire was something you could often prevent. You could not prevent the paparazzi, so they were another thing Mandela said they had to rename as a family.

On the way home from that therapy session, they'd stopped for cupcakes so they could brainstorm names.

"Instead of 'paparazzi,'" Jack said, "how about 'papasmurf'?"

"Papa Smurf is a good guy," Mom informed him.

"He's this old man who hangs around with all these little kids all the time."

"He's their dad," Mom said. "I think."

"Eww," said Jack. "That's even creepier."

"Are there any papas you *don't* like?" Fig asked her.

"Papasmears," she laughed.

"Who's that?"

"A Pap smear is when they stick a little brush inside your vagina and swab cells off your cervix to make sure you don't have cancer."

"I said eww too soon." Jack stopped eating. Jack never stopped eating. "Compared to that, Papa Smurf's not gross at all."

"It's not gross," Mom said. "It saves lives. But it's not a pleasant procedure to undergo."

"What about just smears?" Fig had suggested. "Because what the paparazzis do is smear us. And because it's short for Pap smears, which are not pleasant to undergo."

Therefore they had all updated their lists:

1. ~~Paparazzi~~ Smears

The smears did not just smear them, though. They chased them and stalked them and jumped out and sneaked in and climbed over and lurked. Fig's mother put in a security system with a driveway camera and a speaker and a big gate. It kept the smears farther away but not all the way away, so Fig and Jack had to sneak out the back and keep that a secret too.

"I hate the back way," Jack said. "The hedge has prickers."

"Yeah, but I don't want anyone to see."

"See what?"

Fig bit her lips. She didn't want to tell, but she had to tell someone, and anyway, everyone would know soon enough. "Bex bought a plane ticket." She glanced up at her brother to see how his face would look. "I think she's coming to help Mom."

How Jack looked was surprised. Not glad-surprised. Afraid-surprised. "How will that help Mom?"

"I'm not sure," Fig confessed.

He stared at her. Then he stopped looking alarmed and started looking happy.

"Why do you look so happy?" she said.

"You are going to be in such deep ass, your next turn with the phone will be in high school."

At the end of the driveway, there were lots of smears milling around, but mostly they were just eating breakfast and gossiping with each other. When Fig and Jack came out, they all paused and raised their heads—like in nature films when antelopes are drinking at ponds and lions sneak up—and also their cameras, but they lowered them when they saw who it was. Or probably who it wasn't. They weren't allowed to take pictures of Jack and Fig, and even though they were scary, most of them didn't if their mother wasn't with them. If Fig could have whistled to seem what her mother called "cool as a cucumber," she would have, but she didn't know how to whistle and she didn't think cucumbers were that cool anyway. They were just a vegetable. Instead she and Jack circled around and out the secret back way to meet their sort-of sister.

Bex rode up to the hiding spot in a car she'd called from the airport with an app Fig and Jack weren't allowed to use. Her mask had a picture of a screaming mouth, so when she took it off, she looked like she had calmed down immediately. Fig wished it was that easy.

"Welcome and thank you for coming," Fig said. Bex's suitcase was on wheels—it wasn't like she was carrying it and it was really heavy—but Fig took its handle from her anyway, then held out her other hand to shake.

Bex laughed.

"What's funny?"

"You're so formal for a little kid."

"I'm not a little kid," Fig informed her. "And I'm not formal. Just hospital."

"Hospitable?"

"Hospitable. This is Jack."

He gave Bex a little wave. She gave him a little wave back. Fig saw what Bex meant about her formalness.

"You guys look alike," Jack said.

Fig considered. This was not true. Fig was short for her age and at least half Korean. Bex was tall for any age and white like both her birth parents and her mom.

What was true was that Bex sort of looked and kind of felt like Fig's mom. And Fig looked and felt like what she was, which was dressed and groomed and raised by her mom and also friends with Bex, at least online. So what Jack meant was that they both had long, straight, dark hair in a low ponytail and were both wearing jean shorts and T-shirts and flip-flops, and Fig didn't look short but like maybe she hadn't grown yet, and they were both girls. Jack thought all girls looked alike.

"Now what?" he said.

Fig looked at Bex. Bex looked at Fig. "Go inside, I guess?" Fig answered for them both. "Tell Mom?" Her answers sounded like questions, those questions mostly being how much trouble was she going to be in.

"Suuuuch deep ass," Jack whistled.

ndia had only been asleep for maybe an hour when she heard Jack and Fig get up. It was summer, though, and they could get themselves cereal. Yesterday had been a very bad day, and she had been up till dawn watching Rebecca's video over and over and over and over. So she curled back into bed and fell asleep again at once.

Every time she rewatched the video, she felt something different, not deeper, not a new layer of the thing, not an evolution or a learning or a coming to terms with, actually a new feeling. She expected shock to ease to incredulity then amazement then mild surprise. Instead it toggled to euphoria then anger then hilarity, her sadness to vexation then pride then the-girl-in-that-video-totally-looks-like-my-high-school-boyfriend. It was strange and it was exhausting. Some of those feelings, that last one especially, made a lot of sense. But others did not.

Rebecca was not her daughter, not really, so the anger felt appropriate, what India was used to feeling toward random people saying random shit online. The vexation, though—that special annoyed exasperation reserved for your children alone—seemed misplaced. The euphoria made sense—seeing Rebecca, all grown up, loud and opinionated and self-confident and foolhardy and unafraid—but the pride less so, for Rebecca's loud, foolhardy confidence was nothing India could take credit for. It was all Camille. She could see Robbie around Rebecca's eyes and eyebrows. She could see herself in the way the girl moved and smiled. But mostly, she could see Camille all over her, that surety, that sense of being absolutely right in the world. She wanted to thank

Rebecca because she understood that the video was an effort to help, however misguided. And she also wanted to ground her until after graduation—college, not high school—for acting without thinking or asking permission and for making India's life far, far more difficult and complicated than it had been even eight hours previously, which was saying something since eight hours previously it had already been a colossal mess, not that Rebecca was or had ever been India's to ground.

Therefore, by the time India really woke up, woke up for good, it was already 10:15 and later than she had slept since becoming a parent. She put on a robe and went downstairs and found her children in the kitchen pouring cereal for Rebecca Eaney.

At first she concluded, reasonably, that she was still asleep. She'd only slept a couple of hours, but she'd spent them dreaming of the video so maybe it made sense to see it sitting at her kitchen table. But then it—she—leaped up, overturning her chair, which clattered to the floor behind her, and India could only conclude that she was flesh and blood. Her flesh and blood.

"Rebecca." India's voice sounded asleep still. Dreamy. "You're here."

"She goes by Bex, Mom," Jack said.

"Why?" said India.

"It sounds like sex," Fig informed her. "And it drives her mother crazy."

This was so obviously true it didn't occur to India till much later how Fig would know it. "I meant why . . . or maybe how," she fumbled, "is she . . . are you . . . here?"

"She flew in this morning," Fig said. "We snuck her in the back way so the smears didn't see."

Rebecca wrinkled her eyebrows at Fig.

"'Smears' equals paparazzi," Fig explained. "Remember I said Mandela makes us rename scary things?"

Remember? India's brain alarmed. "But," she began. Then she had to stop because there were too many ways to finish that sentence and no way to choose.

Then finally Rebecca—Bex—spoke up. Her voice sounded different from the one in the video. It sounded different from the one in India's imagination. "I said, 'Should I come out?' and she"—Rebecca, Bex, pointed at Fig—"was like, 'To LA?' and at first I was like, 'No, that's not what I meant,' but then I was like, 'Actually, that's a good idea,' so . . ."

She trailed off, which was fine because that single sentence, half sentence, inarticulate teenager-speak sort-of sentence, raised enough questions to last them the afternoon. India looked at her, bewildered. Here was this child, this being, who lived in her brain, a patchwork of memory and fantasy and possibility. Yesterday she'd gone from that to a real person on a video India could watch and listen to as many times as she wanted, as she needed, miraculous enough, but now here she was at her kitchen table, speaking directly to her. This seemed impossible.

Also impossible but evidently true, it seemed that Rebecca—Bex—knew her daughter. Maybe the thing to do was start there and work backward. "But how do you and Fig . . ." Except she couldn't finish that sentence, either.

Bex looked at Fig. Fig looked at India. Jack grinned around at all of them, happy, India knew, that his sister was the one in trouble for once.

"Okay." India closed her eyes, waited a breath, opened them again. "First things first. Rebecca. Bex. Did you tell your mother you were coming here?"

Bex shook her head.

"In a minute, we're going to call her. Are you okay?"

"What do you mean?"

"I mean it's a lot." India waved her hands around at all of them, the situation, the whole world. It was, if anything, an understatement. "You must have gotten up very early this morning and navigated some pretty daunting stuff all on your own. And I can see that my children have only fed you cereal."

"That's all we're allowed to get by ourselves in the morning," Jack said, reasonably.

"I'm fine," Bex said. "I eat cereal for breakfast too."

India saw Fig's face light with wonder and pride, the shared magic of such unlikely coincidence as both having breakfast cereal for breakfast.

This was going to be hard in so many different ways.

India went into Mom mode. It was her default position anyway, and it made sense—she was the adult here—but it also felt very strange. "If you decide to go straight back home, or if that's what your mother wants, we'll get you a flight right away. If you'd like to stay for a while, you're most welcome. Cam—your mother too. After you talk, we'll get you something more substantial to eat. Then we'll make a plan. Sound good?"

Bex nodded, but she didn't move.

"Do you have your phone, honey?" *Honey?* "Your mother must be very worried. She'll have looked everywhere she can think of, and trust me, here is maybe the last place she'd imagine. So why don't you just bite the bullet, give her a call, and let her know?"

Bex swallowed. "She's probably guessed."

"I doubt it," India said confidently.

"I used her credit card. And her account for the car." Bex wrinkled her nose—she looked so much like Robbie, India felt the kitchen tilt—then added, "And I posted another video on the way over."

Technically this was not the first time Bex had met India Allwood. She met her when she came out of her. She met her, and then her mom had let India hold her. Bex also thought about the nine months she had spent inside India. You might say that didn't count, but India was the only person Bex had ever been inside, so maybe it was a gray area.

The point was, she was too little when she was inside and just barely outside, so now she was meeting her *essentially* for the first time, and it was something she would never forget. India's kids did not look like Bex, no matter what Jack said, but India did, which was surprising. It's not that Bex hadn't known all along what India looked like—everyone in the universe knew what India looked like—but she looked different in person. She looked smaller. She looked slower, like her hands and feet and face weren't pretending to be part of someone else's body, like they did on TV, but were just being part of the body that was actually theirs. On TV, she didn't really look like Bex, and not just because of the Viking costumes. But in person, anyone they met might say, "I bet this is your mother."

The house was not a castle, like where she lived on *Val Halla*, which of course Bex knew but somehow was picturing anyway. It was not even a mansion like where you thought a movie star would live. It was a very nice house, though, with a kitchen her mother would swoon over, and through the glass door, you could see a big pool, big for a backyard anyway, and a pretty view. Or you could see it if you were looking, but everyone was looking at her instead. She sat up straighter and rolled her shoulders back—her mother always said good posture was two things: important and free—and tried to make herself look worthy or at least appealing. She'd gotten up super early, essentially last night, to sneak out of the house to make her flight, and she hadn't really slept because she was worried about being impressive, and excited about finally meeting India, and concerned that her mother's brain was actually going to explode when she found out what she'd done. Now though, she felt porous, like she'd left her covering at home and here she was with her whole body and mind and soul wide open.

She had imagined meeting India a million times. She liked her mom and her life fine, but it was weird when your birth mom was super famous and everyone knew her, and it was hard not to think about what it would be like to live in a giant mansion with an ice rink or a bowling alley or whatever, with outfits famous designers brought over to beg you to wear, with chefs who made you whatever you wanted to eat whenever you wanted to eat it and a private plane you could take to Paris for the weekend with your glamorous friends. It was hard not to think it would be nice to see a pair of cute boots and have a mother who said, "You should get those. We need somewhere to park our giant piles of money anyway," instead of one who said, "But you already have a pair of cute boots." Maybe lots of people looked at movie stars and envied them and thought about what it might be like to live that life, but probably hardly any of them had come so close and yet so far as Bex had.

It was also not quite upsetting but maybe unsettling that no one knew about Bex, not Bex herself, but that no one knew that someone who was her was out there, the baby India Allwood had in high school who grew up to be Bex. She got that India might be ashamed or embarrassed or not want any-one to know about it, but since *it* was Bex, it was hard not to feel like India was ashamed and embarrassed of *her*. Since India clearly didn't want to talk about it, though, Bex hadn't talked about it either. Maybe India would thank her for keeping herself a secret until now. Or maybe she would have if Bex hadn't ruined it by telling the whole world yesterday. Bex had imagined outing herself—well, outing them both—would shut up all the jerks and trolls being nasty about India Allwood's movie and thereby save her career. She had imag-ined that India was probably tired of keeping her a secret and would be kind of relieved for everyone to know. She had imagined that India would be grateful to Bex for fixing her public relations problems. But now that she'd done it, she could see that India might disagree.

Or maybe India thought Bex was the one who was supposed to thank her. For growing her for nine months? For not aborting her like most pregnant sixteen-year-olds would, Bex included when she thought about it, which she did. For giving her to her mom who was a little bit control-freaky but also cool for a mom. Was that the kind of thing someone expected a thank-you for? It seemed like the answer would be no, that that would be awkward and weird, but on the other hand, it was such a big thing. If you said thank you to the barista for handing you your coffee when the barista was getting paid to do exactly that, if you said thank you to someone for holding the door even though you were coming in right behind them and it hadn't taken really any extra effort anyway, didn't it make sense to say thank you to someone who had done such a big thing as make you and give you everything important that was yours? She said thank you to her mom for buying her school supplies and underwear and a new phone case. India Allwood, though, had literally bought her existence, and not with money, but with something way more valuable and hard to part with.

That was what she'd been worrying about on the plane. That was why she made another video in the car on the way over. Since the first one had gone viral, she had gone from a number of followers they indicated with numbers to a number they indicated with a number of Ks. She knew all those new followers were interested in what happened next, and she felt like they deserved to know, kind of as a thank-you for following her, speaking of thank-yous she didn't know if or how she was supposed to give. And she also figured some of them might have the answers to her questions. All she had to do was ask.

She thought of a good first line: "If India Allwood didn't abort you, would you want to say thank you?" And from there it was easy: "I don't know, but I'm pulling up behind her house to find out. Post opinions in the comments, and I'll read them from inside. Updates from there if I can! Thanks everyone!"

And if you thanked random followers you never even met, probably that meant yes, you should thank the person who gave birth to you too.

When Bex called her mom, it went straight to voicemail. Her outgoing message said, "You have reached Camille Eaney and may leave a message after the tone. It may interest a certain caller that the reason I cannot answer the phone is because I have just boarded an airplane," which answered the questions as to whether her mother had seen the video, whether she had thought to look at their shared ride-app account after Bex turned off locate-my-daughter's-phone, and how much time they had left before she showed up and started screaming.

The answer was about two hours.

When her mother arrived, Bex could see through the window—and despite the mask—that she was mad. Probably she was exhausted from the stress of Bex being missing and then found where she was found. Probably she was disappointed that Bex had exposed them all on social media. Probably she was cranky from the various aspects of air travel even Camille Eaney could not control. But when India opened the door, they fell into each other's arms and hugged and rocked and cried like "social" and "distancing" weren't her mother's most-used words for the past year and a half.

When they pulled apart, India reached into her pocket and threw a handful of paper in the air that fell all over everyone.

"What was that?" Bex leaned over to ask Fig.

"Probably a torn-up index card."

"Why did she throw it at us?"

"It's confetti. She's celebrating you and your mom being here."

"She just happened to have a torn-up index card in her pocket to use as confetti?"

"She always has a torn-up index card in her pocket to use as confetti."

"Thank you," India cried.

"Thank *you*," Bex's mother cried back. And Bex's mother never cried.

"No, thank you," India insisted. "You took such good care of her. You raised her so beautifully. Rebecca did an amazing job of growing up."

"Look who's talking," Bex's mother said.

"Who?"

"You! You were sixteen last time I saw you. You did an impressive job of growing up too."

Bex could tell that India was surprised to think of it this way. Bex was too. To her, they were both moms and both adults and both honestly kind of old.

"Some days more than others," India said.

* * *

Bex could have slept in the guest room with her mother, but Fig wanted her to sleep on the trundle in her room, and Bex didn't mind. They were both in trouble with their moms so it was better to share with each other anyway, but also, anyone would expect this situation to be surreal for Bex and India, but Bex could tell that Fig was pretty wigged out too, and she felt kind of bad.

It wasn't like she was using Fig. Fig was the one who found her, not the other way around. Okay, yes, it had occurred to her at first that befriending Fig back might get her more actual accurate information about India Allwood than she could find online. And yes, maybe she had manipulated Fig into inviting her to her house—or at least saying okay when Bex invited herself and claimed it had been Fig's idea. And yes, she had suspected it would get them both in trouble and also that this fact might matter less to her than it would to Fig. So yes, Bex felt a tiny bit guilty. But mostly, she could see that Fig needed a friend in this moment, and Bex saw no reason that friend shouldn't be her. And if it turned out India wasn't grateful to her for posting that video— those videos—maybe she would be grateful to her for being a friend when her daughter needed one.

But it turned out Fig wanted to be more than friends.

"Should we tell secrets?" Fig said as soon as the lights were off. "Isn't that what sisters do in the dark?"

"I don't know. I never had a sister either." Bex was curious about Fig's secrets, in case they had anything to do with her mother, but she felt guilty enough already so added, truthfully, "And I don't really think of you that way."

"Because you're white and I'm at least half Korean?"

"No" —Bex laughed—"because of my mom."

"She doesn't like me?"

"She doesn't know you," Bex corrected. "But we talked about your mother every night when I was little. My mom would tuck me in and kiss me good-night, and I'd say, 'Tell me how you got me,' and she would tell me this story, the same one every night. She memorized it. *I* memorized it."

"Tell me," Fig said.

Bex wasn't sure she wanted to, but then she started anyway. "'Once upon a time, there was a girl named India who was so full of love that some extra overflowed from her heart to her tummy and grew into a baby.'" But it was weird to hear her mother's words coming out of her mouth. "Sorry. I can't. Too embarrassing."

"It's true, though," Fig said.

"You do know how babies get made?"

"I'm not nine. I meant the part about being full of love."

"The point is, my mom wasn't leaving you out. You didn't exist at the time."

"But then you grew up," Fig said. "You must have known about me. We were in magazines and stuff until—" She cut herself off.

Bex rolled over, not that she could see her in the dark anyway. "Until what?"

"Mom had to make a rule. Me and Jack are off-limits."

Bex hadn't noticed, but she realized Fig was right. There were no new pictures of Jack and Fig online. Until they started texting, Bex hadn't seen Fig since she was little. That wasn't Bex's point, though. "It's not that I didn't know about you. It's that I didn't know you knew about me. Not until you DM'd me." She took a deep breath then admitted quietly, "I thought probably she never told you."

There was a pause. Apparently it was due to shock.

"She told me about you before I can even remember," Fig whispered finally. "My mother doesn't lie."

"All mothers lie," Bex regretted to tell her. "Don't feel bad. Mine lies too. Your mother wasn't overflowing with love. She was knocked up and in trouble and miserable. All she wanted was for her life to go back to the way it was. Before I happened."

"That's not true—"

"It is true." Bex couldn't believe she was saying all this out loud, never mind to a ten-year-old, never mind to India Allwood's ten-year-old. "I mean, I get it. I do. But there's no denying I equaled—equal—embarrassment and regret and shame for her."

"I deny it." Fig sat up so quickly her comforter slid off her bed and down onto Bex's. "You're not shameful."

"Not *me* me. She's barely even met me. But, like, the fact of me, out there somewhere, shaming her."

"No. No way." Fig flopped back down. "She talks about you all the time. You and your mom and your family. Our family."

"Okay," Bex said slowly, puzzling it out, "but then why was she keeping me a secret?"

2005

India wanted to take the train from the airport to her dorm, but she had too much stuff and no one to help—they'd decided, optimistically, to save her mother's vacation days for opening night of whatever play India got cast in—so she had to take a taxi. She'd thought maybe she could ask the driver to pull over on the Brooklyn Bridge so she could get out and stand on the shoulder and take it all in, but they went through a tunnel instead, and you couldn't pull over or take anything in in a tunnel. Shortly after they left the airport, though, a break between low brick buildings revealed the whole Manhattan skyline spread out before her, and she knew it didn't matter how she arrived. What mattered, the only thing that mattered anymore, was she was here.

She met her roommate, Dakota Day, and since they both had place names, their new friends on their new hall quickly christened their room the Map, and it became the center of all activity, the room everyone stopped by on their way to take a shower, the room everyone hung around gossiping in instead of doing homework. And just like that, India was popular and had friends and a social life and a million things to do and stayed up talking into the night with everyone about everything.

Except for one thing.

She didn't tell anyone about Rebecca.

It was like Rebecca had never happened. She could not believe it took nothing more than moving across the country to erase the biggest trauma, the biggest drama, the biggest fact of her life so far, a thing so big it had made an actual new human who was actually out there in the actual world. All she had to do was not tell anyone.

Well, not tell anyone, and do what she had come here to do.

The fall main-stage production was a play she'd never heard of called *Arcadia* by a playwright she'd never heard of called Tom Stoppard. She spent thirty minutes railing to her mother on the phone about how woefully behind her peers she was owing to not a single one of her five thousand forty hours of high school being spent on the contemporary theatrical canon.

"India!" her mother finally interrupted to remind her. "You know how to study. You know how to learn. You know how to do hard things."

"I do?"

"This is what those five thousand forty hours were preparing you for. Figuring out what you have to figure out. Don't think about what you learned in high school. Think about what you learned in high school."

Amazingly, this made sense. India went to the campus bookstore and bought a pack of index cards. Then she went to the library, checked out a copy of the play, and read it. Four times. Then she checked out the rest of Tom Stoppard's plays and read them too. A librarian helped her find critical analysis, reviews of productions, articles about Stoppard himself. She was at the library so often, they offered her a job.

Auditions were nothing like they were for Ms. LaRue. No singing, of course. No public humiliation, either. Here, you got a time slot. You showed up for it, walked to the middle of the stage, introduced yourself to someone you couldn't see in the audience, and announced what piece you had prepared. India did her *Merchant of Venice* monologue. She found a wastebasket and rolling desk chair in the wings and dragged them both onstage so she could flip the trash can and prop her feet on it and do the monologue the way she'd done it in high school: power-suited and certain and channeling her mother.

"I appreciate that read," a voice from out in the auditorium called to her when she finished, "but can I see it earnest?"

India blinked. "Earnest?"

"Yes, please."

She didn't know what he meant but also didn't feel she could ask. She took a deep breath and prepared to restart.

"And standing," the voice in the audience said.

"Pardon?"

"Could you please stand when you deliver your earnest read of the piece."

She stood, smoothed the suit even her mother had made fun of her for bringing to college, blinked into the lights, and gave as earnest a read as she could muster on the spot given that she didn't have any idea who she was talking to or what he was talking about.

Then she went back to her room and wept.

When Dakota got home, she sized up the situation—wet pillow, red-eyed roommate, used tissues all over the floor—but was unalarmed. They were drama majors, after all. "Girl, what is wrong with you?"

"Auditions," India moaned into her pillow, "went very, very badly."

"There will be other auditions." Dakota sounded a lot like India's mother: *Give it time; it will pass.* This was not helpful.

"I moved all the way here. I left everything—everyone—behind. The only reason I came here was for the theater program. And I blew the entire thing at audition one."

"Maybe not the *entire* thing."

"Forever," India added.

"Jesus. What happened?"

"I did a monologue I've done like thirty times before, and it's always killed, but that turns out to be because no one in my high school, including the teachers, would know good acting if it crawled on their face in the middle of the night and died because they live in Podunk Middle-of-Nowhere Loserville—"

"You're from Seattle." Dakota had been born and bred a hundred and ten blocks north of campus and felt generally skeptical about anywhere west of Newark, but still.

"They were all, 'India you're so talented, India you could get a scholarship,' when really they should have been saying, 'India, we're pretending the problem is you can't sing, but really the problem is you and your hair and your face and your body and your personality and your lack of skill and talent.'"

"Sounds surmountable," Dakota said.

"I finished, and he just said, 'Do it again.'"

"Who?"

"I don't know. I couldn't see him. He said, 'Do it earnest.'"

"What does that mean?"

"I have no idea."

"What did you do?"

"I did it again."

"Earnestly?"

"Who can say?"

She went to look at the callback sheet the next day with dread in her soul, in the first place because she was sick literally practically to death of going to look at lists posted after auditions and finding her name nowhere on them and in the second place because she'd survived the last time this happened only by meeting the love of her life, letting him woo and bed her, then having his baby, and as far as disaster-survival strategies went, that was a long way to go.

But lo and behold, she'd gotten a callback.

There they did cold reads from the script itself, except in her case they weren't cold because not only had she already read the play four times she'd also copied the whole thing onto index cards. It felt like cheating, but she was more prepared than everyone else, more nimble, didn't have to keep her eyes on the page and could act instead. She didn't want to get her hopes up—she was clearly lousy at judging how auditions went—but unfortunately, her hopes were up anyway.

She went the next day to check the cast list.

And she'd gotten a part. Not *a* part, actually. *The* part. She'd gotten Thomasina, the lead.

It was the best thing that had ever happened to her. It was the best thing that had ever happened to anyone. She tore one of the less important index cards into tiny pieces of confetti and threw them over her own head in celebration.

Then she called home.

"You did it!" her mother crowed. "Was it my advice to think about what you learned in high school instead of thinking about what you learned in high school?"

"Actually," said India, "I think it was Rebecca."

"What was?"

"Who made this miracle occur."

"Rebecca is a baby. Babies don't make miracles occur. Babies don't make anything occur. Exhaustion maybe. Poop. Anyway, this wasn't a miracle."

"It's the most incredible feeling—" India began, but her mother interrupted.

"I have no doubt. But who started researching drama schools at fourteen? Who studied her ass off for four years to make sure she'd get into the program of her dreams? Who prepped the shit out of this audition?"

"Me?"

"Yes you. Certainly not Rebecca."

"Yeah but maybe . . ."

"What, India?" In that voice where she'd anticipated what her daughter was going to say and already overruled the motion.

"Maybe this is my reward," India whispered because she wasn't sure she believed it, and she wasn't sure believing it didn't make her shallow or stupid or selfish or fate-tempting. "Maybe the universe is so happy to have Rebecca in it, it gave me this part as a thank-you."

"That's not how the universe works."

"You don't know how the universe works, Mom."

"True, but I know it's not like that. You are a good person who deserves good things, which doesn't always mean you'll get them, and you are a good actor and a hard worker, which makes landing the star part not only not miraculous but both logical and earned, if certainly not guaranteed. Rebecca had nothing to do with it."

Maybe, maybe not, but she had everything to do with India's success as an actor. When India needed to cry onstage, she thought of giving birth, of giving the baby to Camille, of Camille singing *Guys and Dolls*, of Robbie holding the tiny newborn against his bare skin. When she needed to be angry onstage, she thought of Robbie promising for nine months to do whatever she wanted, then changing his mind and breaking up with her instead. For her first two and a half years of college, she Stanislavski'd the shit out of love scenes by remembering meeting Robbie at the cast list after auditions, making out in the rain under the tree after her *Merchant of Venice* monologue, having sex after the annoyingly competent production of *Guys and Dolls*, slow-dancing at prom with Rebecca wedged snug inside between them.

Maybe it wasn't quite the miraculous intervention she'd suggested to her mother, but for sure she owed her life—the one she had now, the tremendous life where she got cast in every show she auditioned for and landed the lead more often than not—to Rebecca and Robbie. They had taught her, simply, everything she knew about being a human in the wide world. For a while, even, she thought they'd taught her all there was to know, all that was knowable, for what else was there besides love and birth and endings that were also beginnings? It was a lot. It was everything.

Then, halfway through her junior year, it turned out the seeds Rebecca and Robbie had planted reached tendrils further even than that.

TUESDAY

B ex woke in the middle of the night, then wandered around the house looking for the kitchen so she could get a glass of water. When she found it, she also found India sitting at the kitchen table staring out into the night. Bex could see her own reflection behind India's in the glass doors out to the patio. She looked like a ghost with her long white T-shirt and her slept-on hair. She looked like India's ghost—same nose, same mouth—hovering over her in the dark.

India jumped, then met Bex's ghost's eye. "Couldn't sleep?"

"I fell asleep," Bex said, "but then I woke up for some reason."

"I'm the same way." India nodded. "First night in a hotel or a strange house, I can't keep my eyes open, but then I wake up an hour later and can't fall back to sleep." A pause while they both considered that, then, "Can I get you something? Midnight snack? Warm milk?"

Bex wrinkled her nose. "Milk is one of those things I don't think should be warm."

"Agreed."

"I just wanted some water."

India got up and got her some. "Los Angeles is a lot dryer than Seattle. Everywhere is a lot dryer than Seattle, I guess. Sometimes I feel like I've been thirsty since I left."

"Do you miss it?" Bex asked.

"Sometimes. Not as much as I miss New York."

"I've never been."

"Oh, you have to go. The magic everyone tells you about is true. The stuff everyone complains about is not."

"Really?"

India shrugged. "Or maybe I was too in love to notice."

"With . . ."—she didn't think she'd say it, then she did—"my dad?"

For a blink, India looked confused. "No. Well, yes, but that's not what I meant. I was in love with the city, going to college finally, my dreams coming true, all that stuff."

"Getting your life back. You must have been so happy"—*to be rid of me*, she meant—"not to be pregnant anymore."

But India's face lit up. "I loved being pregnant with you." She sounded sincere, but Bex reminded herself that she was a professional actor. "Honestly, I just loved being with you. You kept me company my whole last year of high school."

"Weren't you . . ."

"What?"

"Embarrassed?" Had talking with Fig loosened this so it fell free? "I'd be mortified."

"I'd had three years of practice not giving a crap what anyone in high school thought of me. And anyway, I was oblivious because I was over the moon, all young and in love."

"With my dad?" Bex said again.

"With him. With you."

"Me?"

"For sure. Didn't your mom ever tell you?"

"She did. But I thought she was . . ."

"Bullshitting you?"

"Well. Yeah."

"I was so proud of you. Not proud like a mother is of her child—though I didn't know that at the time because I wasn't one yet—more like proud of something wonderful I'd made, like a poem or a painting or something. Like look at this perfect, beautiful thing I've created. I loved you so much. We both did. I've always hoped you knew that, felt it."

"I just figured you were sixteen and stupid."

"We were that, too." India laughed. "It's funny you call him your dad."

Bex felt her cheeks flame. "It's just because I have a mom." The reason she didn't refer to India that way, she meant, whereas Robbie Brighton was the only dad she'd ever had. "Can I ask you a weird question, though?"

"I'd say that's a reasonable request."

"You took one look at single motherhood and said, 'Hard pass, no way.' So why'd you pick it for someone else?"

"I didn't pick single motherhood for your mom." India shook her head. "She picked it herself."

Of course she did, because her mother picked everything herself, but that wasn't Bex's point. "You could have chosen two parents and you didn't, even though the whole reason you were choosing to begin with was because you knew how hard it would be to have to do it alone."

Bex watched India Allwood consider then reject a bunch of things she might say next before she finally decided on "Me neither, I never had a father. I know even less about him than you do about yours. And I was—am—close with my mom, so I knew what that felt like. But mostly? To be honest, your mother seemed like plenty all on her own."

"She is a lot," Bex agreed.

India laughed again. "It wasn't that I thought single motherhood was going to be hard. It was that I thought *parenting* was going to be hard, that parenting would always be hard, no matter the circumstances. I was right about that, by the way." She shrugged, like it was all obvious. "I was looking for someone who could handle it. And your mom? She seemed like someone who could handle anything."

Bex tried for the millionth time to imagine her mother before she was a mother and could not. What did she control before she had a kid?

"She seemed really changed after you were born, though," India said. "I remember in the hospital thinking you'd turned her into a different person. She was singing show tunes after she'd specifically said she didn't like musical theater. I thought maybe you'd turned her into a flighty hippie or something."

"She is big on recycling," Bex offered. "And we have season tickets to the theater. We love musicals. We wake up a lot of mornings humming the same song from some show we saw years ago. It's weird."

But India did not look like she thought it was weird. "Regardless of how they get made, family is a force to be reckoned with."

Bex took the pause that followed to say, awkwardly, "Thank you."

"For what?"

"Picking my mom for me, I guess."

"No." India shook her head, sure. "You don't have to thank me for that. You get that for free. You were my baby. You deserved the very best I could do for you. All babies do. That's not in question."

"What is?" Bex asked.

"How. Does this baby deserve love and care and the fucking moon is not a question. Of course she does. *How* is always the question. The idea that there's a simple answer or that that answer is the same for every baby, every person who gives birth to one, every family? That's what's absurd."

"That's why you said your movie was bad?"

"Not bad." India looked angry for an instant, then it passed like an exhale. "But yeah. There are infinity different kinds of families. And every member of every one has a different story to tell about it. So the fact that a few stories about adoption are the only ones that ever get told seems like a problem to me. And it leaves you thinking you have something to thank me for when really I should be thanking you."

"For what?"

"Growing up to be so impressive. Making me and your father and your mother proud."

Mothers were so cheesy, but Bex said, "That's what I sort of thought. That's why I came." Part of why, anyway. "I mean, it's not like I think I'm that great, but I turned out okay. You had me when you were a teenager and gave me up for adoption, and I didn't grow up to be miserable and do drugs like in your movie. I'm fine."

"You're better than fine. You're wonderful."

"And, I mean, you became Val Halla."

"What does that have to do with it?"

"You're better than fine too. You didn't get all drug addicted and filled with regret either. The movies all want it to be like your life ended when you got pregnant with me and . . ."

"And you weren't an ending," India finished for her.

"No," Bex agreed. "Not for me, anyway. I was just a baby. Was I an ending for you?"

"Oh, Reb—sorry, Bex—you were barely the beginning."

2008

ndia maybe wasn't even going to audition for *A Doll's House*. It was the kind of play you read in high school English class, not the kind staged by the A-list drama program of a prestigious Manhattan university. She offered to write something instead—a new play that would be timely and envelope-pushy and not over a hundred years old—but the department chair said casting agents were impressed by the classics. He had even hired a new faculty member to direct some.

India was unconvinced. But the scuttlebutt on the new hire was starry. But *A Doll's House* had a good female lead, which was, she had learned again and again, harder to find than it should have been, especially for serious dramatic talent such as herself (aka actors who couldn't sing). Two buts. So here she was.

India and Dakota had the first two slots but then hung around for the rest of auditions. There was a tatty red set-sofa someone had salvaged from some show or other stashed in the hallway, so they lounged outside the audition room all day. Friends showed up, exchanged hugs and cheek kisses all around, went in to do their monologues, then stayed and chatted, caught up, gossiped.

But at 2:57, an actor showed up whom neither India nor Dakota had ever seen before.

"You're not Annabeth Trevor," India observed at once.

"No," the kid agreed.

India got up from the sofa. It no doubt worked better as set furniture than as actual furniture—it was not at all comfortable—so she was glad for the excuse to stretch. "Who are you?"

His face arranged itself into a nice-to-meet-you smile. "Davis Shaw." He reached out a hand to shake. "Who are you?"

She took his hand but ignored his question. "Who's Davis Shaw?"

"Don't be rude," Dakota advised from the uncomfortable sofa, but Davis Shaw grinned.

"I am."

"So you said. But who are you?" India pressed.

"Um. Davis Shaw?"

"I feel like we're going in circles here."

"You're not wrong," he said, then asked again, "Who are *you*?"

"I'm India Allwood."

He grinned wider and played along. "Who's India Allwood?"

"Drama major. Future Broadway star." She flung her arms wide. "Talent of a generation."

"Cool." Davis Shaw pointed to his own chest. "Double English and CS major with—"

"CS?"

"Computer science."

"Like how they work?"

"More like programming. To make them work."

"Sounds boring."

"Sometimes."

"What are you doing here?"

"Auditioning for the play?"

"No you're not. Three o'clock is Annabeth."

"I'm three thirty."

"You're early."

"Yes."

"Why?"

"I've never been to the theater building before. I wanted to make sure I didn't miss my slot."

"Not why are you early," India huffed. "Why are you auditioning? What does *A Doll's House* have to do with computer science?"

"Nothing?" he asked.

"That's what I would guess too."

"*A Doll's House* is my grandmother's favorite play."

India blinked. "*A Doll's House* is no one's favorite play."

"It's my grandma's."

"Has she seen more than one?"

"Yes, but she likes this one best."

"Why?"

"She's Norwegian."

"Norwegians have bad taste in plays?"

"Her grandfather once made Henrik Ibsen a pair of shoes."

India wasn't sure what to say to that. "Really?"

"Probably not," Davis Shaw admitted, "but that's what he said, so she has an affinity."

"For lying Norwegians?"

"Either her grandfather really did make Henrik Ibsen a pair of shoes, or Henrik Ibsen was important enough to her grandfather to lie about making shoes for him."

"Or she's lying about her grandfather saying so."

"Why would she lie about her grandfather saying he made shoes for Henrik Ibsen?"

"I have no idea. Why would dissembling-Norwegian-cobbler ancestry make an untalented computer science major want to audition for a play?"

She watched surprise—and something else—stretch his mouth and eyebrows apart from one another. "What makes you think I'm untalented?"

"Have you ever been in a play before?"

"I was in my high school musicals."

"I rest my case." But she didn't. "This isn't something you can just decide to—"

"My grandmother moved into a retirement community a couple weeks ago," he interrupted.

"In Norway?"

"New Jersey."

"I think I see your confusion," India said. "Are you sure your grandmother's Norwegian?"

The something else bloomed and spread. "Why would I be wrong about my grandmother being Norwegian?"

"It's just that you're . . ."—India paused and wasn't sure it was polite to say then wasn't sure it was polite not to say then wasn't sure she was being polite—"Black."

"You're kidding!" He sounded shocked. Maybe he *was* a good actor.

"Are there many Black Norwegians?" India asked.

"Not that many. But I'm not only Black. I'm also half Black."

"And half Norwegian?"

"On my grandmother's side. She's an old white lady who's kind of bummed about having to move into a home, so I thought maybe if I got Torvald, that would make her happy."

He kept saying things she didn't know how to reply to. She couldn't remember the last time that was true. "So not only are you just waltzing into auditions, you've also decided to be the star."

"I mean, any part would be great."

"To make your grandma happy."

"Cheer her up. Give her a good reason to come into the city. Give us something juicy to discuss on the phone."

"You talk to your grandma on the phone?"

"On Sunday mornings."

"About Norwegian realism?"

"About everything."

She could see him watching her. Not just looking at her. Not judging her. Amused. But also definitely watchful.

"That's weird but sweet," she said finally. "Still, I wouldn't get her hopes up."

"Too late. She has more faith in me than you do."

"Look at the list." She nodded at the audition names and times posted on the door. "How many students are trying out?"

Davis looked. "Lots?"

"I can see it's your precision that makes you a good computer scientist. And how many parts in the play?"

"Not that many?" Davis guessed.

"So almost everyone on that list is going home unhappy."

"But not all of them." He grinned again. "Some of them will get parts. Why can't I be one of the some?"

"These are the best drama students at one of the best drama programs in this city, which means in the world," India said. "Most of them have been in more productions than they can count."

"Theater majors aren't great at math," Davis pointed out.

"We live and breathe this life, dedicate our entire selves to our craft, feel it in our very souls. Whereas you, you've been partying with your frat bros and thinking about computers and kinda wanna do a play to make your grandma happy. I think even she would admit your chances here aren't great."

His face was bright and incredulous and thrilled. And two days of auditions later, he also got the lead in the play.

Well, the male lead in the play.

On the first day of rehearsal, the director, Professor Alan Darden ("You can call me Al. Like the song") asked the assembled company to sit in a single line across the stage. It stretched from wing to wing. The theater/dance double majors all tipped from their hips over wide-apart legs. The crew leaned back on their hands. Knees and elbows took up personal space.

"Closer," said Al-Like-the-Song.

They pushed backpacks and books and scripts and water bottles out of the way. Scooted an inch or two toward center stage by rocking back and forth a few times.

"Touching," Al said.

Theater majors did not have to be talked into physical contact. Elbows were linked, arms flung around waists, legs over legs. Shoulders were massaged. Dakota laid her head in India's lap.

"Aligned," their director clarified. They giggled but did as he asked. India could not truthfully say she hadn't noticed Davis on her other side. She could not truthfully say there wasn't a little frisson of something when touching turned out to mean him too rather than just Dakota. But she wasn't prepared for the jolt that lit up her left side as her shoulder and arm and leg grazed his. She turned to him, stunned, and when their eyes met, she felt that jolt again, less tingle, more electric shock.

"Closer," Al-Like-the-Song said again.

Which at that point seemed impossible without getting naked. They were hip to hip, shoulder to shoulder, crowded already, but when pressed, they could press, not just touching and overlapping but squeezing together, breathing together, sharing the same air and the same space and the same body really, crushed up against one another just shy of painfully. The line that had stretched wing to wing now spanned maybe only fifteen feet or so. It wavered—it was hard to balance that way—but propped itself up, held itself as one.

Al-Like-the-Song nodded, satisfied. "*That* is the kind of *Doll's House* we're going to do."

When he finally released them—not from rehearsal but from physical contact—India felt a little dizzy, a little overwarm, a little overwhelmed, but she followed along as best she could.

"Usually the point of this play is that Torvald"—Al made Davis stand up—"is old-fashioned, hopelessly lacking in passion, imagination, courage. He thinks of his wife"—he made India stand too—"as a child, his child."

"Eww," said Dakota, who was playing Kristine.

"We're going to turn that on its head," said Al-Like-the-Song.

"His child thinks of him as a wife?" said Dakota.

"Nora and Torvald are passionately in love." Al pressed India and Davis lightly on their backs so that their fronts came together. "They can't keep their hands off each other."

India was standing so close to Davis she had to draw her head back so she could see him blush.

"But then why is he such a dick?" said Dakota.

"Men"—Al spread his hands—"are often dicks to the people they love. Passion and even adoration and even deep love are not enough if they are not accompanied by respect, equality, mutuality. She's willing to leave her children. And she's willing to leave her hot husband whom she adores and with whom she has mind-blowing sex. Because they're not enough."

Later India would wonder at what point Al-Like-the-Song had spun this read of the play. Was it his intention going in? Or had everything he planned turned upside down during callbacks when he saw Davis and India act together, as it had for her? She'd been surprised and maybe a little intrigued to see his name on the callback list, but when they were paired up doing scenes during the second day of auditions she felt herself catch fire. Not like she was going to flame away into ash. Like she was sparking into life. He wasn't good for a computer major. He was good, period. And—she could feel this right away—he would make her better.

When rehearsal let out, India and Dakota headed to the dining hall. Davis tagged along. They dropped their bags at a table and split up to get their food. When they got back, India had two bowls of chocolate cereal and one of raw carrots. Dakota had a plate of spaghetti she'd taken to the nacho bar and loaded with shredded white cheese, shredded yellow cheese, and a molten orange substance it would be overly generous to call cheese of any kind.

Davis had a salad. He made appalled eyes at their trays. "I can see my services are going to be required here."

"For feedback on our dinner selections?" Dakota was also appalled. "Pass."

"Carrots strengthen your jaw muscles to help you enunciate onstage," India informed him.

"Really?"

"Or maybe I used to be a rabbit."

"When?"

"In a previous life. I'm a Zen hen."

"I thought you were a rabbit. What's a Zen hen?"

"I don't know. My high school boyfriend used to say it. But like a Buddhist. Like reincarnation."

"Also spare me the sanctimony." Dakota waved her fork at him. "That salad is as big as my head."

"Extra spinach," said Davis.

"And croutons and cheese and dressing and ham."

India reached into her coat pocket and threw a handful of torn-up index cards in the air.

"Hey!" Davis said. "You're getting paper in my healthy dinner."

"Not paper," India corrected. "Confetti."

"She's celebrating the first day of rehearsal." Dakota slurped her nacho spaghetti.

"You brought torn-up paper in your pockets to celebrate the first day of rehearsal?"

"No," said India, "I always have torn-up paper in my pockets."

"You do?"

"Yes."

"Why?"

"In case there's something to celebrate."

After dinner, Dakota headed back to their room, and India went to the library to study. Davis said goodbye, but five minutes after India settled in, he slid in across from her without a word.

She raised her eyebrows at him. He opened a book and uncapped a highlighter like she wasn't even there.

"What are you doing?" she whispered.

"Shh. Studying."

"Why are you doing it here?"

"This is the library."

"I'm trying to work," India said.

"Me too. Could you keep it down?"

Maybe he was teasing her. Maybe he was trying to distract her. Maybe he was only pretending to study. But he kept doing it. Rehearsal was from five to seven every evening. After rehearsal they went to dinner. After dinner they went to the library. They closed it down every night, like closing down a bar, kicked out at midnight when the lights flashed. Then they said goodnight and went back to their dorm rooms to sleep and get up and do it all over again.

"You're very industrious," he said on the walk from dinner to the library one evening.

"You say that like it's a bad thing."

"You hear it like I say it like it's a bad thing."

"You don't get it because you're easy-smart."

"Easy-smart?"

"There are two kinds of smart people," she said. "The kind for whom it's effortless and the other kind."

"Illuminating."

"You read quickly. You understand complicated sentences the first time. You have a naturally big vocabulary. You memorize easily and test well. You do hard things fast."

"How do you know?"

"You work across from me every night."

"Exactly. I spend just as many hours studying as you do."

"Yeah, but in the same hour, I read ten pages and you read thirty. I answer

three questions and you finish your whole assignment. My brow's all wrinkled with trying to understand shit, and you're like, 'No problem. I read
it once, and I totally get it, and I've had some super smart thoughts of my
own.'"

"I have never said that in my life."

"Look how smooth your forehead is," said India.

"So's yours!"

"Because I'm nineteen."

"Me too."

"Yes, but when we're eighty-four, you'll still look like this, and I'll look all
wrinkly and confused."

"I can't wait," Davis grinned, like she meant they'd be looking that way
together. "You're smart."

"I am," she agreed, "but I have to work hard to be that way. That's why I'm
so industrious."

"I didn't mean 'industrious' as a criticism, just an observation."

"That what?"

"That if I said we should skip the library one night and go back to my
room and watch a movie or something, you'd say no if it didn't involve index
cards."

"I'd say no even if it did involve index cards," India assured him.

Davis was talented—widely talented—and smart and funny and extremely
attractive and nice to his grandma. But she believed in the delicate chemical
balance of the play and would never do anything to jeopardize it. Shows were
always intimate. You always had strange relationships with and feelings for
your castmates, especially the actor opposite you. But it was pretend. India
knew this.

Plus, this show was more intimate than usual. Al-Like-the-Song's principal
direction was "All hands." Not like on deck. Like on each other, whenever
possible. Torvald and Nora held hands like teenagers. They wore jeans in some
scenes because Al had reset the play to present-day Oslo, and they forever had
their hands in each other's back pockets. They wore fancy dress for the party
scene, and Torvald took so long pulling Nora's zipper up that Dakota had to
lie down in front of a fan.

"I also want them making out whenever possible," Al directed.

"Aye aye, Captain," Davis said, and tried to french India while Torvald and Nora wrapped Christmas presents.

"Eww, gross!" She pushed him away. "He means stage kissing, not actual tongues."

"Sorry," Davis said, and meant it. "I didn't know there was a difference."

So she showed him how to fake it. Real lips, pretend tongues, real hands slid along the backsides of pretend party attire, real fingers tracing costume costume-jewelry decorating real throats.

One night in the library, he looked up from his work and found her eyes already on him.

"You're staring at me." He smiled.

"I'm studying."

"Studying my face."

"Your face was in a book."

"Studying the top of my head, then."

"You're staring too," she said.

"Not staring. Peeking. Occasionally."

"That's not studying."

"It's studying you."

"I'm not going to appear on the exam."

"Who can say?" Davis spread his hands. "Best to be prepared."

"What have you learned?"

He tapped his pencil on his chin and considered. "That you're crazy talented. Smart. Funny." He paused. "Beautiful."

"Library light is very flattering," she said.

"That you think about things differently than anyone else."

"You got all that from looking at me in the library?"

"I'm a quick study. What about you? What did you learn off the top of my head?"

It was out of her mouth before it was fully formed in her head. "I keep forgetting I'm not in love with you."

It was unreasonable to expect him to understand because he was a computer science major and had no real stage experience save the last month of rehearsal with her, but he got it immediately anyway. "You mean because you spend two hours of play practice a day being in love with me?"

"Yeah." More an exhale than an answer. "Not just in love with. In life with. Besotted by. Aflame from. Heartbroken on account of. Anyway"—she shook her head a little, shook her brain—"that's why you think that."

"Think what?"

"That I'm talented and beautiful and interesting. It's not me and you. It's Nora and Torvald. You'll get used to it. It gets easier during tech week. Costumes. Sets. Lights and all that. She'll stop looking so much like me."

"I see you," Davis said. "I've seen you from the first moment I saw you."

In rehearsal, they weren't getting the final scene. They did it over and over and kept having to do it some more. Whatever Al-Like-the-Song wanted from them, they weren't giving it to him.

"I think the problem is Nora," Davis said finally.

India was instantly outraged. "Who's the rookie here, you or me?"

"I'm not saying *you*. I'm saying the character. She doesn't make sense to me. She's—"

"Me," India interrupted. "She's me."

"Maybe that's the problem. You're so convincing. But then when I think about it, I don't get her."

"This is good," Al said. "Pinpoint it. Use it. This is your wife, the love of your life, but you don't understand her. Why?"

"I mean"—Davis blinked and blinked again—"she walks away."

"She has to," India said at once. "She loves him, but she can't stay. *So* she can't stay."

"With Torvald, maybe. But her kids? What kind of mother leaves her kids? These tiny, helpless people she literally formed from her body, harbored inside her for nine months, brought into the world, the most basic biological, chemical bond, and then she just abandons them. It's unnatural."

"Good. Lean into that," Al said.

But she—maybe Nora, maybe India—did the opposite. She leaned back, leaned away.

"Maybe it would make more sense if she died," Davis mused.

"You think she deserves to die?" India felt like he'd slapped her.

"Not deserves to. Just, you know, like that's how it makes sense for the play to end."

"Ours is not to rewrite the play, Mr. Shaw," Al-Like-the-Song regretted to inform him, "but to look out across the abyss of time and strive for meaning. Let's take it from the top, please."

When the lights flashed at midnight that night and Davis and India gathered up their stuff to leave the library, she found she didn't remember a single thing she'd read all evening. Outside, the March midnight cold was made colder by the fact that she was still dressed for the spring afternoon it had been when she chose her outfit. Or maybe that wasn't why. She hunched her shoulders against the wind and said goodnight.

"Are you mad at me?" He was already shrugging off his jacket and not handing it out to her but wrapping her in it, holding it shut over the front of her with his hands as if the zipper wouldn't work just because it was too big on her.

"No. Of course not."

"I wasn't talking about your performance. I just meant the character as written. These are the perils of the double English major. You're doing a great job."

"Thanks. You too."

"I wasn't dissing the play. Just . . . trying to get the scene right. Don't be mad."

"I'm not mad."

"And anyway, you don't have to defend her. Nora. She's not really you."

"You don't get it—" India began.

"Exactly. That's what I was trying to say."

"But I do." She looked up at him, so close, and back down at her shoes. Took a deep breath. "You said what kind of woman would form a tiny, help-less person from her body and harbor it inside for nine months and bring it into the world and leave it behind. But I did."

"What do you mean?"

"I had a baby. Right after high school. Rebecca."

She wasn't sure why she was telling him. Because Nora and Torvald shared so much? Because she had learned from Nora and Torvald what happened when you didn't share enough?

His eyes went wide, but he did not step back from her. "You were pregnant?"

"Yeah."

"And you gave your baby up?"

"Placed her. Made an adoption plan for her. Yeah."

"Did you . . ."

His expression was so surprised it bordered on pain, and she noticed that her heart was beating very fast.

"What?"

"I don't know. See her? The baby?"

"I saw her. Robbie—my boyfriend—and I both held her." India tried but could not keep her eyes from spilling over. "We said goodbye."

Davis nodded. She could see his breath and hers, white clouds in the tiny space between them, proof they were both still breathing. "Was it hard?" he said finally.

"It was very hard."

"I can imagine." He nodded some more. "Is it still?"

Her turn to be surprised, mostly that that question never really occurred to her anymore. "Not hard, really. Sad sometimes. Or not even sad, because I know the life she got is so much better than the one she'd have had with me. And the life I got is so much better than the one I'd have had with her. But I think of her. I feel her still."

Davis chewed on his lip, and she worried it would bleed in the cold, and she knew there was more, and she knew what he would ask next. "Why didn't you just . . . you know . . ."

"Have an abortion?"

"Yeah."

"I knew giving the baby to someone who wanted a baby would make them really happy." She shrugged like it was simple, but it had been a long time since she'd had to explain this to anyone, and she wondered if it still made sense. "I'd just found out I got in here, so all my impossible dreams were coming true all of a sudden. It felt like . . . a confluence of beginnings I guess. It felt good to make someone else's dream come true too."

"Wow. That's very . . ." He trailed off so she prompted.

"Unnatural?"

"No! That's not what I was going to say."

"That's what you said in rehearsal."

"Nora doesn't give her kids up for adoption. And you didn't abandon your child. It's totally different."

"Then what were you going to say?" India noticed she was still crying.

"I was going to say brave. Or, I don't know, valiant?"

The small space between them had warmed up, or maybe just gotten small enough that she couldn't see him breathe anymore.

"Neither one," she said. "All I had to do was nothing. The baby just grew on her own."

"But to put yourself through being pregnant instead of just . . . stopping it."

"It wasn't that bad. High school was kind of stupid anyway. I mostly just studied and hung out with my boyfriend which I could do anyway."

"I guess. I think I'd just want it gone."

"Maybe you would." India shrugged. "Lots of people do. But not everyone."

"And your . . . Robbie?"

"He wanted to do whatever I wanted to do."

"And then you just . . . gave her up?" Davis still sounded awed.

"She wasn't mine. She never was. I grew her. But she's Camille's. The adoptive mother. She was Camille's all along."

"Did you—do you—ever regret it?"

"Not once," India said. "Not for one minute."

He nodded. And then he shook his head. And then he didn't say anything. The wind picked up, and she shivered in his jacket in his arms. "I think you are the most amazing person I have ever met," he said.

"I'm not."

"You're wrong." He wiped the tears off her cheeks with his fingers. "Your brain and your heart are both so much more interesting than anyone else I know. It makes you such a good actor. But it makes you an even better person."

She noticed she wasn't cold anymore. Maybe it was relief—to have told, to have told *him*, whose opinion she didn't want to care about as much as she did, and been understood, and not just understood but admired.

Or maybe it was something else.

"This is why I keep forgetting I'm not in love with you," she said again.

"Maybe you are," he said this time.

She considered this possibility. "Maybe."

They were standing so close all they had to do was lean forward and they were kissing, her hands on top of his still clasping his jacket closed around her.

When they parted, what he whispered was "Wow," and she was about to agree when he added, "I am a *great* actor."

She laughed. "What makes you think so?"

"Kissing you outside the library is completely different from kissing you in rehearsal."

"Of course."

"And not just because we used tongues."

"Maybe because there weren't three sophomores sitting at our feet pretending to be our children and Al-Like-the-Song standing six inches away saying, 'Okay, but can I see it again stage left?'"

"Or maybe because you were right," he said.

"When?"

"When you said you were her. We were them. In rehearsal, we must be. We must become them. Because Torvald's kissed Nora lots of times. But it was nothing like that. That was a first kiss."

"How was it?" India asked.

"Auspicious."

"Just what every girl wants to hear," she said.

WEDNESDAY

"Oh for fuck's sake, Ajax—" Their mom broke off what she was saying to kiss the top of Fig's and Jack's heads when they arrived downstairs in the morning then push them gently toward the kitchen so they could eat and she could curse.

"Morning, sweets," Ajax said to them, and they gave him a sleepy wave.

"*Val Halla* may be a 'family show' and my 'untarnished' image may be 'important to the network,' though I have to say, this is the first I'm hearing of it, and they're not exactly paragons of virtue over there."

Fig's mother had stopped using just her voice and fingers to make quotation marks and was now using most of her upper body. It was becoming a workout almost.

"But all that has fuck all to do with my being pregnant a decade before they hired me."

"They're not saying it does necessarily," Ajax sighed, "but they have some questions, and they don't like surprises." Fig knew how they felt. She didn't like surprises either. "They feel they've been the victims of a massive cover-up."

"They haven't been the victims of anything. Ever. And no one was covering anything up. If they asked literally anyone I went to high school with, believe me, they'd get the whole story."

"Which makes them wonder why they've been kept in the dark."

"Because it's none of their fucking business!" her mother yelled. "Is it their contention that before they cast me they deserved a blow-by-blow of India-Allwood-the-high-school-years?"

"I believe it's their contention that there's a difference between things one doesn't mention because no one will care and things one doesn't mention because everyone will."

"And anyway"—apparently she didn't care about that contention—"having a baby is not immoral, not even when you're sixteen."

"But lying about it—"

"Not even if you're lying about it. And I wasn't lying about it. And it's not the fourteenth century. It's not scandalous when sixteen-year-olds have sex 'outside of marriage.' What would be scandalous is if sixteen-year-olds were getting married just because they were having sex. It's not scandalous to place a baby for adoption. I wasn't shipped off to a nunnery for my confinement. The fact that the dwebs are calling me a slut and a whore and . . . I mean first of all, they were calling me that anyway, last week, before they knew about the baby, just because I have the audacity to be a female human they've heard of. It's sexism. It's misogyny. And if the network claims otherwise, it's only because they're sexist misogynists too."

"I believe they would argue they'd be given equal pause by any man in their employ undergoing similar . . . shall we say 'challenges' on social media."

"Are they lying," Mom wondered, "or just idiots?" If Ajax had an answer, it must have been a visual since the next words Fig heard were still her mother. "And second of all, if Production's going to fire actors whenever people are assholes online, they're going to have some serious staffing issues."

"Of course." Ajax had on his let's-all-calm-down voice. Fig heard it a lot. "No one's saying otherwise. They just have some questions. Some concerns. And I am merely suggesting that we understand this fact, then answer them reasonably and honestly."

"And I am 'merely suggesting'"—Fig's mother's voice was the opposite—"that I am unwilling to stipulate that their questions on this point are reasonable or honest."

Which was a funny thing to say because when Bex and Camille arrived downstairs, all Fig's mother wanted to do was ask them questions. How did they feel this morning, and what did they need, and how were they handling suddenly being the subject of a Hollywood scandal, ha ha, and did they have any questions or concerns, about that or really anything, and were they hungry? Maybe pancakes or French toast, or did they just want cereal? Yogurt?

Eggs? She could make eggs. Or, no pressure, maybe they just wanted to lie low and chill out and get their bearings before they made any decisions. Did they want to see the photo albums? Or maybe play a board game?

Eventually Bex shrugged. "I'd go see the Hollywood sign."

Everyone looked at everyone else.

"We can send Ajax out first as a decoy," Fig's mother said.

"I'm not a duck," said Ajax.

"Do you want to come see the Hollywood sign?" Jack asked.

He did not. So he sighed and went to be the duck, and everyone else piled into the car, moms up front, Bex between Fig and Jack in the back seat. Bex's legs were longer so maybe they should have given her a window, but they both wanted to sit next to her. When the gate opened to let the cars out, the smears swarmed up like fruit flies when you grab a banana that's been in the bowl too long. A limousine was blocking the path out, which they're not allowed to do, and when Mom put down her window to say so, a woman got out.

She came over and held her hand toward Mom and said, "Evelyn Esponson. We meet at last. It's a pleasure."

Mom ignored her hand and her words. "Please move your car, Evelyn, before I call the police."

Evelyn Esponson ignored her right back. "I have a surprise."

"Not interested," Mom said.

"I think you will be interested." Evelyn leaned over and tried to see inside the car. "I think you all will."

"I don't care what you think," Mom said. "And you can't block my driveway."

"It's not just a surprise for you. It's for everyone. Your special houseguest in particular."

Mom sighed and put the car in reverse. Ajax did the same.

"Honk!" Jack protested. "Flash your lights. Rev your engine. Bash them with our car."

"I'm not bashing anyone with anything."

Jack put his window down, leaned out, and yelled, "Ass off, you smears!"

"Put your window up, baby," Mom said. "We'll wait for them to get bored, call a car, and go out the back. Sorry Bex, Camille. Welcome to the Allwood household."

But Evelyn Esponson had gone back to her limousine and was posing in front of a camera. She took off her mask, applied new lipstick, flipped her hair, and began. "I'm here at the home of India Allwood who has had quite a week. Following efforts to counter criticism from fans, activists, and concerned observers by denouncing her own movie came the revelation of an illicit love child, Rebecca 'Bex' Eaney, who posted a series of videos online revealing her identity and then arrived here sometime yesterday morning. Now, after extensive investigation—and in a *ME* exclusive—the birth father has been found and is eager to meet his new *old* family."

She made a fancy motion with her arm and opened the back door of her long car.

The man who emerged looked dressed for important work. At least, half of him did. His top half had a white button-down shirt and jacket. His bottom half had jeans and sneakers. His mask matched his tie. Fig looked at his eyes, and they looked worried, and then they looked around and looked in the car and looked for a long time at Fig's mother and then they looked more worried. Then they squeezed shut.

All the smears who had been swarming up already swarmed harder. They pushed and shouted and waved their phones and cameras. The man turned and tried to get back in the car he had gotten out of, but Evelyn Esponson held him tight by his elbow. She motioned to her cameraman to keep close on everyone's faces. She tried to lean into Mom's open window and called hopefully, "Rebecca Eaney. What a moment. You've just gotten in touch with your birth mother, and now your birth father's arrived as well. Can you share with us how you're feeling?"

Bex's eyes looked at the man and also looked kind of wide and white and scared, which the rest of her face did too.

"We don't talk to smears," Fig and Jack advised her together, so Bex got it in stereo. She pressed herself back into the seat.

Fig's mother looked at the man. She shook her head. She closed her eyes. Then she started laughing. She laughed so hard she rocked the whole car.

"I think . . ." the man began, and the cameras and microphones all whipped toward him, "there's been some kind of mistake."

"Oh, any number of them." Mom tried and failed to stop laughing.

"Are you saying giving Bex up was a mistake?" Evelyn Esponson said into her mic but to Fig's mom. "Or did you mean getting pregnant with her in the first place?"

"That's not . . ." The man was trying to make his mask cover more of his face.

Evelyn swung the mic back over to him.

"She's all grown up, isn't she?" Evelyn's voice sounded like wind chimes, airy but loud but musical but sharp.

"Evelyn." Mom was still laughing but she was also mad. "You are egotistical and scheming and predatory, but I also took you to be vaguely competent, which was, apparently, a gross overestimation."

". . . my baby," the man finished.

That's when Fig got it. That's when she knew who this man was. "Oh!" she said. "Oh oh oh!"

"Fig," her mother warned from the front seat.

"Pardon?" Evelyn said to the man.

"You've made a mistake. That's not my baby. Not even my baby all grown up."

Evelyn's face got red. Her smile started sliding inside her mouth.

"She looks like a cow," Fig whispered to her mother but not so quietly that everyone didn't hear.

Evelyn narrowed her eyes at Fig and smoothed her shirt and tugged at the bottom of her jacket.

Her mother's eyes looked at hers in the mirror. "Cowed?"

"She looks like a cowed. Why?" It didn't make sense that Evelyn wasn't sorry and embarrassed before but was suddenly sorry and embarrassed now.

"It's hard when you're bad at your job. It's especially hard when you're bad at your job, and that fact is being shared on hundreds of thousands of devices all over the world."

Fig felt kind of sorry for her. "You did a good job finding the birth father," she told Evelyn. She was trying to be positive and encouraging. "Just not the right one."

2008

Closing night of *A Doll's House*, India was unable to stop her final-scene tears all through curtain call and the group hugging that ensued. She cried and cried, and everyone teased her, and she kept crying, and everyone worried about her. And then she disappeared. Eventually Davis found her shivering in the courtyard, crouched against the cold brick wall of the theater building.

"Everyone's looking for you." He sank down next to her. "What are you doing out here?"

"Smoking."

"You don't smoke."

"I know."

"You don't have anything to smoke."

"I know."

"I don't think 'smoking' means what you think it means," Davis advised.

"Smoking's bad for your lungs and shit for your vocal range, and it smells like an ashtray."

"Other way around, I think."

"So I can't smoke," India explained.

"I wasn't pressuring you to smoke. I was just observing that you weren't."

"Yeah, but you know what I mean."

"I don't even have a guess."

"I needed an activity for my hands, fresh air, an excuse to sit alone in the dark for a minute, and something to calm me down. Or wake me up. Or whatever."

"Which?"

"I don't know. Either."

"Do you feel edgy?" he asked.

"No."

"Sleepy?"

"No."

"Handsy?"

"No!"

"I mean, it wouldn't be the worst thing," he allowed.

"I don't feel handsy."

"Then I don't think you need to take up smoking."

He stood and pulled her up and into his arms. There was a furrow in his chest that her forehead fit into like it had been carved especially for her.

"If you're not edgy, sleepy, or handsy, what's wrong?" He had his chin on the top of her head. She could feel his words through her skull.

"The play is over."

"But it was great. Everyone loved it."

"Now we have to break up," she sobbed.

"We do?"

"We loved each other, but we couldn't make it work. I couldn't stay."

"That wasn't us," Davis said gently. "That was Nora and Torvald. We aren't them. Remember you said?"

"When?"

"Outside the library that night. When I couldn't believe how different kissing you for real was from kissing you in rehearsal. And you said of course, because that was Nora and Torvald whereas this was our first kiss."

"That was weeks ago," India said.

"So?"

"In the interim, I became her. She took me over."

"She didn't. Torvald isn't me. Nora wasn't you. They're gone now."

"Dead?" she moaned.

"And my CS advisor said my English major had no practical use," he scoffed. "Literary characters never die. They live on the page as long as you read them."

"Who cares about the page?" She was bereft. "They were warm. They lived and breathed and loved. And now they're gone."

"Now we can just be us."

"Just?" said India.

"You are you." Davis stopped teasing her. "You are more you than anyone I know."

"That's not saying much." India sniffed. "Who could be more me than I am?"

"Not you're more you than anyone else is you. You are more who you are than anyone else I know is who they are. You are so totally, thoroughly unique in the world."

"Everyone is unique in the world."

"Not like you are. In every way I can think of, you, India Allwood, are a star. I'm just lucky I'm nearby enough to catch your light."

"It's not luck." What could she do? She kissed him.

"Do I still feel like me?" he said.

She sniffed, nodded. "Do I?"

"I don't know," he said. "Let me feel you."

She'd spent her first two summers working at the scene shop on campus, but this last college summer, it was closing for two months for renovations, which meant she had to go home and be a barista, far from the theater, far from New York, far from her real life. She acted grateful for meager tips. She acted like it was reasonable for a shift to start at 5:30 in the morning. She acted like it bespoke good taste and intelligence when a customer demanded to know how the beans were roasted. But that was all the acting she did. She was glad to be with her mother. She was glad for home-cooked meals and on-site laundry. But otherwise there was a hole in her where being onstage was supposed to be, except, no, that suggested she was mostly intact except for one leaky pinprick. This was more like she was the hole.

She saw Robbie everywhere. Not saw, actually. Not sensed even. Sense memory would have been a relief. This was some other kind of memory, more like a vegetable peeler. She'd walk by the egg roll karaoke place and feel the sharp cut where the blade nicked in, then the slice as it flayed off a thin piece of the protective outer surface of her. The tree where they first kissed shaved off another shard, his pie shop which had become a bank branch, and of course her very own living room where he sang to Rebecca while she floated inside, her very same bed with the very same sheets even, and knowing they'd been washed dozens of times since Robbie Brighton had been tangled up in them did not convince her nose they did not still smell of him.

Whereas Rebecca she actually did see everywhere. That wasn't sense memory, either. It was sense imagination. India had no reason to believe Camille had left Seattle, which meant every three-year-old India saw that summer might have been Rebecca, and not just every three-year-old, for India wasn't a parent herself and didn't have a good handle on developmental milestones, which meant every child between the ages of two and five seemed like maybe-Rebecca, every high-pitched squeal, every shouted "Mama!," every plea for a cookie to dip in hot cocoa, every pigtail she caught going around a corner, every occupant of every swing in every park might have been Rebecca. She missed her not like she missed Davis and Dakota but like missing a bus, or like missing something that streaked by too fast and when you whipped your head around to see, it was already gone.

She planned to run into Camille, Camille with her child, with India's child, with India's ex-child, so that if it happened, she wouldn't be caught off guard, or really, since she *would* be caught off guard, so she wouldn't have to think of the right thing to say on the spot. She would tell Camille it was so good to see her. She would tell Camille how beautiful Rebecca was. If Rebecca asked— because maybe she would be one of those precocious kids who wasn't afraid of strangers and asked a million questions, since that was the kind of child India had been, or maybe she was usually scared of strangers but wouldn't be scared of India who she'd perhaps recognize at some magical subconscious level—she would say she was a friend of her mom's and she was so, so glad to meet her, and if those two tiny statements, the only ones she would maybe ever make to this child now that she was outside her own body, weren't entirely the truth, they weren't entirely lies either, and India was a gifted actor so surely could persuasively sell them to a three-year-old, even one who was magically subconsciously attuned.

But she did not run into Camille.

On the phone every night, she and Davis talked about their future, not senior year or fall auditions or the future that awaited them ten weeks away. They talked about the future after that: where they would live (where in New York; the city went without saying), what kind of apartment, how long they would wait to have children and how many they'd have and what they would name them and how much fun it would be to be a little kid in the city. They talked about what kind of wedding to have. They talked about how it would feel to be old together, children raised, goals accomplished, glories assured, resting at last. They talked about how their forever would be.

That this forever hadn't started yet, that it did not seem to include the together they were now, should maybe have given India pause. But India never paused.

Instead she had work to do. Al-Like-the-Song had announced before he sent them away for the summer that next year would be the Year of the Bard. He was directing Shakespeare both semesters: *Much Ado About Nothing*, then *Macbeth*. India ordered a gross of index cards and brought them with her to her childhood library. It smelled exactly the same as she remembered, but in miniature. The enormous gilded throne in the children's section was regular-chair-sized and shedding its latest coat of gold paint. The towering cliffs she remembered scaling like boulders were nothing more than carpeted stairs. For nostalgia, she sat in the coveted yellow chair at the rainbow table, even though both were much too small now. She tried to ignore all the little girls who could be Rebecca and got to work.

She used a whole pack of cards for feminist versus feminine attitudes in Renaissance England. She used another for actresses' interpretations of Beatrice through the ages. She got colored index cards and copied down the play in its entirety, twice, the first time coded by character, the second by theme. She rehearsed Beatrice until she had her not just memorized but learned by heart. She remembered that part of herself that was in love but scared of being hurt again, that was quick of tongue but slow of heart. She made herself remember the way second chances were cool balm relief but not unpainful, how it felt when you didn't want to stop but had to anyway.

It was being Beatrice, becoming her for the summer, learning all there was to learn—and there was a lot—that kept India sane and whole in the face of all the maybe-Rebeccas, that made the strange weeks at home tick by, and though it was painful to be away from Davis and away from school and away from New York and away from the stage, she was grateful for the time because she needed it. Shakespeare was hard, and without time enough to research and rehearse and just practice the language, someone else might get Beatrice, which was unacceptable, unthinkable. So hard though the summer was, by mid-August, she was prepared, ready at last.

At the welcome back meeting, Al-Like-the-Song announced he would be gender-swapping all the roles.

B ack in their room afterward, not even unpacked yet, India was inconsolable. "Three months of work down the drain."

"You should eat hay," Dakota mumbled.

"Eat hay?"

"No. Eat hay."

"I think the saying is make hay."

Dakota spat the pins she had in her mouth—she was hanging their posters—into the palm of her hand. "Not eat hay. Be happy."

"And making hay is about working when it's a good time to work—which I did—and look how that ended."

"I don't think it's over yet."

"Why should I be happy?"

"You're always complaining all the best parts are for men."

"I'm behind. I'll never catch up. Auditions are in a week! It took me an entire season to get ready."

"And that it's not fair that there are so many more women who audition and so many fewer parts they're allowed to play."

"And this was my last chance."

"Are you going to die?" said Dakota.

"We're graduating."

"In a year."

"It's like high school all over again. I'll have to sit in the audience and just watch."

"Why would more parts for women make you less likely to get cast?"

"Because I'm not actually talented," India stopped whining to whisper.

"You always get cast." Dakota rolled her eyes. "You usually get the lead."

"Because I prepare. Overprepare. Because before auditions even start I've done all the reading and all the research and memorized the part I want and tried it twelve different ways and practiced and rehearsed."

"Yes, we've met."

"When I show up for auditions, I'm just pretending to be new and feeling my way like everyone else. It's called acting."

"I'm familiar. But auditions aren't for another week."

"A week isn't enough time to learn to be a man."

"They don't seem complicated." Dakota shrugged. "How hard can it be?"

India copied Benedick's lines onto cards then took to her bed to practice under the sheets. Memorizing was easy enough now she had the feel of the language. It was the learning by heart, the becoming, that was hard. Benedick was cocky, a soldier returning victorious from war, a guy's guy, loud and overly confident and sometimes downright mean. He loved Beatrice eventually, but not at first, and India, who had become Beatrice for the last three months, could not fail to take that personally. What he mostly was was male, not in an incidental way but a deep-down one. Whereas she became Beatrice, and Nora before her, by uncovering them where they had been all along—inside her—to become Benedick, she would have to shed every scrap of herself.

She mocked Dakota's outfit and her indecision about her outfit and the fretting she was doing over her outfit on account of the fact that she had a date. She put Davis in a headlock. She bought a Nerf gun and fired foam suction cups at people studying in the stacks at the library. She stood in front of the mirror and spread her legs wide apart and admired how attractive and significant she was. She gave the girls on her hall unsolicited and ill-informed and completely unwavering opinions.

It was hard.

What she did not do was eat or bathe or return Davis's calls or texts or endlessly discuss with Dakota the minutiae of her date or which of the two girls who were in love with her she should ultimately choose. She would be a good roommate and a good girlfriend after auditions when she had more time and could go back to being female. Davis was worried about her, and she didn't want him to worry about her. Dakota was annoyed with her, and she didn't want that either. But worrying about people worrying about you and feeling bad about being annoying weren't very manly, so those were going to have to wait a week as well.

"You smell like shit," Dakota said.

"Hey! I'm the one practicing being rude. And only for pretend."

"I'm not being rude. I'm stating facts."

"Spoken like a man," India accused her. Dakota had already decided not to audition so didn't need to practice being a jerk.

"Not a man. A woman with a nose and a very small room."

"Men smell bad," India explained.

"But I'm gay," Dakota said, "so it shouldn't be my problem."

"You know what would help?"

"Soap?"

"If you smiled more."

She thought about arriving for her audition slot ten minutes late and not apologizing. She thought about showing up in a wrinkled T-shirt with portions of her lunch spilled on it and failing to notice. She thought about replacing her audition monologue with quotes from *Caddyshack*. But she knew acting like a man did not guarantee being treated like one. Instead she decided to demonstrate her masculinity by being underqualified, overconfident, and unembarrassed: she got up on the stage and sang.

Because, like Benedick, it was Italian, she started with "O Sole Mio" despite not knowing what any of the words meant (because it was Italian), then moved on to "My Way" (Sinatra was also Italian, as well as swashbucklingly male) but only got through the first verse before Al-Like-the-Song begged her to stop. She winked, shot him with finger guns, and felt something she never had before: grateful to get off the stage.

After the cast list was posted, after they both found their names on top, India and Davis went out to dinner to celebrate, then came home and changed the sheets and had the kind of sex India imagined you had a lot if you'd been a man all week.

Later she thought it was all Al-Like-the-Song's fault.

If she'd known in May that he was gender-swapping the cast, she could have taken all the long, slow summer to prepare as she liked.

If she'd had longer to prepare, she wouldn't have had to cram or become Benedick so completely.

If it hadn't been exactly a week when she emerged—from the fog of being a man, the nonstop studying, the adrenaline of auditions, the disaster of her not-even-unpacked-yet room, the high of the cast list, the first real food in days, and all the at-last sex—if it hadn't been exactly a week when she finally remembered her pill on the pile of clutter that was her nightstand, she might have noticed that the days on the sticker didn't match.

But it was a week exactly. Her pill said Sunday. And it was Sunday indeed.

WEDNESDAY

"Davis Shaw," India said to him, after she sent Ajax away and herded everyone else back inside. She should never have tried to leave the house this morning, not that staying in would have prevented what happened. What was happening.

"India Allwood," said Davis Shaw. Who was standing in her living room.

She went from window to window and started closing all the blinds, then had a moment where she thought to leave them open so Davis would be impressed by how nice the house looked in the sunlight, then had several moments during which she warned herself sternly not to lose her mind. She noticed she was shaking. She noticed him notice too.

She turned and met his eyes and opened her arms from her sides and left them there—beseeching, though maybe it looked like benediction. "What are you . . . how are you . . ." There were so many directions to go that any one she picked would find them off the path and lost, so she decided to let him lead.

"She told me it was an emergency," he said. Davis said. Her Davis.

"Who?"

"That journalist."

"She's not a journalist."

"I got a text from a journalist asking if I was India Allwood's . . ."

"What?"

"Baby daddy," he admitted.

"Are you kidding me?"

"No, but—"

"No chance this was maybe suspect?" Letting him lead wasn't working, so she took over. "This didn't seem like something you should probably go ahead and ignore?"

"She apologized for the term, said she was just making sure she had the right person, that she'd been asked by the adoptive parents to try to get in touch with me owing to some kind of medical emergency."

"Why would the parents contact a journalist?"

"I don't know. Because she has investigative experience?"

"What kind of medical emergency?" India could hear her voice rising but didn't find she cared.

"I mean, it was a text message. There weren't a lot of details. But there is a global pandemic, you may have noticed, so a medical emergency didn't seem totally out of the realm of possibility to me, and if it was, what kind of an assho—" He saw Jack and Fig and broke off. "Sorry."

"You can say 'ass' on television," Jack assured him.

"Cursing in front of the children is not the fucking problem here!" India shouted.

"I just didn't want to be difficult about identity verification if someone was dying."

"Difficult?"

"Maybe it was some kind of latent paternal instinct."

"*Misguided* latent paternal instinct."

"It's not a muscle I ever flexed before," he said. "Anyway, she said she'd send a car so—"

"This just happened?"

"Like an hour ago. I was getting ready for a meeting when—"

"She picked you up in San Francisco?"

He stopped and looked at her. "I live in Silver Lake." Silver Lake was maybe half an hour away. Davis Shaw was practically her neighbor.

"Since when?"

"November 2019."

"You changed jobs?"

"Opened a new office down here, actually."

"Wow." She tried to decide if she cared that he'd been her practically-neighbor for a year and a half and never reached out to her. "I didn't know."

"I mean, your life is . . ." He trailed off but gestured all around, as if the reason they'd lost touch was she had a nice kitchen and a pool. "Are these your kids?"

"Jack and Fig." She pointed. "And this is Rebecca."

"She goes by Bex," Fig said.

"Rebecca?" Davis said.

"Yes."

"Ahh. That makes sense."

"Yes," India said again, but through her teeth.

"I didn't—"

"She's a white girl!" India was shouting again and still not caring.

"I didn't see a picture." Davis also sounded frustrated. She didn't care about that, either.

"She made a video," Fig said helpfully.

"Two," said Bex.

"It's been all over the internet for the last thirty-six hours," India said. "All over social media, all over everything."

"I don't look at that stuff." Davis shrugged, somewhere between apologetic and smug. "And that journalist—"

"Not a journalist."

"—didn't send me a picture. Didn't in any way describe the child in question, obviously. Though, jeez, when she saw me you'd think she might have realized something wasn't right."

"She's not that smart."

"Yeah, but." He gestured all up and down himself.

"All that Norwegian ancestry must have thrown her off," India said.

He smiled a smile she remembered in her chest. "Listen, let me get out of your hair."

"Too late." Way, way, way too late.

"I'm going to go to work," he said.

"We have wifi. You can work from here."

"But there's no emergency. It was the wrong kid."

"I'm not the wrong kid," said Bex.

"And there is an emergency," India said. "It is simply your understanding of it that has changed."

He looked at her blankly.

"You saw the driveway." She gestured at it. "If you leave, they're going to pounce. They won't leave you alone. They'll follow you to work. They'll follow you home. It would be easier if you just stayed. It would be . . ."—she hesitated—"a help to me. A favor. I'd appreciate it."

"Who is this guy?" Bex leaned over to Fig.

"This is Davis Shaw," said Fig.

"Who's Davis Shaw?"

"Mom's college boyfriend. Lewis's biological father."

"Who's Lewis?"

"The baby my mom gave up for adoption."

"Placed," India said without taking her eyes off Davis.

"I'm the baby your mom gave up for adoption."

"The other one," Fig said.

Bex's face turned the color of vanilla pudding. "There's another one?"

2008

She didn't throw up this time. Not once. She didn't think anything of being so tired because it didn't feel like exhaustion. It felt like stress. Rehearsal was all-consuming. Shakespeare required muscles she had not yet developed. That didn't make her not want to do it. It made her only want to do it. But she also had a full load of courses still, and extra library hours to work now that graduation was in sight and student loans loomed. She was helping Davis apply for every tech job in the city. She was helping Dakota with a documentary she was filming about competing pizza-by-the-slice philosophers. So it didn't seem strange that she was sleeping so hard, that she'd close her eyes for just a moment while Dakota was bitching about her girlfriend and wake up the next morning.

Then she started dreaming about Rebecca. Rebecca as a baby in Robbie's arms. Rebecca as a toddler—she looked nothing like India or Robbie, but India recognized her anyway, maybe in that way you do in dreams, maybe via some kind of maternal sight, unbound by time or distance. Whereas over the summer, any small child might have been Rebecca, now she had no trouble identifying her, no matter what she looked like. Sometimes Rebecca was older than she was now, but India recognized her anyway. She was learning to ride a bike. She was off to kindergarten. She was getting ready for a school dance. Sometimes she was the demanding three-year-old she no doubt actually was, yelling, "Snack! Snack! Snack! Snack!" in the background while Camille tried to explain something on the phone that India couldn't hear. Sometimes Rebecca was still inside her, Rebecca in the womb, but in her sticky, snack-demanding form, banging on India's bladder with a carrot gripped in one fist, pretzel sticks in the other. "India!" she yelled. "Snack!" and when that didn't work, "India! Wake up! Wake up! Wake up!"

India's eyes sprang open—though there was nothing to see but the dark ceiling of her middle-of-the-night dorm room—and she knew.

She managed—just managed—to hold on till the sun was up, which was still hours before Davis would be, but she couldn't wait any longer than that. She called, woke him, made him meet her in the park. It wasn't cold out, just the slight early-fall chill of the day not yet warmed up, but she was wrapped in her winter coat, shivering on the lip of the fountain. Therefore, when he arrived, the first thing he looked was worried about her. She wanted to dispel his concern. And at the same time she wanted to warn him. But there was no gentle way in, no way to prepare, and she couldn't wait another moment anyway.

As soon as he got near enough, she blurted, "I'm pregnant and so sorry." She remembered telling her mother. *I got into NYU and pregnant.* At least she'd got the lede right this time. She couldn't meet his eyes quite, but she looked at his face, watched it fall.

"Oh, India." A whisper.

"I know."

"No," he said. Not quite said. It sounded like an echo of her "know" but was not, somewhere between a moan and a wail. But it was like "no," and "no" was what it meant.

"I'm sorry," she said again.

He shook his head. "It's not . . ." He trailed off. *Not your fault* or *not the point anymore,* sorry or not sorry no longer the pressing issue, it having been supplanted by quite a few others.

"How did this . . . ?" He wasn't finishing sentences anymore. But he didn't need to. Not really.

"The usual way, I guess."

"You're on the pill." Bewildered and more to himself than to her, maybe.

"I am. Well, I was. I'll have to stop now. You have to stop when you . . ."

"Get pregnant," he supplied. "Not a lot of point anymore, either."

She made herself laugh a little, hoping he was making a joke. He ran his hands over his head and left them there, turned in a few tight circles, sat down next to her for a breath, bounced back up again. She watched him. Shivered and watched.

"I guess we should . . ." He trailed off again, but this time she needed him to finish.

"Tell me."

". . . get some coffee."

Not what she'd have guessed. She nodded mutely, then shook her head. She wasn't sure she could stand. "You go. I'll wait here."

"Oh. Sorry. Of course."

"What of course?"

"No coffee if you're . . ." He couldn't say it.

"It's not that." Maybe it was that. "I'm not sure I could manage . . ." She waved in the general direction of her middle.

"I'll just . . ." he began. "Skip it," he was maybe going to say. "Stay here with you." "Give up coffee since everything in the world's been turned upside down, and luxury, to say nothing of sustenance and hydration, has collapsed under the weight of the priority list." But then instead he said, "I'll be right back."

She nodded, glad she didn't have to say anything else while he was gone. She sat on the fountain and tried to stop shaking.

Ten minutes later, Davis was back with a cup of coffee, a sesame bagel, a donut, a croissant, a hot cocoa, and a can of ginger ale. "I don't know what you want"—she thought he meant so he'd bought one of everything, but then he said—"but I was thinking probably we'll get married?"

A question mark at the end.

"Are you asking me?"

But he wasn't. Not really.

"I mean, I will. If that's what we decide." He paused, then blundered on. "I was more wondering if that's what you want. To get married."

She looked at her shoes and nodded. "Someday."

He nodded too. "That's what I thought. That's what we agreed. So I guess the question is . . ."

She looked up at him, waited.

". . . what's the difference between someday and now?"

She blinked. "Everything that was supposed to happen first?"

"But that could happen anyway?" He sounded like he was asking her. "I'll get a job. I'd do that regardless."

"I guess, but . . ." She didn't know how to finish that sentence.

"We'll just have to . . ." He didn't either, apparently.

"What?"

"I don't know. Get a house in New Jersey instead of an apartment in the city. Take the boring job that pays well instead of the exciting start-up that may or may not."

This was so logical. How clever she'd been to get knocked up by a computer scientist. "What about me?"

"Same thing."

"Get a boring job?"

"Stick with the plan. Now instead of someday. Audition a lot and see what happens."

"I can't. I won't be able to."

"Why not?"

"We'll have a baby. You'll be working."

"Oh, yeah, huh." He had his homework face on, the one that solved problems which were tricky but not actually taxing. "Well, maybe someday then instead of now."

"What do you mean?"

"Instead of having a theater career and then a baby, you'll have a baby and then a theater career."

She would have her senior year and then graduation and then the baby would come, which made none of this as dramatic as last time. They were adults now, apparently. Educated. One of them was very employable. One of them was old enough and experienced enough to know she was talented and also to know that talent wasn't enough to guarantee anything and so her career was precarious at best, with or without a baby. If they had gotten married that weekend, maybe they'd have stayed married forever. Maybe they'd have had that baby and two or three more. Maybe they would have grown together and grown up together and never regretted the change in plan because it wouldn't be a plan, it would be a baby, it would be their family.

But they did not get married that weekend.

Instead, India spent some weeks rehearsing the lead role in the Now-Someday

Plan—getting ready to tell her mother and Al-Like-the-Song and everyone, herself especially, that she was tabling auditions, just for a few years, to be a mom instead—but it was acting. She didn't believe it. She tried to. She knew she should. But she did not. Deep down, she believed that a baby wouldn't keep her from her dreams, for nothing would keep her from her dreams. Deep down, she believed she would be reading to the baby in the park, and someone would come over and say, "Pardon me. I'm a big-deal talent scout and couldn't help overhearing, and your impersonations were just extraordinary. You *were* Frog. *And* Toad. Here's my card." Or she would bring the baby with her to auditions and be so good they'd forget she had an infant strapped across her chest. They would believe she was whatever childless heroine they'd asked her to become. They would so clearly see she was the perfect star for their play that they would gratefully rearrange rehearsal to accommodate her childcare schedule. And so having a baby wouldn't change her plans at all.

A few weeks later, in the middle of the night, India and Dakota woke to knocking on the door so gentle they were both at first confused.

"Why are we awake?" India said.

"You have to pee?" Dakota wagered.

It was a good guess these days. "Why are you awake?"

"You woke me when you got up to pee?"

"But I didn't get up." India shook her head, sleepily. "I was dreaming of tap dancing." She had taken tap as her PE credit even though she knew she'd never get cast in a chorus line if she couldn't also sing.

"I was dreaming of woodpeckers," said Dakota.

"I think that means sex."

"Only if you have it with men."

They heard light tapping. Heard it again, apparently. It was coming from the door.

"It's knocking!" India leaped up, triumphant, and threw it open.

Davis stood there, looking surprised.

"What are you doing up?" he said.

"You're pounding on the door."

"Not pounding. Knocking. Not even knocking. Tapping lightly."

"Why?"

"It's the middle of the night. I didn't want to wake your whole hall."

"No, why are you tapping on the door?"

"Morse code."

"Morse code?"

"I have to ask you something, but I don't want to ask you something."

"I don't know Morse code."

"That's why this is effective."

"Only if you don't want an answer."

"I don't," Davis said.

"Go have circular conversations somewhere else." Dakota groaned and put her head under her pillow.

"No circles," said Davis. "Too dizzy."

Dakota sat up. "Is he drunk?" She was delighted.

"Apparently!" India was kind of delighted too. Davis was not usually drunk, especially not on a school night.

"You don't have to go home," Dakota said, "but you can't stay here."

"I live here!" said India.

"You can't go home *and* you can't stay here," Dakota revised.

"Come on," India said to Davis. She grabbed her coat off the back of the door and put it on over her pajamas, slipped shoes onto her feet and her arm through his, and led them out into the night.

"I have a question," he began, formally.

She thought, *I'm in pajamas with slept-on hair and middle-of-the-night breath, and he's going to propose.* She thought it would have been nicer in a restaurant or at a show maybe, something she'd dressed up for, something for which she'd had a chance to brush her hair and teeth. But she also thought it was nice to be so loved even when she didn't look or smell her best. If he wanted to declare himself hers in this moment, he must want to declare himself hers always. "I'm ready," she said.

"India." He looked at her, cleared his throat. "Do you . . ." he began, then corrected himself. "*Did* you take the pill, India?"

She understood immediately what the question wasn't, but it took her a minute to understand what it was. "When?"

"When you were on the pill."

"Of course."

"I saw you take it," he said, "whenever I slept over."

"Yes."

"Did you take the pill . . . every day?"

She saw where this was going. Maybe what was strange was how long it had taken to do so. And upon reflection, this made sense. Why would he have to get drunk to propose? "Usually."

She thought he would yell, but he just nodded. He was not an angry drunk, or maybe he was expecting that.

"You forgot?" he slurred.

"Yes. But not exactly." She had not yet tried to put this into words, not even to herself, and she could see it would be hard to make it make sense, even if he were sober.

He squeezed the bridge of his nose. She recognized this motion not from Davis but from Torvald. It meant *exercising a heroic level of patience with a child*. "How tashing—tashking—*taxing* is it to remember to swallow a pill every morning?"

"It's not that it's too taxing."

"Then what?"

"I think it's that"—she couldn't look at him when she admitted this— "Benedick doesn't take birth control pills."

He squinted at her. He looked confused. Not about what she said. About who she was.

India was not drunk, and she was also not delusional. Benedick didn't do all sorts of things she had to. He didn't have to work at the library. He didn't have to take a useless and impossible stats class just to satisfy his gen ed requirements. He didn't even have to eat because he wasn't a real person. But that didn't mean she didn't consider the options in the dining hall through his eyes. India liked yogurt and fruit for breakfast. Benedick was the kind of guy who didn't consider it a meal unless it had meat.

So it wasn't that he didn't take the pill. It was that he didn't ever think about getting pregnant. Nora Helmer didn't take the pill, either. Nora Helmer would have given anything, truly anything, to have been able to do so. When India was Nora, she thought about her birth control pill with gratitude several times a day, took it every morning first thing after her alarm went off. But such a miracle would never occur to Benedick, and anyway, he was the kind of guy who probably wanted half a dozen children.

"I had to become, really become, Benedick," she tried to explain. "I can only be Benedick on stage for two hours a night by becoming him the rest of the day because I'm not like you. It's easy for you. It's not easy for me. You can turn it off because it's so simple for you to turn it on. You want to be in a play to make your grandma happy? You wander cold into the audition and land the star part. You want a summer internship? You phone in the applications but get an offer everywhere you applied anyway. You spend your time at the library flirting with me instead of studying, but you still get straight As. It's not that you're good at everything, Davis. It's that you're good without even trying."

"What does that have to do with—"

"Because I have to work hard at everything. If I want an A, if I want a part, if I want to succeed, I have to work so hard. I'm not good enough on my own."

"Oh, India, you're soooo talented. You're so good up there." He stopped and smiled then remembered his point and frowned again. "This isn't about that."

"Not for you, maybe. But it is for me. I'd never have gotten that part, any part, if I just waltzed into auditions and gave it a whirl. To win, I have to cheat. I have to get ahead of everyone else. You can be Beatrice for a couple of hours' worth of rehearsals a day. Me? I have to be Benedick all the time. I have to be him body and soul. Otherwise I don't get to be him at all."

"But . . ."

"What?"

"You want to do this for a living." He sounded like he was pleading with her.

"Exactly, so—"

"So you can't go through life like this. No one goes through life like this. It's acting! This is the whole point of acting. It's pretend. It's—"

"I know what acting is."

"I trusted you," he said.

Maybe he was too drunk to realize he'd slipped into the past tense.

"When?" she asked.

But he didn't answer that question. Instead he asked his own. "Did you . . ." he began, looked at her, looked away.

"Did I what?" She genuinely did not know what he would say. So she was totally unprepared.

"Trick me?" She watched his lips form the words, force them out slowly. "Into what?"

"It's okay. You can tell me. It's not like I'm going to . . ." He trailed off, so she didn't know what he wouldn't do. "I just want to know. I need to know."

"Trick you into what," she said. No longer a question. A statement. A dare, almost. *Say it.*

"Marriage, family." He ran his hands over his hair, over his face, seemed like he'd run out of terrible things she might have tricked him into. "Forever."

She felt it all through the middle of her, a rending. "I didn't think I needed to trick you into forever."

"You didn't." He threw his arms out wide. "That's what I can't figure out. That's my point."

India wasn't sure that was his point, but he kept talking anyway.

"India." A whisper. A prayer almost. "A baby is the one thing you can't change your mind about. It's the one decision you make you can never undo. It's the one thing you can never come back from. Did you . . . do this on purpose? So we'd have to get married? So there'd be no going back?"

"Why would you—" She wanted to be angry rather than decimated. "How could you think that?"

"Because maybe, *maybe* this happens to someone once." His voice broke. "But it doesn't happen twice."

"Of course it does. It happens all the time. You think I'm the only woman in the world to have a second unplanned pregnancy?"

"'Happy are they that hear their detractions and can put them to mending.'" Benedick. This did not seem fair, somehow.

"Meaning how could I let this happen again?" she said.

"Meaning how can you not have learned from the terrible thing that happened last time?"

"Because it wasn't terrible last time," she said. "And I don't think it's terrible this time."

"I didn't either." That past tense again.

"I didn't say, 'Let's get married.' You did. And your life's not going to change that much. Mine is. You're going to get the job you were going to get anyway and be with the person you were going to be with anyway and have the child you were going to have anyway. I might have to put the entire point of my entire life on hold. My plan has to change completely. Yours hardly has to change at all."

"That's not what's changed." But he didn't say what had.

India would have stayed and fought—always—but Davis's eyes kept closing, and she walked him back to his room and pushed him into bed. *Let him sleep in his shoes*, she thought. He'd wake up with swollen, sweaty feet, and it would serve him right. *Let him sleep in all his clothes and rise rumpled and stinking and hungover.* Then he would see who the responsible one was, who had drunkenly wrested whom from peaceful trustworthy slumber. She waited for him to show up at breakfast, clad in sunglasses and sorries. She waited for her phone to ring for surely he would want her to hear in his voice how bad he felt and not just send a text. She lingered outside stats till the very last second, certain he would find her and convince her to cut so she could come back to his room and be showered in apologies.

In fact, she heard nothing from Davis till rehearsal. When he arrived, he did look awkward and embarrassed, even a little peaky maybe, but he would not meet her eyes.

"I'm sorry," he said. But he didn't seem sorry. Or maybe it was that he seemed sorry but not desperate: to take it all back, to make it up to her immediately and entirely, to be absolutely certain she knew he hadn't meant it. He was just drunk, talking out loud, fretting pointlessly. Pregnancy hormones, basically.

"Okay," she said. Not that it was okay. More like, okay she understood, though that wasn't true either.

"Last night was hard." Like it was the night's fault. Like its being hard had nothing to do with him. He looked down at his shoes. "I accidentally said some things I didn't mean to."

That's where India's life—and quite a few other people's—turned. On that one tiny word. *To.* Drunk, Davis had said some things he didn't mean to. But he hadn't said anything he didn't mean.

And he turned out to be wrong because this conversation, like having a baby, proved to be a second thing you could never undo or come back from.

When Al-Like-the-Song found out about what he called India's "condition," he decided to scrap the cross-gender casting for spring semester. It was much more interesting to have a hugely pregnant Lady Macbeth waddling around the stage.

"That's why she's so insistent her husband do whatever he must to become king. Not because she's a bitter, ambitious harpy. Because she's nesting. Their family is growing, and she's putting the life and future of her child before her king's, before her husband's, before her own even—she's a very good mother. When she cries about what it feels like to nurse, we'll see the pain of a pregnant woman who's lost previous babies, simultaneously terrified of losing another and already in love with what she knows to be the most fragile thing in the world. Maybe the blood on her hands is real. Maybe it's from childbirth. Maybe this baby doesn't make it either, and that's why she kills herself. This is going to be so much fun!"

Davis did not audition. Because he had no Scottish grandmothers? Because he wanted space from her? Because he was going to be a father and needed to turn away from college diversions toward serious pursuits that would look good on a résumé? Unclear. But India's Macbeth was a fellow graduating drama major. Good, but not as good as Davis. "Doesn't matter," Al-Like-the-Song said. "This Lady M isn't so much in love with her husband as using him to beget and then enrich and enshrine and eventually enthrone her child. That's the point here. It's going to be you and your womb up there, India, and no one will be able to tear their eyes off you."

She should have been thrilled—she had imagined she was going to have to sit her last semester out—except it wasn't just onstage with her that Davis didn't want to be.

She let herself get caught up in rehearsal again. She let herself be a college student for just a little while longer. She let Davis drift away, or maybe "let" was the wrong word, or maybe Davis wasn't the only one floating slowly out to sea.

They stopped talking about getting married and the Now-Someday Plan.

They did not talk about a different plan instead.

In fact, more and more, they didn't talk about anything at all.

India didn't want to think about what that meant. Not didn't want to. Couldn't. Every time she tried, her brain went somewhere else: to sleep, to panic, to anger that had to float around with nothing to attach to. She wasn't mad at him. He wasn't mad at her. But she couldn't focus enough to determine what they were instead.

When they did see each other, they were gentle, subdued. They didn't fight. Maybe they should have, articulated problems so they could be addressed, yelled so the yelling could subside into laughter then quiet talk then intimate whispers. But they didn't know that. They weren't married so they didn't seek a marriage counselor. They were just kids, slow to identify problems, certain they could surmount them anyway, whatever they were.

One day, he was waiting for her after rehearsal, and instead of swelling with love or hope, her heart fell. He should have been with her, not waiting for her afterward. His being there should have been a comfort, not a surprise. She took his hand—out of habit or nervousness she couldn't say—and they walked toward the library, probably for the same reason, whatever it was.

"I'm sorry I asked if you did this on purpose," he began. "I know you'd never do that."

"Thanks," she said, wary, waiting, because obviously that wasn't what he'd come to say.

"I love you so much, India." She could hear the *but* coming, both of them, all of them, all the buts in the world. "I'm so proud of you. And I'm so impressed by you. I don't want you to think otherwise."

"I don't," she said. *Didn't?*

"Every moment is *the* moment for you. You're always present. You're all in.

Full heart. Both feet. It makes you great onstage, but that's not even it. It's that it makes you the best person I know, my favorite person to be with."

His voice broke and he stopped. And she waited.

"You're fearless and exhilarating and brave."

Just say it, she thought. "But?"

"Not but. And. And I thought, I always thought, well, that's the kind of person who gets pregnant at sixteen, right?"

"The kind who's sexually active and menstruating?"

He ignored that because he was making a point. "The kind who's full of life and now and fire."

"So you thought pregnant at sixteen was an unfortunate trade-off." She didn't want to be angry right now—she wanted to hear what he had to say—but she was angry anyway. "Unfortunate but worth it because I'm so fun, and anyway the regrettable bits were behind me so not your problem. Or so you thought."

"I was wrong."

"Yes," she said.

"That's not what I meant. I was incorrect."

"About what?"

"I think I had cause and effect backward," he said as gently as it is possible to say something completely ungentle. "It wasn't that the wonderful way you are got you pregnant in high school. It was being pregnant in high school that made you the way you are."

"The wonderful way I am." Even she couldn't tell whether she sounded sarcastic or hurt or confused or enraged.

"You lost so much. Being a kid. Dances and parties and nights out with friends. Robbie. Rebecca. You grew up before it was time, India. How can that not damage a person?"

"How did we get from 'wonderful' to 'damaged'?"

"Because look." He met her eyes, but he meant look at her wide, rounding belly. "Look what happened. And I guess I'm starting to realize maybe the fact that this happened before is what made it happen again."

It wasn't the point really, but India asked anyway, "Who cares why it happened again?"

He squeezed his eyes shut. "Because I don't know if I can do this forever."

"Raise a baby? Be a family?"

"Be with someone for whom neither the past nor the future really exists. Be with someone so focused on one goal that taking care of anyone, even herself, isn't possible. I believe too much in consequences and learning my lesson. I don't want to drag you down with my pragmatics and practicalities. But I don't know if I can scramble behind you our whole lives trying to hold everything in both arms."

"Do you think when you grow up"—her voice caught but she held his eyes—"I won't grow up too?"

"Anyone can make a mistake once," he whispered, "even a terrible one. But then . . ."

"What?"

"To let it happen again?"

Again, it wasn't maybe the issue, but she felt the need to point out, "It wasn't terrible."

"I think it was." He was whispering still, maybe because he didn't trust his voice, maybe because it was too horrible to say out loud. "I think it was so terrible it made you unable to notice. It wasn't that you did this"—he waved at her midsection—"on purpose. It's that after it happened, you therefore couldn't prevent it from happening again. I'm not blaming you. The opposite, in fact. I just don't know how to be up for it forever."

She went with the only bit she knew for certain. "I loved Rebecca. I got to make sure she would have a good life. It wasn't terrible. It was wonderful."

"But you didn't want a baby."

"I did. I just didn't want her for me."

He nodded and stopped walking and there were tears on his cheeks, but his voice did not shake when he said, "I think that's how it is for me too. I love you. And I want you. But I don't want you for me."

She found, for the millionth time, that New York City had everything, in this case an adoption agency with parent profiles posted online. She didn't look through every one. She didn't have to this time. As soon as she found the Andrews, she knew they were the ones.

Andy Silverman was stuck on the very first question of the application. This seemed like a bad sign. When they'd met, Andy wasn't Andy. He was Andrew. And Drew wasn't Drew. He was also Andrew. At first, this was just meet-cute, and honestly only to the two of them. It was a popular name (top twenty in 1979, the year they were both born), so not that much of a coincidence that they shared it. And it wasn't really a problem practically. If they were in the common room of the dorm studying, and Drew whispered across the table while also running his foot up his inseam, "Andrew. Hey. Wanna take a break and head up to my room for a bit?" he was hardly going to be talking to himself. Their friends called them Stache (once—*once!*—he'd left breakfast with chocolate milk on his lip) and Penny (Drew had eventually gotten into Lenox off the waitlist, thank God, but he'd already bought a Penn sweatshirt by then and claimed it was more comfortable).

One night their senior year, though, Drew had said, "Race you for it."

"Race me for what?"

"Your name."

"My name?"

"*Our* name. I'll race you for who gets Andrew."

"We're doing fine sharing," Andy had observed. He couldn't picture them calling each other Penny and Stache. He couldn't picture them calling each other honey and sweetheart. He couldn't picture calling or even thinking of this boy, this man, this love of his life as anything other than Andrew, and honestly, it felt apt to him that they shared a name, that aloud they were indistinguishable, because that was how it felt to him, that they were part of each other, that they were one.

"In college, sure," Drew said. "But what about what comes next?"

Andy stopped breathing, practically. "What comes next?"

"When we have to get an apartment together. And a car. And babies. When we get married. When we meet each other's bosses. When our friends are actual adults."

This litany spilled out in a strange order. Andy's ear and heart had snagged on marriage and gone no further.

"Then we'll need different names. Real ones," Drew concluded. "So I'll race you for it. Up to the park and back. Winner takes Andrew."

They'd pulled on shorts and shoes and nothing else and were outside running through the frigid night before he'd said okay, before he even knew what they were doing, pounding pavement, laughing and yelling after each other, people on the street staring like they were crazy, but not that crazy because it was a Saturday night and they were college students and this was New York City, down three blocks of sidewalk, across four intersections, over two piles of dog shit, four bags of trash, and one tower of carryout noodle boxes, around the fountain, through the park, cutting back down an alley, neck and neck, retracing the final block, Drew just ahead of him at the front door, swiping his card then pulling it shut behind him, Andy just getting his hand in, good thing because he didn't have his card on him, the sudden heat of being inside again after a hard run drenching them both at once with sweat, stumbling up the stairs together but Drew winning, undeniably, back in the room first by a body length, two, then turning to grin triumphantly at Andy who did not even pause but barreled into him, taking them both down, panting, heaving chests pressed together, Andy's heart pounding in every part of him. They were wearing nearly nothing so were naked instantly. They fucked with their sneakers on.

Later though, after, the first thing Andy said was, "Congratulations, Andrew."

"Thank you, sir."

"Is that who I have to be now? Sir?"

"Better than Stache."

"Agreed," he'd agreed, "but I guess I was thinking Andy."

"Andy. How do you like it?"

"Weird. But okay, I guess. I'll get used to it."

"I was thinking I'd be Drew," said Drew.

"If you lost?"

"Starting now," he said.

"But you won."

"I was just trying to get your heart rate up," he said.

"There are other ways," said Andy.

"Well, I did those too."

"They worked."

"You didn't think I was really going to take Andrew just because I'm a better athlete than you?"

"One of us should be Andrew. No point in both of us suffering."

"Sure there is."

"What?"

"Solidarity, sister," he said. "Share and share alike."

"Drew and Andy," Andy mused.

"Drew and Andy Silverman," Drew corrected.

Andy's heart rate went back up.

Drew—newly Drew—sat up on one knee.

"I figured when we got married, you'd take my name."

Andy could not think where to start. "You did?"

"Yeah. Because it's not a political thing. You're not a woman."

"I mean, yeah."

"And because my parents love you whereas your parents . . ."

"So I'd be Andrew Silverman too?" Andrew Silverman. The love of his life. And the man in the mirror. It was very strange but also not that strange.

"Officially, you'd be Andrew Silverman. And I'd be Andrew Silverman. But mostly we'd be Drew and Andy."

Andy could not actually believe it. "Are you asking me to marry you?"

"Are you crying?"

"I asked you first."

"I'm not so much asking you to marry me as telling you to marry me."

"Yes."

"Yes you're crying, or yes you'll marry me?"

"Yes," said Andrew Silverman.

"Andrew!"

Except when he was fucking up. Then he got the full name.

He looked up with his eyes but kept his face pointed at his laptop.

"You are overthinking this," Drew said.

"These forms are hard."

"You're stuck on 'Name.'"

"Maybe it's a sign."

"It's not a sign."

"If we can't even fill out the forms to apply to be parents, how will we ever parent?"

"We *can* fill out the forms," Drew said. "And ability to fill out forms has nothing to do with fitness to parent. And you don't believe in signs."

This was all true, of course, but Andy believed in all sorts of things he didn't believe in. Should he ever get to page two, there loomed a question about religion, the space for which was a small one, like for name, like for city, like for date of birth, as if an inch were plenty sufficient space in which you might describe your soul's relationship with the infinite and the divine. That he'd fled the church as soon as he had a choice, that he'd never believed, that he'd never—never never never never—subject any child of his to it, or really to organized religion of any kind, was not the point. Religion, Andy knew, was something you were born into and could not escape. Belief had nothing to do with it.

This did not, however, suggest it made any sense because it didn't. For one thing, there was too much sin in the world to imagine everyone who engaged in it was going to hell. How could they all fit? Even granting that the laws of physics probably didn't apply to afterworlds, hell would have to have space for very nearly everyone who had ever lived. Whereas heaven needed room for his sister and Jesus. The pictures they showed—clouds stretching off into infinity, wide expanses of angels and sunshine—seemed entirely the wrong scale. Ditto the cramped caverns of hell looking like someone's creepy unfinished basement. Hell would have to be the size of a galaxy. Claire and Jesus would fit in the linen closet.

When his father kicked him out, finally, Andy was only fifteen and therefore scared but also relieved. Faced with being disowned and homeless, he was, ironically, as unemotional and unsentimental as his father had been begging him to be for his entire life. He went to the library to figure out what to do, but mostly to have someplace to be. It was late spring, so maybe days at school, evenings in the library, nights on a bench would work until it got cold out again which gave him five months, more or less, to find a better arrangement. Maybe while he was in the library, he could do some research and figure it out. Maybe the library would even give him a job, as long as he was there all the time, and that would help too.

He wasn't quite ready to be that brave yet, so he headed for his usual spot in the fiction stacks and figured reading about other people who'd overcome parents who didn't love them—and the fiction stacks were full of them—was a good start.

That was where his sister found him.

"Hi," she said, like she'd run into him in the living room.

He jumped an inch off the floor, even though he was sitting on the floor.

"How'd you find me?" Andy was staring at his sister like she'd tracked him down in a tent in Antarctica.

"Where else would you go?" She braced herself and slid awkwardly down the wall, her pregnant belly making her a little wobbly, to sit on the floor beside him.

He gave her the list of places he'd considered—the mall, the bus station, somewhere a bus went—but she was unimpressed.

"Not where else would one go. Where else would *you* go."

He didn't need to ask how she knew their dad had kicked him out. Their mom would have called her before he reached the end of the driveway. Technically Claire was living two and a half miles away in her own house with her own husband and her own child, another in her belly, who knew how many more on the way. But she and his mother talked on the phone every few hours it seemed like, and Claire came by every day to check on her. Or, it occurred to him now, maybe it wasn't their mother she was coming to check on.

So how she knew to look was not Andy's question. Andy's question was whether she knew why.

While he was figuring out how to ask, she told him she didn't know what the Bible said.

"What are you talking about?" he raised his eyes from the floor to ask her. "You know everything the Bible says."

"I mean I've read it," she allowed. Understatement. "I go to church. I try to live as I think and believe God wants. But . . ."

She trailed off, and he couldn't imagine what the end of her sentence was, so he just sat while his head swam and waited for her to finish it.

"The Bible says love your brother. It doesn't say love your brother unless he's gay." So she did know why. He could feel his face burning like the flames of the basement caverns. But she went right on. "It doesn't say love your brother unless your father doesn't."

"But being gay is a sin," he managed.

"Yeah, but everything is a sin. Eating a hamburger on a Friday is a sin. Thinking it would be cool to have a pool in my backyard even though there's no way we could afford it is a sin. Enjoying sex with your husband is a sin but so is not wanting to do it. Wishing your dad wouldn't hit your brother is a sin. Honestly, wishing anything is a sin because you should be praying, not wishing, and praying for your father is allowed but praying against him isn't."

"Yeah, but isn't gay, like, higher on the sin spectrum?"

"Who knows? I don't think there's a ranked list. But when you think of all the really horrible things people do to each other, gay has to be further from murder and torture and closer to hamburgers, right?"

"I guess?"

"Anyway, Jesus loves you regardless. That's the whole point of Jesus. And if Jesus loves you, who am I not to? Who am I to speak for him? He's Jesus. I'm just Claire. I do what I think he wants. You should too."

He couldn't believe it.

"Let me ask you a question, though," Claire said, and he felt his heart seize because what kind of God would offer this sort of love and then take it away? The kind he'd been taught, that's who. But she said, "Have you thought about where you'll sleep?"

He told her about the bench plan.

His sister said, "Come on."

"Come on where?"

"Home."

"No way." He scrambled away from her. That was the one thing he absolutely could not do.

"Not your home," she clarified. "My home. You can sleep in the nursery."

"What about Carley?"

"She sleeps with us."

Andy wondered how Claire could possibly be pregnant again already then, but for obvious reasons, he didn't want to think about it too hard. On the way through the garage, she grabbed a sleeping bag, and he followed her into the house and up to the nursery. Inside, it looked like a flamingo had exploded. Pink walls, pink curtains, pink sheets in a crib piled with pink pillows and pink teddy bears. Pink carpet and, at its center, a darker pink rug. A rocking chair and rocking ottoman, both lined with pink cushions. A pink dresser. A changing table with pink drawers and a pink pad on top, pink towels hung from knobs alongside, a mobile dangling pink baby animals from the ceiling.

They stood in the doorway looking in.

"What do you think?" she said.

"Well, if I wasn't gay before . . ." It was out of his mouth before he could consider the wisdom of these words, but she knocked her hip against his, giggling.

"Shut up!"

"I just . . . I mean . . . are you worried she'll play a sport or something if she sees the color green?"

Claire was cracking up now. They could joke about this. This was something they could joke about. It was a feeling like floating.

Claire tried to stop giggling and failed. "When she was born she was just so . . ."

"What?"

"Bald! And I thought . . ."

"That pink leads to hair growth?"

"That we could compensate by being extra . . . I don't know . . . girly."

"So you decorated her room like a vagina?" Andy said.

"You're going to make me pee my pants." Claire was laughing so hard her face matched the nursery. "My pelvic floor muscles have forgotten their job lately."

"Hang out in here more. Maybe it'll remind them."

"I just thought out in her stroller or whatever people were going to keep mistaking her for a boy. Doesn't matter anyway, though. Carley has not spent a single night in here. Not one."

"I mean, she spent nine months in the vagina room before she got here. Maybe she's over it."

"Maybe that's what I should try." Claire cracked up again. "Maybe if I painted in here, the girl would shut up and sleep more than three hours in a row."

They laid the sleeping bag out on the pink rug in the middle of the pink carpet. "The dresser is full of clothes she doesn't even fit into yet," his sister said, "so you can just shove them in the closet and use the drawers for your stuff."

He opened his empty palms outward.

Claire looked at the floor. "Mom packed for you. Craig'll go over and get it later."

Claire's husband, Craig, was the silent type, less the strong silent type than the fat silent type, and not really fat, but in that way men got when they were more interested in beer than in the gym. Claire seemed not to mind, though. Claire was also fat now because she was pregnant, or maybe Claire was above such shallowness as caring about bodies now that she was a mom, or maybe Claire felt that God wanted her to marry a man with a hairy potbelly. Andy had nothing against Craig, but if Craig was going to his parents' house to get his stuff, it meant he knew now too. It meant Andy had to add Craig to the list of people who would find out about him and be repulsed and disgusted and appalled.

But after dinner, which Andy couldn't eat, after Claire went to bed at 8:30 because Carley would be awake again in a few hours, after Craig cleaned up and headed for the stairs without a word, he paused, hand on the banister, and turned back toward Andy.

"So," he said, "you're gay?"

"I . . ." Andy couldn't think of anything else to say. "Yes."

It was the first time anyone had asked directly. So it was the first time he had ever answered. He was having trouble breathing.

"Whew," Craig said. "Hard."

"I . . ." Andy began and, horrified, felt his eyes fill up. "Yes," he said again. It wasn't what he had expected Craig to say in response to the news. It wasn't what he expected anyone to say in response to the news. But it was true. And it had not occurred to him before. And it was nice to have this fact acknowledged—not quite as nice as joking about it with Claire, but only because Craig admitting it was hard meant he had to admit it to himself.

"Need anything?" Craig asked, and because he'd been thinking about it, Andy thought he meant help with being gay, or with not being gay, or help on account of the fact that he was gay.

"I . . ." Why did he keep starting sentences that way? "No. Thank you."

"Okay," Craig said. "Cool." He started up the stairs then turned back, held out his hand in that hooked vertical way guys did when a handshake isn't appropriate but they don't want to hug you either. Andy held his arm upright as well and entwined forearms into clasped hands for a moment. "Glad you're here, man," Craig said, then turned and went upstairs. It was the most masculine moment of Andy's young life.

Like the adoption forms, the ones Andy had to fill out to apply to college had also asked questions that were difficult to answer. So he drew a comic book. He drew his father, navy and horned, his dark ink bleeding into the white borders between the panels. He drew his mother hidden in each square, behind a tree, beneath a chair in their kitchen, barely visible around a door or a corner or encased in a curtain. He drew himself walking away from home after his dad kicked him out, the smooth sidewalk outside his house turned rubble-strewn and hole-pocked and smoking. But then his salvation. In the scene where Claire found him on the floor in the stacks, the library looked like a church, soaring ceilings, prismatic light from stained-glass windows, his sister a backlit pregnant angel, a savior sent by God.

He drew her home. The sight of his rebirth, the vagina room, was a little on the nose symbolism-wise but required no reimagining. He sat in there and sketched it just as it was. He drew himself drawing his admission comic alongside Carley drawing him drawing it, which also required nothing but sketching what was.

And then the part that did require imagining. His comic turned speculative. Maybe fantastic. Andy at college—taking notes in class, lying on the quad in the sun, joining a club, touring the city (for he only applied to colleges in New York: big enough to be lost in should that prove necessary again, big enough that he had reason to hope it wouldn't be). In every panel, at every activity, he was surrounded by friends. In one small square, toward the end, he drew himself holding hands with another student, a boy whose face you could not see but whose grip he could almost feel, whose touch was gentle as the pencil lines that traced it, and who was out there, somewhere, waiting for him.

When he found him, though, it turned out Drew hadn't actually been waiting. Andy realized this in bed, telling the stories you tell in bed in the early days when there's still so much you don't know about each other. He had assumed they'd have the same story. He assumed every gay kid had the same story.

But no. Drew's parents loved him. Everyone loved him. Drew was popular in high school. He was president of student government without actually running for student government because so many kids wrote in his name. He played varsity soccer in the fall and baseball in the spring; and in the winter, because he was too short for basketball, he joined the bowling club.

"Because heaven forfend you went two months without being on a team of some kind," said Andy.

"Heaven forfend," Drew agreed.

He had friends, loads of friends. He even had girlfriends.

"I don't understand," said Andy. "How were you straight?"

"I wasn't *straight* straight." He bit Andy's nipples to demonstrate.

"You were bi."

"No."

"You were passing?"

"I was high school straight," Drew explained.

And when that didn't work anymore, when he stopped being even high school straight, he talked to his parents.

"Your *parents*?" Andy was incredulous.

"I was just like, 'You guys, I think I might be gay.'"

"Whoa."

"Yeah."

"How'd they take it?"

"My dad was all, 'We know!' and my mom was like, 'Well, we didn't know, but we had a hunch,' and then my dad was like, 'No, we knew,' and then my mom said, 'We pretty much did. We were just waiting for you to know too. Mazel tov!'"

"Mazel tov?"

"It means congratulations."

"I know what it means."

"Not congratulations for being gay. Congratulations for figuring it out, for becoming, you know, who I was or whatever."

"They weren't upset?"

"Why would they be upset?"

Eternity in fiery hell, Andy thought. But what he said was "Lifetime of getting picked on. Lifetime of disappointment."

"I wasn't picked on," Drew said and leaned his face into Andy's neck. "I'm not disappointed."

"But, like, the gap between what they imagined for you—what you imagined for you—and what you actually got, what you'll actually get."

"I got into my first-choice college." Drew spread his arms wide to indicate it. "I met the boy of my dreams," around whom he encircled them to prove it. "Have you seen my GPA? I'm going to get into my first-choice law school too. I don't think my life's disappointing anyone. I think it's working out exactly like I planned."

"You thought you'd grow up and fall in love with a woman and have babies together," Andy pointed out.

"Sure, but that's just a detail."

"Kind of a large detail."

"No, like if you grew up fantasizing about a blond, but when you met the love of your life he had dark hair. Or in your fantasy you had a stucco house in Southern California, but you ended up in a colonial in the Bay Area. I'll still grow up and fall in love and have babies, but instead I'll do it with you."

Andy remembered a conversation he'd had with Claire shortly before he left. Craig was late at work. She was nursing Clyde who was too fussy to eat because he was too hungry. Cash was in his high chair, also screaming, also hungry because he was throwing spaghetti on the floor. Carley was suspiciously quiet, and when Andy went to investigate it was because she'd used his good and permanent markers to draw all over herself and the white tile floor of the bathroom, the tub, the cabinets, the wallpaper that predated their tenure in the house and which Claire told herself might be vintage. It probably wasn't but that was hardly the point.

It took hours to get everyone cleaned and fed and asleep. Craig came home finally, declared himself exhausted as if he were the only one who was, and went straight to bed. Andy and Claire hadn't eaten anything yet. While they were waiting for the pizza to come, he said, "Is this what you thought your life was going to be like?"

He meant it rhetorically. He meant it so rhetorically he meant it as a joke.

But from the other end of the couch, without opening her eyes, she said, "Oh yeah."

"What? Really?"

"Definitely. Adored husband who adores me. House full of kids. Family. Church. This is exactly what I pictured."

"But weren't you hoping for more . . . ?"

"What?"

"I don't know. But as far as fantasies go . . ."

"I mean in my fantasy, Craig looked less like Craig and more like El DeBarge. And my kids never misbehaved. And I had shinier hair. But you know, basically this."

Whereas Andy, asked to picture his future, had no idea what came between high school and the fiery hell pit. He never pictured marriage because he wasn't that way. He couldn't be. He'd tried. So he never pictured children either. He didn't picture jobs he might hold because all the jobs he knew required a man to be like his father—brutal, hard, mean. He didn't picture friends—he hadn't had any so far, and why would people start liking him now? He knew he wouldn't go to church anymore. He knew he would lose his nieces and nephews who wouldn't want him around once they learned what he was. He pictured himself crouched against a brick wall being rained on in the cold dark, homeless maybe but it wasn't that specific a scenario, just the permeating chill and the surety that he was alone in all the world.

So you wouldn't think it, but maybe Andy was luckier than Claire, luckier than Drew. Claire got what she thought she wanted, what she mostly wanted, and if it was harder than she'd imagined, the Scriptures had prepared her well to deal with it. Drew was getting what he'd imagined too and was finding the substitution of men for women to be essentially cosmetic. But Andy? Andy'd won the lottery because his life was nothing, *nothing*, like he'd imagined. Their life together was what Drew had fantasized; it was beyond Andy's wildest wild dreams.

"Wait, what?" On the bed in Drew's dorm room that day, though, as his mind wandered and snapped back again, Andy remembered what he'd said. "Babies?"

Macbeth performances began the first weekend of May. Commencement was two weeks later. India was due at the end of the month. She thought she might not deserve to graduate, though. Graduation was meant to be a confirmation of her learning and growth, and if she was still making the same stupid mistakes four years of higher education and coursework and reading and essays and exams later, could she really be said to be learned? So she was happy to skip graduation.

But she had to see *Macbeth* through. It was a dream part. She knew that. And she was great. She knew that, too. But she was so tired. Huge. Heartbroken. And right on the cusp. Which was also the edge.

She thought about inviting the Andrews to opening night but worried it might be weird to have to watch your future be a prop and a theme, upsetting to see it turned to blood, even if it was just stage blood. She knew it would be upsetting because she herself could not stop crying. She cried when she ran lines in the shower. She cried from act three onward. She cried so hard during "Out, damned spot!" she shorted her mic in tech rehearsals. But her voice never wavered. You could hear every word. It was only a college show, but later, when India got famous, people who were there all swore they knew, they knew for sure, that she would be a star.

After the final bow of the final performance, after she let herself watch from a chair across the room rather than participate in all the frenzied hugging, after promising thirty different people that of course she would come to the cast party, after showering off all the fake blood, she found a business card in her backstage cubby, tucked inside her left sneaker. In hot pink script on a yellow background it read:

Ajax Axelrod.
Agent. Maker. Impresario.

On the one hand, it might have been a prank because Ajax Axelrod seemed such an unlikely name.

On the other hand, scrawled on the back was "India, I may have a part for you. Or, if you prefer, may I have you for a part? Do be in touch sooner than later," which was exactly the sort of eccentric, incomprehensible missive one expected from an agent. So India let herself believe probably it was not a trick after all.

Suddenly she had the energy to keep her promise to those thirty cast-party goers.

Hours later, high from the promise of that card, from her last show, from her last college cast party, from exhaustion that had crossed over into delirium, India stumbled back to her room. It was nearly two a.m. Before she let herself sleep, though, she did some calculations. Powerful agents probably didn't get to work until at least nine on Monday mornings, and overeager might be off-putting as a first impression. Plus, maybe it was considered rude to call first thing as if Ajax Axelrod didn't have meetings and emails and colleagues' weekends to catch up on before he got to the business of new clients. She resolved to get some sleep and call him at 9:48 the next morning, late enough not to seem desperate, early enough not to seem disinterested, off the quarter hour enough not to look like she was trying too hard.

Just before dawn, she went into labor.

WEDNESDAY

"There's another one?" Bex's own voice echoed in her own head.

India Allwood had given birth to her and then given her to her mom. End of story.

Except then it turned out it wasn't the end of the story. It was only chapter one.

Suddenly she had a thousand questions with their hands up, waving frantically to be called on. She was used to that because she'd had so many of them for so many years, but when she got here yesterday, they'd all evaporated. Everyone was just so . . . normal, too normal to ask about. India didn't seem like a glamorous movie star *or* a recovering knocked-up teenager. She seemed like every other mom Bex knew in that frazzled way mothers are, either about or because of their kids, and what was there to ask about that? What was there to ask about India before she got pregnant and gave birth to Bex? India was only sixteen then, and Bex knew, from being sixteen herself, that whoever India had been at the time was some weird combination of pretend and hiding and still deciding and trying too hard and completely clueless. So it didn't make sense to ask about that either. And Fig was right about herself: she seemed like a little sister. But whereas Fig also seemed to think that was special, sister was definitely ordinary. Lots of people had one. Sisters were everywhere.

Now, though, her questions were back because Davis Shaw changed everything. The questions he raised didn't even have their hands up waving frantically. They were hunched in the back of the classroom praying not to get called on. They were questions that had detention for being answered wrong the first time.

For instance, Davis Shaw meant you had to ask—re-ask, re-ask for the millionth time—why India had hidden Bex (and Lewis!) from the world. It turned out the reason wasn't remorse or shame. It wasn't because India regretted not getting an abortion, and it wasn't because she regretted having Bex, and it wasn't because she regretted giving her up for adoption. Davis Shaw proved all of that because if India had been regretful and ashamed and sorry, she wouldn't have done it again. She might have accidentally gotten pregnant again—Bex understood this, she was not stupid—but she would have made a different decision the second time if she felt bad about the first. And she didn't. Which meant Bex—her presence, her existence, the very fact of her—had not ruined the life of the person who had caused hers to occur.

But if shame and regret weren't the reason for the secret—secrets—what was?

It was a big question, but big as it was, it was smaller than the other ones because the fact that Davis Shaw had a baby with India Allwood and that baby wasn't Bex meant there was another kid out there who that baby actually was. Which meant Bex had a real sibling. Well, half a real sibling anyway. And who was he? Even though brothers were just as ordinary as sisters, she shared something with him she didn't share with Fig and Jack. She shared something with him no one shared with anyone. Having the same genes as someone else was kind of interesting, she guessed. India Allwood was hot enough to be a movie star, so that was promising for Bex. But what was really interesting, way beyond genes, was that someone else was out there who could understand— who shared with her—the incredibly strange, heretofore unique, central fact of her life. She was literally the biological child of literally Val Halla. And now, it turned out, she was not the only one.

2009

India would not say *mourn*. She would not say *grieve*. Not even to herself, no matter how often the social workers and adoption counselors advised it. You have to give yourself a chance to mourn this baby, your son, they said. You will be devastated, they said. You have suffered a tremendous loss. Give yourself time to sorrow, a period of lamentation that might last a lifetime.

India objected to this advice and this characterization and, especially, to being told how to feel. She had chosen this of her own free will in her own right mind with her own big brain, so did not appreciate the intimation, however sympathetically intended, that placing the baby with the Andrews was something she'd been cornered into, owing to being lost, wronged, depressed, misled, maltreated, poor, unemployed, woebegone, and/or without any other options. That read made her character a tragic figure and a disempowered one, infantilized and victimized, and she was none of that. Would not be. Refused.

The anguished parts, the heartbreak, were obvious so did not need belaboring to ensure observation. The euphoric parts—the Andrews got a baby, the baby got a stable, lovingly given, ardently sought family, India and Davis got . . . not what they wanted, exactly, but more of what they wanted given the available options—were the parts that would get lost if no one insisted on them. So she did. She insisted. There was cause for heartbreak, yes, but there was also cause for celebration. If she could have eaten anything, she'd have asked for birthday cake.

But she couldn't. She couldn't eat. She couldn't mourn. She could barely move. It didn't feel tragic; it felt apocalyptic, a life lost—hers—the baby and college and Davis, the stage lights and star parts, the world she commanded and years of well-laid, well-loved, well-executed plans. For what seemed the first time since she was ten, she didn't know what would happen next. So it felt like that, like the world was ending, even though it was not, no one's was, and in fact by every measure—every one—the world was much improved by what had happened here.

Still.

She was sore and bleeding and leaking milk—leaking fluids of all kinds, in fact, because also she could not stop crying. She was empty. Emptied. She lay on her bed in her dorm room like the college student she essentially no longer was anymore, like the person she had been two days ago who she also no longer was anymore.

Dakota brought her a can of cream soda and two slices of pizza so greasy they turned their box translucent.

"I can't eat."

"You didn't try," said Dakota, but she ate the pizza herself then replaced it with an entire chocolate babka and a bagel sandwiching two full inches of lox.

"I'm not a tourist," India said.

"You have to eat New York food while you can," said Dakota. "We're graduating in four days."

"And moving eight blocks away."

"Maybe they don't have as good bagels over there."

"Then we'll walk back over here."

But it was the pickle too fat to get her fingers around and the lump of whitefish salad in a seeping cardboard container that finally got India vertical. No matter how sore she was, no matter how sorry and sorry-looking, no matter how much she knew Dakota was just trying to help, she could not inhale through her nose in that room a moment longer. She made her way outside and limped around campus.

Move-out was underway, and she watched sweaty students shove overfull trash bags into overfull cars. She watched all the hugging and tears from friends about to be parted for three mere months before they got to return in the fall. She watched crews of workers polish the campus for graduation and the expected onslaught of parents and guests and potential donors. Flower beds got new-blooming bulbs and fresh soil. Dumpsters overflowing with left-behind dorm detritus got emptied and filled again. Ivy was trimmed (but not removed—it was too good a photo op). The sun shone in a world-continuing-on way, and everything was glittering and hot and changing forever.

She found a bench outside the drama department and had her own very small, very private graduation ceremony. She made herself remember that she knew better than most how goodbye could be sad but needn't break you and why endings were so often marked by commencement. Then she called Davis.

"How do you feel?" He arrived and lowered himself beside her gingerly, as if jostling the bench might be what hurt her.

"Terrible. You?"

"I didn't just give birth."

"Still."

"Also terrible," he conceded.

"I'm sorry." She was.

He nodded. He knew. He was also sorry. "Are you okay, though? You know"—he waved at her, her body—"physically?"

"A little sore." That this was an understatement was not the point. Nor that the distinction he was making—physical pain owing to birthing a baby and giving it to the Andrews versus emotional pain owing to birthing a baby and giving it to the Andrews versus emotional pain caused by everything else in general and Davis himself in particular—was indistinct. "Congratulations," she said instead.

He looked surprised. "For what?"

"Graduation?"

"Oh. Thanks. You too."

"And, you know, moving on. From everything. It's over now."

"In some ways." His face closed a notch, and she said nothing to that. They had tried enough times to know there was no way through it.

"They named him Lewis," she reported.

"Lewis? He sounds like an old man."

"He looked like an old man, actually." India understood why Davis hadn't wanted to—couldn't—be there. But she wanted him to know.

"Did he . . . ?"

"What?"

"I don't know," Davis admitted.

"Look like you? Like me? Seem happy for a newborn? Seem destined for a wonderful life?"

"Yeah," Davis breathed. "All of those, I guess."

"For sure," India said. "All of them."

Davis nodded. He wiped away his own tears, then hers, which didn't take. Eventually he said, "I heard you got a big-shot agent."

"Maybe. I haven't . . . I haven't been able to call him yet."

"India." He pulled back to look at her. "This is important."

"Yeah, I know, I know, I—"

"No, I'm not nagging you. Extenuating circumstances, for sure. I'm just saying this is important—"

"I know. I just—"

"This is why we did this."

"No it's not."

"Gave up the baby, I meant."

"Placed him. I knew what you meant. And no, it's not. We did it because we didn't want to have a baby together right now."

"Yes. And this is why. At least some of why. So you could get an agent. So you could get a job. So I could get a job. So we could have our lives. So don't let the aftermath of this ruin that."

"No. I won't."

"You might have to make yourself, you know?" Very gently. Knowing her. She felt this in her chest. "It'll be hard, but you can't call this guy a month from now and say, 'Sorry, I was really busy giving birth and breaking up with my boyfriend and graduating and getting my shit together emotionally, but thanks for your patience and I'm ready now.'"

Breaking up with my boyfriend. "Yeah. I know."

"So just suck it up and breathe deep and call him. You don't even have to get dressed. You don't even have to stop crying." He reached over and wiped her eyes again. "You just have to act like you're not crying."

"That's my best thing," she cried.

"I know," he said. Then added, "I did."

"Cried?"

"That too. But I meant I got a job. A great one. A dream job."

She unfolded herself to face him fully and felt the joy branch out from her center into every part of her. "Davis!"

"Yeah." A little sheepish.

"*Fuck* yeah," she corrected.

"Yeah. It's great. Thanks."

"Tell me about it."

"It's an education start-up that uses performing arts—plays, musicals, operas; ballet, I guess?—for after-school programs. So the job is programming but also theater."

"Musicals?"

"They were really impressed with all my acting experience. So I have you to thank. I'd never have gotten this job without you."

"Sure you would have."

"Nope. I've thought about it a lot, and I don't think so."

She reached into the pockets of the hoodie she'd tied around her waist in case she bled through her shorts and threw a handful of a shredded *Macbeth* program over his head.

"Thanks," he laughed, but then he said, "It's in San Francisco."

Since it didn't matter anymore, she was surprised to find that this knocked the wind out of her. "Oh. I didn't . . . I didn't know you were looking out there."

"I wasn't. I was only looking in New York because . . ."

. . . because we were going to live together and get married together and have more babies together and you needed to be in New York and I needed to be with you and we love it here . . .

"But then when . . ."

. . . when I didn't want to be with you anymore . . .

"I expanded my search," he finished.

"I thought . . ." She didn't know how to finish that sentence honestly and kindly, for honesty and kindness were called for here. She settled on "I hear it's nice out there."

"I'll be the opposite of the song. Instead of leaving my heart in San Francisco, I'll bring it there and see how it goes."

They were holding hands, all four hands—she did not know when or how that had happened—and leaking again.

"You'll have mine with you too," she said.

He put one hand on it. "And I'll leave most of mine broken here with you."

"I know." She slotted her forehead into the notch in his chest where it belonged, and he held her, and they cried.

And then he kissed her goodbye and walked away.

B ecause she had promised Davis she would, because it was her dream and her destiny, maybe just because the show must go on, on Wednesday India forced herself out of bed and into clean clothes. She could only wear sweatpants because nothing else fit, and only black ones because she was still bleeding, and a terrible sports bra she lined with cabbage leaves because, in their understandable confusion, her breasts were as painful as her singing.

She kicked Dakota out of their mostly packed-up room. The walls without their posters and programs and photos felt naked. The desks without their piles of books and paper and highlighters and scripts felt obscene. Her index cards were all in careful boxes. Their room felt bereft. Or maybe that was India herself.

She managed to tell whoever answered the phone that she was calling for Ajax Axelrod, but after he picked up, her voice broke on her very next line. "He-llo." Inauspicious, but she kept on, professionally. "This is India Allwood."

A moment of nothing on the other end. "India Allwood?" Another too-long pause. "Who are you?"

It had only been maybe sixty hours since he'd slipped his card into her shoe. It's true she had become a different person in that time. But he probably hadn't.

"You left me your card Sunday night?" Nothing. "I was Lady Macbeth?"

"Ahh, yes, Lady M," Ajax Axelrod remembered, and then, "Sunday? Bacon, lettuce, and tomatoes, you took your time."

"Something came"—*out*, she wanted to say, but went with—"up."

"More important than landing the hottest agent in the city?"

"Not more important than," she hedged, "but—"

She hadn't been sure going into that sentence how she'd get out the other side, so it was good he interrupted.

"This is why I do not ordinarily take on students."

"I'm barely a student anymore. Graduation is this weekend."

"You were very good." Not praising her. Informing her. "In all my years, I have never seen a pregnant Lady M. Clever. That Alan Darden's doing? I forget this about him. He's smarter than you think. College professors, eh?"

How to answer that? Fortunately, he didn't wait for her to do so.

"Well, Al gets credit for a good idea, then. But the genius was in the execution. You really sold it. I truly believed, truly *felt*, you were about to have a baby."

Shit.

"You *were* pregnant. Desperate, hormonal, heartbroken. Everything about you screamed, 'I am overlarge, ungainly, uncomfortable, formidable. I labor under the burden of impending labor. I am carrying the progeny of a too-weak, too-frightened, too-deluded man.' It was an impressive performance. Shed real light on a play I have seen, truly, dozens of times."

She ran quickly through the pros and cons of coming clean, but again, her response seemed not to be required.

"I represent actors, singers, dancers, directors," said Ajax. "New York. LA. I do the whole thing really. I'm very good."

He paused. So she said, "Wow."

"Yes, wow," he agreed. "But I don't do playwrights. I draw the line at writers. All the ego of actors but more neuroses and less money. However, one of my clients has written himself a vehicle, one he will star in and direct, so I've been forced to make an exception. We're scheduled for ten weeks at the Public, but there's already buzz that we'll transfer."

"Transfer what?"

"Transfer *where*, dear. Broadway."

"Ahh," she said, half I-understand, half holy-fucking-shit.

"Indeed." He seemed to get both meanings. "But we're worried about casting. The female lead is proving tough to fill. It calls for not just young but ingenue, so we don't want a Hollywood starlet looking to slum it onstage for the publicity. It calls for real, gritty, not too pretty." But while India was coming to terms with that, he added, "And mostly, it's a killer role, let's hope not literally but it's not out of the question. The play's in two parts, six-plus hours total, and she's onstage the whole time. There are acrobatics. Flame work. Live animals. Eight shows a week. Tight schedule. It's a big ask. Impossible, maybe. But then you, Sunday night, you were the first flicker of hope I've had that there exists someone capable of pulling this off."

"What's it called?"

"*Nestra*. Technically *Nestra: Imagined After Aeschylus*. You see what I mean about ego. Honestly. Nestra is the part we want you for. Unless I've scared you off."

Off? No. But scared didn't even begin to cover it.

He arranged for her to audition Friday afternoon. She spent the fifty-two hours in between trying to figure out whether she'd been very, very lucky or this was the worst thing that would ever happen to her. On the one hand, it obviously didn't bespeak extraordinary talent that she was believably pregnant when she was actually pregnant, a fact he would surely have noticed at the audition if she hadn't had the baby almost three weeks early in the heartstoppingly narrow window between being discovered and having to prove herself. Lucky.

On the other hand, she was thus being given a chance she didn't merit, and once word got around about her lack of talent, she'd be ruined before she had time to learn and improve and work her way up, and all of this, all of it, everything in the world, would be for naught, and her dream would be dead, and so would she.

Worse still, there were no index cards to be made, no performance history to research, no lines to learn by heart in advance. The play was unpublished, as yet unperformed, existed nowhere but in draft form on the actor-turned-writer's computer. She had to go in cold. Cold and less talented than advertised.

She put on a very thick pad and a very padded bra, packed two entire changes of clothes—outfits she'd had to buy the day before, since ratty black sweatpants were not appropriate—and arrived with enough extra time to, if necessary, remodel herself down to the studs. But on the way up to the audition room on the tenth floor, the elevator got stuck and ate all her extra time. The man who came to fix it played improv games with her through the door to keep her calm—at a professional rehearsal studio in New York, even the maintenance workers had Broadway dreams, apparently—and when the doors finally opened, she had only enough time to thank him for freeing her then run, leaky and sweaty and panicked, to the audition. There, she channeled all she'd learned in four years of drama classes, four years of college productions, twenty years of her short-so-far life, and tried her best. It was all she could do.

Ajax Axelrod called Saturday morning to tell her she had the part.

Ajax's actor-turned-playwright-and-director was named Henri LeClerk. When India showed up the first day, she realized she knew him.

"Hey. You're the guy who unstuck my elevator."

He bowed deeply, then rose to admit, "Also the guy who stuck it."

She blinked, waited for this statement to clarify itself in her brain. "I don't get it."

"I'm not really an elevator repair specialist."

"What are you really?"

"An actor. I was acting like an elevator repair specialist."

"I still don't get it." This was not how India had envisioned her first moments at her first job.

"I am not just an actor. I am also a playwright and a director."

She still looked at him blankly, now tinged with irritation.

"*The* playwright and director," he clarified. "I needed to know what you sounded like before I knew what you looked like, to hear you before laying eyes on you. And I wanted to audition you in a situation where you'd be under pressure but not trying too hard to impress."

"That's . . ." *Creepy? Insane? Actionable?*

But before she could decide how to finish that sentence, he said, "You had the job before you set foot in the audition room."

So she had to allow it.

As someone in charge of building maintenance, he was exactly what you'd want, but as a writer-actor-director, he was terrifying: a giant, tall and muscled, with flashing eyes, simmering machismo, and barely contained volatility. She understood that was acting, but she doubted anyone was that good an actor, and beneath that, he was cocky and entitled and confident, swaggering, and that was also terrifying.

"Welcome," he began once everyone was assembled that first morning. They were sitting at an enormous U-shaped table with cards in front of them indicating their characters' names and, much smaller, their own. India peeked at everyone while trying not to stare. They looked unfazed. No one looked panicked. No one looked starstruck or overwhelmed or in over their head. No one looked stunned to find out that the elevator repair specialist was actually the director, so she must have been the only one to get that audition treatment. "For those of you who don't know me"—his tone suggested this was an unlikely state in which to find oneself—"I am Henri LeClerk." He pronounced it ON-ree. "Soon we'll get to know one another. In the meantime, I must let you know that at the moment this play makes no sense whatsoever. We will put it together together."

He handed out the script. First they did yoga. Then they did a table read. Then he sent them home. "Tomorrow, we will discuss. We will explore. We will find out all this play might mean and all it actually does. Get some rest."

"*Get* some *rest*!" India shrieked at Dakota. "Is he fucking kidding me? Is he kidding *himself*? Is this a joke he's perpetuating for his own amusement? Is it a joke the universe is perpetuating against me?"

"I think you can rule out that last one." Dakota had her head on their tiny kitchen table. Since she didn't have an Ajax, she was working at a coffee shop she opened at five o'clock every morning so as to leave her afternoons and evenings free for open-call auditions.

"First of all, what kind of man traps women in elevators for an audition?" India was chopping carrots into such tiny pieces they were approaching juice.

"Or really for anything."

"Second of all, he thinks he's so great. He's an actor and a director and a playwright, and he's so handsome, and he's barely thirty, and isn't everyone so impressed? Well no, I'm not, because I'm sure he's not that great an actor, and I'm even more sure he's not that great a director. Yoga? That's not the first thing you do on the first day of rehearsal. 'Get some rest'? That's his advice?"

"Sounds amazing," Dakota mumbled.

"Are you even listening?"

"One ear is. One is getting some rest."

"And a playwright? Hardly. Playwrights write plays that make sense. Playwrights write plays that can actually be performed. Plus, he didn't really write it. It's an adaptation. Yes, the original is lost, but it's not like he made the whole thing up."

"Did you figure out what it's about?"

"Nestra." India waved her knife around. "Hypermnestra, actually."

"What does that mean?"

"Extra Nestra? Super Nestra? Really fast Nestra? How should I know? It's about twins. One has fifty sons. One has fifty daughters."

"Multiples are more likely to have multiples," Dakota said.

"How do you know?"

"Remember that semester modern dance was full so I had to take biology?"

"The father of the sons wants to marry them to the daughters." India had moved on to destroying leeks.

"They're cousins!"

"Yeah, but the numbers work out."

"Gross."

"And nonsensical. This is my point. Anyway, the daughters agree with you, so they try to escape."

"Good call."

"But they can't, so their dad is like, 'Look, I have all these daggers. Everyone take one, get married, and then just kill your groom on the wedding night. Problem solved.'"

"Tough family," Dakota said.

"So they have this giant group wedding, and then that night, all the brides kill all the grooms. All except one."

"Hypermnestra?"

"Hypermnestra."

"Why?"

"She doesn't like blood? Killing is wrong? She loves her cousin?"

"I mean, I love mine too," Dakota said. "He taught me how to turn my eyelids inside out, but I don't want to marry him."

"You're gay."

"I don't think that's why."

"He says we're going to put it together together, but it's not even close. We open in six weeks. And I don't see how this thing is so buzzy when it doesn't make any sense."

"Maybe he doesn't realize because English isn't his first language?"

"It's not?"

"Isn't he French? Henri LeClerk?"

"Are the French egotistical megalomaniacs who trap women in elevators and stage plays literally no one understands?"

"*Mais oui*," said Dakota.

For the whole first week, they started every morning with yoga, then sat around the big table and talked about the play, tried to make sense of it, discussed. For the whole second week, after yoga, the designer came in with a mock-up of the set, and they spent every day on the space of the play. Anytime anyone said anything that wasn't about the space, Henri would declare it off topic, but what was and wasn't the space was a mystery to India. Week three was back to table reading again, interrupted every few minutes by Henri editing in real time, his laptop plugged into a projector, India reading new lines aloud as he wrote them. They were three weeks into a six-week rehearsal process, and no one was off book because the book wasn't finished yet, nothing was blocked, nothing tried, not even tried and rejected never mind tried and adopted and honed. Rehearsed. India didn't understand her lines. She didn't understand her character. She was starting to panic. She wrote the whole play on index cards—her evolving lines and everyone else's—and made notes on the back as to what they might mean. She was only guessing, but it was better than nothing.

On Friday of week three, they fell out of her bag and scattered all over the floor.

Henri picked up a few that had settled at his feet, turned them over front and back. She held her breath and waited to see if he was offended.

"This is all wrong," he said finally, "but I like it. Right isn't the goal after all."

"It's not?"

"The goal of writing is not to give the audience answers. It's to ask them questions, throw out some possibilities. I've been thinking of rehearsal as an excavation we do as a cast, a process of discovery and creation we undertake together. But I'm starting to see we need somewhere to start. And quickly."

She was weak with relief that he'd finally noticed.

"Fuck yoga," Henri began first thing Monday morning. *"Voilà!"* It was the first French he'd uttered, and he used it to reveal an enormous piece of butcher paper that took up the entire floor. "We shall unspool the whole play on this thing, block it for the stage, and then hammer it to the walls as well as our souls until it stalks our waking moments and haunts our very dreams."

They made notes, sketches, arrows; they pasted pictures, articulated connections, exploded small ideas into stars. It was like dancing, but with colored pens. And afterward, suddenly, a miracle occurred, which India supposed was the way of miracles. She was used to the kind that took nine months and were mixed blessings at best. But surely *suddenly* was the traditional way. Suddenly, the words on the page made sense. Suddenly, they went with movement and motion and intonation that also made sense. She didn't have to memorize them because the words were hers. She was able to imbue them with the subtleties of Nestra's emotions and relationships, which were as complicated as emotions and relationships always are—love but fear, scorn but admiration, loyalty but a loyalty you questioned constantly and berated yourself for—and she could make Henri, playing opposite her or sitting at the table watching his cast roam the floor he'd taped off to the dimensions of the stage, hear all of it.

Also suddenly, Henri proved a more interesting character. For one thing, all the preening, simpering egoism turned out to be acting too. He was very good. He was not even French but actually from Oklahoma where his real name was Henry Clark Smith. He was as lost and terrified and excited and ambitious and wonderstruck as India—he was young and new in the professional theater world too—but unlike her, he had only himself to blame if this show's hype proved unfounded. But they were not alone. They had a whole cast and crew of wildly talented, madly hopeful, much more experienced people with whom to get down to work.

And what work it was.

India would try things twelve ways, even things that were working well enough the first time, and see which worked best, or maybe not even best, maybe most interestingly. She could do this because the people she was working with were just that talented. It was not that Al-Like-the-Song and Davis and Dakota and all her friends from school weren't good. It was that they'd prevented her from knowing, really knowing, how good *good* could be. Davis was good, but his heart was never in it. He'd done it for his grandmother or to woo India or because she wanted him to, never because he loved it. Al-Like-the-Song's job wasn't to do a good show as much as it was to teach them to do a good show or, failing that, as good a show as they were able.

Whereas these people could do anything. Henri would say about a character, "Okay, but what if he's lying?" And they'd try it like that. And then, after they worked the rest of the scene, he'd say, "Or what if it's not that he's lying but that he's fudging certain aspects. It's mostly true, just not all the way true, though he thinks it's less true than it is," and India would sit and watch the actor give you that, that tiny change in attitude and aspect, clear as exposition, as if he'd held up a sign telling you. And slowly, play and questions and trying things were hammered into specificity—life-and-death specificity, because the technical aspects of the show were such that if you weren't at the exact right spot at the exact right moment, you would fall through a trapdoor or be crushed in a fold of scenery or catch fire.

India recognized Nestra. She recognized her in herself. And she recognized her the way she'd recognized Robbie all those years ago: *Oh, it's you. I've been waiting for you.* She was Nestra who said no, no to her father and no to her sisters and no to the chaos and hysteria that erupt when everyone in your entire family agrees to something you do not. Nestra who understood that sacrifice was not the point with marriage, no matter that everyone said it was. Nestra who understood that family ties are more complicated than mere genes, that blood can bind and also unbind, unwind, unravel until it is gone.

But more than recognizing Nestra, India invented her. She stopped acting by channeling her own life—acting sad by remembering Davis, acting torn by remembering Rebecca, acting benevolent by remembering Lewis and the Andrews—and starting acting sad and torn and benevolent by being sad, torn, benevolent Nestra. It was like making a baby: you sparked her into life, you grew him until he was ready, but then you delivered to the world someone new, someone else. This was also how India learned to be India. Learned to stay India. Nestra didn't take birth control, but being Nestra was acting. India was so thoroughly Nestra onstage that it was clear how not-Nestra she was everywhere else. At home, on her commute, on the phone with her mother, hanging out with Dakota, she was India.

She was India who, among other things, thought about calling Davis every day to tell him the good news. "I figured it out," she wanted to tell him, "how to act and take birth control, how to be good onstage but keep my shit together off it, how to star in a play but also consider the future, consequences, and other people." She wanted to tell him, "I'm fixed. You can come back now. Please come back now."

But instead of telling him, she decided to invite him to opening night and let him see for himself.

WEDNESDAY

Davis looked like an adult now. India had a mirror so knew she did too. She also knew how many years twelve was and the difference between being a college student and a thirty-two-year-old. But when she thought of Davis, she thought of him as last she saw him, on the bench outside the drama department. She thought of him the day they met. She thought of him onstage: himself, but also not himself. So it was very strange to have him here, the man she remembered but also not quite, the man she told stories about but who kept growing after those stories ended, like if you came down for breakfast one morning and Little Red Riding Hood was an adult and in your kitchen.

Everyone had questions. At dinner, Camille asked them politely and appropriately. The kids asked them impolitely and inappropriately. They learned Davis was at the same job programming software for theater kids, but that that wasn't really what the job was or had ever been and it was funny that India had thought so all these years. They learned he was heading up the new office in LA so had had to buy his first car, electric and blue. They learned he had two dogs, both mutts, Rachel and Rachel Junior. Fig clutched her chest at the prospect of puppies, but Davis said they weren't even related. "The intake worker at the shelter named all the dogs after his grandmother."

India braced herself, but they learned Davis had no children, that he was not married, that he was not dating anyone so his neighbor would have to watch the dogs till he got home. They learned—even though, or maybe because, he turned so red when they asked—that yes, he thought about Lewis every day and yes, he supposed he did miss him, even though he had never met him.

They learned, though India could feel her own face catch flame when they asked, that yes, he also thought about her every day and yes, he missed her too. That's when India interrupted the kids' interrogation and said maybe Davis had some questions of his own.

But he smiled and shook his head. "I already know all about you."

"How?" Jack said.

"I own a phone. And a TV. And I'm alive in the world."

"This morning you said you don't look at that stuff," Fig said.

"What stuff?"

"News, social media."

"When I can help it," Davis said. "And not at the beginning."

"The beginning?" said Jack.

"When your mother first started showing up on my screens, I couldn't look away."

India felt her face flush deeper, half with embarrassment, half with weirdly pleased gratification.

Fig was unimpressed, though. "We know just as much about you."

"Not possible." Davis shook his head sadly. "I'm very boring. And not famous."

"We know you think you're a good actor but actually you're an excellent actor," Jack said. "We know you like musicals, swimming, thin-crust pizza, nineteenth-century British literature, flirting in libraries, and cinnamon raisin bagels, even though sweet bagels are an abomination."

Davis's eyes flitted from Jack to India and back again.

"We know your dad's lactose intolerant," Fig added, "and helped you build forts when it snowed, and your grandma likes to talk on the phone on Sundays, and your great-great-grandfather may or may not have made a pair of shoes for Henrik Ibsen."

India clapped her hands and declared it bedtime, never mind it was too early, and sent Jack and Fig to their rooms and Bex to Fig's trundle bed. Camille said goodnight too, and since she was staying in the guest room, Fig asked where Davis would sleep. India told her he'd sleep in the pool house, but when she got back downstairs from tucking the kids in, he was sitting on the sofa right where she'd left him.

"Did you do lullabies and bedtime songs?"

She laughed. "It hasn't been *that* long."

She opened a bottle of wine and poured two glasses. It felt like playing house, like pretending at being adults. She thought about sitting in the wing-back, but that was too much pretending, too absurd, so she crawled onto the sofa and wedged herself into the armrest opposite him, her legs drawn up but provisionally, in a way that suggested they were amenable to overlapping in the middle at some point in the near future.

"You talk about me," Davis said. He wasn't asking, but he sounded surprised.

"Of course."

"A lot."

"I mean, don't get a big head about it."

"Why?" He still sounded awed, but it was incredulity edged with something more pointed.

"You're part of Jack and Fig's story."

"I met them two hours ago."

"You better catch up."

"How can that be?"

"If we hadn't had Lewis. If we hadn't decided to place him with the Andrews." Her voice caught but held. "If we had stayed together. If you hadn't made me think about all the ways having Rebecca changed me, how being pregnant and pregnant again changed me. If you hadn't helped make me into the actor I am. If you hadn't helped make me into the adult I am."

"Then?"

"Then I wouldn't have Fig and Jack." This was the most obvious thing. Was it not clear to him? "Kids like to hear where they came from, how they arrived. You're part of their birth story, their how-our-parents-got-together story."

"But I'm not part of either of those things. I wasn't there."

"By that logic, me neither."

"There are aspects of the story of us that aren't especially suitable for children," he pointed out.

"Too sexy or too sad?"

"Both, actually."

"I leave those parts out," India said. "It's gross to think about your mother having sex."

"You're telling me."

"And they've had enough sadness in their lives, enough love lost."

"You're telling me," Davis said again, in an entirely different tone. "I read all about it at the time."

"Everyone did." India winced. "I was young and naive back then, so I answered journalists' questions when they asked. Jack and Fig had only been mine for a few days, and I had bigger things to protect them from than invasions of their privacy, but honestly, I should have been protecting that too. I just didn't realize. They tell you motherhood is natural and you'll know what to do, but it's all lies. You have to learn how the hard way, and even then, you screw it up."

"Are they okay?"

She nodded. "They're okay."

"They're lucky."

"They're the opposite of lucky."

"What happened to them was the opposite of lucky. But anyone would be lucky to have you. And anyone who has you is lucky."

She noticed that they were sitting very close together, though she couldn't say how they had gotten that way. "Davis," she whispered. "I'm so sorry." About her missteps with the press back then? About her missteps with the press today? About pulling him back in? About letting him out in the first place? About being so lucky, so blessed, and not protecting it with her whole entire life? About having that life without him? She honestly didn't know.

"That's not what I meant," he said.

"I know. But I am."

He put his hand on the back of her neck, pulled her forehead against his. "Me too," he said. Then he said, "It's okay."

"It is?"

"I forgive us," he said, and she nodded, her head still pressed against his so they had to affirm the veracity of their unspecified but mutual forgiveness together.

Eventually he cleared his throat and fixed his smile and said, "So how does it feel to realize every single dream of your nineteen-year-old self?"

She snorted. "My nineteen-year-old self was a moron."

"You became a rich and famous and wildly successful actor."

"Yeah, but the dream was Broadway, Shakespeare, branching into writing or directing maybe. Not TV and green screens and problematic movies."

"Close enough," Davis said. "You were absolutely, no doubt about it, going to become a professional actor, and you did."

"My dream was to be a classical actor and married to you. And New York and our children and living our lives together."

He nodded. "Mine too."

She thought of something more concrete to apologize for. "Sorry the kids asked if you missed Lewis. And me."

"Don't be. I do."

"Yeah, but—"

"No, it's a fair question, just a hard thing to explain. How can I miss Lewis when I never met him? I don't know, but I do. Not in an I-wish-we-hadn't way. More . . . wistful than that, more imaginary, or . . . speculative, I guess." He was choosing his words very carefully. "That's not how I miss you."

She licked her lips. "It's not?"

"Remembered is the opposite of speculative. Lived is the opposite of imaginary. I miss the life that had you in it. And I'm missing your life, which is something I am also pretty keenly aware of."

"Me too. Yours, I mean."

"Totally different."

"What makes you think so?"

"You don't read about me when you're waiting in line at the grocery store."

"Don't believe everything you read in those magazines," she laughed. "In fact, don't believe any of it."

"I don't. But it's nice to page through and look at the pictures."

"The pictures are lies too." She was laughing still, but softer now. "In real life I have pores. And laugh lines."

"We're not as young as we used to be."

"True of almost everyone," she said. "Though half my wrinkles are from this week."

"You're a great artist," he shrugged.

"Meaning?"

"Misunderstood in your time."

"Like Nora Helmer," she said.

"And look how things turned out for the Helmers."

She tucked her lips inside her teeth and felt like she might cry, but instead she let them out and kissed him. Or maybe he kissed her, it was hard to tell. Her brain spun and spun, then found purchase and held. She expected it might feel familiar, but it did not. She expected it might feel jarring, too different from something that *should* have felt familiar, but that wasn't it either. Maybe it was both at once. It was electric like a first kiss, slivers of ecstatic light shooting like stars behind her closed eyes, but she knew her way.

They kissed for a little while, fervent but gentle because the possibility of escalation was off the table, at least for the moment. Her children were just upstairs. That—not growing up, not all they'd given up, not all the impossible years in between them—that was what was different from before. She remembered when she couldn't have sex with Robbie because her mother was home. It turned out to work both ways. So eventually they had to stop.

"Actually," he said when they did, "I think all the time how much Val Halla is like Nora Helmer."

"You do?"

"Strong. Brave."

"I guess."

"Viking adjacent."

She laughed but also wiped at her eyes. "I'm a long way from Nora Helmer these days. Too far. I miss her too."

"So what happened?"

"I had kids." She smiled. "They changed everything."

"About time," he said, but he was smiling too.

She shoved him with her foot.

"Anyway, I didn't mean what happened eventually," he said. "Your life at present isn't exactly cloaked in secrecy. I meant what happened after the last time I saw you. When we said goodbye, I didn't really think it was goodbye."

"Me neither," she admitted.

"I thought I'd break down and call you or you'd break down and call me within the week."

"You moved to San Francisco."

"I thought maybe Broadway would be too hard, and you'd call and we'd get back together, and you'd move in with me and try acting out here, something regional maybe, just to break in, just to get started."

"You did?" Never mind the thousand reasons it was ridiculous for her to do so, she felt hurt by this lack of faith.

"Not really. But I did think maybe you'd make it big on Broadway, and you'd call and we'd get back together, and you'd convince me to move home."

She laid that vision on top of the years and considered them. "Would you have?" She wanted to know, and she didn't want to know, and besides, she knew she couldn't know.

Him too. "Maybe?"

She knew the sinking feeling was an old one, an answer to questions—Was he following her career? Might she spy him in the audience one night and then he'd be waiting at the stage door?—she had asked and asked but not in years.

"I didn't know either," she said. "I was going to invite you to opening night but . . ."

"But what?"

"But we broke up." Her voice broke too, like it had just happened.

"That's only one," he said.

"One what?"

"One but."

She'd forgotten how it was with people who'd known you too long and too long ago. "At first," she conceded. "But then there was another one."

2009

Tech week was full of disasters.

"They always seem worse than they are," Ajax said when he checked in to see how it was going.

Half the beds' trapdoors refused to open, leaving dozens of wiggling husbands tossing red ribbon in death throes not choreographed beyond the fifteen-second mark. Aegyptus's cassock caught fire with Aegyptus inside. He was fine, but everyone became skittish and self-conscious around the open flames.

"Probably a good thing," Ajax suggested.

The sieves in the finale drained too quickly and flooded the stage, and Athena sprained her ankle slip-sliding into the boat, a boat which shouldn't have been onstage at that moment anyway but was stuck, a boat which, when it became unstuck, snapped three of its oars, one of which ripped a giant gash through Aegyptus's backup cassock.

"That is why you have tech week," Ajax said.

"In college," India began, "tech week is more like—"

"Welcome to the big leagues, kid." And then, pleased with himself, "Ooh, a sports reference."

It was in the held breath between previews and opening night that India understood at last what it meant to be a parent. She had created this child, loved and nurtured it, coaxed its development, strengthened its heart, and ironed its core. Served as its center and also built her life around it. And now, now she had no choice but to send it into a cruel, unsafe world where she could neither control nor protect it. If they didn't open, they kept the play in their hands, kept rehearsing, improving, fixing, refining. But once they let an audience in, no matter how good the production was, it would be misunderstood, the work and love that went into it discounted, its art disregarded, harsh words uttered against it, hearts hardened to their gift. And she did not think she could bear it.

But opening night would come anyway. She knew this. It always did. For the whole last week of previews, the first thing she did every morning was rewrite the email to Davis inviting him to come. "I miss you. I'm better now. I'm changed. Everything's changed." All true, none quite the point she wanted to make. "Just come. Come and then you'll see, you'll know" was closer. But really it was beyond her or, she suspected, anyone's ability to put into words. "I've left a ticket for you at the box office" was maybe the romantic, dramatic approach, and that seemed what was called for. But before she could convince herself to press Send, a knock on her dressing room door:

"These came for you." The AD held a bouquet of flowers almost too big to carry. "You know you're a star when you're getting flowers before we're even open."

The note read:

Step #1: Tear up card
Step #2: Throw over head
Love, Rob (bie) (Brighton)

When she started breathing again, India wondered if it was possible to refall in love with someone based on parenthesis usage alone. Also whether a flower shop would give you a customer's address. Was a florist legally obligated to protect client privacy? Could she convince them based on the mountain of love he'd squeezed onto their molehill of a card? She would even settle for his zip code, say, so at least she could picture where he was living now. She'd thought being famous—not that she was, not yet anyway—would be all upside, but this part had not occurred to her: that Robbie Brighton could know so much about her, where she was and what she was doing, her successes and failures, her (please God) soaring reviews as well as any soul-shriveling ones, while she wouldn't know a single thing about him.

She considered where a thank-you note, if she figured out how to send it, would start. "Thank you for the flowers. Thank you for the congratulations and celebrations." Or would she go back further than that? Her mother had disagreed, but India remained grateful to Rebecca for the cosmic, unfathomable way she got her *Arcadia*. Dakota said it was just good timing, but India was grateful to Lewis for the literal, actual way being pregnant with him got her an agent and his graciously coming early got her *Nestra*. Maybe all that was magic afoot in the universe or maybe not, but no one could argue about the gratitude she owed Robbie Brighton. "Thank you for making sure I arrived by letting me go," she would tell him if she could. "Thank you for knowing the only way I could get here was if you didn't come." Because she loved him, she would have stayed with him forever. Because he loved her, he had made her leave alone. How could you thank someone for something as big as your self and your life and the granting of your every childhood wish but one? You couldn't, not even if you had their address.

But what she could do was not email Davis. She could do for him what Robbie Brighton had done for her: let him live his life unencumbered and unrestrained, love him enough to let him be, grant him his every wish but one.

Opening night, then, Robbie and Davis were there in spirit. Rebecca and Lewis too, she was pretty sure. Her mother and Dakota and Ajax attended in the flesh, of course, and out beyond the lights, what felt like ten thousand strangers, a hundred thousand, filling every seat in the house and every corner of her soul. It was a flooding, her senses wider, keener, so they could take in every moment and the ones to come and to come, the beats of which lay before her like a well-lit path, the story they were telling, the three thousand years that had come before of actors doing exactly what she was doing right now which even she had never done before and would never do again, the eternal ancient newness of her every breath onstage.

But at the same time, it boiled itself down to a single moment, a single India-shaped atom of space, which she commanded exclusively and entirely, and then it was gone. She had to find her light, say her line, perform the action that carried her on, communicate to the audience the message of that instant, and that was all, that was all there ever was to do, every, every moment until you ran out of them, at least until the next night. She was self-conscious enough not to say so out loud, but she thought she might have achieved enlightenment, transcended, be ready for her higher plane now, except she would elect to stay here on this one please, living this night every night from now until forever.

The reviews were . . . *rapturous!*, the ovations standing, the house full, the tickets oversold. Four months later, they did indeed receive word they would transfer to Broadway. Her castmates, though they were far more experienced than India, were ecstatic, giddy. Henri was acting calm by exuding congratulations-to-all energy that India wasn't buying even for a moment.

"You know," Ajax told them both, "after this, I'll be able to get you work in Hollywood instead if you want."

"Instead of Broadway?" India was incredulous. "Why would anyone ever pick anything instead of Broadway?"

"More money," he answered. "More fame. More stability. More opportunities for people who can't sing."

"But . . . Broadway," she protested, the argument made in a single word.

That was how it felt, just that way, every night, for every one of the 452 performances of *Nestra*'s Broadway run.

A nd yet?

It turned out a dream job was still a job. At least it did when she had a job. Once *Nestra* ended, she was often—too often—between them, so when she did have work, she was grateful and gracious.

"This is soooo fucking hard." She laid the back of her hand on her brow for dramatic effect, but that was all the movement she could manage.

"You should try coughing," Dakota countered. They were lying on their floor because they were too tired for chairs.

"Coughing?"

"Coffee-ing."

"Oh, coffee-ing. I have tried it. It is hard."

"Thank you. Your thing is hard too." Dakota didn't sound like she meant it, though.

India understood this. She'd had three hours of blocking that morning for the circus-themed *King Lear* she was doing at Cherry Lane followed by an hour of movement coaching followed by an hour of weights and an hour on the treadmill, and she was sore everywhere, but still her body didn't ache as much as it did after seven hours of pulling espresso shots.

"Today a customer wanted to know how many calories were in a latte with nonfat milk versus two percent milk versus whole milk versus soy milk. And then ordered a slice of cake on the side."

Cake did sound dreamy, but the *Lear* choreographer had spent the morning mumbling to himself (loud enough for everyone else to hear) that it wasn't his fault the jump wasn't working because he'd designed it for someone smaller. "Sort of like these pants," the costume designer had commiserated.

"And then her friend sent her first cappuccino back because it was too cold and her second cappuccino back because it was too hot and her third cappuccino back because it was the right temperature at first but then it got too cool. And then she didn't tip."

India thought it made more sense to change the jump and the pants than her person—she had had two babies so her stomach didn't flatten all the way anymore, like when you tried to get an air mattress back in the box it came in—but apparently she was wrong about that.

"Then a guy refused to pay for his skim latte because he thought 'skim' meant 'foam.' He said my big-city coffee terms were discriminatory."

And it wasn't just her outside that was deemed unsatisfactory. She had to trill her tongue for twenty minutes a day because her vocal coach thought her mouth was unlimber. She had to do dead bugs and butterfly crunches because apparently her strength trainer hated insects.

"His friend wouldn't pay either. He claimed to be a farmer and therefore an expert in how real zucchini bread doesn't taste of zucchini."

"Tourists." India's eyeball muscles were the only ones that weren't sore, so she rolled them sympathetically. "Move over." They were soaking their feet in dish soap and once-warm water in a dog bathtub left behind by whoever had lived in their apartment before they did.

"I can't. I'm too tired."

"The water's too cool now," India whined. "I want my money back."

It wasn't fair. India knew this. She was lucky, beyond lucky, luckier than her dreams, at least the realistic ones. Dakota had to work at a coffee shop, whereas she got to be an actor for a living. Dakota had to suffer open-call auditions, whereas she had Ajax. Dakota had to be up for work at 4:30 in the morning, whereas rehearsal often didn't start until ten.

At least it didn't when she had rehearsal.

That a dream job was still a job should not have been so surprising since it was right there in the name, but all you ever heard was the dream part. It was different, though, doing it for a living instead of doing it as a hobby, a school activity, a class. Instead of being one thing, it was the only thing. Instead of being the break, the treat, the reward, it was the bedrock, which sounded solid but also had to be. You can fuck up a hobby. You cannot fuck up the foundation that underpins your entire life.

Part of the problem was that she was talented enough to have advanced to a level where she was no longer the most talented person in every room. She would go to auditions and totally nail them, reach heights she hadn't known she was capable of, bathe in the glowing, mind-blown praise of directors and producers, and still not get the part. It was more crushing than frustrating, but only barely.

She resorted to the only thing she knew to work: controlling the tiny amount she could control. She prepped audition material into oblivion, towered index cards on every flat surface in the apartment, memorized roles she was probably never actually in the running for, honed performances she would never give. When she didn't get a part, she discovered her detractions and put them to mending. Everyone said that when your agent reported back, "They went a different way," or "They loved you, but you weren't quite right for the part," the thing to do was move on, nurse your wounds somewhere pampering, and figure out where God had opened a window. But India made Ajax press for notes.

"Remember, we could always get you a movie," he'd open with when he called her after auditions she didn't land. "TV if you preferred. No one in Hollywood expects you to be able to sing."

"Is that why they're saying I didn't get this one? It's *Waiting for Godot*!" It felt, every time, like her chest hollowed all the way empty, her stomach bottomed to the bottom of the sea: deep shame, deep dread. Sometimes, though, on top of that, it was also absurd.

"They're flirting with Estragon singing, 'You Can't Hurry Love.'"

"That's appalling."

"So look at it as a dodged bullet," Ajax advised. "I'm just saying, you have options. Higher-paying options. There is not a single reason to despair."

"No," said India. "There are a thousand."

There were months between shows when she was sure she'd never work again, the doubt and dread of having peaked at twenty-one, of last time being the last time. She thought maybe she'd write her own play—her own star vehicle, yes, but also her own words and ideas, a story different from all the usual ones—but Ajax said she'd never get funding.

"Henri LeClerk did," she protested.

"Henri LeClerk was the exception that proved the rule, the cream that creamed the crop, if you will. The straw that broke my back."

"I could cream a crop."

"What did I say about writers the very first time we spoke?"

"More neuroses, less money."

"Correct. And you, my dear, have neuroses enough already."

Since she could neither write her own part nor sing anyone else's, what she had to be was a Serious Actor. Shakespeare, Chekhov, Shaw, Pinter, Ibsen, O'Neill. Tennessee Williams and Arthur Miller. Noël Coward, maybe. Not many good, strong female characters in these repertoires and even fewer good, strong female playwrights. The contemporary stuff was better, but not as much better as you'd like to think. There were too few decent parts for women, too many that were the star's wife or mother or daughter or girlfriend, jilted or abused or forgotten or depressed or misunderstood or sidelined. It was hard to be raped, even for pretend, night after night. It was hard to be left for dead. The plays that did have decent parts for women were often written by women, which was great, but they were also often relegated from the main stage to studio spaces and experimental black boxes: lower budget, lower production values, lower quality, lower pay. Updating classics updated the costumes and the sets, but Ophelia with a briefcase and a power suit still went mad for love, then died.

When she complained to Ajax, he said, "There's always TV."

"Oh yes," India agreed, "because television is a bastion of feminism and empowered women."

When she did land a part, rehearsal was eight hours a day plus an extra hour with a coach or a specialist beforehand and an extra couple with a trainer afterward. Tech weeks upped the rehearsal schedule by fifty percent. Performances were eight a week, two on Wednesdays and Saturdays. It was totally, completely, encompassingly, entirely, unreservedly bone-deep, blood-curdling, cellular-level exhausting.

And it was also the most energizing thing she had ever done in her life. She loved the night after night of it. She loved losing herself onstage, or not losing so much as shedding herself, sloughing herself off, emerging as someone new. She loved the sheer terror of live performance that never went away and the relentlessness of it and how all-consuming it was. So it was a dream, yes, for sure, no question, but it was also a job, and it wasn't an easy one.

Nonetheless, she might have done it—gratefully, joyfully—forever. She might have grown old onstage. She might have received a Lifetime Achievement statue at the Tony Awards a month after her ninety-seventh birthday.

But then her life turned upside down for the exact same reason as most people's did, just not in the same order. India Allwood was going to have a baby.

THURSDAY

When Fig and Jack came down for breakfast, it was like a party, first of all because there were so many extra people—Bex and her mother were talking intensely in the living room, Davis and their mom were talking intensely in the kitchen—but mostly because someone had ordered three huge bags of bagels plus lox and cream cheese and regular cheese and those pickle-y things that look like rabbit poos plus coffee and tea and hot cocoa. It was like craft services had come to Fig's very own home.

But before she could help herself to any of it, her mother wanted to do a little speech.

"Thank you all for being here."

Fig didn't know who she was talking to, but it wasn't her and Jack. They lived here.

"Thank you for coming," she said toward Bex and Camille. "Thank you for staying," she said toward Davis. Fig noticed their eyes held each other.

"I want to acknowledge this is a weird situation, and I appreciate your patience and support, all of you. Of course you're free to go at any time." She sounded like one of those police shows she didn't let them watch. "But if you could stay a little longer, that'd be great. This will die down—the smears have short attention spans—but until it does, it would be good to lie low. It's a lot if you're not used to it."

"It's a lot if you are used to it," Jack said.

"It's not that we don't want to help." Bex's mother was laying down a circle of cream cheese so perfect her bagel looked like a bagel in a magazine. "But

we have things to do at home of course. We have a life. We can't just indefinitely—"

"I'm staying," Bex interrupted.

Fig felt glad. She wanted Bex to stay. And she wanted Bex to stay because
of her. But that turned out not to be the reason why.

"She's right and you know it." Bex was talking to her mother, but really
everyone was listening. "Remember *Annie*?"

"This has nothing to do with *Annie*," said Camille.

"Don't even lie, Mom. This has *everything* to do with *Annie*."

"Who's Annie?" said Jack.

"When I was your age," Bex said to Jack, and Fig shivered because Jack's
age was her age and she didn't want Bex to think of her as a little kid, "my
Girl Scout troop went to see *Annie*, and afterward the troop leader wanted me
to tell everyone about my time in an orphanage. I was like, 'Hello. I've never
even been to an orphanage,' and she was all, 'Tell us. Educate your sisters
about adoption. You can earn your public speaking badge.'"

"Musicals." Fig's mother rolled her eyes. She looked like Bex.

"Everyone's always 'Blah blah blah, representation matters,' but it's all bullshit."

"I don't know where she gets that language," Bex's mother apologized.
"Maybe it's hereditary."

Fig's mother pointed her finger at herself. "Ladylike and demure." Then she
pointed her finger at Bex's mom. But it was a different finger.

"There are like a thousand orphans in the books you read at school." Bex
wasn't done being upset. "There are tons of adopted kids on TV or pregnant
girls whose babies get taken from them. The problem isn't lack of representation. It's bullshit representation. 'Oh, poor adopted kids! Let's rescue them.
They're so troubled and abused and setting stuff on fire. Boo hoo.'"

Fig wished Bex wouldn't say fire. She wished she wouldn't even think it.

"It's so embarrassing," Bex said.

"Be that as it may"—Bex's mom seemed like she'd heard all this before—
"we can't just relocate to Los Angeles until—"

"Someone had to say something. Why should she get in trouble for it?
Everything she said was true."

"Kid's definitely related to you," Davis said quietly, but not that quietly.

Bex looked happy about that. Mom looked annoyed at Davis. Davis looked like he had more to say, but before he could, Jack yelled, "Cake!"

"Cake?" Mom said.

"They have cake!"

"Come away from the window. Who has cake?"

"The smears."

"The smears have cake?"

"And balloons."

"Technically they're at work," Fig pointed out. "Maybe it's like an office party."

"Ignore them," Mom said.

"But I'm hungry," Jack whined.

"Have a bagel."

"Bagels aren't cake."

"We can go to Cupcake Conniption later."

"They've got tables and chairs," Jack moaned.

"Why is he upset about tables and chairs?" Bex asked Fig.

"If they're camped out in the driveway," Fig explained, "we won't be able to leave."

"They have a banner," Jack said. "Two banners!"

Which did not belong at a driveway office party, even a smear driveway office party, so they all went to the window to see.

Jack was right. There was a long table set up with lots of chairs and lots of people lounging in them. There was a giant cake in the middle of the table plus plates and napkins and forks and cups. There were big bunches of balloons tied to each table leg. And there were two banners. One had a picture of a pregnant belly with a whole smiling baby inside wearing Val Halla horns and giving a thumbs-up and thinking a thought bubble that said "Horns for the Unborns!" The other just had words, but the words were "Congratulations India Allwood, Pro-Life Hero of the Year!!"

"Oh, for fuck's sake," Mom said.

"See?" said Bex's mother. "Hereditary."

2014

One Wednesday evening, the rarest of confluences: India and Dakota both found themselves at home at the same time. This called for drinks. And an overdue conversation.

"I have news." India clinked her wineglass into Dakota's. "I'm having a baby."

Dakota stopped with her glass halfway to her mouth. "You're pregnant again?"

"No."

"How can you possibly be pregnant again?" Dakota sounded incredulous and appalled, but not as incredulous as one might have ideally hoped. "Mary Mother of God."

"I'm not pregnant."

"I'm not swearing. I'm saying you're not Mary Mother of God."

"True."

"So to get pregnant, you have to have sex."

"Usually."

"I don't have time to have sex." Five years post college, Dakota was now managing the coffee shop—still working the morning shift, though; still leaving as much of her day as possible to audition and rehearse when it came to that, which it did sometimes, like now when she was appearing as one of the lesser brides in an off-off-Broadway production of *Seven Brides for Seven Brothers*, a show that reminded India of *Nestra* in the obvious way and offended her in all the others. Nights, after auditions or rehearsals or even performances, Dakota had to finish all the paperwork parts of coffee-shop management and then get up and do it all again just a few hours later.

"You don't have a lot of downtime these days," India sympathized, "though, strictly speaking, your not having time for sex wouldn't keep me from getting pregnant anyway."

"Nothing keeps you from getting pregnant anyway," Dakota said. "The last time I was offered backstage hanky-panky was at school."

"Maybe it was offered and you didn't realize they updated the terminology."

"Professional theater's so . . ."

"Professional?"

"Exactly. It's annoying. When am I going to have sex if not backstage?"

"I'm not pregnant," India repeated.

"About time," said Dakota. And then, finally, "Wait. Then what do you mean you're having a baby?"

India smiled her India-smile. "I'm adopting."

"What?"

"Adopting."

"I heard you."

"Then why did you say, 'What'?"

"It was an abbreviation for 'What the fuck.'"

"No fucks," said India. "That's the beauty of this plan."

"What plan?"

"My plan to adopt a baby."

"At least you made a plan this time."

"I even made index cards."

"I'm stunned."

She wasn't, but India had been—not about the index cards, obviously, not even about wanting a baby, which was something lots of people seemed to want, one way or another, one time or another. But India was not naive. She wasn't even optimistic. She knew having a baby changed you and your life, every single part of it, and not just changed. Cost. She maybe didn't know *how* everything would transform so completely, but she knew it would. She had thought it through, far further through than most not-yet parents ever did, but she still couldn't avoid the bewildering conclusion that somehow she wanted to be one.

It wasn't because she saw babies on the street and felt a tug in the middle of her. Maybe you couldn't say Rebecca had nipped that in the bud—if Rebecca was a plant, she had definitely been allowed to flower—but when Al-Like-the-Song used to bring his baby to rehearsal and other girls swooned, India rolled her eyes. She flirted with babies fussing next to her on the subway only because their parents' eyes felt empty, not because her uterus did. If her uterus felt anything, it was that it had already served.

It wasn't because it was time. She had no overeager husband drumming his fingers, no anxiously waiting in-laws. Her mother was definitely, definitely not pressuring her to have a baby, and though she would no doubt welcome grandchildren—another thing you could say about almost everyone—she had earned never getting a pregnancy announcement from India ever again. The ticking clock bemoaned by castmates a decade older than she was felt as remote as planning for retirement.

It wasn't a revelation, either. She didn't wake up one day and just know. She didn't play a mother role—nor a childless one—and just know. She didn't hold someone's baby and just know. She didn't have a dream or cry at a commercial or see Rebecca or Lewis—maybe-Rebecca or maybe-Lewis—on the street and just know. She didn't just know. She didn't know at all.

It was a state without a verb. Not *knowing*. Not quite *wanting*, either. Not *needing*, certainly. She didn't feel tempted, fated, cornered, wooed, tricked, or exhorted into having a baby. She didn't feel resigned or relieved or relegated into motherhood. It was more like the idea burned her brain, less niggling notion, more sun-bright possibility, too much glare and heat to get anywhere near but too pervasive to escape.

For shade and a hat, she turned to what she knew: index cards.

She remembered the simplicity of Robbie's, of the choices available to them. Now they were not so stark. Now she needed a stack of index cards six feet high and a rubber band as big around as a cow. She didn't play them like Baby War. She read them like tarot cards: to know her future, to meet it forewarned, twice shy. She wrote them as they occurred to her, in rehearsal, on the subway, as an excuse to get off the treadmill and catch her breath. She wrote them without thinking, without knowing whether they were true, even. She wrote them to see what they said.

One read, "I wasn't ready before, and I knew it, so maybe not knowing now is an indication of readiness." But another replied, "Everything that's easy now would get hard. Everything that's hard now would get harder." One read in its entirety, "I am so single," but another reminded her, "See Mom and Camille: parenting need not have anything to do with partnering," and a third piled on, "*Nestra* lesson: if you have the right husband, fine, but odds favor the dagger forty-nine to one." One said, "I have given up two children," its point as slippery and clouding as milfoil. Another, just as opaque, replied, "I did right by them both."

But soon, a pattern developed. One card read, "I already made two children. Why make more?" Another: "There are babies who need families." Another: "Benedick was joking when he said, 'The world must be peopled.' There are plenty of people already."

That was how parenthood came to seem right: adoption came to seem right. Again.

But when she tried to explain all this to Dakota, she couldn't. She didn't think that was so unusual, though. It seemed, in fact, like the whole human race was predicated on people having babies without quite being able to articulate the reasons why. Or to heed the reasons why not.

"Maybe that's all the more case for it." She topped off both their glasses. "I'm not doing it because it makes sense or looks right on paper or it's well reasoned and logical. I'm not doing it because it's time or I'm out of time or someone else in my life is ready or everyone I know is doing it. I'm not doing it because I'm pregnant. I'm doing it because it feels right. What better reason could there be?"

"Those other ones," Dakota said. "Can I ask a question you won't like before we get too drunk?"

"Better hurry."

"Didn't you just go to considerable lengths to avoid this exact situation?"

"Not just," said India. "It's been five years since Lewis. It's been nine since Rebecca. I've lived more than thirty percent of my life since then, and probably the first two-thirds don't count since I was a child. I'm a person now, and a different person. And, also, my own person."

"Meaning?"

"Meaning it wasn't this exact situation. Not even close. I didn't want to be a parent with Robbie. I didn't want to be a parent with Davis either, as it turned out. Having a baby with someone ties you to them forever."

"Everything about a baby is forever."

"I am ready for forever with a baby. I am not ready for forever with anyone else."

"What about me?"

"Except for you," India allowed. This was true. And it was what made what came next so hard to say, and not even because of the wine. "Which especially sucks because I'll be living across the country."

"I think the pregnancy hormones are addling your brain." Dakota's face showed not even a trace of believing her, that was how impossible this was.

"I'm going to have to quit my job," India whispered.

"You don't have a job."

"I'm going to have to quit Broadway." Her eyes swam as she said it. "You can't be on Broadway and have a baby. The schedule is not conducive to baby-having. When you have work, you're at work from five p.m. to midnight, plus matinees. When you don't have work, the baby has nothing to eat."

"Tons of people on Broadway have babies."

"*I* can't be on Broadway and have a baby," India revised. "Maybe the people who can are married. I won't be married. I'm going to have to prove I have a steady income and a childcare plan all on my own."

"No one goes into baby-having with a plan," Dakota protested, "least of all you."

"Yeah, but I'm not going to tell them that. Some of the people who have both Broadway and a baby are megastars who can demand flexible schedules or limited runs. Or they make enough money from their flexible schedules and limited runs that they can take a decade off afterward and raise children. I am not a megastar."

"Babies don't care!"

"You can't move a kid in foster care out of state." India shook her head sadly. "You can't move if your adoption is pending. Maybe there will be visits with the birth family. Maybe the kid will be settled in school and not want to leave. If I have to move there eventually, I have to move there before I start."

"But why would you have to move there eventually? Why can't you get stuck not being able to move away from New York? Where you live? Where you have me?"

"Ajax says he can get me work in Hollywood."

"You can get work here. Want a job at the coffee shop?"

"He says it could be commercials that shoot in a few days or a movie with a three-month schedule that would pay enough I wouldn't have to work for a couple years."

"You don't want to not work for a couple years. You don't want any of that."

"True. But I'm going to be a mom."

"That doesn't mean you have to give up your life here, everything you've worked for, every goal you've ever had. All your hopes and dreams. Me!"

"I'm keeping you."

"Three thousand miles away?"

"We'll visit," said India. "It won't be forever. Just until I get Hollywood-famous enough they're begging Ajax to book me for a flexible, limited run of something highbrow and high-profile on Broadway."

"And the rest of it?"

"I think this is that whole thing they tell you about parenting involving sacrifice."

"It sucks."

"I think that's the sacrifice part."

"What about having it all?"

"I think 'all' means 'some.'"

"'All' is the opposite of 'some.'"

"I think 'all' means 'a few.' I think it means 'Pick two.' I'm picking adopting. And I'm picking acting. But I can't also pick New York and Broadway and passion projects and job-to-job and crossed fingers and you."

Dakota narrowed her eyes. "You don't sound like you."

India swept imaginary flowing locks behind her shoulders. "Motherhood changes a person."

"I don't think you're doing this in the right order."

"What else is new?"

THURSDAY

What India told her kids on the way out the door was "Don't watch on the driveway cam," though this was futile and she knew it.

What she told herself on the way out the door was *Calm and composed, calm and composed.* She knew from long experience that what you wanted to be in situations like these was not forceful or indignant or even right. What you wanted to be was unfazed. Unfortunately, she was about as likely to heed her good advice as her children were.

When she got to the strange assembly at the end of the driveway, a blond girl not very much older than Jack and Fig stood to greet her. She had big eyes and hope in her heart and pink ribbons at the ends of very long braids. She clasped her hands to her chest. "It's such an honor to meet you, Miss Allwood. I'm Leslie. You're my hero."

"Pleasure to meet you, Leslie," India said ironically, though Leslie looked like she had yet to encounter irony in her young life. "Can I ask what you're doing in my driveway?"

"We're here to congratulate and celebrate you?" Leslie asked. She waved at the cake and balloons.

"Thank you," said India. "For what?"

"For being such a great pro-life role model and spokesperson?"

"I am not a pro-life role model and spokesperson."

"Unofficially?" Leslie clarified.

"Even unofficially."

"We're just very proud of you is all." Leslie blushed. India wished it was because she was embarrassed but could tell it was pure bliss. "You are so amazing."

"I'm really not."

"Defending unborn babies? Taking a stand against"—she had to whisper the word—"abortion."

The intercom crackled to life. Fig's voice said, "She looks scared out of her tits, Mom."

India pressed the button so she could talk back. "Wits."

"You say potato," she heard Camille say.

"Everyone says potato!" she heard Bex reply.

India turned back to Leslie. "How have I taken a stand against"—she dropped her voice to a whisper too—"abortion?"

"By being a public advocate?"

"For what?"

"Having your babies anyway?"

"Having my babies anyway?"

"You were a poor, troubled teenager who found herself in a state of . . ."

"A state of . . . ?" India prompted.

"Well, disgrace." It was Leslie's first declarative sentence so far. "But instead of murdering the innocent babies inside you, you brought them into the world and gave them up—"

"Placed," India interrupted.

"Placed them up for adoption. Would you like to invite them out?"

"Who?"

"Your children. And the child you gave up—"

"Placed."

"—who we know is visiting. She must be so grateful to you? We have cake."

"We are not interested in cake," India said.

The intercom crackled again. "We are very interested in cake," said Jack.

Which reminded India she was talking to a child. "Who's in charge here?"

"In charge?"

"Who is staging this performance with snacks, balloons, and an award for my supposed pro-life bona fides before the supposed press?"

"Bona fides?"

"I believe you mean me." The woman who stood slowly was wearing a navy suit, full makeup, expensively done hair, and an expression that carefully and pointedly said she was unimpressed by India. She looked overdressed for cake at the end of the driveway. She looked like she had definitely encountered irony before. "Velma Robinson, president, LAMA Life."

"Llama life?"

Maybe these people were even further off their rockers than she'd feared. On the other hand, perhaps they'd be appeased if she said she had no position on llama abortions—though, so far as she knew, no one had a position on llama abortions.

"Los Angeles Mothers Advocate for Life," Velma Robinson explained, dry as the driveway asphalt. India began to suspect she would not be able to out-unfaze this woman. "I am the bestower of the prestigious title you've just been awarded. I am also Leslie's mother. Adoptive mother, in fact."

"Women like you saved my life," Leslie said. "Think what would have happened if my birth mother had aborted me."

India did so and concluded the current situation might have been marginally improved.

"Instead she gave me up for adoption, and it's all because of people like you who are brave enough to just say no."

"I think you're mixing misguided PR campaigns there, Leslie," India said. "And while I don't know why your birth mother chose adoption, I can tell you it had nothing to do with me."

"We simply want to express our gratitude to you for taking a stand and welcome you to our fight." Velma Robinson's tone suggested something else entirely.

"Incorrect. You want to exploit me and my family to promote your agenda."

"*Our* agenda," Velma insisted.

"Incorrect," India repeated. "I am not anti-abortion."

"You're pro-abortion?" Leslie gasped, but Velma did not look at all surprised.

"I am unambiguously, unreservedly, unconditionally pro-choice," India said to Leslie, "as I imagine your mother well knows."

"But you gave your babies up—"

"Placed them."

"Placed them. For adoption," Leslie stammered.

"Correct. For that was my choice. That's what 'choice' means."

The intercom crackled to life. "You tell her, Mom," Jack cheered.

India looked back at the house, then pressed the button. "Didn't I say to stay off the damn driveway cam?"

"I'm not on the damn driveway cam," said Jack. "I'm on the damn phone. It's my damn turn."

Shit. "How are you seeing this on your phone?" But India scanned the crowd and had her answer. Evelyn Esponson was filming the whole exchange.

"Look." India dropped her voice and turned back to Leslie and her mother. "You can't have a party in my driveway because it's my private property and you don't live here, and you can't give me a pro-life award because I am one hundred percent pro-choice. So it would be great if you could just leave."

Anger flashed through Velma's eyes, quick and bright as lightning. "Twice—that we know of—you have faced unplanned, indeed unwanted, pregnancies, and both times you have chosen not to have an abortion, and do you know why?"

"I do," India sighed, "for I am me."

"Because you *believe* you believe in abortion," Velma answered anyway, "but you can't bring yourself to have one, can you." It wasn't a question. "Your objections to abortion are innate, instinctive, visceral, indeed biological. Your brain may have been so indoctrinated that it no longer recognizes abortion as murder, but your gut and your womb certainly know. We're here to help clear up your confusion."

"No you're not," said India. "And I'm not confused."

"Confused and embarrassed and ashamed to be secretly pro-life." Velma, to no one's surprise, was undeterred. "And no wonder. You graduated from an elite East Coast university. You work in a notoriously liberal, amoral industry. You have a fan base of entitled, perpetually offended, also-confused young women who consider themselves modern and empowered, without being either one, and who are loud and opinionated about their imagined and imaginary so-called rights without the self-possession to realize they have been brainwashed, misinformed, and misled to their own great harm. No wonder you want to hide your feelings of revulsion and horror toward abortion publicly. But in the privacy of your heart, you carried two unwanted pregnancies to term. We want you to be proud. You, of all people."

"Why me of all people?"

"Because you're pro-adoption. You know as well as anyone that adoptive families are just as good as birth families, which means no one needs an abortion. Anyone who finds herself pregnant but unable or unwilling to be a mother can resort to adoption, rather than murder, with a clear conscience."

"Being pro-adoption doesn't mean pregnancy isn't life-altering," India said. "Hell, being pro-adoption doesn't mean adoption isn't life-altering."

"Perhaps women who don't want their lives altered shouldn't be generating new ones," Velma pronounced.

"Which, among a thousand other reasons, makes it unconscionable to force them to do so." Arguing with Velma Robinson suggested she had an argument, the right to make it, and the right to do so in India's driveway, none of which did India wish to concede. Plus, she knew better.

"No, what's unconscionable"—Velma wasn't listening anyway, of course—"is allowing a woman to end her child's life simply because the consequences of her actions are inconvenient. This would be true even if adoption weren't such a wonderful alternative, but as you know so well, it is. Do you have any idea how many loving, stable couples, childless through no fault of their own, are desperate to adopt a baby? Do you know how long they have to wait? The pool of healthy infants available to adopt has dwindled to essentially none. And yet there are millions of women out there destroying them."

Leslie added sweetly, "Think of what an incredible gift you gave two families." She had a line of tiny paper cups she was trying to get punch into using a ladle the size of a cat. Between the braids and the red liquid she was covered in, you'd guess her birth parents were Pippi Longstocking and Elmo.

"You didn't think your biological children should be aborted." Velma went back to winning the calm-and-composed game. "You didn't think your adopted children should be aborted. So who do you think should be aborted? Is it my baby you wanted to murder?"

Leslie paused mid-dribble to look up at India with huge wounded eyes.

"I do not want to murder Leslie." India smiled at the girl. She was trespassing, manipulative, and catastrophic at beverage service, but she was only a child and did not deserve to die for it.

"Think what would have happened if this baby had been destroyed. She could be the one to cure cancer, solve world hunger."

India turned—as did Evelyn's camera—to consider the baby in question who had given up on punch and moved to cake but was finding it hard to cut because every time she leaned over with the knife, her braids fell in the frosting.

"She could be the next Albert Einstein," Velma said.

The camera cut back to India whose reaction shot did not require words. She managed to communicate all the moment demanded with one particularly skilled and articulate eyebrow.

She had not even made it all the way inside before her phone rang. It was a long driveway, but it wasn't that long.

"Wine, women, and tacos!" Ajax yelled. "Have you lost your mind?"

"I don't know what you're talking about," India said.

"You went on television and said that poor child should never have been born."

"One, I didn't go anywhere. Two, it wasn't television—"

"It is now."

"Three, I didn't say a word."

"You are a gifted actress, India."

"Thank you."

"That wasn't a compliment."

"It was an insult?"

"It was a warning. And don't play innocent because I know you are completely cognizant of and in control regarding the power of your face."

"Thank you," she said again.

"Still not a compliment. The internet says you're being ableist. They say you want forced sterilization and involuntary pregnancy termination. They say you want to abort anyone under a certain IQ."

"Based on fetal SAT scores?"

"The pro-life mob is angry you're pro-choice. The pro-choice mob is angry you're advocating adoption. The adoptee advocates are angry you're not acknowledging their trauma. The adoption advocates are angry you're downplaying the inequities in the system and the lasting emotional and psychological pain on all sides."

"I don't think anything about this situation could reasonably be described as 'downplayed.'"

"Somehow you have managed to make a whole lot of people who agree on absolutely nothing, including the problem, agree that whatever it is, it's all your fault."

"Good. They cancel each other out."

"You are not a child, India. You know goddamn well all it takes is one pulled ad by one spooked advertiser and your entire career is in the toilet. You'll never work in this town again or—because I know what you're thinking—any other. Every time I get up to take a piss, I get back to my desk and you've dug this hole deeper."

"I'm not the one digging. I'm the one being dug. Buried. And not in dirt either."

"Well, at least we can agree it's shit," Ajax said. "The studio wants a meeting."

"No."

"Yes. It's scheduled. Tomorrow at noon. I'll send a car."

"What do they want? What could they possibly want me to do here?"

"I have no idea," Ajax said, "but find out. And then do it."

She called her lawyer. "They want a meeting."

"Who?" her mother said.

"The studio execs. Or their goons maybe. I don't know."

"I'll come down."

"You can't," said India.

"Of course I can. Why can't I?"

"Because either they just want a friendly chat followed by a gentle warning, and I've lawyered up for it. Or it's a come-to-Jesus meeting and I've brought my mommy along."

"Swap them," her mother advised. "Bring me to the friendly chat and your lawyer to meet Jesus."

"I won't know which it is till I get there. And anyway, I don't want them to think I'm scared."

"Are you?"

"They could ruin my life."

"I doubt it, but regardless, I certainly can't do anything about it from here."

"I have to work." India started ticking needs off on her fingers, even though her mother couldn't see her over the phone. "I have to get paid for my work. I have to get more work in the future. If these things don't all happen, I can't take care of my kids. They're threatening my career, my family, my children's safety and privacy, our well-being, our confidence in our continued well-being, our—"

"I agree, which is why you need counsel and—"

"But I'm not going to sit back and take it, either." It wasn't that she didn't want her mother's advice. It was that she was too worked up to listen to it. "If I'm baited by disingenuous anti-abortion nutcases in my own home, I'm not just going to cop to it. I have opinions—actually informed opinions based on hard-won experience—about adoption, and I'm not going to be cowed into silence on that front or really any other."

"I don't think anyone doubted it."

"None of this is my fault."

"No one said it was."

"Many, many people said it was," India groaned. "Three days ago, this was a couple of bellyachers on the internet, bellyachers who had eaten too much chocolate."

"Too much chocolate?"

"They had legitimate bellyaches. They had a point. Fine. Good. Now, though, it's hundreds of thousands of random chimers-in who are complaining their stomachs hurt even though they've avoided gluten, dairy, and cruciferous vegetables."

"You may have reached the limits of this metaphor," her mother advised.

"Ajax is furious. So, apparently, is everyone involved in the show and the movie, the production company, the network, the studio. These losers are trying to set fire to my career and make sure I never work again. In the name of life and protecting children, they'd like mine to starve to death?"

"I'll feed Jack and Fig," her mother offered.

"And meanwhile, *meanwhile*, I can't leave my house, which would be unreasonable under any circumstances, but at the moment means I'm trapped inside with the world's most stressful houseguests. Oh here, how about on top of a pointless, groundless, career-ending scandal, we pile your biological daughter and your ex-boyfriend? That'll be fun! These are not the circum-stances under which I wanted to see Bex and Camille again. It's not how I wanted to see Davis again, either."

A brief pause. "Did you want to see Davis again?"

"That's not the point!" India shrieked, then reminded herself that all the aforementioned houseguests were nearby and lowered her voice. "The point is I have enough stress at the moment without going in for an official scolding. What if I just refuse to get in the car Ajax sends?"

"Do you want me to be your lawyer right now or your mother?"

"Surprise me."

"Those jerks are big meanies. It's no fair."

"Thanks, Mom."

"You're welcome, baby. Please hold for Sarah Allwood, Esquire." A dra-matic pause she'd learned from her daughter. "I strongly advise you to go to that meeting, India. Apologize generally but admit nothing. Agree to what-ever they ask of you but only out loud, not in writing. Be nice, but neither confirm nor deny their accusations, no matter what they are. Swallow your pride and your rage and your righteousness, and wait to start throwing things until you get home."

"I hate that answer."

"I know."

"I don't want to."

"I know."

"I'm not wrong."

"Act like you are."

"I'm not that good an actor," India said.

"You're the best actor in the whole wide world," said her mother.

India hung up the phone and screamed into a pillow.

All of which would have been bad enough, even if Fig hadn't overheard the entire thing.

2015

Los Angeles was completely different from New York—sunny and blooming and warm, palm trees and ocean breezes and cheerful citizens who smiled and made eye contact. It was depressing. Among all the other indignities, India had to get a driver's license.

Also completely different was moving someplace new as an adult, which apparently she was now. No perfect algorithm-selected roommate. No bustling cafeteria or packed library or dorm full of friends eager for the slimmest of excuses to play instead of work.

But of all the differences, the biggest was the difference between acting for the screen and acting onstage ("real acting," India called it). Acting for the screen denied you the power and range of your body. The camera was too close. You had to mute the rest of you and act with only the tiny muscles on the outsides of your eyes. Your wide arms and swinging elbows and strong shoulders were replaced with fingers which had to indicate the full sweep of human emotion in the distance between fist and clenched fist. You could not roam or dance or crouch or leap—if you did, you would no longer be in the shot—so your legs grew roots, which managed occasionally only to wrap around the leg of a chair. Your body was paramount, insisted upon, intensely circumscribed, not a cell of it off-limits to the camera's cocksure eye if anyone wished, but its use and employ was off-limits to you.

"You're thinking of this the wrong way around," Ajax insisted. "You have so many more options. You can raise an eyebrow and know it will be seen in the back of the house. You can whisper without worrying you won't be heard."

"When I whisper onstage," India said, "it is crystal clear in the back row of the upper balcony."

"Yes, but it's a trick, and think how hard you have to work to do it."

"It's acting," said India.

"It's stage acting," Ajax corrected. "For the camera, you can whisper or weep or mumble or say not a blessed thing, and everyone will still understand. And if not, they'll turn on the subtitles."

"Which is not acting," India said.

"Don't mention it at the audition," Ajax advised.

She didn't. But she didn't get cast anyway.

She didn't get the intellectually promising but emotionally confused law student because she was too loud. She didn't get the intellectually promising but emotionally confused surgical resident because she moved her hands too much. She could come in for a second look for an intellectually promising but emotionally confused detective who had risen through the ranks of the toughest police squad in LA if she was willing to lose thirty pounds. She was not.

"It's not that you're fat," Ajax hedged. "It's that the character's suffering from an eating disorder in season one. You'll probably be able to gain the weight back if it gets picked up for more seasons."

India politely declined.

She was surprised, at twenty-six, to learn she was still in the running to play high schoolers—the distance between current-India and high-school-India was one that felt best measured in multiple decades, never mind it hadn't quite been even one yet—but she didn't get those parts either, not the lead-girl series regulars she went up for, not their hangers-on or enemies or ex–love interests either. Too old, they said, with which India could only agree.

She was surprised, given that she was still in the running to play high schoolers, that she was also in the running to play the girlfriends and even wives of men in their fifties. These she didn't get owing mostly to misunderstanding.

"They said you were too creepy," Ajax reported.

"I thought that's what they were going for."

"The role was PTA secretary and soccer mom of three."

"Married to a man three decades older than I am."

"You might be inventing backstories that aren't serving you," Ajax suggested.

"Or I might not be the one who's creepy."

And those were the ones where Ajax was able to ask and someone was willing to give them an answer. Often there wasn't one. They went a different direction. She wasn't what the director had in mind. They needed a bigger name. They wanted someone with more experience. They wanted someone more able to follow their lead.

"They asked me to read the sides, and I read the sides," India protested. "No one even offered direction."

"They want someone more impressionable."

"I can take direction. I love direction."

"Impressionable like moldable, hollow maybe."

"Hollow?"

"So you can be built, filled up, rather than arriving already full. I told them you could do that too, but they weren't buying it."

"Me neither," said India.

She might have liked to do a movie, but she couldn't very well submit an adoption application then be on location for six months halfway around the world. Children, with good reason, were no doubt nondeferrable.

She might have liked to do a filmed-before-a-live-studio-audience sort of TV show since they were rehearsed all week during regular, conducive-to-child-rearing work hours and then performed. For people. Like a play. But there weren't very many anymore, and they were all comedies, and, Ajax regretted to inform her, "You're not funny."

"I'm funny."

"Yeah but not funny funny."

"I can be funny funny."

"But not sitcom funny."

"Anyone can be sitcom funny," India said. "It's getting people to laugh at *Antigone* that's impressive."

"Only to you," said Ajax.

One evening he called and said, "I've got a good one. Pilot. Series regular. Great part." It must have been because it was late New York time for him to be up working. "But you've got to go in first thing tomorrow."

India had reluctantly but long since retired her reliance on index-card audition prep, but this was still tight. "What is it?"

"*Val Halla*," Ajax said triumphantly. "They're casting for the titular role."

"You want me to play a cafeteria for dead Vikings?"

"Not Valhalla," said Ajax. "Val Halla."

"Oh good. Puns."

"Don't be a snob, India."

"I am a snob."

"Shakespeare used puns."

"Used, but did not rely upon."

"It's a good part."

"Is Val a Viking?"

"Metaphorically."

"What's a metaphorical Viking?"

"I think it's warriors and gods and such fighting evil. Like she's captain of a new breed of superhero."

"Would I have to wear horns?"

"I don't think so."

"Spandex?"

"Possibly. Look, I don't think it's superheroes like *Spiderman*. I think it's superheroes like *Buffy*. Like ordinary girl finds the strength and courage to change the world."

"Is Val intellectually promising but emotionally confused?"

"Just try," said Ajax. "It's a cold read. All you have to do is show up and see what happens."

What happened was they liked that she looked "more real," Ajax reported, to which he added, when she pressed, "More strong than thin." They liked her "unique physicality," which he took to mean she could move more than her eyeball muscles and clenched fist. They thought her "vocal qualities" were "inspired," which was confusing since no one had ever thought so before.

"I think they mean you can be loud," Ajax translated.

"Projecting for the back of the house," India said.

"They like that you sound different."

"Different how?"

"You . . ." he searched, and settled on ". . . stand out in Hollywood."

"Is that a good thing?"

"Not usually. So try to use it here to your advantage. Callback's next week with the director."

She auditioned for the director. She auditioned for the producers. She auditioned for different producers.

"Network test," Ajax said when he called. "Good news is this is it. Last round. This means you're in the final running. Bad news is everyone else there will be too. Added bonus is a surprise for when you get there."

"I don't like surprises. What surprise?"

"You know the meaning of the word, India, do you not?"

The casting team and the director and the producers she'd already met were all there, plus seeming teeming hordes of suited, unsmiling execs, and writers who did not have the air of playwrights quite but were recognizably mussy haired and laptop toting and ink stained, if only, like the Vikings, metaphorically. What had started as a room full of women who looked like her had dwindled now to only four of them. The other three looked nervous and awkward. She knew how they felt because the first many rounds of this audition had all been awkward. This round, though, perhaps owing to all the additional bodies, was being held in a screening room, which looked and felt for all the world like a small theater. It was like coming home.

They auditioned solo—again—but then, the casting director explained, they would be paired up in rotation with the actors in the running for the male lead. India could see how this would be important to trial—did you two work well together? look good together? inspire each other? give off heat and light?—but she'd never before had an audition that depended on someone else's talent and skill and level of preparation, and it seemed grossly unfair that after all this, she could be perfect but still not get the part because the partner they chose for her didn't cut it. On top of which, he was late, which did not seem like a great sign.

Then a side door opened and a PA bustled in full of apologies and protestations that it was all her fault. The reasons went on for a long time, but India caught not a word.

"Anyway sorry. So sorry," the PA puffed, then made introductions to the room. "India Allwood and Henry LeClerk."

"ON-ree," India and Henri said together. Every muscle in her body coiled to launch herself into his arms and demand to know how the hell Ajax had gotten him to forsake Broadway—was he adopting a baby too?—and how long had he been in California and why hadn't he been in touch and how bananas was Hollywood and when could they catch up and did he know what a sight he was for sore eyes amid all these glaring, weary, terrifying ones and thank God he was here because now, finally, she was at last being asked to do something she knew how to do: act with Henri LeClerk. But the AD called, "Action," so it would all have to wait.

When Ajax called later to tell her that she—they—had gotten the part, she was not at all surprised. Which was good, because she did not like surprises.

She celebrated by submitting the adoption paperwork. She'd already gathered references and recommendation letters, taken the classes, assembled portfolios and dossiers, completed the background checks and interviews and home visits and certifications. She'd already answered all the hard questions about why she wanted a child and why she wanted to adopt; how she'd deal, and help a child deal, with any attendant challenges, now and in the future. She'd speculated answers to countless potential eventualities, such as how she would incorporate a child's birth culture into their lives if it differed from her own and how she would respond if the child begged to go "back home" to his or her "real mother" and what she would do if the child tried to set fire to the family pet.

These questions she had pondered and researched and meditated on and spoken to experts about and drafted and honed and finally answered. The ones she could not were the easy ones: job, salary, work schedule, childcare arrangements. Among all the other things *Val Halla* meant, it was also the final puzzle piece. She pressed it into place, admired the completed picture for a moment, poured herself a glass of wine, and pressed Send, the email icon a little paper airplane, which seemed about right: precarious, fragile, unlikely to fly straight. She had been pregnant enough to know this didn't feel like that, but it felt like something.

"Thx!" The reply came not even a minute later and seemed underwhelmed by the many miracles at play here. "Now we wait."

After months and months of discussion and preparation, meetings and interviews, homework and paperwork, countless emails and texts, India All-wood was now officially in the running to be someone's mother at last, a status she was granted thanks to landing the title role in what promised to be a new superhero franchise and major Hollywood property, and her social worker, Regina Starlite—in Los Angeles, even the social workers had stage names—could not be bothered even to type out the entirety of "Thanks."

India appreciated that Regina had a hard job and worked hard at it. Still, she wanted a little bit more. "When will I hear from you?" she typed.

Again, the reply came almost at once and without fanfare. "When there's news."

THURSDAY

It was bad.

It was very bad.

Fig fled the hallway, where she'd been pressed against the wall listening to her mother on the phone.

Ruining her life, her mother said.

Threatening her family, she said. Threatening their safety. Starving to death.

Setting fire to, she said.

Fig tried to remember what Mandela said to do when she couldn't remember what Mandela said to do because she couldn't remember anything because she couldn't breathe. She was supposed to do slow deep breaths, and her mouth was wide open trying, but her lungs were closed and wouldn't let anything in. She was supposed to count them, but that didn't work if you couldn't count because you couldn't breathe. "You can," Mandela said. "Your brain is just tricking you in these moments into thinking you can't." But Fig could not fight with her own brain. Fig *was* her own brain. She ran into her room into her closet into her nest and tried to block out her mother's voice saying "ruined" and "threatened" and "fire."

Then the closet door opened.

"Fig?" Bex dropped into a squat and put her head around the weird half wall that made Fig's nest.

Fig couldn't say anything, but she realized she was panting, which probably meant she was also breathing.

"Are you okay?"

Fig couldn't answer, but she shook her head no.

"Yeah, I get it." Bex seemed like she understood. "If I had a closet this size, I'd hang out in here all the time too." Or maybe not. "You could fit your whole bed in here and then use the rest of your room for . . . whatever. Or you could do one of those hair-and-makeup counters with a light-up mirror. Not that you need makeup. You have perfect skin. Lucky."

Fig nodded like of course she knew this, but she had not. She did know Bex was trying to distract her with conversation and compliments and making her laugh. Fig didn't want to be a bad host or a bad sort-of sister. There was no way, though, that Bex would understand what was happening, and even if she would, there was no way Fig could explain. Bex didn't seem to mind waiting, though. She started slipping Fig's shoes one by one over her toes and making them do little dances. After a while, Fig realized she could breathe again, which meant she could probably also talk again, so eventually she admitted, "My mom was really upset on the phone."

"About the people in the driveway?"

"She said they're ruining our lives," Fig whispered.

"I think all those people are ruining is their cake."

"She said they're setting her career on fire."

"She's Val Halla!" Bex said. Then she said, "Was it because she used the F-word? It's just a figure of speech, you know."

Fig did know. Knowing had nothing to do with it. Then she told Bex something she had never told anyone. Some people knew—her mom, her grandma, her brother, Mandela—but the words had never come out of her mouth before. "My birth mother set the car on fire with us in it."

She heard Bex breathe in. "You and Jack?"

"Me and Jack and her too. She said overpopulation, pollution, people were ruining the planet so she was going to remove as many of them from it as she could."

"Oh, Fig." Bex sounded sick.

"And then she took us in the garage and we all got in the car and she set it on fire. We were four."

"You remember this?"

She thought she did. It was all documented in the police reports and witness statements and court papers, but she also thought she remembered. But she wasn't sure. Mandela said with a trauma like that, no wonder she remembered, but she also said it was the sort of thing that was easy to picture and hard to unpicture, which meant maybe Fig remembered or maybe she just thought she did. Either way, Mandela said, of course it was traumatizing but also healthier to remember than repress and healthier to picture than imagine and also really, really sad. She also said it was okay to be upset that her birth mother tried to hurt her, while also understanding that she didn't do it because she was a jerk but because she was very sick, while also being a little bit proud that her birth mother took a stand against the climate crisis.

"What happened?" Bex said.

"The neighbors called 911."

"God, no wonder you hate fire," Bex said. "What about Jack?"

"Jack doesn't remember."

"Lucky," Bex said. Fig had never thought of it that way before. "What happened to her? Your birth mother?"

Which was the part Bex would never understand. Bex had left her birth mother at birth—maybe that's where the term came from, maybe that's how adoptions were supposed to go—but Fig had stayed with hers for years. Bex's birth mother had made a careful, thoughtful plan for her adoption, whereas Fig's birth mother had made an uncareful, unthoughtful plan for her destruction. "She lives in a hospital. A judge took us from her. It's called involuntary termination of parental rights. But it's kind of a lie because she was voluntary too."

"She was voluntary?"

"Or volunteery?" Sometimes Fig said the wrong word. "She didn't fight or scream or cry or demand to get us back before they took her to the hospital. She was really sick then, but even after she was in the hospital for a while and off drugs and had lots of therapy, she still didn't try to get us back. She still said, 'Whatevs, no worries, I don't really want them anyway.'"

Bex was quiet for a minute. "Or yes."

"What do you mean?"

"It could be 'No, I don't want them back,' but it could also be 'Yes, I want them to stay in their new home in their new family.'"

Fig had never thought of it that way before, either.

"It was the same way with mine," Bex added. "Well, yours. My birth mom. You know?"

Fig did not know. It was not the same way. It was the completely, totally opposite way.

"Your mom gave me to my mom," Bex said slowly, "so she would have a better life and so I would have a better life too, right?"

"Yeah?" That was true. Fig knew that was true. "So?"

"So when she could, maybe your birth mother did the same thing."

2015

The call came in the middle of the night. That was right. That was, she knew, when labor started. That was when children came. At half past midnight when India's buzzing phone read "Regina Starlite," she knew there was only one reason she'd be calling this late. She answered without preamble, "You have a baby," already out of bed and pulling on clothes. That she was wrong—making erroneous assumptions without even realizing she was doing so, having to revise on the fly every single thing she'd planned for and thought she knew—was actually her first lesson in parenting.

It would be a frequent one.

"Not a baby," Regina said. "Kids."

That "s" on the end! India's breath caught. "How many?"

Underwear. No, not those. Clean underwear.

Jeans. Sure, those. Jeans didn't have to be clean.

"Two. Twins."

Twins! "How old?"

Socks. Or, no, sandals and then no need for socks.

"Four."

Two years younger than Lewis, six younger than Rebecca. "Identical?"

T-shirt.

"No. Boy and a girl. Jack and Fig."

"I'm on my way."

Sweatshirt, though last time she was outside, six hours ago, it had been eighty-two degrees. But it was chilly at night, even in LA. Or it might be air-conditioned at the— "Where am I meeting you?"

"Hospital." Regina Starlite stopped.

India also stopped. Sat back on her bed and noticed the sandals she'd slipped on were not a matching pair. "Are they okay?"

"We think so. Smoke inhalation. Some abuse. Some neglect. Some trauma for sure. You should prepare yourself, India."

"I'm prepared."

"There's a lot of loss here. I know we've talked about this, but even more than usual."

On the way to a hospital India had never heard of, she tried to do what she'd been advised: prepare herself. She had gone into the process cocky. She'd been through adoption before. Twice! She knew what she was doing better than most adoptive parents. After all, she'd seen it from the other side. But in fact, Regina's take on adoption was the opposite of India's: all doom and gloom and downside and tragedy and regret. Loss.

Best-case scenario, Regina had explained, the birth parents were being forced—one way or another or another—to relinquish children they longed not to. The children were losing their real families, losing their ancestors, losing their homes, losing, sometimes, their culture, their country, their homeland, their people, losing their sense of place and belonging. Adoptive parents were mired in loss too, finally giving up on the idea of having their own children once and for all and settling for these instead.

India thought it was so much bullshit. She had not been forced to relinquish children she longed to keep. Not in any way, from any angle. If some birth mothers were, it didn't mean all of them were, any more than anything else that was true for some mothers was true for all of them. To decide they'd all been forced was insulting, disempowering, and condescending. It was possible to lose but not be lost, to be sad without wishing things were other than they were. It seemed to her that women did this all the time, weathered things that were hard and heartbreaking but also chosen and even strived for. It seemed to her they often made tough decisions to let go, to lay down, in order to pick up something else because they knew—maybe in their bones, maybe having learned it again and again—that having all the things you wanted all at the same time was rarely on the table. It seemed to her that the people who had decided all birth mothers were regretful and unhappy and had been forced to do something they didn't want to do were probably men.

She also knew she was quite fertile. Some might have said too fertile. If she wanted to get pregnant and make her family that way, she could. She wasn't adopting because she had no other choice and was settling. Adoption was her first choice. It had always been her first choice. She wasn't settling for anything.

These children, these particular children, if they had suffered smoke inhalation, abuse, neglect, and trauma, clearly had some loss going on. But not because of adoption. If she got to adopt them, that adoption would not erase their loss. That adoption might be occasioned by their loss. But the adoption itself, joining a new family, was not a loss.

India knew, she did, that the foster care system was different from the adoption agencies she'd used with Rebecca and Lewis. She knew Rebecca and Lewis were the reason she'd been picturing a baby, even though she'd said she was open to older children. She knew this same over-identification (or was it under-imagination?) was also why she was envisioning a birth mother like her, like she had been: sad but also at peace, sorrowing but hopeful, choosing this with her whole heart. Deep down, she knew it was unlikely. Deep down, she knew that this birth mother, whoever she was, whatever her circumstances, was not—could not possibly be—as lucky as she was. But for all (well, many) practical purposes, India was in labor, so she forgave herself her blind spots.

None of this was the "prepare yourself" Regina recommended.

When India reached the right room finally, she found Regina outside it talking in hushed tones to three other adults, all looking mournfully through the window into a semi-dark hospital room. Inside, sharing a bed with the sides raised, were two sleeping children. India looked at them through the window and lost everything—her heart, her plans, her unaltered-since-she-was-ten dreams, all her certainties, everything she knew and believed. As she looked in the window, they all went out the window.

"Can I go in?" Was she whispering because it was a hospital or because it was so late? There was no one else around.

Regina shook her head. "They're finally asleep. And we have a lot to talk about."

India listened to Regina's story, then went in anyway. The room smelled of hospital, but the kids smelled of smoke. They were scrunched, each against a bed rail, so she couldn't scoot herself onto an edge and perch there maternally, and besides, she would have had to pick a side and what a way to begin. So she kicked off her shoes and climbed up onto the middle of the bed, between the two children, and stood, hands on hips, looking down at them. If they woke, though, they'd think her some kind of towering giant, so she eased herself between them and lay back on the pillows, one arm hovering over the girl, but not touching, not yet, one over the boy, and waited.

She woke sometime later, with sun streaming through the window and a small finger poking her ribs.

"Who are you?" said the finger.

"I'm India. Who are you?"

"Fig," said the finger.

"Nice to meet you, Fig." India stuck out her hand, but not very far. It was a small bed to be so crowded. The finger was still deployed, so India unfolded the rest of the set and joined it with hers to shake. Then she pointed at the sleeping child on her other side. "Who's that?"

"That's Jack."

"Is he your brother?"

Solemn nodding.

"I can tell you've done excellent work taking care of him, Fig. Super job."

"How?"

"How can I tell?"

More solemn nodding.

"Because he's sleeping so soundly. He must feel safe and loved and warm."

"Or tired," Fig said.

India laughed out loud and woke Jack.

"Who are you?" said Jack.

"India," said India. "Who are you?"

"Jack."

"I've heard a lot about you, Jack."

"Oh."

"How do you feel?" she asked, turning back and forth between them.

They looked away from her then. They shrugged their tiny shoulders. They folded right into themselves like portable children, like those jackets that disappear into their own pockets.

"Let me ask a more specific question," India tried. "How do you feel . . . about waffles?"

After waffles and hot chocolate in the cafeteria, then a trip to the gift shop for a puppy and a panda, the kids had to go with a nurse for more tests. India felt already as if part of her body had been summarily removed and shipped off without her.

"This match is being offered to you, not forced upon you," Regina said.

"I know."

"This will be a tough placement. You do not have to accept it."

"I know."

"If you say no to these children, it means nothing more than waiting for a better match. No one will look down on you for saying this one is too much. No one will hesitate to match you when a child with fewer challenges to negotiate comes along needing care."

"I know."

"You do not have to accept siblings just because you said you were open to siblings. I would not be doing my job if I talked you into this."

"You didn't talk me into anything."

"If this is too much, it's better for them and for you and for everyone involved for you to say no rather than 'I'll try' or 'Let's see.' I would not be doing my job if I talked you into this just because these children will be hard to place and need a home right away. I would not be doing my job and neither will you if we gloss over the challenges they will face. The difficulties they will pose, even. You might not be up for this, and that's okay."

"I get all that, Regina, but—"

Regina Starlite held up a stop-and-listen hand. "India, they've been through a lot. There are going to be attachment issues. They have significant trauma to recover from. We'll never know all that went on in their household these last many years. And who knows what they were exposed to in utero. There's a lot of uncertainty here, very little of which is likely to clarify either neatly or quickly."

"I know, but—"

"You can't think of yourself as their savior."

"I won't. I don't."

"You can't think of them as yours, either."

"I know," India said. Again. Then before she lost her turn to talk, "What about their mother?"

"Her parental rights have been terminated."

India understood that. That wasn't what she was asking. "Is she okay?" Probably a stupid question, though. How could she be? "*Will* she be okay?"

"No. And I don't know. She needs help and a lot of support on any number of fronts."

"Will she get it?" India asked. A better question at least.

But Regina said, "I'm afraid I don't know that, either."

India tried to think of a question that *would* have an answer. She remembered wanting to close her ears so she wouldn't hear what Camille named the baby because even at sixteen, even at that moment, she'd known that letting go while holding on would be exactly as impossible as it sounded. She'd been right that a name made someone harder to forget. But she'd been wrong to think she'd want to. She didn't know much about what would happen next, but she did know Jack and Fig would remember—would want and need to remember—their mother. "What's her name?"

Regina had to look at her notes. Her job was the children, not their parents, though India wondered who had decided those were separate departments. "Sarah."

India's mouth hung open.

"What?"

"That's my mother's name too."

"It's a common name." Regina was unimpressed. "Don't read anything into it." Her eyes were still on her folder. "That's also what the kids call her."

"Sarah?"

"Apparently."

"Why?"

Regina shrugged. "That's her name."

In the books India had been assigned and the classes she'd had to take, opinions as to what would happen next varied widely. Children are like rubber, people said. Bad things bounce right off them. Children are like plastic, easy to wipe down and resistant to stains. Children are like dogs, they said, always shedding. They can't remember before they can't remember. They're more malleable than adults, more willing to take the present as it comes and not worry about the future or wallow in the past. You'll be stunned at what a kid can get over, they said. You'll be amazed how it will be like the bad things never happened.

Other people said you were never too young to remember trauma. It got in your blood. In your bones. It didn't even have to happen to you to ruin you—maybe it happened to your mother or her mother or hers and you just inherited it. There are some things you can never get over, no matter how young you were, no matter how loved you become.

Fortunately, these were opposite philosophies, so India thought it would be simple enough to tell which applied in Fig and Jack's case, develop an appropriate approach accordingly, then research the indicated strategy and how best to implement it.

Unfortunately, parenting quickly proved itself unindexcardable.

THURSDAY

People always told Jack that he and Fig were lucky to have each other. What they meant was that even though he was adopted, he got to have someone he was DNA-related to. But he didn't know why it mattered that you shared blood and genes and were actually even twins with someone if they were completely different from you in every single important way.

Unlike Fig, Jack did not think about the fire or their birth mother or their birth father. His sister could not understand this, but Jack could not explain it because you could only say—*sometimes* say—why you did think about something, not why you didn't. He thought about pizza because he was hungry. He thought about books he'd loved when he was little because he had an assignment in language arts to make a collage of books he'd loved when he was little. Whereas think of all the things you never think about. It can't be done.

What Jack did think was some people were lucky, and he was lucky to be one of them. He saw how thinking this was like not being able to think of everything you weren't thinking of, but he still thought it was true. Some people did drugs, and he was lucky not to live with them. Some people did drugs, and so when they did terrible things like almost set their family on fire, it wasn't their fault, but it still sucked to be their kid. There were some things that some people thought were bad and some people thought were good, like taxes or putting pineapple on pizza, but setting fire to your children wasn't one of them. Everyone thought that was bad, probably even his birth mother when she was able to think about it.

She was Korean. Well, Korean American. What his birth father was was not known for sure—his mom said he could do one of those DNA tests when he was older—but in the meantime you could guess he was probably half white and half some kind of Asian because Jack and Fig looked a little white and mostly Asian. When people asked what he was, he said Korean, and the only people who challenged him about it were Fig, because she knew it was not the whole truth, and his best friend Oddney's mom because she was actually Korean from Korea and also because she wished he would call her son by his given name which was Rodney. Jack thought Korean was close enough and that people wanted a one-word answer not a life story when they asked you what you were, and he also felt that if you named your son Rodney you should be prepared for people to call him Oddney.

Jack would like to have been able to ask his biological parents what it felt like being Asian American drug addicts when everyone thought Asian Americans were smart and quiet and well behaved and everyone also thought only Black people and poor white people did drugs. No one thought Asian Americans did drugs, and no one thought Asian Americans had twins, but his birth parents had done both.

He did not do drugs and he never would (he might have twins someday because it was hereditary), but he definitely felt strange sometimes about being the weird combination that he was. Oddney was smart and quiet and well behaved, though maybe it was a coincidence, but Jack was not a model minority or really a model anything.

Fig could not understand all this, despite being his DNA twin, because Fig was a model everything. She loved books and homework and listening quietly in class. She never got in trouble at school for talking to her neighbor or coloring the bottom of her shoe when she was supposed to be looking at the board or falling out of her chair when she was not even allowed to be leaning back in it.

Through the wall, though, Jack could hear her in her nest, which meant that even though she never got into trouble, trouble had gotten into her. But when he went to find out if she needed him, Bex was already in there.

"Come on in," she sang when he peeked his head around the door. "The water's fine."

"What water?"

"It was a joke. We were just thinking about cool things Fig could do with her giant closet, though. You could put in a pool."

"That's a weird thing to think about," Jack said.

"No it's not." Bex rolled her eyes. "What were *you* thinking about?"

"Lewis." He was stunned to hear himself say this and even more stunned when he thought about it and realized it was true.

Fig and Bex must have agreed because they both yelped, "Lewis?"

He couldn't see Fig because she was still in her nest, but Bex's eyes got a big bright look in them. "Why?"

He was about to explain how you can't always say why you're thinking about what you're thinking about when he realized he could in this case. "Probably because you're here."

"Me?"

"He's just as related to our mom as you are and just as adopted. Maybe he even gets in trouble in school sometimes. Plus he's a boy and not white. No offense."

"Why would that be offensive?"

"I dunno." Who could say what girls thought was offensive?

Bex rolled her eyes some more. But then she said, "We should find him!"

"What?" Jack and Fig said together, though her "What?" sounded scared and panicky, but his, he could hear, sounded more like how it felt, which was "Hmm, interesting, tell me more."

"We should find him and get him to come. It's time to get the band back together."

"What band?" said Jack.

"Joking. Again."

Since he hadn't understood the first joke, he wasn't surprised that he didn't understand this one either. Sometimes girls were bad at knowing what was offensive *and* what was funny.

"We don't know where he is." Fig crawled half out of her nest, but her eyes looked wild.

"You didn't know where I was," Bex pointed out, "and you found me."

"Two buts," Fig said, so Jack slapped one hand on each butt cheek. He couldn't help it. "*But* he's only twelve."

"So?"

"So probably he's not allowed to have social medias which is the only way I found you. And even if we did find him, he's too young to come by himself."

"His mom could bring him," Bex said.

"He doesn't have a mom," Fig told her.

"His dad could bring him."

"Dads," Jack corrected. He used his hands to wiggle his butt to remind Fig to tell her second one.

"*But* Mom's already upset, and everyone's already mad at her, and the whole thing is already out of control."

"But that's why I came," Bex said. "To show everyone how adoptions turn out fine, so people wouldn't be mad at your mom anymore. Lewis could help with that."

"It didn't work." Fig sounded like she had a stomachache.

"Two buts," Bex said, and Jack and Fig looked at her with shock. "What? I catch on quick. *But* we can't just do nothing while your mom gets canceled and treated like crap. Do you have a better idea?"

Jack and Fig shook their heads.

"Don't you want to help her?"

Jack and Fig nodded.

"*But* maybe we won't even find him. So we can try without worrying what will happen if we do."

2015

People liked to talk about life with small children as high drama involving lots of make-believe. "Let's play house" or "Let's pretend the ground is lava," but also "Shots don't hurt" and "You like broccoli" and "I don't even mind taking only one shower a week." But as far as India could tell, it was the opposite of acting. It involved saying, "Not perfect, but good enough." It involved saying, "Not good, but good enough." It involved saying, "Well, that sucks shit, but whatever, good enough." Sometimes it involved saying, "That's not good enough, but I'm going to have a glass of wine and go to bed anyway."

There was no workshopping with parenting. You said the wrong thing, and you couldn't go back and give a different read, try it again smiling instead of glowering, gently instead of shouting, with a deep breath before delivery. You had to live with your first read, even though it was often appalling. There was no rehearsal, either. You were live onstage from the moment you got the part. There was no curtain call. There wasn't even an intermission. It was just an endless, endless dance number, and never mind you couldn't sing, you had to sing anyway. There was no playing to your strengths with motherhood. There was no understudy nor, in her case, even a scene partner let alone a director. It was just you, monologizing unscripted to an unruly audience until you died.

The first problem was the twins did not sleep, and they did not not-sleep alone. No matter how many stories she read, how much milk she warmed, how vigilantly she stuck to a routine, Jack couldn't fall asleep. Eventually, he'd grow tired of trying and get up to roam the house at one, two, three in the morning. Once, she closed her eyes for just a minute and jolted awake at dawn to find his bed empty and Jack crashed out in the bathtub. Once, she closed her eyes for just a minute then couldn't find him anywhere, tore through the house with alarm bells pealing in her head, until she found him finally under a shelf in the pantry cuddled up with a box of graham crackers. She couldn't lock him in his room. She couldn't tie him into bed. But then she also couldn't sleep because it wasn't safe for him to wander on his own.

Whereas Fig had trouble staying awake until bedtime. She would fall asleep during dinner. She would fall asleep in the bath, her brain too tired from flitting from worry to worry during the day to keep her eyes open by dark. But then she would wake in the night shrieking. Not wake, actually. Her eyes were open, her mouth was open, but she was not awake or asleep or quite of this world. She would cry and scream and quake and not be quieted or comforted or roused. "Night terrors," the pediatrician said, "they usually grow out of them," as if they were just another childhood phase, as if they didn't shake the whole house, the whole world.

Jack and Fig were a little young to articulate all they were thinking about, never mind all they couldn't stop thinking about, but India figured it had to be their mother. Their other mother. (First mother? Former mother?) India couldn't stop thinking about her either. Perseverating, really. She had the questions anyone would, like had someone told Sarah her kids were okay, and was someone helping her get the care and support she needed, and who were these someones and were they good at their jobs.

But she also had stranger, harder-won worries, like how—literally *how*—Sarah was thinking about Jack and Fig. Belatedly, finally, India understood this was the point of those prospective-parent dossiers she'd pooh-poohed all those years ago: so you could picture and remember and think about your kids. On the one hand, she'd had nine months with Rebecca, nine more with Lewis. But on the other, she hadn't seen either since the day they were born, had no idea, all these years later, what they looked like or loved, were good at or afraid of. She thought of them—she thought of them every day—by thinking of them with their parents, whom she *could* picture, who had grown less since she saw them last.

But Sarah hadn't been the one to choose India, hadn't gotten to peruse her binder or meet and get to know her. So how was she supposed to manage her brain and her memory and her imagination? India knew she couldn't invite Sarah over for coffee. She knew she couldn't meet her for a glass of wine. She knew her own situation and Sarah's were more different than the same. But she also knew something Sarah was probably just finding out: that just because the children you began and grew and loved were no longer with you didn't mean they were no longer with you. She would have liked to be able to offer commiseration, birth mom to birth mom, solidarity, a few dearly bought survival tips. She knew this was not possible. And she knew why. But knowing didn't seem to have a lot to do with parenting. Especially not at three in the morning.

So they were all tired.

Also hungry. India might have been a first-time parent, but she was a realistic first-time parent so she wasn't expecting Fig and Jack to like kale salad and sushi. But they refused chicken nuggets and fish fingers, pasta and string cheese, pizza and cookies, pretzels and animal crackers, and not consistently, so she'd hit on something they liked, and they'd devour homemade nachos all week, demand them three meals a day, and she'd go out and buy a cart full of chips and beans and cheese and avocados, and then they'd refuse to eat nachos ever again, and not just refuse. India would happily have taken meltdowns, tantrums, throwing food even, because what she got instead was silence, vacant stares, children who sat at the dinner table and could not eat and could not be roused.

"They don't like white food," she texted Regina Starlite. Cottage cheese, yogurt, rice, mashed potatoes. "Any thoughts as to why? Did something happen?"

"No idea," Regina replied. "Does it matter why?"

India supposed it did not.

"I just thought if I knew more, I could avoid upset, feed them stuff that makes them happy."

"Not how children work," came the reply.

And never mind how much they had to learn about one another and all the healing and settling-in required and all the missed time that needed making up for, there were still so many hours left to fill. She bought pencils and paints and glues, stickers and construction paper, tiny scissors with fat handles and rounded tips, but Jack and Fig just sat at the table staring at all of it, clutching a crayon in each damp, overwarm hand. They did not want to pretend they were on safari and their stuffies were animals they could spy behind the couch. They got agitated if you stacked more than two blocks together and caused them to wobble. Play-Doh and clay were too sticky, games too loud, cartoons too scary, puzzles too in-pieces. When India showered them with pocket confetti to celebrate finishing their ice cream cones without dripping, they flinched. They didn't even like *Guys and Dolls*.

India called her mother. "I just feel like if I knew more about the first four years of their lives, I could be as good as everyone else."

"At what?" said her mother.

"Parenting."

"Everyone else who?"

"Normal parents who have their kids from birth so there's no mystery, nothing about their children they don't know or understand."

"In the entire history of time, India, throughout the wide vast universe, there has never been a parent for whom that is true."

"You know what I mean. If they'd been with me since birth, there'd be no surprises. I wouldn't accidentally give them things that set them off. I wouldn't innocently make smiley-face pancakes without realizing smiley faces—or, hell, maybe pancakes—were triggering for them."

"What is your favorite kind of ice cream?" her mother said.

"Strawberry."

"What was your favorite kind of ice cream when you were little?"

"Strawberry."

"Once when you were about the twins' age, I gave you strawberry ice cream after dinner and you screamed that you hated strawberry ice cream, so I took it away and then you screamed that you wanted it back, and when I gave it back you dumped it on the floor."

"Why?" India was truly baffled.

"Who the hell knows. For a while, you went through a phase where you'd poke through the ice cream with your fingers and pick out all the strawberries and eat them first."

"Gross."

"You were five. Everything you did was gross. Then you'd cry because your fingers were cold. So I gave you a fork. Then you ate out all the strawberries and cried because it wasn't strawberry ice cream anymore."

"What did you do?"

"Opened a bottle of wine."

"About me?"

"Waited for you to grow out of that phase and hoped the next would be more rational."

"And I was easy and reasonable from then on?"

"You may recall getting pregnant your senior year of high school."

"But other than that?"

"You might be confused about what parenting means."

"I don't care what it means," India said. "What do I do?"

"Talk with them. They're not babies. They can understand."

"Exactly, they can understand," India said. "If you have a newborn, you can tell it anything. It won't understand. It won't remember. But if I talk to Jack and Fig, they'll understand everything I say."

"Not to," her mother said. "With. Talk with them. Discuss what they're scared about. Discuss what you're scared about. Be honest with them. Tell them everything you can think of."

"Why?"

"They're family." She could hear her mother's shrug over the phone. "They've got a right to know."

So after bath every night, before bed, they told each other stories. India did not elide the fire and the trauma and the sad parts. She wouldn't lie to them. But those parts were only just that: parts. Jack and Fig told all they could about Sarah and their home and life with her, what had been scary and hard but also what had been fun and funny and quiet. India added the scant winking details she had about their biological father, about the neighbors who had seen trouble and called for help and saved them. She told them about Regina Starlite and the hospital. She told them about Lewis and Davis and the Andrews. She told them about Rebecca and Robbie and Camille. She told them about their grandmother and her clients. This is your wide, strange, remarkable family in the world, she said. These are your ancestors, progenitors, and forebears. This is your story.

"I want four bears!" said Jack.

Principal photography started in two months and eight days.

THURSDAY

F ig reminded herself they probably wouldn't even find him. One reason
she knew was she had already tried when they first got their phone and
she found Bex. Another was, it turned out she was right: it seemed like Lewis
wasn't allowed on social media yet. It would have been a relief to just give up,
but Bex didn't want to and neither did Jack, and if it might help their mom,
Fig didn't have a choice.

So instead of finding Lewis they would have to try to find his fathers.
At least one of his fathers. But their name was too common. They shared
it not only with each other but hundreds of other people too. If they had
different names, even just different first names like normal married people,
maybe they would have been easy to find. But even Google didn't know what
Fig meant by "Andrew Silverman and Andrew Silverman." They tried to look
through the feeds of all the Andrew Silvermans, Andy Silvermans, Drew Silvermans, A. Silvermans, and D. Silvermans for pictures of kids who might
have been twelve and also looked like their mother and/or Davis, but lots of
parents do not post pictures of their twelve-year-olds on social media. Probably for exactly this reason.

They made a list of everything they had learned about the Andrews from
their mother's stories. They knew the Andrews had been Lenox students too—
that's why she chose them—but they didn't know exactly when except that
it was in the olden days, years before their mom was there. They knew one
Andrew Silverman was a lawyer and one was in advertising. They knew they
lived in New Jersey (so Lewis could have sidewalks and a yard) and commuted

into New York City (where there were apparently no sidewalks or yards?). It wasn't much to go on. They didn't even really know those things because they might have become untrue in the last twelve years. Maybe the Andrews had changed jobs or homes or coasts. Maybe they had changed their names again or fled the country.

They could not ask their mother for more information. Probably she had already told them everything she knew anyway, but she absolutely could not know about this plan. She would take away their phone. She would say she did not need Fig and Jack to take care of her because it was her job to take care of them. She would lecture them that Lewis and his dads were entitled to their privacy. Fig agreed. If the Andrews said they wanted to be left alone, Fig would respect their wishes. She just had to find them first so she could ask them what their wishes were.

Which left only one option. They needed to get Davis alone and not standing next to or sitting beside or talking with or eating near or gazing weirdly at their mother.

Fortunately, after lunch he opened the door to the backyard and went by himself to the pool house.

Unfortunately, it was so that he could have a meeting for work.

It was the best shot they were going to get, though, so they took it. Fig and Jack waited till their mother went to the bathroom and followed him out. They did knock on the door, but they opened it at the same time. It was their door, after all.

Davis looked up. "Hold on," he said, maybe to them, maybe to the people on his computer. He raised his eyebrows at them. "You okay?"

"We need to know any unusual but distinct things you know about the Andrews," Fig said.

Davis told his computer he would call back.

"Bex wants to know. She just found out Lewis exists, so she has a lot of questions." This was true, so it was a good lie.

"What sort of unusual but distinct things?"

"Like maybe if you knew some surprising stories about them or unique tributes."

"Attributes?"

"Unique attributes," Fig agreed.

Davis looked at her like he thought she was strange. Eventually, he said, "They really loved each other. We could tell that immediately. We could tell they were stable, loving. Would make great dads."

"Obviously." Fig didn't want to be rude, but of course there was no way her mother would make an adoption plan for Lewis with un-great dads. Also, you couldn't Google "stable in love great dads" and expect to turn up anything useful at all.

"They drove an MG MGB." Davis sounded pleased with himself for finding this detail in his brain.

Fig nodded encouragingly, but it was annoying how whenever you wanted to talk about anything, boys wanted to talk about cars, and whenever you asked boys a question, no matter what the question was, "cars" was always the answer. Fig didn't know what an MG MGB was, but cars guys thought were cool were always two-seaters, so they'd probably gotten rid of it when Lewis was born anyway.

"They were Lenox alums," Davis offered.

"We know that." Fig was losing her being-encouraging battle. "That's why Mom picked them."

"No it's not."

Fig was pretty sure Davis was wrong but did have to admit he was there at the time and she did not yet exist.

"She picked them because of their Christmas tree," he said.

Suddenly Fig felt hope in her heart.

"One of the photos they submitted was in front of their Christmas tree. Drew is a Buddhist Jew and Andy is a recovering Christian, so I guess they didn't have many ornaments. Instead they'd hung corks with little colored tags."

"Corks?"

"Like from after you finish a bottle of wine or champagne. The writing on the tags was mostly too small to read, but the one you could make out said, 'Finished Sunday crossword before Monday!' And that's how she knew."

"They loved wine?" Fig didn't get it.

"That's what I said." Davis laughed. "I said if they pop the cork for crossword puzzles, they can't need much of an excuse. But your mother said no, it means they celebrate and encourage and honor each other. It means they'll find ways to support and cheer their kid, not just at graduation or the finals or whatever, but the little things too. It means they keep confetti in their pockets, just in case." He looked at Fig and Jack. "Does your mother still do that?"

"It used to scare the ass out of us," Jack admitted.

"Me too." Davis laughed again. "The first time it got in my salad."

"Now we love it," Fig said.

"Me too." Davis looked halfway happy and halfway sad.

A Google search turned up lots of cork trees decorated for Christmas and lots of Christmas trees made out of corks and lots of tips for making ornaments out of used wine bottles, none of which helped them, but when they went back to look at what all the A. Silvermans posted in December, they found a photo of a tree with presents underneath, a Jewish star on top, and corks with colored slips of paper on every branch.

"We found him!" Jack cheered. "One of him, anyway."

"Maybe," said Fig. "And even if it is, we still don't have any way to get in touch."

"Yet!" Bex said. She looked on her phone. Fig and Jack looked on theirs.

This A. Silverman's account had no posts of Lewis or any child. It had no posts with any people in them at all. It had only twenty-three photos total. Two of the Christmas tree. Two beach pics. One jack-o'-lantern. One skyline. One sunset. One rosebush. The rest were mostly food.

"No wonder he only has nineteen followers," said Jack.

"Did he tag his location in any of them?" Bex asked.

"He probably doesn't know how," Jack said.

"Can you tell what city that skyline is?"

They could not, but it didn't matter anyway. Maybe he was just visiting. Even if he lived there, wherever it was, it would only narrow their search down to everyone else who did too.

"Maybe someone else tagged him?" Bex wondered.

A few other people had, but that got them further away, not closer, and then they had to look through those feeds too. A. Silverman was tagged by someone at a winery in upstate New York. He was tagged by someone at a pool with lots of kids at a swim meet in the background, all too blurry to see. He was tagged in a restaurant, at a zoo, at a wedding, at a party. At least they could see what he looked like now. He looked like a dad.

He was tagged at a baseball game, but he must have had bad seats because you couldn't see where it was being played or what teams were involved. The hashtag, though, was #WorkOuting. There were seventeen people in the group photo, and Fig looked at the feeds of every single one. One of them mostly posted photos of shoes. One's daughter was a ballerina. One was in a book club. One was learning to surf. One of them had a crush on her barista. She posted pictures of the drawings he did in her latte foam every morning. Sometimes she put the coffee on her desk to take the picture. In one of them you could see a bulletin board with a cheat sheet about how to work the voicemail. It was printed on letterhead. The letterhead had the company name and phone number.

Fig called it and said as professionally as she could to the receptionist who answered, "May I please speak to Mr. Silverman?" If the receptionist said there was no Mr. Silverman there, she didn't know what she would do.

But the receptionist said, "One moment please, I'll transfer you."

Then it turned out Fig did not know what she would do anyway.

She had just enough time to think she shouldn't start by saying, "I'm looking for Lewis. Are you one of his dads?" because that might scare him, but she didn't have time to think of what she should say instead. When he came on the line, she blurted, "Hello. This is Fig Allwood." Her voice wobbled a little bit. "Do you know who I am?" She sounded like when someone was a mobster on TV. But even though the last time he knew her mother Fig didn't exist yet, he'd probably at least heard of her. This was one of the hard things about having a famous mom, but it was sometimes one of the convenient things too.

"Fig! Are you okay?" he said right away. Fig had often noticed that when you were someone's parent you acted like everyone's parent.

"I'm fine," she said. "I'm looking for Lewis."

"You are?"

"Yes."

"Why?"

Once when Fig had to do the climbing wall in gym, she lost her grip, and while she was skidding all the way back down (it wasn't a very high wall, but still), she tried to catch hold of something, anything, but she was going too fast.

"*I'm* fine." Slipping, sliding, falling.

Then, just in time, a toehold. She remembered how Evelyn Esponson got Davis to come by referring kind of vaguely to a medical emergency and how Davis said asking too many questions at that point made you a jerk. Probably whichever of Lewis's dads she was talking to didn't want to be a jerk.

"But Bex—Rebecca—isn't. Might not be."

Also this was not a lie. Bex might not be fine because anyone might not be fine.

"Oh no," said one of Lewis's dads. "I was afraid of that."

"You were?"

"When we saw you all on the news, we thought . . ."

Fig waited. If she knew what he thought, she could do a better job with whatever she said next.

"Well, I could just tell something about the story wasn't right. I said to Drew it didn't make sense. And then Davis? We thought maybe diversion tactic, but that didn't really make sense either."

Fig didn't know what that meant exactly, but she could see that asking wasn't going to help her cause.

"Is she okay?" Lewis's dad asked, but sadly, like he already knew the answer was no and he was trying to prepare himself. "How can we help?"

"Bex needs . . ." Fig's mind slipped and slid and clutched and landed on ". . . stem cells."

"Stem cells?"

"From a relative. A blood relative."

"Slow down, Fig. Tell me from the beginning."

She couldn't tell him from the beginning because she was still making it up, but she was grateful for the instruction to slow down. She took a deep breath and then a couple more like she was collecting herself. She had almost said "kidney transplant" which would have been a disaster because of course that was something they would look into thoroughly before getting on a plane, and also something Camille or a doctor would probably call about instead of Fig, and could twelve-year-olds just give kidneys to their half-siblings? Fig had no idea, but it seemed, at best, complicated.

But a few years before, a kid in her class cured his sister of cancer just by donating some of his blood which was bone marrow which meant stem cells. Fig had remembered a convention they went to with their mom where there was a blood drive van painted to look like a Tardis, but her grandma explained that was a different kind of blood that was good for strangers whereas if you needed stem cells it didn't happen in a Tardis and worked best when it came from a blood relative, preferably a sibling.

"So she came to your mom but she wasn't a match," Lewis's dad said, halfway between a statement and a question, like he was explaining it to himself.

"Right," Fig agreed.

"And they can't find the birth father."

"Exactly."

"Is Rebecca . . ." He trailed off like he didn't want to say. "She looked . . ."

Healthy, Fig finished in her head. She forgot that like everyone else on the planet, he had seen Bex's videos and he had seen her in their car on TV looking healthy as . . . well, healthy as the healthy teenager she was. "She's fine for now," Fig said quickly. "They just don't know for how long. They wanted to see if my mom was a match . . ." Fig didn't know the word.

"Prophylactically?"

Fig had learned about those in sex ed but didn't know how they applied here, so she kept right on. "Like just in case, before it's an emergency, so when Bex really needs it, they aren't scrambling."

"Makes sense," Andrew Silverman said. Fig was stunned.

"No one knew where you were, and everyone's really upset and busy, so Jack and I thought we could try to find you because we're better at computers than Bex's mom."

"Digital natives," Lewis's dad agreed.

Fig didn't know what that meant either, so she just kept on talking. "It's a lot to ask, but we wondered if he—if all of you—could come."

"It's not a lot to ask," Andrew Silverman said. "You shouldn't even have to ask. We'll come right away. Of course we will. We'll get a flight out first thing tomorrow. And if it turns out Lewis isn't a match either or they're not ready yet or whatever happens, at least we'll be there. I bet we can help some other way."

"I really, really think that's true," Fig said.

2015

Eventually India found something Jack and Fig liked: a tiny kitchen with faucet knobs that turned and an oven door that opened and closed. They liked India to sit at the miniature café table and chairs so that her knees were level with her head. They liked to make menus by covering sheets of construction paper in scribbles then taking her order. They liked to dice the velcroed carrots and bring her plates of a slab of wooden steak, a whole plastic chicken, a stick of neon-yellow butter, an unpeelable banana.

And so, one evening, India announced they were going out for dinner.

She made a reservation, but they still had to wait. The kitchen was backed up but annoyed anyway when they went through four baskets of rolls. Jack's spaghetti came with green stuff on it and Fig's french fries with aioli, so India had to trust in the talents of her dry cleaner and pocket the side of white sauce then pick each fleck of basil off with the precision and patience of a bomb disposal unit. But they had left the house. She was eating something she hadn't prepared herself somewhere other than her kitchen. The risk of public meltdown—and the ways the public led to meltdown—had been hazarded and vanquished.

The table next to theirs ordered bananas Foster, and while India finished her own ice cream and watched the kids take polite turns sticking their fingers into the pitcher of hot fudge, she tried to remember whether bananas Foster was essentially a snooty banana split or what the difference was. Ice cream, bananas. Was there caramel? Was it wrapped in a crepe? Were ladyfingers involved?

The waiter wheeled out a cart, poured rum then liqueur over sliced bananas in a silver pan, and lit the whole thing on fire. There were delighted gasps around the room, applause from their neighbors, and then, of course, it burned itself out moments later. It happened so quickly it took India a breath or two to notice that Fig was shrieking underneath the table.

She was not crying, she was howling, a sound India had never heard a human make before. She was drenched. Blood? That would explain the sound she was making, but it wasn't red, and a rough check revealed nothing cut or broken. A spark of banana on a bare arm frantically doused with a glass of water? But no, it wasn't blood or soggy ash, just ordinary wet—sweat, tears—and by then India's brain had caught up and understood what was happening here, what was happening again as far as Fig's mind could tell. The whole restaurant was horrified, assuming, as India had, that Fig had been burned somehow. But when it became clear it was just a tantrum from a child who should have been left home with a babysitter, everyone fell silent or to piqued whispers, appalled and disapproving. India crawled all the way under the table on her hands and knees to comfort her daughter, but Fig couldn't hear her, not over her own shrieks, not over the inside of her head. Eventually, India pried her from the furniture, hoisted her limp and raging body, grabbed Jack's hand, and fled.

It wasn't just flambé desserts. Fig was anxious anywhere enclosed with lots of people or lots of noise or spaces she couldn't see all of at once. She didn't trust mirrors or other reflective surfaces because it was scary to look around a crowded room and catch a glimpse of someone familiar who turned out to be you, and it was scary to sit across from someone and be able to see their face and the back of their head at the same time. India could scan menus for wood-fired ovens and flaming dishes, could avoid restaurants with a reputation for overbooking or cramming in, but there were a lot of reflective surfaces in LA, so they mostly ate at home.

Jack was fine with flames, crowds, loud noises, large rooms, mirrors, and windows. But his first encounter with the paparazzi ended with the arrival of the police. Hype for *Val Halla* had barely begun, so they were all three surprised when a photographer jumped out from behind a trash can in the park and started snapping pictures. India put a hand to her hammering heart, and Fig hid behind her leg, but Jack bent to the gravel of the path they were on and started throwing it by the handful in all directions. The photographer fled, which convinced Jack only that it was working—he was protecting his family and should not stop—until someone called 911, which only made it worse. They were both afraid of police and police cars, the red-blue lights, the sirens.

"It's over now," India assured him, assured the cops, assured everyone gathered around. But, of course, it was just beginning.

"Maybe I was wrong." Even at night she spoke to her mother only in whispers. At least one child was usually awake, and she didn't want them to overhear. "It turns out love is not all you need. It turns out love is not what makes a family."

"That didn't turn out to be the case," her mother corrected. "That was never the case. It was never that simple, and you never thought it was. You're not a greeting card. You're not an after-school special."

"Maybe your blood-related-to-you kids have problems you're genetically set up to handle. Like if your kids inherited pyromania, your ancestors knew how to handle that so your genes are naturally selected to know what to do."

"By definition, I don't think pyromania is hereditary."

"Or maybe not genetically set up to handle. Maybe genetically set up to recognize, to find familiar, a mark of belonging, and therefore not mind so much."

"Even if it ran in your family," her mother said, "I think you'd still mind pyromania."

"But maybe not night terrors."

"This is what parenting is, India. Solving impossible-to-solve problems while also experiencing deep crises of faith while also being kind of annoyed while also never getting enough rest. These problems only ever go away by changing into different equally impossible problems. This is how it always is for all parents, no matter how you came by your children."

"No, everyone says motherhood is natural and beautiful and magical and life-altering."

"The life-altering part is true."

"And effortless," India added. "They say effortless love."

"They mean you don't have to work hard to love them." Her mother was whispering now too. "They don't mean loving them isn't extremely hard work."

Principal photography—and kindergarten—started in one month and twelve days.

FRIDAY

Lewis had been allowed to wear his cape to California. Encouraged, even. Lewis had been encouraged to wear his cape to California. This was suspicious because his fathers hated his cape. His dad said it wasn't sanitary because he wore it every day. His other dad said starting seventh grade next year would be easier if he didn't go in costume. When Lewis said it wasn't a costume but a *manifestation* of his *soul*, his dad said maybe he could manifest his soul at home. His other dad said middle-schoolers didn't have souls anyway.

One of his dads had grown up with popularity and tons of friends and a family who adored him. His other dad had not had a family like that or friends like that or friends at all. So Lewis was really the perfect average of them, just like if he'd gotten half his DNA from one parent and half from the other like most kids. He wasn't as adored and celebrated and well-adjusted as his one dad, but he was way more adored and celebrated and well-adjusted than the other.

Lewis was not clueless. He knew it was embarrassing to wear a cape at age twelve. He knew wearing a cape to seventh grade was not going to help his social standing.

But.

But he was not easily embarrassed, a quality which anyone would admire. But his social standing was already lower-middle, not great, but not the basement, and he had two friends, which was enough for anyone. But in movies and TV shows, the geeky weird kid who dresses funny is always secretly the cool one.

264 | LAURIE FRANKEL

One reason he'd been allowed—encouraged—to wear his cape was because early in the pandemic he'd used his sewing machine to make a cape *with a mask!* So it was good for all the airports and airplanes and taxis a last-minute cross-country trip required.

But the real reason his dads had let him wear it was because he might be called upon to save a life, the life of India Allwood's other biological child, his actual half-sibling, who might need the marrow from his actual bones, and if that wasn't being a superhero, honestly what was?

His dads did not believe in keeping information from him, so he'd always known he was adopted, even before he realized neither of his dads was a mom. He'd also always known his birth mother was India Allwood, but then she got famous so Lewis had an opportunity most adopted kids never got, which was to watch his birth mother use a no. 2 pencil to blind a clairvoyant lizard demon in high-definition. He still had questions, but not as many as he would have had otherwise.

It was weird, though, to go your whole life never knowing anyone you were biologically related to and then be all of a sudden standing with two of them explaining that a third was off "doing battle with the studio execs," which was not really an explanation because he had no idea what it meant. Two adults and three kids all staring at you would make anyone feel weird, so feeling weird didn't make him a weirdo (in this case), and being a normal person in a famous person's house was weird in a normal way, which sounded weird but actually wasn't.

His dad hugged the man who was his biological father and sounded like he might cry. "Davis!"

His other dad also hugged him and also sounded like he might cry. "It's so good to see you."

"You guys too," the man said from inside the hug while also looking confused and surprised and concerned and at Lewis. Mostly this last one.

After they stopped hugging, his dad held his hand out to the woman and said, "Andrew Silverman, pleased to meet you."

His other dad also held his hand out to the woman and said, "Andrew Silverman, pleased to meet you."

They never didn't think this was funny.

She shook both of their hands, one at a time. "Camille Eaney," she said.

"And you must be Bex," his dad said to the girl who was Lewis's half sister. "It's nice to meet you too." He half shook her hand, half grasped it, and Bex looked like she thought that was weird.

"We're so glad to be here." His other dad also shook-grasped Bex's hand. "And so glad you're . . ." —his eyes went wide and Lewis thought he was going to say "alive" which even Lewis knew was not the right thing to say— ". . . here too," his dad finished, and though that was a less wrong thing to say it also wasn't right. Lewis saw what he meant, though. She looked not just regular alive but extremely alive, whereas his dads had been expecting—he knew because they'd prepared him—a girl who was weak, sickly, in bed, in a hospital, and possibly practically dead.

Bex wasn't even a little bit dead.

He could tell this, even though he could not look at her. He knew she was a girl, a teenager, only four years older than he was, but she looked like an adult woman, not in that she looked old but in that she had . . . well, boobs. His dads wanted him to say "breasts," but Lewis was weird enough already, and anyway his dads weren't really experts on boobs and boob terminology. Lately, Lewis had been starting to suspect that he was probably not gay because, for instance, he didn't think boys who were gay would be afraid to look at Bex because they knew if they did they would not only stare, they would stare *at her boobs*. Soon he would have to tell his fathers that he probably was not gay, and even though he knew they would be okay with it, the fact was that being not-gay was one thing, but being not-gay for your sister, even if she was only half a sister, even if you'd never met her before, was a whole different thing altogether.

"Hi," he said to the floor.

"Hi," she said.

He glanced at her quickly, then away again, and thought she did look a little pale and not very much like him. When people looked at Lewis, the first word they thought was "weird." The second was "confusing." They thought maybe he was a white kid who was really tan, or a Black kid with light skin, or maybe he was Hispanic or Latino or South Asian or Native American or Native-Some-Other-Country or Middle Eastern, or once a new kid at school had moved from Hawaii and thought Lewis was from there too. When Lewis explained he was actually one-quarter Black and three-quarters white, the new student wasn't interested in him anymore and immediately got brainwashed by the cool kids and said Lewis looked like a black-and-white cookie, which he did not. So maybe Bex looked pale because she was sick, or maybe she looked pale just because she was paler than he was.

He didn't think either of them looked much like his birth mother—*their* birth mother—but it was hard to tell because he'd only ever seen her on TV where she wore a lot of makeup and sometimes horns and armor. Still, as far as looking like Bex went, he probably didn't. Among other things, he didn't have boobs.

Whereas even with only quick glances, he could tell that his dad did look like him. Not his real dad or his other real dad. Yet another dad. He looked worried or maybe a little bit afraid, but definitely, he also looked like him, like Lewis, even though Lewis took only tiny peeks so no one, especially this dad, would accuse him of staring.

It was hard, though, because Lewis wanted the opposite. He wanted to stare at Davis for a long time. He wanted to watch him somewhere no one could see him, and Davis himself could not see him, like if Davis was under arrest and had to sit in one of those rooms with a one-way mirror so Lewis could just look and look and look for a few hours until they determined that a mistake had been made and let Davis go. Lewis knew it was bad to wish someone was under arrest, especially if he was a Black man, especially if he hadn't done anything wrong, but he also knew you shouldn't stare—staring was one of the things that made other kids call you weird—and he had twelve years' worth of staring at Davis to do.

"Nice to meet you, Lewis," his biological dad said.

"You too," Lewis said, even though it was not exactly the truth. It was not nice to meet him. It was weird to meet him. It was overwhelming to meet him. But Davis looked like he thought so too, so maybe that was the normal way to respond to this moment.

Or maybe Davis was also weird and it was hereditary.

Lewis felt guilty about being more excited to meet his birth mother, whenever she got back from her meeting, than he was to meet his birth father and birth sister, though he also felt this was kind of understandable. For one thing, neither of them was Val Halla. For another, he already had a lot of dads and did not need more. Lastly, it was not his fault or even necessarily a bad thing that he couldn't look at Bex's boobs.

"Does this mean I'm going to be tall?" he said.

Everyone looked at him.

"I'm sorry?" said Davis Shaw.

"Because you are?"

He couldn't call him Dad because it was confusing enough already. Plus, his dads were his dads in at least hundreds and possibly thousands of ways, whereas Davis was his dad only in one way. His dads had chosen to be his dads and had worked very hard to become his dads, whereas Davis had not chosen to become his dad and then, after that, had worked at least a little hard not to be his dad.

"I'm not . . ." his not-dad said, and trailed off. Then he finished, ". . . that tall."

"How tall are you?"

"Five eleven."

"That seems tall. Can you dunk?"

"A basketball?" said Davis.

"Or really anything," said Lewis, "but into a regulation-height basketball hoop."

Davis shook his head. "Sorry to disappoint you." Then he winced.

"I'm not disappointed," Lewis reassured him. "Did you grow late?"

"What do you mean?"

"How old were you when you reached your current height? I'm twelve."

"I don't think I was this tall when I was twelve," Davis said. "I remember a winter formal where I was embarrassed to ask the girl I liked to slow-dance because she was taller than me."

"Was she a giant?"

"I . . . don't think so."

"That's something you would probably remember," said Lewis. "So probably it's that you were short rather than you were tall and she was a giant."

"Mom is short," the kid named Jack put in suddenly.

"Size is relative," said the sister, Fig.

But before Fig could explain what that meant, Bex spoke up. Finally.

"Ahem," she said. She did not cough or clear her throat. She actually said, *Ahem.* "Speaking of relatives."

Everyone waited to see what speaking of relatives would lead to, but it didn't lead to anything. She rolled her eyes. "We've been waiting for you, Lewis." Like he was late. Like they hadn't dropped everything and rushed all around and taken a last-minute flight practically the second his dad hung up the phone.

But Lewis knew that when you were sick, all you wanted was to feel better as quickly as possible. "Sorry," he said.

"We have much to discuss." She turned around and kind of bounced off down the hall like she lived there. Jack and Fig looked at each other, then scrambled after her. So Lewis tossed his cape out behind him like Thor and headed down the hallway too. He knew what happened when you didn't do what the other kids did and they thought you were weird, and he suspected it didn't matter one bit whether you were related to them or not.

2015

Call varied, but usually India had to be on set from six in the morning to six at night. Then she went home to do dinner and bedtime and receive the next day's script and learn her lines. Then she got up and did it again. Steady work had been an adoption prerequisite. Plus, it turned out kids needed a lot of stuff like clothes and toys and food and a house. So India had to have a job to be a parent, but she couldn't parent because of her job. She didn't understand why she was the only one who saw the impossibility of this. Maybe the balance was easier if your children were born to you or hadn't suffered breathtaking trauma, but for the life of her she couldn't figure out how. Even if she'd had a job with more normal hours, school wouldn't even almost cover them. She needed a morning nanny and an evening nanny. She needed Mandela assuring her that it was good for kids to see their mother work and for Jack and Fig to get comfortable with other adults. "Kindergarten's not really about learning how to sound out letters and write their names," Mandela said. "It's about learning how to meet new people and follow new rules. It's about learning how to adjust and grow and change."

Which made India think she might usefully enroll in kindergarten herself.

For one thing, her new job involved hardly any acting. She had to be there so early because wardrobe and hair and makeup took forever, but then she just sat in her trailer for hours—sometimes hours and hours—waiting for them to get to her scenes. Then they called her to the set where she got to rehearse maybe once—*once!*—before they did four or five or six takes of whatever shot. And then more waiting while they reset the camera and lights and makeup and costumes and hair and sound for the next shot of the scene. It was something like five hours of waiting for five minutes of acting.

Even when Henri was willing to run lines with her—maybe he came over for dinner and played with the kids and after bedtime they did a read-through—it wasn't really rehearsal. Often they didn't get the script for the next day until late the night before. Often it had changed by the time they showed up in the morning anyway.

There was also the fact that they weren't in many of their scenes. They had to be there to mime, say, screaming, but the actual screaming was done in post, and the causes of the screaming—normal things (chases, fights, attacks, jumping off cliffs) and not (shipwrecks, battles with dragons, plunges into icy seas, anything involving artillery or a bird of prey)—were performed by stunt doubles.

"I have stage combat training and experience," India insisted to anyone who would listen (usually only Henri). "They don't have to bring in someone else to fake it for me."

"We don't need stage magic," Henri said with the conviction of a convert. "We have actual magic. That's the beauty of television. You can have it all."

India disagreed—vehemently—but *having it all* gave her an idea. If the job was mostly sitting around waiting, why couldn't she sit around and wait with Jack and Fig? She transitioned her evening nanny into an afternoon driver who dropped the kids off at the *Val Halla* set after school. In her trailer, while India waited, they all recovered together from the stress of the day and being apart, from all the new people and rules Mandela was right about. They listened to music or read books or watched movies. They played dress-up with castoffs from Wardrobe. They competed in cooking shows like Top Allwood where you had to use snacks from the craft table to make a dish (Fig layered veggie sticks, cashews, and cheese slices and called it lasagna; Jack arranged cookies he'd chewed into triangles and called it pizza) or the Great Allwood Bakeoff Mystery Centers Challenge (Fig cored an apple and filled it with brownie; Jack ate a banana, stuffed the peel with olives, and put it back on the oatmeal bar. He spent a whole afternoon waiting for someone to slice it into their cereal unawares).

Ajax was skeptical about Jack and Fig being on set, but India thought there were lots of good lessons for kids: Even superheroes need stunt doubles.

Beautiful people on TV require hours of work by teams of people to look that way. But the biggest one was this: it is not necessary to do things in order. They often shot an episode's climax before its opening, the kiss before the falling, the comeuppance before the sin. Narratively it didn't make a lot of sense, and if Jack and Fig had been trying to earn MFAs, she'd have been concerned. But Jack and Fig were trying to learn that it was okay if your family came to you not moments but years after you were born, if being a carefree little kid came after being a tortured old soul, if first you got a sad ending and then you got to start again.

And not right away, but slowly, eventually, they all started settling in, to the mirrors in the kindergarten classroom, to the need to sleep at night in order to get through the days, to the work that was green screens and dragons instead of Shakespeare and Broadway. But just as India was showering them all with pocket confetti, it turned out they were losing everything.

Val Halla would not be renewed.

Critics loved the show. Audiences were less convinced.

"A clever title and conceit are elevated to the highest of upper echelons," one reviewer wrote, "by the astonishing acting and chemistry of its costars."

But viewers either didn't notice or didn't care.

"Who doesn't want to cheer on kick-ass Viking girl power (and its hunky sidekick), especially when it's this much fun?" asked one critic.

"We don't," yawned the collective.

Val Halla season one made all the good lists: "Best Shows You're Not Watching," "Sleeper Hits Ready to Take Off," "Cult Favorites That Deserve a Wider Audience."

But TV watchers didn't want to join a cult.

"The show's just not getting eyeballs," Ajax tried to report gently. "Don't take it personally."

"I'm Val," India said. "Of course I'm taking it personally."

"It's not your fault," he assured her.

"No," she agreed, "it's the network's. If the show were bad, it would be our fault. If the writing were good and the costumes were good and the effects were good, but the acting was bad, it would be our fault. But it's all great. The only people not doing stellar work are the ones whose job it is to promote the show."

Every week they waited to hear they were getting picked up for a second season.

And every week, they didn't get picked up.

And then, finally, they did but with caveats piled on provisos piled on bad faith and low expectations and lackluster support. To no one's surprise, season two numbers were even worse. The rumor was the powers that be regretted their decision and would kill the project mid-season without warning.

Ajax stopped promising everything would be fine and started promising that finding her work would be easier now that she had a Hollywood track record.

"On a show no one watched," she said.

He could only nod grimly and admit that this was true.

Maybe instead of bringing Fig and Jack to work with her, she could go to work with them: get certified to teach theater, head up a school drama program where she could stage serious plays and cast talented student actors who couldn't sing.

The writers started to wrap things up in case each week was their last so that at least there weren't so many mysteries left open, so many threads still dangled. She and Henri had no choice but to go through their motions. It was like digging up a garden you'd just planted only because it hadn't grown yet. It was hard, and it was heartbreaking.

But then, like one of the show's own plot twists, just when all seemed lost, India and Henri fell in love.

FRIDAY

Fig knew you could trick an adult into flying all the way across the country, but you could not trick them into discussing matters of life and death—even matters of life and death you had made up—in front of kids, and never mind she was a brilliant mastermind, if she stayed and tried to manipulate the conversation, they'd get suspicious.

So they found out. Probably right away. Probably the conversation went:

CAMILLE: What are you guys doing here?
ANDREWS: We came to (potentially) save your (potentially) sick kid.

Fig doubted conversations could use parentheses and also doubted that whichever of Lewis's dads she'd talked to would remember she had not said Bex *was* dying and Lewis *was* the only one who could save her but rather suggested that Bex *might* be slightly a little bit ill and there was a *chance* maybe perhaps that Lewis could help in some way.

CAMILLE: What are you talking about? Bex is fine.
ANDREWS: That (rotten) kid Fig told us it definitely was an emergency.
DAVIS: I knew that India Allwood was trouble and would raise a kid who was also trouble. Also, you can't use parentheses in conversation.

"Mom's going to kill you." Jack wasn't even looking at her. He was rummaging inside the pantry. "No offense," he popped out to say to Lewis. "She'll be glad to see you and your dads. But she's going to kill Fig."

Lewis had a cape. Or really, Lewis's mask had a cape, but now that he was off the plane and away from the airport and could take it off, he didn't. Fig saw why he loved it, though. She saw how it would be comforting to have wings to curl around yourself if you were sad or scared or needed to hide from your mother.

"Do you think they know yet?" Jack said.

"It's only been like thirty seconds." She didn't know how he could eat when her stomach felt so nervous.

"They're going to find out."

"I know."

"Right now Davis and Camille are being polite, but soon they're going to ask what Lewis's dads are doing here."

"I. Know."

"And then Lewis's dads are going to be all, 'We're here so our son can save your daughter.' And Bex's mom is going to be all, 'Save my daughter from what?' And Lewis's dads are going to say, 'From being sick,' and she's going to say, 'My daughter isn't sick.' Aha!" He emerged with two bags of popcorn, one cheese and one caramel. He liked to combine them.

"Wait," said Lewis, "you're not sick?"

"I'm fine." Bex, for instance, looked like she could use a comfort cape. She kept looking at Lewis and looking away and looking back again.

"And then the whole story's going to come out." Jack dumped both bags of popcorn together in the yellow bowl. "And then they'll tell Mom, and then Mom will kill you."

According to Mandela, this was just something siblings said to each other. *Mom is going to kill you.* It came from a place of love, Mandela said, and meant "As your brother, I am devoted to you always and therefore warning you that your behavior might get you in trouble." Mandela also insisted that Fig's birth mother hadn't been trying to kill her or really trying to do anything but was merely out of her mind when Fig happened to be nearby, and so telling herself that Sarah had tried to kill her was not serving her.

"No one needs . . . saving?" Lewis looked like he might cry, and Fig hoped he wouldn't. "No one needs me?"

"We do need you," Fig assured him. "We do need saving. It's just not because Bex is sick."

"Minor detail." Bex rolled her eyes.

"We're getting the band back together," Jack explained.

"What band?" said Lewis.

"It's a joke," Bex groaned.

"We needed the whole family," Fig clarified.

"I'm not family," Lewis said.

"Not family family—" Fig began.

"*We* share blood." Bex wiggled her finger back and forth between herself and Lewis.

"Blood is gross." Jack licked each of his cheese-and-caramel-encrusted fingers, then reached back into the bowl for more.

"Mom's life is being ruined." Fig tried to get them back on track. She felt a sad feeling she had said all this before. She had dreams like this, where she couldn't scream loud enough to make anyone hear, where she couldn't run fast enough to get help. Mandela said everyone had dreams like that, but Fig thought this was probably a lie because why would they.

"She means *their* mom," Bex translated for Lewis. "Our birth mom."

That *our* sounded strange to Fig's ears. Bex and Lewis looked like they thought so too. But Fig went on. "They're getting our family all wrong. The smears think—"

"'Smears' means paparazzi," Bex interrupted to explain again, "and the press and so-called journalists."

"—that adoption is scandalous and ungraceful—"

"Disgraceful," Bex corrected.

"So we're going to save Mom by setting the record straight and showing them how fine we all are."

"Oh," Lewis said. "You want me to be a commercial for her."

"A commercial?" said Fig.

"One of my dads is the senior creative strategist for an ad agency," Lewis shrugged modestly.

"Kind of?" Fig didn't know what a creative strategist was but thought a commercial might be a great idea. "Is it hard?"

"No, it's simple," Lewis said. "First, you brainstorm ideas. Then you discuss with your team and narrow down to the good ones. Then you storyboard and present to the customer. Then you write and edit a script, scout a location, cast actors, hire a director, hair, makeup, props, effects, art. Then you—"

"It sounds hard," Fig interrupted.

"Well, there's no client. My dad says the client is who ruins everything. And if your family is who you're advertising, you probably don't need actors. Your phone camera isn't as good as the ones they use, but it's fine if you're just going to post it online or whatever. Probably you could do writing, editing, and rehearsing in one week and then filming and postproduction in another and then—"

"We have to do it before our mom gets home from her meeting." Fig looked at their phone to see what time it was. "We have an hour and a half."

"She might hit traffic," Jack said hopefully.

"An hour and a half is not enough time to do anything in advertising." Lewis got a thinking face. "Maybe you could hold a press conference?"

"How do you do that?" Fig said.

"In your case"—Lewis's shoulders climbed up to his ears—"I guess you just go out to your driveway and start talking."

The meeting was not over lunch. It was not on set or anywhere on the lot. It was not at a discreet but elegant but modern but timeless restaurant. The meeting was on the eighteenth floor of an imposing glass-and-granite office building. Studio headquarters. India had never been there before.

The room she was ushered into was similarly imposing with clearly expensive but wildly uncomfortable chairs and a wide view out over the city and the hills that managed somehow still to feel claustrophobic. She suspected this was the point.

Claustrophobic and also empty, the latter so she would be the one waiting for the executives to come importantly in (she knew a staged entrance when she saw one). There were three of them: one woman, two men, all white and wearing suits and anyone's guess whether they were thirty or sixty. She recognized them vaguely from being introduced at an awards show or small talk at a party or bumping into them on her way through a restaurant with Ajax. They reintroduced themselves anyway, names and titles, information that went through India's brain like a plane on a runway that then departed into the clouds.

"India Allwood," the tall one began. "We are such enormous fans. All of us. It's a true pleasure to properly meet you."

"*Such* enormous fans," the short one echoed, "of your work *and* of you. You're an incredible talent. We're so grateful to you for taking the time to get together today. It's a real treat."

"I might geek out a little," the female one admitted. "Watching the pilot of *Val Halla*—the pilot!—I decided this was the only thing I wanted to do for a living."

India saw that this was meant to be a compliment, but she had the instinct to apologize. Imagine being moved and inspired to become a studio exec.

"I'll tell you a secret." The short one leaned in. They all leaned in. "I saw *Nestra*. In fact, I saw it before it transferred." He turned to the other two. "India was unbelievable, truly transcendent. I said to Liza"—back to India— "my girlfriend at the time, now my wife"—back to the execs—"'This India Allwood is a star, no doubt about it, sky's the limit.' And I was right."

India sat back in the uncomfortable chair. Maybe this wasn't going to be so bad after all.

"However," the female one plunged in.

No, it definitely was.

"Not even 'however,'" Tall corrected. "Therefore. Because. *Because* we are such fans of your work—"

"—and of you," Short added.

"—therefore we want to make sure," Female went on, "that you get to keep doing it."

She stopped. They all stopped. They all looked at India.

"Keep doing it?" She felt her uncomfortable chair tilt away from the floor. "Are you firing me?"

"No!" Tall laughed. They all laughed. Then they all stopped laughing. "The opposite. We want to get rid of all the things that are making it difficult for you to do your job."

"It's not difficult—" India began.

"All the barriers in your work and indeed"—Short cleared his throat— "your life that are getting in the way of doing what we know you were born to do."

"Barriers?"

"The studio feels"—Female clasped her hands on her knee, which caused Short and Tall to do the same—"that you've gotten into a little bit of trouble here, and we'd like to help you—"

"—and," Short put in, "help you help us—"

"—clean that up," Tall finished. "And get you back to doing what you do best."

"Promoting your movie?" India guessed.

"Acting," Female corrected.

"Same thing," India said.

Tall's eyes flashed. "It's been quite a week for you, hasn't it." Not a question.

"It's not that we necessarily disagree with your positions or what you've said," Short emphasized.

"It's just that we think we can help manage the message and assuage some of the concerns," Female explained.

"Can and must," Tall corrected.

"You don't disagree with what I said?"

"Not at all," they concurred at once.

"I mean, it isn't really a thing you agree with or disagree with." India made sure her hands were steady then poured herself a glass of water from the pitcher on the table beside her. "I did have a baby I placed for adoption my senior year of high school. I did have another baby I also placed for adoption my senior year of college. It's not really a matter of agreeing or disagreeing. That's kind of not how it works with facts."

"Be that as it may, we have some concerns with the way that information was shared with the public and the *opinions*"—Tall emphasized the word like a producer's niece at a table read—"you have managed to communicate along with these facts."

"Opinions?"

"About adoption, abortion"—Short cleared his throat again—"certain projects with which you have been involved."

"Projects you are contractually obligated to support," Female reminded her, "though of course we hope you will do so as we do, out of genuine passion and pride."

"We think it's time to do more than just play defense," Short said.

"*Strongly* think," said Tall.

"Can we tell you what we had in mind?" Female's clenched knuckles were the same color as her clenched teeth. India was fairly certain that if fifteen penguins were to waddle though the door at this moment, it would not prevent the execs from telling her what they had in mind.

"We'd like to set up a sit-down," said Tall.

"An in-depth interview," Short explained.

"In your home," Female added.

"With your kids," Tall said pointedly, and when India opened her mouth to object, he raised a hand that meant *Listen to the costs of saying no before you proceed.* "We need to see humans here, not just sensationalism, not just reactionary takes. You are that human. But you are not the only human."

"My kids are off-limits. You know this. You've agreed to this."

"You brought them into it," Female said quietly. "Maybe not explicitly but implicitly. You didn't have to drop that bombshell—"

"—revelation," Short softened.

"—history," Tall settled on. "But once you decided to share it, you raised a great many larger issues. Why did you choose adoption? Where are those children now? How did those adoptions play into the one you undertook to become a parent yourself? These are significant questions."

"Which are none of anyone's business," India finished for him, though he was done.

"Maybe not," Tall said. "Call it an opportunity, if you like. You've stepped in some shit, India. We're giving you a towel with which to remove it from your shoe. You'll sit down with an interviewer—we're working on who, but it'll be someone big—"

"—and good," Short assured her.

"You'll give viewers a tour of your home," said Female. "Sit in front of a fire in your living room. On your turf. In your comfort zone. Just have a conversation, like with a friend. Take the opportunity to go a little more in-depth, explain a little more thoroughly, apologize and clarify."

"And introduce Jack and Fig," Tall's words said while his voice brooked no discussion of that or any other matter. "Your real daughter too."

"I don't think 'real' means what you think it means," India advised.

But Tall kept listing people he wanted viewers introduced to, as if she hadn't spoken. "Your real daughter. Her mother. The other birth father. We understand these people are all at your home, so this shouldn't be burdensome. In fact, it means you don't have to send them away for the taping. They won't stay for the entire interview, just say hello at the beginning and the end. We're writing the questions ourselves, of course, and will get those to you by end of day. We'll ask you to stay on script as far as your answers go as well."

"Which will be?" India asked, mostly out of curiosity.

"That you're sorry for encouraging adolescent promiscuity and advocating teenage pregnancy," Tall said.

"That you're sorry for downplaying the traumas of adoption and the traumas of abortion as well," said Short.

"That you're sorry for misleading the public about your personal history and past experiences," said Female.

"But I'm not sorry about any of those things," India pointed out.

"Doesn't matter." Tall's hands turned up.

"It does to me," India said calmly. "As does the safety and well-being and privacy of my children, as you are well aware, and as, frankly, should go without saying."

"We're not broadcasting their SAT scores," Tall snapped. "We're not filming them in the bath. We're not invading their privacy in any material way, so please spare us the self-righteousness." Short and Female eyed him frantically, but he kept going. "We're not endangering your children, any of them. We are throwing you a lifeline. Take it."

"I thought you were getting shit off my shoe."

"Look, India." Female took the baton. "We get it. We do. Think of it as getting ahead of the story. Taking back control. Doing this on your terms—"

"You mean your terms," India said.

"If you like," she sighed. "Our goal is the same as yours: to clear your name and—"

"Hold on," India interrupted. "I haven't done anything wrong here. You do know I haven't done anything wrong here?"

They did not.

"I've not been casually racist. I've not been caught in a sexual harassment scandal. I've not broken the law or anyone's trust or even an NDA. You can't punish me if I haven't committed a crime or even an indiscretion, and you can't clear my name if it hasn't been sullied."

"As a woman in this industry, I know how hard it is"—Female leaned forward—"to be a woman in this industry. Standards and expectations aren't always equal. Perceptions and reactions aren't always fair. But it is what it is. And we women have to stick together so that—"

But Tall cut her off. "This matter is not open for discussion. If you refuse the very small, very sensible concessions we're asking of you, it will be the end of your career. Simple as that. *Val Halla*'s season ended on a cliff-hanger. If you think we can't have you written out of the show, you are hugely mistaken. If you think you can leave and have your pick of jobs, you are laughably mistaken. If you are imagining that the pick of jobs will come not from *Val Halla* but owing to your talent and personal appeal, you're uproariously mistaken. If you don't do what we're very reasonably asking you to do, you will never work in this business again, India."

"He doesn't mean to be mean," Short lied. "It's just that 'Difficult,' 'Not a team player,' 'Talented but ego is a liability' . . . these are hard accusations for an actor to get past."

"Especially an actor who's an actress," Female added sadly.

"And this needn't feel so dire," Short continued. "We know you don't want to imperil *Val Halla* or *Flower Child* or all the good, hard work of all the many wonderful people involved in these projects. We know you're a good sport and a team player and a terrific mom. We just want to get to know you a little better and let the rest of America get to know you a little better too."

"You," Female said, "and your family, your real daughter, your adopted kids, your home. These are all things to be proud of. We just want to help you show them off."

"Don't say no now," Short begged. "Think about it and let us know. Think about it, and really weigh what you're objecting to. Maybe you're just standing on principle, and you can let it go. Maybe when you really sit down and look at it, none of this will be as distasteful as you're imagining. I hope so. I really do. Just . . . give it some thought."

"Quickly," Tall added.

Then all three rose and left the room.

The car took back roads so they wouldn't hit traffic, but they hit traffic anyway. India was glad. She needed time to talk herself down before she got home. She was shaking, rage or fear or maybe both, so she took deep breaths and tried to be objective. The good thing about studio executives, the only good thing, was they weren't actors, so it was easy to tell what they were lying about. They weren't really enormous fans, but they also weren't really all that appalled by her high school pregnancy or her driveway dramas, even by what she'd said about *Flower Child*. It was all just posturing. They had to be seen—by whom was anyone's guess—expressing their concern, taking decisive action, scolding her. That done, she was betting they'd move on now. They wouldn't actually fire her. There were hundreds of wildly talented people employed by *Val Halla*. They wouldn't punish all of them just to punish her. They couldn't actually expect her to put her children on camera.

Now that the pro-lifers had left, now that Bex had stopped posting videos, now that Davis had arrived and stayed, surely the worst was behind them and the melee would subside and the smears would move on, and then the execs would forget all about this meeting. Or maybe they'd remember and feel embarrassed and contrite. Maybe they would even apologize to her, an apology she would graciously pretend to accept, and then everything could go back to normal. She took some deep breaths, and her hands stopped shaking, and she felt a little better.

Then she pulled into her driveway.

Fig changed into a dress. Bex said she wouldn't wear a dress, but she would put on jeans with fewer holes, and she also said she would do Fig's makeup. Fig's mother didn't let her wear makeup, but when all her problems went away owing to their smart plan followed by their practically professional press conference, she probably wouldn't mind. She might not even notice.

Fig wished she had one of those tall tables people stood behind when they had press conferences on TV. She wished the anti-abortion awarders had left their balloons and cake, which at least looked festive. She wished Jack had brushed his hair. Mostly, she wished her mother were here to stand with her and hold her hand and tell her everything would be okay. But her mother was not here. That was the point. And unless she hit a lot of traffic, she would be home any minute. They had to hurry.

They snuck into the foyer holding their shoes. Fig wasn't sure if any of the adults who were in the house would care what they were doing, but in case they did, she didn't want them to know about it.

"Everyone ready?" she whispered.

Two heads nodded, and Bex didn't roll her eyes, so Fig took that as a yes too.

"Everyone remember what you have to do?"

"Look super," Lewis whispered.

"Just stand there," Jack whispered.

"Back you up, sister," Bex said, too loudly, but it was such a perfect thing to say, Fig didn't mind.

"I'm really nervous," she admitted.

"Want my cape?" Lewis held its hem toward her.

"It doesn't go with your outfit," Bex advised, so Fig shook her head, took the deepest breath she could, and opened the front door. She went out on the stoop to put her shoes on, then she walked down the driveway. Strode. She strode down the driveway to the smears.

As soon as they saw her, they all rolled upright and started moving like if you accidentally kicked a box with marbles in it. They called, "Look over here!" and "Do you have any comment?" and "How does it feel to be together?" and "What does your mother think?" But as soon as Fig opened her mouth to talk, they all got very quiet to hear and record what she had to say.

"We have a press conference," she announced as loud as she could, which was not that loud because her whole body was shaking, even her lungs.

She looked at her brother. Brothers. Bex took her hand and squeezed it. When Fig looked up at her she winked. Fig had to let go of her hand to take out her index cards. The first one was on top, right where it was supposed to be. She opened her mouth again and took another deep breath and began.

"Thank—"

Her mother's car screeched up and her mother got out of it. She was running and waving her arms and saying, "No no no no no no nonononono." When she got close enough, her arms grew long as ladders and wrapped around all four of them to squish them together and turn them like one wide, rotating kid. Then she pushed them toward the house. Over her shoulder while she pushed, she shouted to the smears, "You are all hell spawns from hell."

"I mean, where else would hell spawns be from?" Bex rolled her eyes.

"Lewis said it would take a long time to make a commercial," Fig tried to explain, but her mouth was muffled from being squished into Jack's shoulder, "so we decided to make a press conference instead."

"Lewis?" Her mother was still pushing.

Lewis wiggled his hand free and held it up to her. "Lewis Silverman. Pleased to meet you."

Fig's mother stopped pushing. Her face was very red from running and squishing and steering them, but when she stopped it became very white. She swallowed and took Lewis's hand and blinked her eyes a bunch. Then she took a deep breath and restarted pushing all of them toward the house.

"It wasn't the smears' fault." Fig felt that unfortunately she had to be honest. "Don't blame them. Blame me."

"Why choose," her mother managed, "when you can do both?"

Inside, Fig discovered Jack was right for once. All the adults *had* figured it out. Her mother *was* going to kill her. First, though, she was going to do a lot of enthusiastic hugging of Lewis's dads and of Lewis himself, who looked a little overwhelmed and also a little overmashed. She apologized to them for Fig's actions and said really they were all her fault, which did not fool Fig even for a minute because she knew her mother wasn't going to ground herself. Lewis's dads waved their hands while her mother was saying sorry as if flying all the way across the country to save one stranger/sort-of sister a mere fifteen hours after another stranger/sort-of sister asked you to under false pretenses was a minor inconvenience not even worth mentioning.

Fig knew that wasn't going to save her from being grounded either.

"Lewis," her mother sighed. She put her hands on his shoulders like they were going to slow-dance. They were exactly the same height. "You're so . . ." She trailed off, and Fig worried what she was going to say, and she could see Lewis was worried too, ". . . beautiful," she finished, even though that was not what you were supposed to call boys.

But right away Lewis replied, "Thank you. You too," which was true, but not what you were supposed to say back.

Her mother laughed. "I'm so glad to meet you." She also had tears in her eyes, though, and also on her face. "Well, meet you again."

"Thank you," Lewis repeated. "You too." Which made more sense this time.

"You were beautiful the first time we met too"—the corners of her eyes scrunched—"but it was an eventful day, and I can't remember all the details."

"That's okay," Lewis said. "Me neither."

Her mother laughed again. "I'm grateful you're here, Lewis. I'm grateful you came."

This may have been true, but Fig could see that in addition to feeling grateful her mother was feeling angry (at Fig), overwhelmed (by Fig, or at least by things and people Fig had caused to occur), exhausted (by the events of the week, which were not all Fig's fault, but the percentage was definitely higher than usual), and worried.

Worried worried Fig. She had known all along that finding Lewis would get her in trouble. She'd just thought it would be worth it because Bex said it would help her mother.

Fig was looking at her mother, though, and she could tell it wasn't working.

2018

In fact, it was not Henri and India who fell in love at the end of season two, but Henri and Ajax. Or maybe they'd been in love for years and only became, after season two, ready to do something about it, which for Ajax meant the one thing he'd always sworn he'd never do. He left New York and moved to Los Angeles. The difference this made in India's life was that Ajax was in a better mood, and now she got lectured in person sometimes rather than only over the phone.

Far more momentous, at least for more people, India and Henri also fell in love. Except it wasn't them, of course. It was Val Halla and her co-captain, Rune Erickson. The producers had at first tried to hide the fact that Henri was very gay ("I'd like to see them try," said Ajax) and India very much a mom (and therefore unsexy by definition) but finally realized, on the brink of cancellation, the value in pointing out that these two were definitely, absolutely, unambiguously, not remotely sexually attracted to each other, and yet you watched them on TV every week and simply did not believe it. They gave off heat through your screen. When their hands brushed then held for an extra moment, viewers swooned. When she fought a family of evil mermen, wrestling Rune out of a watery grave that soaked both their shirts to clingy translucence, legions of fan-fiction writers set to work. When the writers' room contrived to have Val and Rune slow-dance at an elf wedding, tens of thousands of shippers took to social media to declare they could not go on living if these two didn't get together.

And a job that had been tenuous, yes, but doable and manageable and sane suddenly became none of the above.

They were America's sweethearts. Every carpet they walked was red. They were invited—begged, really—to every morning program, late show, charity ball, A-list opening, and Hollywood event. At one convention, they told the story of how they met at India's *Nestra* audition, and "stuck then unstuck her elevator" became internet parlance for all sorts of debauchery India had been perfectly happy living in ignorance of all her life so far. They appeared on dozens of magazine covers. One styled them in matching head-to-toe leather from high heel to horn tip. One dressed them in matching *bunads* for a photo shoot in a Norwegian fjord on one of the *Val Halla* tours that were popping up all over Scandinavia, never mind the show was filmed on a soundstage in Studio City. On one, they wore the soaked-through shirts. On another, they were strategically naked in a treasure chest. (Henri had gained thirty pounds since *Nestra*, but it was India's having a second bagel at breakfast one morning that occasioned an emergency meeting of the production team.)

Fans loved them, finally, in the way only superheroes could be loved: obsessively and with a willingness to spend money. There were Val Halla dolls and action figures and Lego sets and T-shirts and yogurt cups and french-fry sleeves and water bottles and board games and fan events and academic conferences and comic books and online forums and bobbleheads and a hundred thousand internet memes. And India Allwood's face was on every single one of them.

On the one hand, this meant job security and financial security, and both were nice and necessary. She was finally getting the hang of TV acting, schedule balancing, working while mothering. She'd grown close with not just Henri but also the rest of the cast and crew. With *Val Halla*'s future on surer ground, the writers started taking some chances on edgier plotlines, timelier subtexts, more complex character arcs, and it started to feel like real acting again. Henri even got to write and direct two episodes, and though India was rebuffed when she asked for the same, she had hopes for the future. (India: "How come Henri gets to write and direct, and I don't?" Ajax: "Henri has experience writing and directing." India: "How am I supposed to get experience writing and directing if you only let Henri do it?" Ajax: "Maybe you can just be content with being a superstar for a while before you demand more." India: "How long?" Ajax: "We'll see.") (Like her children, India interpreted "We'll see" more optimistically than it probably warranted.)

On the other hand—and it was a huge hand, a giant's hand—suddenly there was nowhere India could go without being recognized, approached, yelled at or at least near, sometimes serenaded, sometimes proposed to, twice stalked, twice assaulted, constantly followed, frequently threatened or propositioned, and photographed, photographed, photographed. They took her picture when she pulled out the recycling, got into her car, checked the mailbox. They took her picture when she stopped for coffee, shopped for groceries, dropped books at the library. These photos appeared in tabloids and online as proof she was depressed, despairing, too fat, too thin, had had plastic surgery, needed to have plastic surgery, had given up, and had it all figured out.

It would have been a lot for anyone, but it was more when the anyones in question were so young, were living in an aftermath, were right, unfortunately, to believe danger lurked and they could be grievously harmed and it might not always be okay. Jack was still alarmed when people jumped out unexpectedly, and they did, a lot. Fig was still freaked out when people approached loudly or too enthusiastically, unkindly or overkindly. They got tougher over the year, less inured than expectant: Most bushes hid someone. Most strangers approached them. But India sometimes wondered if that was worse, the lesson that people will be callous and uncaring and self-centered, and all you can do is not be surprised by it.

And then one day, school called.

"Sorry to disturb," the attendance admin apologized. India was on set, having her hair and makeup touched up between takes. "Jack and Fig's father is here to take them to their doctors' appointments, but for some reason we don't have him on the approved pickup list. Are we okay to release them?"

India's throat jammed. Like in a nightmare, she couldn't scream. She couldn't get so much as a syllable to come out.

Mrs. Olson's voice dropped to a low laugh. "He's a little agitated they're going to be late, but I said, 'Honey, you know doctors are never on time.' Honestly, they make you get there fifteen minutes early, but have you ever been seen by your appointment time? Never. And then you're just shivering in that horrible little gown. Fig's over in the music building third period so I've sent someone to fetch her, and Jack was in gym so he's having a quick shower which I expect the doctor will consider worth a slight delay in—"

"Noooo!" India finally managed, more strangled wail than word. "Call the police. Do not release the kids to anyone but me. Do not get them out of class. I'll be right there." She leaped from the makeup chair, face blue for a scene in which she was half-frozen, bobby pins scattering like beads from a broken necklace. School was twenty minutes if there wasn't traffic, but there was, plus lights that wouldn't change fast enough and pedestrians who could not be run over even if they did deserve it. When she screeched in finally, she was dismayed to find no phalanx of armored vehicles abandoned askew with their doors open, no shrieking sirens, no red and blue flashing lights, only a single silent police car, carefully parked parallel to the curb as if all, or really anything, was right with the world.

She abandoned her own car half in the loading zone, half on the sidewalk, and tore inside to find Jack and Fig seated in the cheery orange plastic chairs outside the front office, both in tears—*but!*—both there, right there. The look that washed over Mrs. Olson's face when India ran in was part relief, part horror.

"I'm so sorry," she was saying before India even reached her children, never mind she felt like she flew there, like no time elapsed between seeing them, safe and whole, and having them in her arms. "I didn't know. He was very believable. Goddamn actors! No offense. It's just this town is full of people really good at convincing you—"

"Don't apologize." India had to project so Mrs. Olson could hear her from beneath her children. "You did exactly right. You did perfect."

"I wasn't even going to call you. I know you're busy, and he was so rushed and so . . . persuasive. I can't tell you how many times I call parents because someone's not on the approved pickup list and everyone's just irritated but—"

"You saved them," India interrupted. "I'm so grateful."

"You look scared to death," Mrs. Olson said.

"It's the makeup." She was meant to look half-dead, but that's how she felt too. "Where is he?"

"He left."

"When you called the police?"

Mrs. Olson looked sheepish. "Jack and Fig were already on their way to the office when I called you. He tried—"

"He tried to take us, Mom," Jack interrupted. "He grabbed our hands and tried to drag us. He said you sent him to take us to our appointments. He said you were his friend. Fig screamed."

She looked at her beautiful daughter. "Good girl," she whispered, but Fig was still crying.

"So I bit him," Jack finished.

"You bit him!"

"He wouldn't let go of my hand! So I bit him and Fig screamed and he ran away."

"By the time the police arrived . . ." Mrs. Olson trailed off and eyed a uniformed officer who was in the front hallway with a walkie-talkie to his mouth. "His partner's searching the building, but I don't know why—the guy ran. He jumped in a car and tore off. They keep asking me what kind of car, but these two were upset so I was seeing to them and"—she dropped her eyes—"I'm so sorry. I feel terrible."

So he would walk free. So he could come back. So he would continue to draw breath when India wanted him drawn and quartered, insofar as that was what she felt herself, pulled to breaking in all different directions: comfort her children, chase down this monster, grill the whole school about a strange car *someone* must have seen, bend on grateful knee and kiss Mrs. Olson's feet.

She did this last, if only metaphorically, then talked to the police officers. One seemed a little starstruck and kept enthusing, "Think how much worse this could have been!" which India was trying, valiantly if unsuccessfully, not to do. The other seemed the opposite of starstruck, more like star-annoyed, as if India's rage and panic were overreactions, unreasonable diva behavior. He rambled skeptically about security footage until she took her kids and left.

"He almost got us, Mom," Jack said breathlessly on the way out of the building. Then, when he saw her parking job, "I don't think you're allowed to leave your car there. Can we stop at Cupcake Conniption?" Like a jump scare. He had been frightened for a moment there, but now the fear was gone, and he was fine. She'd take it.

"Sure. Fig? You okay?"

Nothing from Fig.

"Who was he?" said Jack.

"I don't know." Best to downplay, maybe. "Just some guy wanting to stir up trouble."

"A smear?"

"Maybe."

"What did he want?"

My soul, India thought, *my loves, my life*. Maybe money? It would have been a ransom. Maybe fame, and she didn't want to think what that would have been. "He probably didn't know himself," she told Jack. "The important thing is everything worked exactly as it was supposed to. Mrs. Olson knew he wasn't on the approved list. She called me right away. You both did a great job scaring him off, but even if you hadn't, school would never have let you leave with him. They would never have let him take you. You're safe."

Over cupcakes, she said it again. "You're safe." She was relieved when Fig found her voice enough to pick a double vanilla with strawberry cream and appetite enough to eat it and to whack Jack when he tried to take her cupcake liner. But she hadn't said anything else.

They had as normal a night as possible. But while India was tucking them in, Fig said her first real sentence since breakfast: "How did he find us?"

It was a good question. Really, it was the only question. Who was he? Some asshole. What did he want? To be an asshole. But how did he find them? It's not that the question itself was that revelatory, but its answers were ones she could maybe do something about. You couldn't stop assholes from being assholes. But at least you could try to cut off the path between them and your kids.

India did not Google herself. Not ever. The dwebs were mean. That's why they called them dwebs. She didn't care what they thought, but she didn't want it rattling around in her head anyway. Besides, it was like researching international travel. You went in with a simple question and vague wanderlust, and three hours later you had a headache, eighty-five open tabs, and no progress whatsoever toward a vacation. A Google search for India Allwood turned up more hits than a normal person could get through in a lifetime.

An asshole, however? Not a normal person. Maybe he had more patience. After bedtime, she sat down with vodka and popcorn and Googled not just herself but herself and her children. That was when she found the person whose fault the near miss at school had been.

It was her.

"Tell us about a day in the life of India Allwood," one interviewer had said, and she'd spoken of the coffee shop across from school and how they tried to save time on mornings she didn't have early call to stop and get hot cocoas on the way.

"How do you balance work and motherhood?" another asked, and she'd name-checked the Korean dance studio Jack and Fig walked to after the last bell on Monday and Thursday afternoons.

"Does being a superhero for pretend help you single-parent for real?" a reporter had wondered, and India talked about the power of storytelling and the kids' favorite bookstore in an old fire station they'd visited on a walking field trip in kindergarten.

The answer to Fig's question was: Easily. He had found her kids with no trouble at all and plenty of help from her.

That was when she made the new rules. No photos of her kids. No interviews about her kids. No reporting on her kids. Her kids were off-limits. Period.

FRIDAY

Lewis thought India in real life was like Val in season two, episode nine, "Opposite Day," where she meets a *nøkk* who lures her to the bottom of a lake and steals her powers, but it only works when she's wet, so mostly she's her regular, happy, powerful self, but then she goes to a beach party and then it rains and she even takes a shower before she figures it out, and in those scenes she's someone else.

She was happy-surprised-excited to see Lewis and his dads and to welcome them to her home. She was happy-weepy-grateful when she learned why they had come and that they forgave Fig anyway because she was only a child and just trying to help. She was happy-sappy-touched that his dad thought it was sweet and loving of his other dad to insist they drop everything and rush here the moment he learned there was a sick kid, and yes, a more cautious man might have asked some questions before buying plane tickets, but that was why he loved him. She was happy-awed to meet Lewis again at long last.

But she was also angry. She was sad-angry at Fig for lying and tricking his dads. She was regular-angry at Jack for encouraging Fig. She was worried-angry about the meeting she'd just come from regarding a situation which had been dying down but was now, Lewis guessed, dying up.

Fig got grounded, and India got on the phone with her agent, but everyone else went in the pool. Jack was trying to catch food with his mouth, so the water was full of soggy popcorn. Lewis solved this problem by swimming underwater. If he took a breath at one end, he could swim all the way to the other without coming up. But when he surfaced at the end of his twenty-third lap (it was a pretty small pool), he ran into legs, and the legs belonged to Davis.

"You're a good swimmer." Davis had his pants rolled up and was sitting on the side, swishing his feet in the deep end.

"I can just hold my breath a long time," Lewis said modestly. He realized the goggles he'd borrowed were one-way mirrored so now was the looking-at-Davis moment he'd been waiting for. Davis looked like an adult.

"Plus drag," Davis said.

Lewis glanced down. It was true his T-shirt seemed pink but it was just faded red, and his shorts were more puffy than a real bathing suit would have been, but he had been to drag brunches with his dads, and he looked nothing like that. "It's more manly when it's not wet."

Davis laughed. "I meant the extra drag from your cape. When I was on swim team in high school, we'd shave our legs for meets."

"Even the guys?"

"Yup, because even that tiny bit of reduced drag makes a difference. Whereas you're swimming in a cape. I'm impressed."

"Other kids think it's weird." Lewis was suddenly worried he looked like a bug. He raised the mirror goggles to his forehead.

"There are worse things to be."

"Like what?"

"Like boring and unimaginative. Like so worried about what other people think you change how you dress and swim."

Adults always thought that, that being yourself was the best thing to be. Lewis wasn't sure if that was just something they said because they knew you were stuck being you so might as well make the best of it, or if it was something they believed because being yourself when you were an adult was great and they forgot that being yourself when you were a kid usually wasn't.

"Once, I told everyone Val Halla was my birth mom, but no one believed me because she's so cool and I'm so weird."

But Davis laughed again. "India's pretty weird."

"She's a movie star!"

"A weird movie star," Davis said. "Weird was one of the things I loved most about her. And I loved everything about her."

Lewis looked down at his hands and feet treading the warm water. "It might also have been because I don't look like her."

"I think you do look like her."

So Lewis clarified, "Like hers. Like I could be hers." He looked up at Davis. "No one knows what I am."

Davis puffed up his cheeks and blew the air out slowly. "Yeah. Boy do I get that." And Lewis knew right then the whole trip was worth it because whenever he tried to explain this to his dads they said, "You're a kid" or "You're our baby," but that wasn't the question people were asking when they said, "What are you?"

"Me too," Davis said, "no one ever knew what I was. Or they assumed I was someone I wasn't unless I was with both my parents."

"Did people stare at you?"

"Oh yeah. I don't know how it feels to be adopted, but it's real strange to not be adopted and have everyone assume you are. When I was out with both my parents, people stared maybe, but they got it. When I was out with just my mom, no one thought I was hers."

"That's what I did too," Lewis said.

"What?"

"Switched parents. Birth parents. Sides of the family. Since no one believed Val Halla was my mom, I told them about Henrik Ibsen."

Davis's laugh was so loud it echoed.

"I said my great-great-great-grandfather made Henrik Ibsen a pair of shoes, and no one believed that either. Kids don't know who Henrik Ibsen even is, but I got in trouble for lying anyway because my teacher said it couldn't be true because Norwegians are all blond white people."

Davis whistled and shook his head a little. "Well, your classmates might be right, but your teacher definitely wasn't."

"Your grandmother lied about the shoes?"

"No! At least, not on purpose. Just, you know, family lore, stories that get handed down. Maybe they're lies, maybe they're exaggerations, maybe her grandfather was wrong and it was just some guy who looked like Henrik Ibsen. Or, hell, maybe it's true. Everyone needs shoes. Henrik Ibsen must have bought his from someone. What I do know for sure is that my grandmother was born and grew up in Norway. She moved to the US when she was a teenager. She had a daughter—my mom—who's a blond white woman who grew up and married a Black man, my dad. All of those things are one hundred percent true, no matter what anyone says. Which is why it's good we've met."

"Why?"

"Because we're both . . . rare. 'My Norwegian ancestor sold shoes to Henrik Ibsen' is not a thing most Black men can say."

It wasn't a thing hardly anyone could say, and no one would look at Lewis and think he was definitely Black or remotely a man, but he could feel himself glowing that that's how Davis saw him.

"So we should stay in touch. If you want." Davis was picking popcorn out of the pool instead of looking at him, but Lewis nodded. "Sometimes when things are hard it's because you're in a situation so strange, it seems like no one else has ever been in it before."

"Like being a Black Norweigan American? Or the birth child of Val Halla?"

"Exactly. So you have to find other people who've been there too. Like me and Bex."

"Do I make you feel less alone?" Lewis asked.

Davis looked up from the popcorn and into his eyes. "Well, I think you will, but I only met you today."

"What'd you do before that?"

"Before that," Davis said, "I had to look very, very hard."

2018

Davis could not remember India ever having much to say about Robbie Brighton, but everything she did say was kind of vague and airy and unspecified, as if she couldn't really remember and couldn't be bothered to try. From his self-centered, self-congratulatory, totally besotted perch by her side, Davis had therefore assumed Robbie was either surpassingly boring and tiresome or possibly kind of a jerk. Either seemed like the best explanation for why India had so little to say about someone with what was clearly an outsized role in her life.

Had he been honest with himself—which he wasn't until much, much later—Davis would also have admitted that Robbie had to be all wrong for India so that he, Davis, could be both right for her and different from him: Davis had to be the vanquishing suitor, the happy ending. And if he was really honest with himself, he'd have had to admit that it was necessary to think of Robbie Brighton as boring or boorish because otherwise it had to be all India's fault, the utter failure to avoid what could so easily be avoided.

When it turned out Davis wasn't the happy ending, he started to think maybe he'd been wrong about Robbie Brighton. It seemed clear that the failure to avoid what could so easily be avoided was India's fault after all. In the immediate aftermath, Davis concluded that Robbie Brighton wasn't the bad guy or the good guy or even the entirely-bland-and-unremarkable guy. He was more like a warning shot. And Davis had missed him altogether.

Soon enough, though, he stopped thinking very much about Robbie. He stopped thinking very much about India. He stopped thinking very much about the baby and the Andrews. He didn't *not* think about them. He never forgot. He would never forget. But a year on and a year after that and a year after that, he found himself thinking of the baby only two or three times a day, of India only three or four. He had a whole new life, a job, a new hometown on a new coast, new friends, new girlfriends. As he got to know people, as he exchanged with them details about his life and stories from his past, the broad strokes and the shading work and the filigreed lines, he simply never mentioned the baby, there having been a baby, or India Allwood.

Over those years, he told two serious girlfriends. He told a coworker he was close to. He told an upstairs neighbor who used to come down for beers some nights after they both got home from long days. He told a woman he slept with at a conference and knew he would never see again. And he found that they never understood, no one understood, the same way he hadn't understood when India told him. They had questions he couldn't answer. Some of them were practical questions (what plays had characters who *did* take birth control?) and some were personal (how did he feel now?) and he couldn't answer either one. Which was when it occurred to him: the one person who might understand, who would get the maddening magic of India, the things she made you forget and the things she made it hard to remember, was Robbie Brighton. But it occurred to him idly. He certainly didn't do anything about it.

And then India got famous, which complicated matters. Thoughts of her had dropped down to only a couple times a week maybe, not painful, not even wistful, just lazily passing through his brain. But suddenly her name and face and body and presence were everywhere. Then, on the one hand, he definitely couldn't talk about it. He didn't want to hamstring her burgeoning career with dark secrets from her past, certainly. He didn't want to get dragged into a scandal himself. He couldn't tell anyone because that wasn't the sort of secret you could expect someone to keep. And the extent to which no one understood was ratcheted to such heights now that the air was thin around it.

But on the other hand, he was desperate to talk about it. Not in a gossipy way. More like here he had—was having—this exceedingly strange, all but unique experience, and how often did that happen? Never. New girlfriends, new close coworkers, new upstairs neighbors had taught him that everyone had the same stories, the same heartbreaks, the same near misses and lessons learned, more or less. But no one but Davis had ever loved and lost and had a baby and then given that baby away with Val fucking Halla. Except for one person.

A Google search of Robbie—then Robert, Rob, Bob, Bobby, Bert, Burt—Brighton turned up no one—or rather, it turned up too many someones who could have been anyone. He realized he knew nothing about Robbie, really, none of the useful identifying details that might have helped him narrow down—what he looked like, where he went to college, where he lived, what he did for work—and none of the ephemeral stuff it would have been comforting just to know somehow. He half hoped, half dreaded that Robbie Brighton, wherever he was, would emerge either to ride India's coattails or drag them through the mud by screaming from the rooftops the same story Davis was burying in the backyard. He didn't want that to happen to India, of course, but then at least he'd have found him.

And then, one night, a beer and a half in with his upstairs neighbor, looking out from his balcony at the bay and the bridge and the ocean beyond, a detail he never remembered having known emerged from his brain. Like a cabbage falling off a truck into the middle of the road in front of you, it was just there all of a sudden, whole and clear and green. India and Robbie going to karaoke. Robbie secretly being a good singer. India embarrassed and rueful about this betrayal, especially since what did she expect given Robbie Brighton's father was a professor of musicology, not that musicology meant singing, not that ability to sing was hereditary anyway.

"Nor a betrayal," Davis had allowed at the time.

"I will break up with you immediately if it turns out you can sing," India had retorted.

So Davis reminded her he'd been in his high school musicals and warbled "Something Good" from *Sound of Music* as tunelessly as he could, and she hit him with a pillow, and he said that was as off as he could manage, and she said that song was only in the movie, not in the show, and was therefore apocryphal, and he said that wasn't what "apocryphal" meant, and then they had sex.

What were the odds that the number of Professor Brightons of musicology was low, that finding him would somehow lead to his son? Poor. But, as it turned out, good enough.

It seemed like it would be awkward. It seemed like it would be an impossible email to write. Chances were also quite good, maybe even likely, that

Robbie Brighton didn't want to be contacted, didn't want to talk about it, didn't have anything to say, maybe hadn't considered it since, hadn't given India Allwood or the baby they'd made together another thought since India got on a plane and flew to New York all those years ago.

In the end, Davis had boiled the whole thing down to the truest, simplest statement he could manage.

Dear Robbie Brighton,

You don't know me. My name is Davis Shaw. India Allwood was my college girlfriend. Nine years ago, she and I had a baby who we placed for adoption. It was and remains a hard, strange thing, difficult—and increasingly so—to understand. But I thought you might. Please forgive me if you do not wish to discuss or revisit, which I would certainly understand. If I do not hear from you, I will not contact you again. If you are interested, however, in chatting with a kindred spirit, it's probably me.

Sincerely,
Davis Shaw

FRIDAY

India Allwood's house wasn't the *MTV Cribs* situation Bex would have guessed, but it was still pretty big. There were getting to be a lot of people in it, though, so the kids all moved into the rec room for the night, and in this case, Bex was a kid.

In her sleeping bag, she considered how the house wasn't the only thing about India Allwood that was different from what she'd imagined. Of course she knew *Val Halla* was total fantasy, and of course she also knew what professional hair and makeup and a made-to-fit-you wardrobe could do for your natural face, hair, and body (one of the things Bex's overprotective mother was overprotective about was body image issues), so it's not like she was surprised that India Allwood her birth mother wasn't India Allwood the movie star. It also wasn't like she thought India would have big secrets to reveal and finally Bex would have all her questions answered and know how to treat her dry skin. She knew: use more lotion more often. She also knew: India hadn't wanted to be a parent at sixteen. Who would?

So maybe what was really different from what she'd imagined wasn't India, but *meeting* India. Being the child of a celebrity turned out to suck. There were no red carpet after-parties or private planes or glamorous outfits after all. All there was was you couldn't go anywhere or say anything or have any opinions, and you had to stay a big secret. So any lingering sadness Bex had about almost but not quite being India Allwood's daughter had been squashed. She tried not to be disappointed—it was actually good news because who wanted lingering sadness?—but she was disappointed anyway.

And then there was her brother. Half brother. Surprise half brother. She hadn't been imagining anything about him because she hadn't known he existed, but now that she did, she wasn't alarmed exactly, but you couldn't say she was feeling relaxed. She could already tell he wasn't someone she'd ordinarily hang out with in a million years. The cape, obviously, but he couldn't even look at her, and every time he opened his mouth, something weird came out. She didn't know if she should feel lucky that she hadn't inherited the nerdy, awkward traits her genes apparently carried or whether she had some kind of sisterly obligation to try to help him. She knew lots of girls whose annoying little brothers were geeky and embarrassing, and you couldn't even believe they came from the same family as their beautiful, fun, cool older sisters. She'd just never thought she'd be one of them. And she didn't need surprise geeky-younger-brother energy in her life any more than she needed extra-mom energy.

Dad energy, though, was another matter. She'd been thinking of India all these years, probably because India was famous, so easy to have a fantasy about, and India's face was everywhere, so easy to picture, but what about her biological father? She could not deny she felt disappointed when the man who got out of that reporter's car turned out not to be her bio dad after all. She had to admit it didn't feel great when he said she was the wrong kid. And since her birth father wasn't famous or on TV every week or the subject of eighty billion articles and interviews and fan sites and social media posts, she had no expectations. Which meant she literally could not be disappointed.

"I think families are like flashlights," Fig said.

She was whispering so she wouldn't wake Jack and Lewis, but that wasn't why Bex couldn't understand her. "Huh?"

"It's good to have extra," Fig whisper-explained, "because sometimes they break and you don't want to wait until you need one to find out. Plus, if you have extra, you can risk one on something that's probably not a great idea—like spelunking—and know that if you drop it in a cave or bash it on a rock, it's okay because you have more."

"Jesus, Fig. Which one of us are you planning to bash on a rock?"

"No one," Fig giggled. "I'm just saying Mom's mad now, but I still think calling Lewis was the right thing to do. Sometimes less is more, but not with family. With family, more is more."

"I was just thinking the same thing," Bex was surprised to discover.

"Really?"

"I was thinking about finding Robbie Brighton."

Fig sat up in her sleeping bag. "How?"

"I don't know."

"I've Googled him," Fig whisper-warned. "A lot. I've never found anything."

"Me too," Bex had to admit. "Me neither. But you found me. We found Lewis."

"You're a teenager. And we found out some new things about the Andrews. We can't find out any new things about Robbie Brighton."

"Shit," Bex whispered.

"Shit," Fig agreed.

Then, from out of the darkness, Lewis piped up. "You shouldn't say shit."

"I won't do it again," Fig promised at once. "Please don't tell the FCC."

"No, I meant instead of feeling hopeless," Lewis explained, "you should just go there."

Bex was surprised to hear from him. "You're awake too?"

"Everyone is awake," Jack moaned from underneath his pillow. "You two are damn loud."

"We're whispering," Fig whispered.

"Damn loudly."

"Go where?" said Bex.

"To Robbie Brighton's house," Lewis said.

"I could if I knew where he lived." Were all little brothers this annoying?

"I know where he lives," Lewis said.

"Don't be stupid," said Bex. Then she said, "What do you mean?"

"I know where he lives. In the house behind the bookstore in Seaside, Oregon."

"How could you possibly know that?" Bex was no longer whispering.

"Davis told me."

2019

Robbie—most folks called him Rob these days, he said, but he happily answered to anything—had not gone far. Davis found him in a little beach town in Oregon, only one very long day away if you rented a car and drove up along the coast, which was what Davis did.

In fact, Robbie had been far and wide. He'd left India, donned a backpack, and seen the world, living in tents, hostels, friends of friends' extra rooms, busing, hitchhiking, taking last-minute travel deals to who cared where and volunteer gigs in exchange for room and board. He'd seen the country that way, plus most of Europe and Central and South America and lots of Asia and Africa. In Mozambique, he'd met a fellow American traveler who was taking a gap year before med school. They came home and got married and had five children. Then they got divorced. Now he parented and ran a community center.

"What kind of community center?" Davis asked the first time they met. They sat on Robbie's back porch drinking tea and looking over his garden, then the scraggled grass, then a wide beach to the ocean out beyond. It was January, chilly but clear, the beach not crowded but not empty either, the sun setting already at four. Davis could not make out which of the silhouetted beach walkers were Robbie's five kids and two dogs, but Robbie seemed unconcerned.

"Emphasis on community," Robbie said. "Or, hell, on center too, I guess. We're matchmakers really. We pair people who need warm clothes with people cleaning out their closets. Old folks who want company with parents who need a break from their toddlers. Teenagers who need math help with retired engineers."

"Wow," said Davis. "You founded this place? Just saw a need and filled it?"

"Saw a lot of needs and filled them with each other, more like. Half a dozen stones, giant heap of dead birds. Ugh, sorry."

"Why?"

"That was a gross analogy. I would never kill a bird."

"I never thought of you as a hippie." Davis blew on his tea, watched the steam swirl around his hands in the cold air.

"A hippie?" Robbie laughed.

"Vegetarian, tea on the back porch, socialist-community-center gig."

Robbie laughed harder. "Big brood of muddy, wandering children and dogs," he added.

"Cottage behind the town bookstore with a garden and a view of the sea."

"I am a Zen hen," Robbie conceded. "It's funny you've been thinking of me at all. I didn't even know you existed. But it's like you picked up where I left off. Was she angry?"

"India?"

"Yeah. She was so angry when she left."

"You broke her heart."

"Other way around," said Robbie.

"She didn't know that, I don't think."

"Lucky her."

"She was pissed you could sing," Davis confided.

Robbie laughed again. Even a decade and a half later, Davis could see why sixteen-year-old India had chosen him. He was easy, kind, and wide open.

"I'm so happy for her," Robbie said. "How many sixteen-year-olds who swear they're going to grow up and be actors actually do? How many sixteen-year-olds who swear they're going to grow up and do anything actually do? What did you want to grow up and do when you were sixteen?"

Davis frowned. "I don't remember. You?"

"Live happily ever after with India Allwood."

"And you're still happy for her?"

"What do you mean?"

"You're not . . . mad? Jealous? Resentful? Something?"

"Of course not. It's been years. Years and years. Are you?"

"Not exactly," Davis hedged.

"But?"

"I'm not mad at her. I certainly don't begrudge her her fame. But I do have . . . mixed feelings."

"Free-floating anger?"

"I'm not angry at her, but maybe I'm angry in her general direction? It's different for me."

"Why?"

"Because she'd been through it already once with you. She'd been warned. So she shouldn't have ended up there again. You guys were so young."

"Whereas you two were what when you were together? Twenty? Still pretty young."

"Old enough to be responsible. And experienced enough to know what it felt like to be pregnant and not want to be a parent and have to bring a whole other human into the world and then give it away."

"How did it feel?"

"It felt like shit. How'd it feel for you?"

"Confusing," Robbie admitted. "India, though . . ."

"India loved it. I know. She told me. Over and over, she told me how great it was and how happy you'd made Camille."

"That part was true."

"What part wasn't?"

"None of it. It was all true. That was how she felt."

"But it wasn't how you felt?"

"Maybe not quite. But it was her choice, you know? It had to be hers."

"You wanted an abortion?" Davis wrapped cold fingers around his mug.

"I didn't want anything. Or, really, I wanted everything." Robbie got up to get the kettle, poured hot water over their spent tea bags. "I wanted an abortion, and also I wanted to marry her and raise our baby together and be in love forever. I wanted always to be a teenager and also to grow old with her. I wanted to go back in time and prevent her from ever getting pregnant. I wanted to make it all go away. I wanted never to have met her. I wanted to die. I wanted everything. She didn't get to choose because she was the girl or the mother or the body in question. She got to choose because she was the one who could figure out what she wanted." He paused to take a sip, then asked, "Do you watch her show?"

"Yeah," Davis admitted. "You?"

"Oh yeah. Never miss it. But I think that's what makes her such a good actor."

"What?"

"Her ability to figure it out. She wanted to be onstage, but she couldn't sing. She wanted to get into college, but the guidance counselor wouldn't help her. She wanted acting and New York, but she loved me and was having a baby. She figured it out. It's like she could embody all the possibilities in her imagination, and then she didn't have to guess because they were all there before her."

"I don't think that's what makes her a good actor," Davis said.

"Why not?"

"I acted with her."

"You're an actor?"

"Not really. I dabbled in college. Opposite India."

Robbie grinned at once. "That must have been quite a thing."

"It was." Davis knew then that he had been right, right to come, right in his guess that in all of time and space Robbie Brighton was the one person who would understand. "Fighting with her onstage in front of the whole world. Being in love with her onstage in front of the whole world."

"Getting to stand next to her while she did her thing," Robbie added. "So what is it, then, the key to her success? Just raw talent?"

"She's not figuring it out. She's not anything. She disappears. She's just totally replaced by the character she's playing."

"I can't imagine India ceding herself to anyone, even someone pretend."

"Because they weren't pretend to her." Davis shook his head.

"What do you mean?"

"That's what happened. We were doing a gender-swapped *Much Ado About Nothing*. Benedick didn't take birth control, so India didn't either."

Davis could hear the bitterness in his voice still. Robbie raised his eyebrows briefly and said nothing.

"Does that sound hard to believe to you?" Davis pressed.

Robbie sipped his weak tea and considered for long moments. "I haven't known her for so many years."

"Right, but the years in question weren't that long after you did know her. You'd think she'd have learned from her previous experience, her experience with you, and I think she did, but maybe she learned the wrong thing."

"Wrong thing?"

"That she could get pregnant and it would be okay. Fun even. A mitzvah. A good deed. A gift."

"It was okay," Robbie pointed out, then corrected himself. "Is." Then added, "Isn't it?"

"I'm not sure." Davis had his chin in his hand. "I'm not sure I'm over it."

He wasn't explaining this well, but then this was why he'd come, so that he wouldn't have to.

Robbie nodded. "Maybe you never get over India Allwood."

"And your baby? Rebecca?"

Robbie looked startled for a moment, surprised that Davis knew her name or maybe at the pronoun. *Your.* "I think about her."

Davis exhaled a cloud of white breath. The temperature was dropping with the sun. "How?" He wasn't even sure what he was asking.

But Robbie seemed to get it anyway. "I think it must be like how babies dream, you know?"

Davis did not know. He had no babies. He did not know how they dreamed.

"I mean, babies dream. You can see them dreaming. But what could they be dreaming of? They have no memories because they're brand-new. Never mind they don't have anxiety yet about forgetting to prep for their history final. Never mind they don't have houses yet in which to find extra rooms. They can't even be dreaming about people because they don't know any yet. They can't be picturing anything because they haven't seen anything. But they must be dreaming something. That's how I think of Rebecca. I can't picture her because I don't know what she looks like. I can't hear her voice. I have exactly one memory of her, and she wasn't even a whole day old yet. So, to answer your question, how I think of her is with love. With frequency. With curiosity, I guess. And very vaguely."

"You've never Googled her?" Davis asked. "Social media or whatever?"

"I haven't. It seemed—seems—creepy I guess, stalking a little girl online. You?"

"No." Davis shook his head. "India felt strongly about doing a closed adoption."

"I remember."

"And I guess I felt like, I don't know, the least I could do was just let everyone move on."

"Move on?"

"From the trauma, the shame."

"Was it traumatic? Or shameful?"

Davis raised his eyes to Robbie's. "Maybe only to me?"

"That's what I realized too. It took a while, but eventually I noticed there wasn't anything to be angry about. Rebecca got a great home, a great life. Camille got a great baby. India and I got our lives back to normal. What was there to be mad about? Or traumatized or ashamed?"

Davis knew the answer was meant to be "Nothing. Of course nothing! Why did I never see it before?" But unfortunately it wasn't. "Did you know even then . . ." he began, and then stopped, tried again. "Or, I don't know, does none of this surprise you?"

They were quiet for a while, watching the ocean, the darkening sky, before Robbie said, "None of what?"

Davis took a deep, cold breath. "Did you somehow suspect India would go forth and keep making babies for other people? Was this thing already in her?"

"Fertility?"

"Benevolent fertility. Fertility with an inclination toward charitable giving. A proclivity not to care or not to take care on this particular front."

"I just thought we were teenagers and kinda stupid," Robbie admitted.

"Yeah." Davis tried not to be disappointed. He didn't know what it would have meant anyway if Robbie said yes, absolutely, he had seen this coming, had pictured India accidentally getting pregnant dozens of times to give dozens of babies to dozens of needy would-be parents.

"I don't know about you"—Robbie looked over at him, then back out at the ocean—"but when I was twenty?"

"Yeah?"

"I was still pretty stupid."

Eventually the kids came back, cold and sandy and loud and happy. While Robbie made homegrown tomatoes into homemade sauce and the kids set the table and told their father about their adventures on the beach, Davis wondered what the proportionate response was to getting pregnant with India Allwood but not keeping her or the baby. Five children or no children? He could see the argument for either one. He begged off dinner and said good-bye. Robbie walked him out to his car in the driveway and did not pressure him to stay, did not say he must be hungry and should for sure join them for dinner, did not note he had a twelve-hour drive in front of him and should, at the least, wait till morning. What he said was "Keep in touch." The two men hugged goodbye, to the surprise of both, and Davis got in his car and drove through the night all the way home.

But they did. They did keep in touch.

SATURDAY

Fig was panicking.

Bex was packing and unpacking and repacking her backpack.

"Why can't you just ask Davis for Robbie Brighton's email?" Fig could hear that she was whining but couldn't do anything about it. "Or even his phone number? You could text him like you text me."

"Because Davis would tell my mother"—Bex took her sweatshirt out of the backpack and tied it around her waist instead, then stuffed an extra T-shirt in—"and she wouldn't let me go."

"But if you had his email and his phone number you wouldn't have to go."

"I want to go. It'll be a grand gesture. A surprise."

"Some people don't like surprises." Fig spoke from experience.

"Maybe not." Bex filled the head part of a baseball cap with two under-pants and two pairs of socks, then shoved that in too. "But if it's a surprise, he can't say no."

"No?"

"No, he never thinks about me. No, he doesn't want to be in touch. No, he doesn't want to know anything about me or for me to know anything about him."

Fig thought about how it would have been if Bex had said no, if she'd learned who Fig was but ignored her DMs and texts anyway. It would have been like Fig had moved to a cold, dark, drippy cave all alone forever. "Okay, I get that. But why do you have to go now?"

"Why not?"

A question Fig could answer! "Your mom's already mad at you."

"Exactly, so I might as well consolidate. This way I won't have to piss her off again some time in the future."

"But now she's on alert. She'll catch you."

"But not till I'm already there."

"But she'll be paying attention to your ride app this time." Fig noticed they were both full of buts. "But she'll be paying attention to your credit card and notice if you buy a plane ticket."

"Which is why I'll be using cash. And taking a bus."

"But we'll tell." Fig was sorry, but it was true. It wasn't a threat but an admission.

"What!" Bex looked mad and hurt. But mostly mad.

"Not on purpose. At least, I won't tell on purpose. Jack won't either." She didn't really know Lewis well enough to say. "But as soon as they notice you're gone, they'll make us tell them everything. You know they will. They'll catch up to you before you even get to the bus station."

"You'll say you don't know anything."

"They'll know we're lying."

"Shit." Bex stopped packing and put her hands on her hips and her bottom lip between her teeth. Fig could see she wanted to argue but knew there was no point because Fig was merely stating facts. Their parents would know they knew, and they would know if they lied, and then they would know everything.

"Maybe you should ask permission," Fig suggested quietly.

"Oh sure. 'Hey Mom, is it okay if I take a two-day bus ride to sneak-attack Robbie Brighton?'"

"But then you wouldn't have to take a bus," Fig said, even quieter. "Or sneak."

"Or . . ." Bex frowned, thinking. "The three of you could come with me."

"No," Fig breathed.

"Yes."

"We'll get in trouble."

"To review, we're already in trouble."

"We'll get caught. Even faster than if you went by yourself."

"Not if we travel incognito."

"But we don't have a cognito. Or any money."

Bex rolled her eyes in her eye sockets and her fingers on her temples. "Let me think."

She did, but not for very long.

"Okay, good news. The plan doesn't really have to change. It was a stealth mission already. We don't have to get all the way there before they realize we're gone because you guys will be with me, so there won't be anyone around to interrogate. We just have to make it as far as the bus. Go get the boys, and I'll explain everything."

Bex's stealth plan was no phones (which could be traced, she said), no credit cards (same reason), no ATMs (ditto), no cars (borrowing, renting, ordering, or getting in any, which meant at least Fig could take hitchhiking off her list of worries), no luggage bigger than a backpack (which meant yes to extra under-wear but no to a real change of clothes because they also had to carry food). The bus left from the station downtown super early in the morning, but they would go in the middle of the night tonight so no one would notice them leave. Fig had a lot of objections, but Bex had answers for every single one of them.

"How will we get to the bus without a car?"

"We'll walk to the bus stop."

"No one walks anywhere in LA."

"So they won't be expecting it. Besides, we'll take a bus to the bus. We only have to walk to the first one."

"How will we buy bus tickets?"

"We're going to borrow my mom's ATM card and get cash here before we go."

"How will we find our way without our phones?"

"We'll look up directions before we leave and then erase our search histories."

"What about Covid?"

"We'll wear masks."

"What will we do about the fact that our parents are going to kill us?"

"Oh, there's nothing we can do about that." Bex waved her hand like this was no big deal. "We just have to do what we have to do before they find us."

"Let's take a vote," Jack said.

He barely got his whole sentence out before Bex's hand shot up in the air. It was her plan, though, so of course she was going to vote for it. Then Jack put his hand up too. Maybe he was trying to look cool. Maybe a stealthy bus trip sounded fun to him. Fig looked at Lewis. Lewis looked at Fig. She could tell he wanted her to vote no so he could vote no. That was what Fig wanted too. But Fig was often scared about things Mandela insisted she didn't need to be scared about, and maybe this was one of those. But Bex was her sort-of sister. *Their* sort-of sister. Two buts. So Fig slowly raised her hand too. And then Lewis did—had to do—the same. It was not a fair election.

Fig could not tell for sure but suspected and hoped the plan was stupid, and her mother would realize what they'd done right away and pick them up from the side of the road when they were still within sight of the house. But it was also possible the plan was actually stupidly simple: it was easy to walk a mile to a bus, easy to ride a bus to another bus, easy to ride on that bus for one day, five hours, and forty-seven minutes, easy to walk from the bus stop to the bookstore and knock on the door of the house behind it. Maybe there were kids all over the world sneaking away from their mothers to go somewhere they wouldn't be allowed if they asked. It sounded like one of the fantasy-adventure books her mother read them before bed. But it felt more like one step they could do then another then another, all the way to Seaside.

She left an index card for her mother. In her very neatest handwriting, she wrote:

Dear Mom,

1. I'm really sorry.
2. Don't be mad.
3. We'll be home soon.
4. I love you.

Love, Fig

She wasn't one hundred percent sure about number three. Bex said nothing about getting home, only about getting there, which made Fig think Bex would let her call her mother and tell her everything eventually. She knew her mother would be mad, even though Fig asked her not to be, but she also knew she'd come to Oregon to get her right away.

But when Bex saw it, she ripped Fig's index card into pieces. And not so she could celebrate.

"Why did you do that?" Fig thought maybe Bex wasn't her sister in any way, blood or parental or familial or anything, because sisters loved you and never tortured you on purpose or destroyed your important documents and belongings. "You think she's not going to notice we're missing unless she reads it?"

"We need the head start." Bex stuffed the pieces of index card into her pocket. "If you don't tell them we've left, it might be hours till they even notice we're gone."

India said goodnight to the kids, but it was less like bedtime routine and more like hosting a party. She had a brief old pang of wishing she were the sort of mom who could stand in the doorframe, backlit by the hallway, and sing a lullaby that would simultaneously win the admiration of children and put them soundly to sleep. Instead she thanked them for not grousing about the crowded conditions, found Fig an extra pillow since she'd relinquished hers to Lewis and was using a towel, wished them all pleasant dreams, and turned out the light. It was probably too early for a sixteen-year-old to go to bed, but she heard no complaints. It had been a hard week for all of them. It was no surprise the kids were as exhausted as the adults.

"So," she said when she got back downstairs. "Drinking?"

Three-quarters of the way through his second glass of wine, Drew said, "You're like the old lady who swallowed a fly."

"Don't tell an actress she's like an old lady," Andy advised from the corner of his mouth.

"You swallowed execs because of pro-lifers. You clashed with pro-lifers when Davis showed up. Davis showed up when Bex came to your house—"

"You had to grouse, when she came to your house," Andy chimed in.

"She came to your house when you talked to that journalist."

"Not a journalist," India said.

"You talked to that . . . woman when you upset adoptees. You upset adoptees when you blew off hard issues."

"They cried into their tissues, when you blew off their issues," Andy added.

"But they don't know why I swallowed the fly," India said, "the reason I made the movie in the first place."

"Me neither," said Camille, "since you didn't like the script."

"Because I am sick to death of the miracle of life." India waved out the window with her glass. "Everyone's always on about it, but it's pretty common for a miracle. It's being performed right this second by the grass in the yard. Anything that happens to every species that ever was or will be is probably not all that miraculous. Whereas adoption isn't rare, certainly, but it's rarer, and no one ever talks about the miraculous part."

"Because it's not a miracle," Andy said. "Trust me: I suffered a decade of Sunday school. Adoption's great, but it's not miraculous. For one thing, we all chose it, and miracles aren't chosen, more like visited upon you."

"Not the kids." Davis looked down at his wine like it was to blame for his saying this out loud. "They didn't choose it."

"No," Camille agreed. "But that's true for all kids. Kids don't choose their parents even if they're born to them."

"Plus"—Davis was still talking to his wine—"miracles are good things, all upside. There's no loss in a miracle."

Because of course he hadn't chosen adoption, either. India knew this, had always known it. Selecting from a list of options you don't want isn't a choice. Nor is going along with someone else's choice just because she has the right to one, or just because you're mad at her, or just because you love her.

But Andy said, "Have you even read the Bible? Miracles are complicated as fuck. That's not how they put it, but all sorts of shit gets lost."

"That's what you should have said to that journalist." Drew pointed a chip at India. "Miracles are complicated as fuck. Just because adoption isn't all sunshine and light for all parties all the time doesn't mean it shouldn't be celebrated."

"I mean, jeez," said Andy, "look at Easter."

"Easter?" Camille was winding and unwinding the corkscrew.

"We celebrate the miracle of Easter, and big parts of that whole situation really sucked for all the key players."

"Joseph!" Drew banged his fist on the table. "There's another one."

"Another what?" said Camille.

"Jewish adoptive dad. Just like me."

Not that they seemed to need it, but India went to the kitchen to grab another bottle of wine and some snacks. Davis followed her in.

"I could have sworn there was more food in here," she called from inside the pantry. "Are potato chips less weird with salsa or cheese?"

"They've had enough wine they won't care what you feed them," Davis said, but she emerged from the pantry with one jar of olives and one of peanut butter. "Never mind. No one's ever been that drunk."

"I have twelve boxes of graham crackers in there but nothing to serve adults."

"You didn't predict company this week."

"I didn't predict anything about this week."

"Not even Val Halla could have predicted this week," he said. "How was the meeting really?"

"Bullshit. Posturing. Wall-to-wall absurdity. But really pretty scary."

He raised one eyebrow. "I mean, what's the worst that can happen?"

"I could lose my job."

"You're Val. No one's ever even heard of these execs. You can do *Val Halla* without them. They can't do it without you."

"Sure they can. They could have a sorcerer transmute Val's face. They could have her survive a fight with a dragon but be left unrecognizable. She could go through a time portal that spits her out in a new body. They replace actors all the time."

"But you're so good."

She understood that this was meant to be comforting but also that he had no idea what he was talking about. "Trust me, they haven't noticed."

"That *Val Halla* is an enormous, groundbreaking, revenue-raining hit?"

"No, they've noticed that. They just don't think it has anything to do with me."

"Who else would it have to do with?"

"Them." She threw her arms wide. "Their business savvy and creative acumen and industry insight and risky but brilliant decision-making. And as if that weren't bad enough, part of what they think they're so smart about is shit like this. They'd fire me because they're pissed. But they'd also fire me because they think I'm costing the network advertising dollars. Or they don't think that, but they think they can get more advertising dollars by pretending they do."

"So you'll go do some other show."

"It's not that easy. Actors who get fired for this kind of thing don't work again. Well, actresses anyway."

"Because they disagree with your opinions on abortion and adoption?" He sounded incredulous.

"It's not my opinions." India shook her head—not like no; like trying to dislodge something. "It's the fact that I have opinions. It's not that I got in trouble. It's that having gotten in trouble, I wasn't sorry enough. They'd like me contrite and quiet."

Davis raised his other eyebrow. "Have they met you?"

She laughed because she knew he was teasing her, but she also knew he wasn't, not entirely. "I'm not sorry to them. But I'm sorry to you."

"I didn't mean—" he began.

"I'm sorry about all the loss in your miracles."

He came around the island and took the peanut butter and the olives out of her hands and set them on the counter. "Love is pretty common too, you know." His voice was full, more rasp than whisper. "Maybe not as common as birth but not exactly rare. And it's complicated and messy and difficult to talk about." His hands were on her hair, her face, the sides of her neck. "But you were as close to miraculous as I ever had in my life."

India swallowed. "Are," she corrected. She might have been laughing a little or crying a little. It was hard to say. "And adoption's not why you lost me, you know. Lewis wasn't why."

"No." He wiped her eyes. "I know. That's not what I meant."

"And you know what else?"

He kissed her like he didn't care what else. He kissed her like her life wasn't falling apart and she didn't have a living room full of company or a house full of children. Her many children. All their children. It felt closer to miracle than loss, but she was older now and knew there could be both, knew miracle and loss were swings not seesaws. They went down as well as up, yes, back as well as forth, but in tandem, up together and down together, or at least not always in opposition. More of one usually just meant more of the other too.

When they stopped kissing she found, right where she'd left it, the notch in his chest where her forehead fit perfectly. He rested his chin in her hair.

"What else?" he asked finally, and she remembered the feel of his words in her head.

It took her a beat to recall what she'd wanted to say. "'Lost' doesn't mean gone. It means lost. Like you don't know where you are or how to get where you're going. Like you're wandering in the woods."

"That doesn't sound great either."

And not just in her head. She remembered the feel of him in her chest and in her hands in the small of his back and in her shoulders where his arms held them and in her legs, shaking a little at the knees and ankles.

"Maybe not," she said, "but it's completely different. Opposite."

"How do you figure?"

Reluctantly, she drew her head away so she could meet his eyes. "'Gone' means gone. 'Lost' means given time you can figure it out, find your way, come out the other side."

They stood and looked at each other some more long moments. Then she went upstairs to check on all their children.

On a map it looked like Oregon was up, but the bus stop was down down down the hill. Bex was right that four kids dragging suitcases down the side of Sunset Boulevard in the middle of the night would have looked suspicious, but four kids with backpacks just looked like they were going for a hike. Or they would have, if it hadn't been dark and you could see them.

It was past their bedtime, so Fig should have felt sleepy, but instead she felt scared. She could hear an owl. It might have been following them. (If a wild animal followed you, was it actually called hunting?) She tried not to think about other animals that might be following/hunting them in the night: coyotes, mountain lions, raccoons, bats. All were terrifying. Why was the day—when someone could help you—all bunnies and squirrels, and the night—when no one could—full of animals with giant teeth and claws and fangs? Still, the walk to the first bus stop was easier than she thought it would be, and the bus came and they got on it, and no one stopped them or took their picture.

Bex walked to the back of the bus, which was practically empty, but instead of sitting, she wrapped herself around a pole, leaning so far back her hair was at risk of touching the sticky floor, hanging first with one hand, then the other, switching back and forth so Fig worried she would fall in between but always catching herself just in time. "It's all downhill from here," Bex sang, almost upside down.

"It was all downhill already," said Jack.

"No, it means the hard part's over, and everything will be smooth and easy from here on out."

But Fig thought it could also mean it would be worse from here on out, like the best part of the day was the part where she was in her very own home with her very own mother and it was all downhill from there. She watched out the window, and though it was dark out and she'd never been on a city bus before, she was still in her neighborhood. They passed their grocery store and their coffee shop, closed with empty parking lots and dim lights inside but still recognizable, still theirs. They passed their second- and fourth-favorite carryout places and their school and their library and the place with the best frozen yogurt toppings (though not the best frozen yogurt, which her mother said was just one of those things). So far, everything was familiar and ordinary, but already, nothing felt either one of those things anymore. Maybe it was because she was looking at it out a bus window instead of from the back seat of her mother's car. But probably it was because they weren't stopping here, and this strangeness was as familiar as this trip was going to get. It was all downhill from here.

When they got off at the big bus stop downtown, it was only eighteen miles from her house. If she found a pay phone and could make it work, her mother could be there to pick her up in less than half an hour. It was the middle of the night so there wouldn't even be traffic. Fig knew that, but she didn't believe it because the bus station was closer to a *Val Halla* set than to home: spooky and too lit up and mostly empty. The chairs were bolted together in rows of webbed metal benches flaking blue paint onto the dingy floor. There were vending machines with the kinds of drinks and snacks they weren't allowed to have and winding ropes to make organized lines of people who weren't there. There was a couple sleeping on a pile of backpacks and suitcases. There were a few people staring at their phones. It was not clean, and it did not smell nice. Fig took Jack's hand, and he let her. Lewis wrapped his cape around himself. Bex looked at them like she wanted to tell them all to stop doing what they were doing, but instead she said, "Wait here while I buy tickets." Fig thought someone would say, "I can't sell tickets for a one-day, five-hour, forty-seven-minute bus trip to Oregon to four kids," but maybe Bex looked old enough and they wouldn't ask who she was buying them for. Then she went to a machine to buy the tickets anyway, and Fig's last hope that someone would notice she was not where she should be and call her mother vanished. In only three hours and sixteen minutes, the sun would come up and their new bus would leave and they would all have to be on it.

ndia's first thought was *Don't scream. You'll wake the kids.* But there were no kids to wake, not in the rec room where she'd left them, not in any of the other rooms either.

She flew downstairs. "The kids aren't here." Not yelling. Not yet.

"What's that quote?" Drew laughed and got up to pour her more wine. "'There was never a child so lovely but his mother was glad to get him to sleep.'"

"Not sleeping. Gone." India was pulling on shoes, though she didn't know why because she didn't know where to go look. She watched everyone's faces fall to ashen panic.

"Call them." Camille already had her phone out, and current-India gave sixteen-year-old India silent thanks for choosing someone so competent and in control and good in a crisis.

But the answering ring came from upstairs. They all ran up to Fig's room and found Bex's phone on the desk. Lewis's and Jack and Fig's too.

"Shit," said Drew. An understatement.

"It's a big house." Camille spread her arms wide. "Lots of grounds outside too. Let's look around before we panic."

"Too late," said India.

"They're not toddlers."

"Doesn't mean they can't get in trouble."

"Of course not," Camille said. "But it does mean they didn't fall in the pool and drown. They're not somewhere sticking their fingers in light sockets.

Maybe they're playing a game. Hide-and-seek or something. Or holed up watching a movie with headphones on."

There followed ten minutes that felt like ten hours of calling their names, looking in every room and closet, under every bed and pile of blankets, around every corner and behind every door, the bottom of the pool too, just in case, God forbid, the driveway even though India knew they would never, never go out the front. There were no kids in any of those places. Then India remembered the snacks she swore she'd shopped for but couldn't find and felt her stomach drop. "They might have packed food."

"Why?" Davis said.

Everyone shook their heads. No one knew. Or no one wanted to say.

"Where would four kids go in the middle of the night?" Andy was pale as paper.

"Good question," said Camille, "but not the first question. Do they have any money with them?"

"My kids are ten," said India. "They don't have any money."

"Lewis has our account on his phone, but without it . . ." Andy trailed off.

They all looked at Camille. Of all the kids, Bex would be the one with money. Maybe, India prayed, electronically accessed and therefore traceable money. But Camille flipped over her daughter's phone to show her credit and ATM cards snugly in their pockets on the back of the case. But then, "Wait! Hold on." She tapped at her own phone for a minute. Then all the blood left her face. India watched Camille's irritation tinged with minor concern turn to panic tinged with nothing because the panic took up everything. *Welcome to hell*, she thought, and then *About time you got here*. "She withdrew seven hundred and fifty dollars, cash, from my account earlier today."

India collapsed to the sofa with a huff, all the air leaving her lungs and none coming back in.

"Could she be buying drugs?" Drew asked hopefully.

"No," said Camille, "definitely not."

"Can you see her search history?"

"She's cleared it. I can see that she didn't order a car. I can see that she hasn't charged anything to the credit card. I can see"—Camille opened her hands helplessly—"where her phone is."

"Do you have a driver?" Davis asked India.

"No, I don't have a driver. Who do you—"

"A car service?"

"I mean, sometimes Production sends one. Or Ajax if he wants me to—"

"Call him!" everyone said together.

Ajax was not happy to hear from her. ("Earth, wind, and fire, India, it's one a.m.!") When she explained why she was calling, though, she heard him wake up, sit up, turn the lights on. He had heard nothing from her kids. Henri hadn't either. "We would have called you," he said.

"I know."

"I'm on your side, always."

"I know, I know."

"I'm sure they're fine, India. But call us when you find them, no matter what time it is."

"Ask the people at the end of your driveway," Drew said.

"What people?"

"The press or the paparazzi or whatever."

"They don't live there," India said. "I'm sure they went home hours ago. Besides . . ."

"What," Camille insisted.

"Fig and Jack know how to sneak out the back. They know how to evade the smears and anyone else. They know how to be invisible."

"Look." Davis ran his hand over his eyes. "They don't have a car. They didn't order a car. No one's going to rent them one. No one's going to sell plane tickets to four kids with no adults, no IDs, and a handful of cash. So they can't have gotten far. Maybe they went for a walk."

"They didn't go for a walk," India snapped. "It's the middle of the night. There's nowhere within walking distance to go. They're not out for a stroll. Fig doesn't like the dark. Neither of them likes getting in trouble. These kids didn't just leave on their own."

"Are you saying they've been . . ." Davis wouldn't finish.

"Kidnapped?" India shrieked. "You think they've been kidnapped?"

"Well, they're not here. So if they didn't leave on their own, what are the possibilities?"

"We've been here all night. The front door didn't open. The back door leads to the pool and a gated backyard. There's a significant security system. No one could get in here without our knowing."

"If the kids know how to sneak in and out," Davis said, "someone else might too."

"They live here. A stranger wouldn't—"

"A friend of theirs? A friend's parent? Someone with a grudge? Those pro-lifers, maybe?"

"I don't think they're pro-kidnapping. And I don't think they could mastermind making a sandwich, never mind an abduction."

"Someone from your past?" Davis said.

The man—the *monster*—who'd tried to take Jack and Fig from school! He had never been identified, let alone arrested, tried, and locked far away from her children.

But Camille interrupted. "Can we please be rational?" India thought of her third-grade teacher correcting anyone who said, "Can I go to the bathroom?" with "Let's hope you can, but you may not." The Andrews genuinely did not look like "rational" was a thing they were able to be anymore. India knew how they felt.

"There's food missing." Camille counted off on her fingers. "The cash. Bex's sandals are still here, and her makeup, but her backpack is gone, her running shoes, her sweatshirt, her Mariners hat. You don't pack for a kidnapping. And you don't snatch four kids from the house without five adults noticing."

The Andrews were nodding and nodding because it was all true, and it wasn't good, but it was better than the alternative. India was shaking and shaking her head, not because she disagreed with Camille's points, but because the inevitable conclusion was just as hard to believe and nearly as heart-sinking.

"They left," Camille concluded. "Willingly, not unpreparedly, and seemingly on foot. Which means the question is twofold: Where are they going? How are they getting there?"

They all looked blankly around at one another.

Then India knew. "Bex wanted to see the Hollywood sign. Remember? I bet they went to see sunrise at the sign."

Camille and the Andrews stayed at the house in case the kids came home.

India and Davis drove to the Hollywood sign, scanning the sidewalks and road shoulders and parking lots all along the way, because Jack and Fig were good at hiding from smears and the public but less good at hiding from their mother. It was a shitty plan, but it was better than no plan, and it was better, if only marginally, than overreacting—assuming that was what it proved to be—by calling the cops and having them descend in a storm of officers and sirens and smears and gawkers on two kids with no experience facing this sort of circus and two more who were deep down afraid, variously, of crowds, noises, surprises, melees, and, especially, cops and sirens.

It was also better to be doing something than nothing.

Never mind he was probably the love of her life and definitely the father of a child she had brought into the world, India had never been in a car with Davis before. One of the many ways New York was better than LA was you didn't have to drive, especially if you were a college student. But a car is small, warm and close, dark and intimate, and they found themselves alone again, again. Not alone in another room. Not alone downstairs while her kids were asleep upstairs. Actually alone, together, for the first time in twelve years. If she hadn't been so distraught, she would have been distraught.

They drove in silence for a while, focused on seeing anything there was to see. Eventually she said, "It's not always like this, you know."

"What?"

"Frenetic and terrifying and full of drama."

"No, what's not always like this?"

"Parenting."

"No," he agreed. "Of course not."

"But there's always the threat of this, which is maybe worse." She wasn't sure why she needed him to understand—or why she needed him to understand now—except for how narrowly they'd missed doing this together. She didn't want him smugly relieved he'd dodged the bullet that was her, them, family. But she didn't want him cavalier about the gun either. "Everything's fine. Everything's *great*. But you're always aware that at any moment, with no warning at all and no way to head it off, you might have to throw clothes over your pajamas and head out into the night, scared out of your mind, to battle whatever demons have come. It's always this serrated edge of scared for them and because of them, angry at them for getting into trouble and angry at whatever trouble had the audacity to get into it with your kids."

They checked all the viewpoints for the Hollywood sign and then checked them all again, but they were empty. It had been a long shot, but it had also been their only shot, and she didn't know what to do next. She reversed out of the last lot and headed toward home.

His face was turned away from her, searching the predawn light. "That's what I was trying to say too."

"When?"

"Back at the house. About loss. Not parenting is hard, but it's not hard every day. It's hard, but only on one side of the coin."

"Parenting isn't hard every day, either. You just never know which ones till after bedtime."

He nodded in her peripheral vision. "Not parenting is the opposite, I think. It's quiet, but not like peaceful, more like . . . haunted."

The feeling that washed over her was part memory, part something else, for it was always like this with Davis, the wonder that all the unutterable things were things he understood. She remembered the summer of maybe-Rebeccas, all those little girls who might have been the one who might have been hers. She considered the hole Bex had cratered in her life this week. In addition to everything else, she'd killed sixteen years of maybe-Rebeccas, wiped them out en masse like the dinosaurs, ushering in a new age.

"When we made the decision we made," Davis said carefully, "I was half sure it was the right choice, half terrified I'd regret it forever. But in fact, it's been neither. Or maybe it's been both. I was worried it would be too sad, knowing there's this kid out there who's secretly mine, but it's not that. That kid's too real and he isn't mine. It's knowing there's this *life* out there that's secretly mine, not out there in New Jersey, out there in another timeline, another version of my life."

"Our," India corrected. That life was impossible for her to mourn, though, impossible for her even to imagine, because Jack and Fig weren't in it. "Anyway, life is full of those, right? Other versions? Roads not traveled? Not to be a Zen hen."

"Yeah but—" Davis began. And then he stopped. Hard stopped.

"What?" She took her eyes off the road to take in his face. "Did you see something? Davis?"

"I don't know where the kids are," he said, so slowly she wanted to reach into his mouth and yank the words out, so fast he had fired her every nerve before he finished speaking. "But I think I know where they're going."

SUNDAY

At first Fig was relieved because the big bus was more like an airplane than the city bus had been, its tall seats in twos with tray tables and headrests and a place to put your bag overhead, but it smelled worse and came with none of the reassuring aspects of an airplane, such as adults whose job was to make sure you were safe.

"It's weird how no one recognizes you two," Bex said. Lots of eyes roved over them—four kids traveling alone—then slid away. "If we were with your mom . . ."

She trailed off, but Fig didn't need her to finish. If they were with their mom, everyone would recognize her and Jack. If people were paying more attention, they might recognize any of them, really. Bex had posted those videos. The smears took photos they weren't supposed to. But no one did pay attention.

Five minutes after they pulled out of the station, Fig already didn't see anything familiar anymore as they made their slow way out of the city, high above the sidewalks, looking down on the tops of people's heads. There were lots of red lights and streets that parked cars made almost too skinny to get a bus through. Every time they stopped, the brakes shrieked like something had leaped out at them from behind a bush. Every time they started again, the brakes sighed like letting go was too hard and you were being unreasonably demanding. Fig thought she saw her mother's car.

Every car Fig saw, she thought might be her mother.

But once they were on the highway, very quickly what should have been a grand adventure became the most boring adventure in the world. Bex let Fig have the window, but all there was to see was miles and miles of the same thing: cars and trucks and billboards, then brown hills and green hills and fields, then trees and trees and trees. Hours went by, and they were no closer to anything. It was like floating in an ocean in the dark. It was like being dead. Fig had come close enough to know.

The biggest difference, though, between alive and dead—she guessed, anyway—was that dead people did not get hungry or thirsty or need to pee, and the four of them did all three. The bathroom on the bus was too scary to use—too small, too smelly, too much risk you might fall in, a risk which even Bex admitted was legit—but the bus made a rest stop every few hours, and they quickly learned that if they hardly ate or drank they could wait. This solved two problems—the bus bathroom and running out of food—but brought up new ones.

There were lots of mirrors in rest-stop bathrooms, many more than in your house bathroom, many more even than in normal public bathrooms, and what they reflected, in flickery, hummy, dim light, was each other into infinity. Once, Fig pressed into a stall whose door was half-open only to have it slam shut in her face with a snarled "Someone's in here, asshole!" Once, someone asked if she'd prefer a ride instead of the bus, and when Bex came out of her stall and put her arm around Fig and said, "She's with me," the ride-offerer grinned with brown teeth and said "I've got room for you both." Fig knew to say no to that.

While they were waiting to transfer in Portland, though, an old man looked at them then looked away then looked back then looked away then eventually came over and said they looked cold (which Bex and Lewis were not because they weren't LA kids used to year-round warm weather, but Fig and Jack were shivering) and hungry (which they were because their food stash was down to half a bag of tortilla chips, a baggie of crackers, and thirteen dried apricots) and alone (even though they were together and had each other) and asked if he could buy them some breakfast, and that answer was harder because they didn't know what he knew. Had their mother panicked and told the smears they were missing? Were they headline news, their pictures posted everywhere? They didn't know because they didn't have phones, but if they were recognized, they would no longer be missing, no longer almost there, but instead all the way back at the start again.

So they kept their heads and eyes down and said no thank you to breakfast, and Lewis shoved his cape into his backpack because a cape was good for hiding inside but bad for hiding in general, and Bex put on sunglasses and a baseball hat and tucked her hair up inside it. Fig and Jack already had lots of practice being unnoticed and hidden right in front of everyone. Their new bus arrived and they climbed onto it to head west, back toward the ocean.

The third bus ride was long and loud and smelly, but not as long and loud and smelly as the second one. They were closer now to where they were going than to where they'd started. They were out of California, off the Five, headed toward water. The bus was half-empty. Fig could hear her own voice again. She was still surprised, though, to hear it say to Bex, "Are you jealous of us?" She hadn't meant to ask. It just popped out.

"Who?" said Bex.

"Me and Jack. Or like . . ." She didn't know how to say it really, but she'd already started so she kept going. "Do you not like us as much because you hate us a little?"

"Why would I hate you any amount?"

"Because we get to have India Allwood for a mother and you don't."

"You mean because she's rich and famous?"

That wasn't what Fig meant. From afar, with only what you saw and read from the smears, Fig could see why being placed for adoption rather than raised by India Allwood would seem like you got lucky, but now that Bex was here and could see what her mother was really like, maybe she felt bad.

"I used to." Bex took off her baseball cap and shook her hair out. "Who wouldn't want to be rich? And Hollywood parties, private jets, dating some guy you met after the Oscars or whatever."

"We don't have a private jet," Fig said. "Or go to those kinds of parties."

"And you for sure don't make famous seem fun. Are you jealous of me?"

"Why?" Fig hadn't meant to sound so surprised.

"Because I know everything about my birth mother and I even got to meet her, and I know why she gave me up, and any questions I ever had, I could get answers. Whereas you . . ." She trailed off.

"I remember mine." Fig looked out the window.

"You do?"

"We were four when we . . . changed mothers. I remember lots about her." Fig paused to see if she was going to be able to keep talking about this. "We called her Sarah, but I can't remember why."

"My best friend in middle school called her parents by their first names too."

"Really?"

"They were cooler than normal parents." Bex shrugged. "Maybe your birth mom is really cool."

"Maybe." Fig took another pause. "I know some things about my birth dad too."

"Like what?"

Fig felt stupid. She knew way more about Bex's birth father than her own. "He loves fruit. That's what Sarah told the social worker, anyway. They did a lot of drugs together so she didn't remember too much about him and never even knew his real name, but she told the social worker he had a thing for fruit."

"What kind of thing?"

"I don't know," Fig admitted. "But if he bought a peach or an apple or something, he'd take a picture before he ate it. And he named them. Like, if he had blueberries he'd say, 'Thanks Josh,' and pop one in his mouth and then, 'Nice to meet you, Penny,' and pop in another."

"Weird." Bex shoved her hat into her backpack and pulled her hair into a ponytail so it looked like Fig's again.

"He was gone by the time Sarah knew she was pregnant, but that's why she named us after fruit. I think"—Fig had never said this to anyone—"it was nice of her."

"You do?" Bex sounded like she did not.

"She could have gone with Banana or Cantaloupe or something like that, but instead she thought till she came up with fruit names that could also be kid names."

It wasn't totally fair because when people heard Jack they thought of a boy or at worst a boy and a beanstalk whereas people heard Fig and thought of drizzling it with goat cheese and honey. But it was proof that Sarah wanted to protect her from being bullied and also pass on a little piece of her past and her parentage.

"Do you want to find him?" Bex said.

"My birth father?" Fig could hear that she sounded alarmed, which was also how she felt. "We don't even know his name. He doesn't even know we exist."

"So he'd be surprised." Bex made it sound like a good thing.

"He might not like surprises." Fig knew, though, that the reasons she didn't probably had nothing to do with her genes.

"Okay, but if it wasn't a surprise? Like you found him, and then you sent him a letter, and then you waited a few months for him to get used to the idea. Then would you want to meet him?"

Fig tried to picture this and could not. She tried to peer past the part of herself that was panicked just thinking about it, but there wasn't enough of her left after that. "I don't know," she confessed. "Why do you want to meet yours?"

Bex blinked. She looked surprised. Then she looked across the aisle, out the window. "I don't know either."

They were quiet some more miles. Then Bex said, "Remember the first time you texted me?"

It felt to Fig like years ago, like she had grown up a lot since then, but it had only been six months. "Yeah."

"You said you were family, but when I didn't know what you were talking about, you said not family family."

"I just meant—"

"I know what you meant. It's not like there's a name for your birth mother's adopted daughter."

"Yeah," Fig agreed again. She wasn't sure where this was going. She wasn't sure she was going to like where it was going.

"Now that we're about to meet my bio dad, though . . ." Bex trailed off.

"You think he's the one who's family," Fig supplied.

Bex turned her face from pointing out the window to pointing in at Fig. She looked surprised again. "The opposite, actually. I think you were wrong back then."

"Me?"

"We are family family. We must be. Who else would follow along with a plan that's going to get us in as much trouble as this one?" Bex laughed, so Fig laughed too, but then Bex asked, serious again, "Why did you come, anyway?"

"You made me!" Fig said.

"You could have said no."

"I did say no!"

"You could have said no harder. You could have refused. You could have told your mom. Or mine. You didn't have to come, but you did."

Fig hadn't realized it, but Bex was right. She didn't have to come. So why did she? "You wanted to go," she said finally. "I wanted to help you. I didn't want you to have to go alone."

"Exactly." Bex turned her face back out the other window. "Family family."

2020

"Shakespeare in the Park," said Ajax.

India was putting away the Christmas decorations finally. The kids were back at school, also finally. Ajax and Henri had come over bearing cheese and chocolate for a little post–New Year's celebration, they said, but really they wanted to see her face when they told her.

"Shakespeare in the park?"

"You and Henri will headline." Ajax was speaking too slowly, savoring this apparently. "It's a four-week rehearsal, starting early May, as soon as *Val Halla* wraps, two weeks of previews, then the run."

They were glowing, both of them, like they'd told her they were pregnant.

"What play?"

"*Much Ado*," said Ajax, "but you're saying it wrong."

"Saying what wrong?"

"It's not Shakespeare in the park. It's Shakespeare in *the* Park. Central Park."

"The *Delacorte*?" She leaped into his arms, and he spun her around in her kitchen. "Ajax, you are a worker of miracles." She felt like her own house-plants, which she forgot and forgot and forgot to water and then did. Like she was getting what she needed most after far too long. Like she was coming back to life. It would be real acting, live theater, a play.

"I am excellent," he agreed, "but in this case, they called and asked if I thought you might be willing."

Willing? She'd have given her firstborn. Not that her firstborn was hers to give.

"This one"—Ajax hooked a thumb at Henri—"had to be talked into it."

"As you both know damn well," Henri sniffed, "live theater is terrifying."

"Yes," India agreed. Rapturously.

"But I assumed you'd be an easier sell," Ajax drawled. "They like to get big names to headline, and given the developments of this season, Val and Rune are perfect for *Much Ado*. That in this case, you happen both to be classically trained actors is just a bonus, as far as they're concerned. At the moment, they're thinking of a Roaring Twenties theme for the new decade—flappers and such—but it's only January, so obviously that could change half a dozen times between now and then."

India didn't care. It could change as much as they wanted. It would still be Shakespeare, New York, night after night in front of an audience.

"We'll probably stay at my apartment." Ajax had kept it when he came to LA, not bet-hedging, he'd assured Henri, but for when they moved back. *If*, Henri insisted. *When*, Ajax insisted back. "But they'll put the three of you up somewhere swanky and—"

"No need." She was giddy. "We'll wander the streets by day, perform by night."

They raised their eyebrows at her.

"You two are starting to look alike," she warned. "We'll stay with Dakota. And wander the streets by day and perform by night."

She was making plans already. Where to take the kids for pizza first. How early a flight they'd need to get to the bagel place before it closed. She was going over all her favorite parks in her head, scanning for playgrounds, something she had not considered last she was there.

Then suddenly, she interrupted her own reverie. "Who's who?"

"You mean who else have they cast?" Ajax waved a cracker around. "Only Benedick and Beatrice so far. The stars. The leads. The draw. They'll cast the rest with whoever. I'm sure they'll be excellent, but—"

"No, I mean, who am I playing?"

"What do you mean? Beatrice. You're Beatrice."

In the fullness of time. She wondered how much of it she remembered, how much was stowed away in some dusty crease of her brain, waiting, ready, full of faith.

She had heard her detractions.

She had put them to mending.

She had arrived at last, and she was going home.

It would be the best summer of her life. It would be the best summer of anyone's life.

MONDAY

The fourth bus was better, just a little regional one, smaller, quieter, and smelling like rain. There was almost no one on it, either, no one scary and no one to recognize them, just a kid Bex's age with a surfboard, and a couple with giant backpacks and hiking boots, holding hands. The road was only four lanes and then only two, winding gently under giant evergreens, the dry dead colors out the other bus windows—tan grass, brown fields, white sky—replaced by green everywhere, everything sparkling with wet.

Fig's butt hurt from being sat on for so long. Her stomach hurt from being anxious and empty. Her head hurt from bouncing against the window. Her heart hurt with worry about her mother worrying about her. But she perked up a little from the new view, the clean air, the lack of people, and being close finally. And then Bex yanked a wire over the window, and the last little bus pulled over and let them out.

There was no bus station. There was no waiting room, no bathroom, no water fountain. There wasn't even a bus shelter with a bench they could rest on. There was just a sign on the side of the road.

"Now what?" said Jack.

"Now we walk," said Bex. "It's less than a mile. Flat. Easy."

Maybe. Maybe if they hadn't been so tired and aching and thirsty and cramped and hungry and worried and scared and in trouble and hiding from everyone with an internet connection. But they were all of those things.

Lewis got his cape out and put it on so it flowed over his backpack.

"You look like the guy from that cartoon," Jack said.

"Batman?"

"The Hunchback of Notre Dame."

They trudged in single file, first along the highway, which was small for a highway, yes, but the cars that passed were driving fast and not expecting anyone to be along the edge. Then they turned off onto a smaller road with hardly any cars, but they had to walk on the white-striped rim where the weeds had prickers no one ever trimmed down. Then they turned onto an even smaller road where there was still no sidewalk but also no cars, and if any came you'd have plenty of time to get out of the way, so they walked right down the middle of the street.

The rain was just stopping, so there weren't many people around, but sometimes someone came out of a house and held a palm up to feel for rain or looked up at the sky or waved to them and called, "Hiya. Nice day. Glad it stopped raining," and all you had to say was "Hi," or "Yeah," or "Me too." There were two kids on a swing set, one complaining that his underwear got soaked on the slide and the other one laughing about it. There was another kid chasing a dog around a yard. There was another in a wet suit, holding a surfboard over her head, calling, annoyed, to her brother (Fig recognized the tone).

They came over a tiny rise, and there was the ocean. Fig could not believe they'd traveled all these hours all this way only to be on the same shore of the same body of water. It still looked gray and blue and green and giant, though, and light still broke the surface of the water into a million dancing, shining pieces. Then the road went down again and the ocean hid away, and there were a few stores with beach toys and T-shirts and a couple of cafés and a rental shop and a coffee shop and a fudge shop and an ice cream shop. And a bookstore.

"This is it," Bex said.

"Will he have food and a bathroom?" said Jack.

"I don't know." Which meant Bex wasn't really listening, since of course he would have food and a bathroom. Whether he'd let them in to use them was another question, but Fig suspected he probably would because no matter who they are or why they've come, when four hungry children travel one day, five hours, and forty-seven minutes to your front door, you probably let them in. Especially if you don't want them to pee in your bushes.

"What should we do?" Lewis pulled the mask part of his cape over his mouth and nose.

"Knock," said Jack.

"No!" Bex's eyes were too wide and not rolling for once.

"How will he know we're here otherwise?" Fig asked her.

Bex shook her head. "What will I say to him?"

"'Hi, I'm Bex who used to be Rebecca,'" Lewis suggested. "'We've come a long way to find you.'"

"Don't be stupid." Bex squeezed her too-wide eyes shut.

Fig could not see why this was stupid. She patted Lewis's arm so he didn't feel bad.

"Hi, I'm Jack Allwood, and if you don't let me in, I'm going to starve to death on your damn driveway."

The sky was getting bluer, but Bex was getting grayer. "I'm scared," she whispered.

Fig held out her hand. Bex took it and squeezed. They headed down the little road, and the boys did not hold hands but did follow them, and they found the right house and walked up the driveway and onto the front porch and stood for a minute just breathing, just waiting, amazed at where they were, amazed that they had gotten there, all by themselves, after so many miles and so many hours, amazed at Robbie Brighton's little sea house, all soft wood and peeling paint and sand tracing the cracks in the driveway and shells in a pile under the porch swing and the door painted faded blue, like Fig's favorite jeans, like everyone's favorite jeans, no buzzer, no doorbell even, so they took deep breaths, all four of them, all together, and Fig and Bex squeezed hands again, and then Bex took the last step forward and her hand was shaking but she made a fist with it and knocked on the blue door. They heard feet inside at once. And then the door flung open wide.

And there, bright red and panting on the other side, was Fig's mother.

2020

Everyone had the same story.

Everyone had a different story.

India's was mostly gratitude. She couldn't work from home, but she didn't need to, and she wouldn't be replaced or fired as a result. She was grateful to have money. She was grateful to have a big house with a pool—plenty of room and plenty to do. She was grateful *Val Halla* wasn't in its infancy, those tenuous first seasons when they'd nearly been canceled. *Val Halla* filming would resume. She was grateful her kids didn't like to go out for dinner anyway.

She missed her mother, but lots of people's mothers wouldn't survive this thing or wouldn't live long enough for it to go away. She missed her work but was keenly aware that lots of people missed their paychecks and that that was a different thing altogether. She missed her kids leaving the house, but lots of people had to work from home while their toddlers climbed the bookshelves and their five-year-olds failed to learn to read. Her children had already learned to read and were happiest at home anyway. At first, Jack was rattled by the interruption in routine, but India instituted a new one, and since it involved more swimming and less math, Jack adapted. At first, Fig was rattled by increasingly alarming footage on the news and headlines in the paper, the incredulity then sobering of the adults all around her, but India turned off the TV and left it off, secreted the newspaper away to her bedroom. They were only nine. They understood, but they didn't understand.

She was grateful even the smears weren't willing to get anywhere near them anymore.

She was grateful, at the grocery store, in the park, carrying out from Cupcake Conniption, that almost no one recognized her in a mask.

She was also grateful this thing hit in March so it wouldn't derail their summer in New York. Surely, it would be gone by summer. And anyway, Shakespeare in the Park was in the park. If indoor events were still iffy, outdoor ones would therefore play to packed houses. Maybe they would extend the run. Maybe school and filming would both be delayed a few weeks in the fall and they could stay in New York an extra month.

She was already packing when Ajax called. She'd gotten used to his coming by, so it was weird to go back to phone calls only. True, she was packing a week too early, but she was too excited to wait. She was contemplating how many pairs of sandals she'd want when the phone rang.

"They pulled the plug, India. I'm sorry."

"But outside," she protested. "But summer."

"The whole city got clobbered. You know this. And outside where you can spread out is one thing. You can't spread out in a theater, even an outdoor theater. You can't spread out when you rehearse, never mind perform."

"We could start socially distanced rehearsals and see what happens. Maybe it'll go away in time. People are saying summer will be better."

"We couldn't even get out there. It's not safe to fly. They couldn't get a cast or crew together. It's not safe to work. And there's no audience. It's not safe to attend."

"I'll take my chances."

"You won't. Even if you were willing and even if I were willing to let you, it's out of our hands. And it's the right decision. I'm sorry. I know you're disappointed."

She was not disappointed. She was bereft.

At night, after she put the kids to bed, she watched videos of graduating seniors who finally got the lead in their high school musical but would never get to go on. She watched virtual graduation ceremonies, kids in caps and gowns alone in their backyards. She watched ice skaters practicing their routines in socks in their living rooms. She watched whole villages out on their balconies serenading one another.

She watched Dakota on Zoom.

New York seemed so far away suddenly that texting became insufficient. It was necessary one night to hear Dakota's voice, to look into her eyes, read her face. And then it was necessary again a couple nights later and then a couple nights after that, and soon they were talking almost every night.

For a few years, Dakota had been running acting workshops as team-building exercises for corporate retreats, work that had been lucrative in February but was now snuffed like a candle: gone but for the wisps of smoking memory, impossible to imagine rekindling. She was thinking—miserably, incredulously—about going back to the coffee shop. Was it safe if it was carry-out only? Were enough customers willing to risk it to make it worth finding out? Would they not prefer to stay home where they didn't have to put on pants or risk the plague? And if so, what would become of coffee shops without caffeine addicts, New York with dark theaters, LA with silent soundstages, restaurants without diners, subways without riders, cities without commuters and tourists, lovers and playdates? Friends with no way to reach each other? What would happen when everyone stayed home with their streaming services, but there was nothing for them to watch because filming couldn't resume?

These were questions with no answers or terrible answers or pointless ones. They asked them of each other around in circles as India listened to sirens scream ceaselessly by on the other side of the country.

She did her *Merchant of Venice* speech, and she and Henri did a scene from *Much Ado*, into their webcams for charity or morale or distraction or who knew what. She watched theaters mount strange remote performances. She appreciated that they were trying, but it just made her feel farther away and more alone. As spring stretched into summer stretched into fall and winter, but the days kept on the same one after the next, and *Val Halla* stayed shut down and theaters stayed dark and school stayed closed, she turned to putting on skits with the kids, doing soliloquies in the shower, making Henri run lines with her over Zoom for a play they both knew might never be rescheduled.

"You've got to do something," Henri told Ajax. "She's making me crazier than quarantine. The very hardest part of this whole very hard situation is India."

An envelope arrived at her house the next day. She called Ajax for an explanation. "A movie script?"

"Just read it."

"I'm not a movie star."

"You could be."

"I have to leave my schedule open for *Val Halla* and the kids. And *Much Ado*."

"It's a quarantine project. You'll Zoom with the director and the rest of the cast. It's a film about isolation, being alone in any number of senses, so it speaks to the moment, and they think they can mount a skeleton crew and film it safely under current restrictions."

"The whole thing?"

"Ninety percent maybe. It's lots of scenes of your character walking on a lonely beach and making dinner for one in an empty apartment. And doing drugs, but by herself. No stunts, no hair and makeup. You can wear your own jeans and an old sweatshirt."

"Hey!"

"What?"

"I'd need hair and makeup and wardrobe to look like a drug addict."

"I'm just saying they think they can film most of this movie right now. Edit it in their homes. Even for the group scenes, they think they can keep actors six feet apart."

"Sounds like a fun story."

But Ajax was used to ignoring India's sarcasm. "Since it's about the only thing going, they'll be able to get good people on it. Plus it's a great part. A serious part. That's why they want you for it. When you got *Much Ado*, lots of people in this town learned for the first time that you're not just a superhero. This is the opposite of green-screen acting. It's going to take someone with chops who can carry the whole project. And it's going to be nominated for everything."

"I don't know, Ajax. I'm not sure a quarantine project is how I should break into film."

He paused. "It's about adoption."

She felt the earth shudder to a stop for a moment. "Really?"

"And you'd be great in it. Read the script. See what you think."

She got off the phone and sat down and did so. Then she read it again. Then she called Ajax back.

"It's a great part."

"But?"

"And I see how it could work. I see how they're going to be able to do most of it quarantined and distanced."

"But?"

"And I love that it's about adoption. Truly. We need more stories about adoption. We need to talk about it more. Lots more."

"Just tell me the *but*, India. You're killing me."

"Welcome to my world," she heard Henri say in the background.

"But*s*," India said. "Two of them."

"Do I look like your mother?" said Ajax.

"But its portrait of adoption is a little problematic. But its resolution of its portrait of adoption is a little pat."

"How is it problematic?"

"Everyone's miserable."

"It's a movie about drug addicts."

"It's a movie about drug addicts who get addicted to drugs because they're so broken by adoption," she corrected.

"They recover," said Ajax. "They come around."

"Sort of. At the too-pat end. And they don't come around. They go to rehab."

"It's a metaphor."

"Yes, and the metaphor is that being adopted is like being addicted to pills and there's never enough and you always need more and it destroys you. The metaphor is that placing a baby for adoption is as self-destructive as heroin. The metaphor is that the only cure for the misery of adoption is to undo it."

"I see that read." Ajax had on his indulging-India voice. "But I think it will become more nuanced in performance. Your performance. This is one of the reasons you're so perfect for this. It's a hard story. It's a hard part. It needs someone who can see—and make the audience see—all the gradations of gray."

"Sure, but there's only so much I can do within the confines of the script." She held for a beat before she ventured, "Would they hire me to do a rewrite, maybe? I do have some thoughts on the topic, you know, not to mention first-hand experience and, speaking of hands, lots of time on mine."

"Two buts," Ajax said. She couldn't see him, of course, but she could tell he was pleased with himself. "But you're not a writer."

"Because every time I ask, you say no."

"But it's bad form to go into a project tearing everything up and remaking it in your image."

"That's not what I'm proposing. You know that's not what I'm proposing."

"That's what it will look like. You're a debut film actress, and you want to rewrite their script? They're taking a risk on you—and at a very difficult time—and you're being a diva before you've even got the part?"

"No. That's not what I'm saying—asking—offering! I just think I could maybe make some . . . useful suggestions if they'd let me."

"Look, it's a hard topic," Ajax hedged—fudged, really—"which too many people know too little about. You want a real conversation about adoption? This will start it. It's not the whole conversation, so it doesn't need to say everything. It's not the end of the conversation, so it doesn't need to wrap up. It's the start. Who better to fire the opening salvo than you?"

MONDAY

There were adults everywhere. Fig watched Lewis's dads close around him like a clam. Camille's expression was like the Phantom of the Opera, one half super angry and the other half super relieved. She held Bex's face in her hands and kissed her forehead and her cheek and her other cheek and her eye and her other eye.

"Eww," said Bex.

"You're grounded forever," said her mother.

Davis was hanging farther back with a man Fig realized must be Robbie Brighton, first of all because he was the only one she didn't recognize, but also because he was barefoot, and adults are only barefoot in their own house. Davis and Robbie stood together like they were a couple and watched everyone with hard-to-describe expressions on their faces.

Her mother hugged her and Jack both at once, mashed together like a sandwich, and like when she put too much jelly on the jelly side of a PB&J and some squished out, Fig wiggled free to demand, "What are you doing here?"

"What are *you* doing here?" her mother replied, all panty and sharp, but Fig didn't know what to say because her mother obviously knew the answer to that question because here she was.

"You're here," Fig said.

"You're not here because I'm here! I'm here because you're here!"

"How?" Fig could hear the wonder in her voice.

"Not me how. You how. How are you here? Why didn't you tell me?" She was looking from Fig to Jack to Fig to Jack.

"There was a vote," Jack told his mother. "You lost."

"No, how did you know where we'd be?" Fig clarified.

"I understood you the first time," her mother said. "I am not prepared to stipulate that the position we currently find ourselves in is one in which you ask the questions and I give the answers."

"We rode four damn buses," Jack put in helpfully.

"I'm aware of that," her mother said. It was like she really was Val Halla, that mighty, that magic. "Davis said he'd just told Lewis where to find Robbie. You didn't have a car. You couldn't fly without more money and IDs and adults than you had. You were stupid but not stupid enough to hitchhike. Call it a series of educated guesses."

"But . . . you beat us here," Fig stammered.

"Because we got on a plane. We called the bus company, and then we called Robbie, and then we got on an airplane."

"A plane would have been awesome," Jack sighed. "The bus was ass."

"Not ass enough!" said their mother. Then she took a deep breath in. Then she let her deep breath out. Then she said, "Are you all okay?"

They all four nodded.

"Are *you* all okay?" she asked the adults. The adults nodded too.

"I might starve to death," Jack allowed.

"I really, really have to . . ." Fig trailed off and hoped her mother got it. She didn't want to say "pee" in front of Robbie Brighton.

"Here's what's going to happen," her mother said. "Bathrooms will be used. Showers will be taken. Pizzas will be ordered."

"Hot damn!" Jack cheered.

"And then we are going to have a discussion."

"Just damn," Jack revised.

"Yes," their mother agreed, "just damn."

Even though Robbie Brighton had five children, there were only two showers, one of them outside. Those five children were with their mother at the moment, but Bex wondered how they managed when they were here. Or when it was winter. She got first shower, though, because everyone else wanted to eat and Bex wasn't hungry. She was the opposite of hungry. Not full. *Full* sounded like satisfied and well-fed. She was more like congested, like when there were too many cars or too much snot. There was too much stuffed inside her for food to fit in too.

In the space of a week, she had gone from having no siblings to arguably still having no siblings but just as arguably having up to eight, and even if you didn't count Fig and Jack, and even if you put asterisks next to the other six, she still had five biological half-siblings she hadn't known she had half an hour ago. She had spent so many years knowing everything about India Allwood and her kids that it had barely occurred to her that of course Robbie Brighton might have children too and that he might not have adopted his. A week ago she hadn't met a single blood relative since the day she emerged from one. Now there were so many she couldn't even remember all their names.

She didn't dry her hair in case other people needed the bathroom, but when she got downstairs, damp and overheated, she was the only one there. She could see everyone else out on the back deck, Lewis pretending a slice of pizza was a kite, Fig breaking off pieces of crust to throw to the seagulls, Jack breaking off pieces of crust to throw at Fig. The walls of the hallway were covered in photographs, dozens of them: kids on beaches in front of sunsets, kids burying each other in the sand, a toddler gazing at an infant in his lap, gap-toothed sisters elbow deep in cookie dough, an elementary schooler with a lunch box boarding a yellow bus. Kids in Halloween costumes. Kids dressed up for a fancy occasion. Normal except for how many of them there were. Was this another life she'd almost had—being one of half a dozen, like an egg, nestled, also like an egg, with her brothers and sisters in a little house by the sea?

Bex had her face right up to a picture of the whole family together on a ski trip when she heard India in the living room tell someone she'd call them back at the same time as the slider opened and Robbie Brighton came inside, and suddenly she was standing barefoot in a stranger's house, her hair dripping on the floor, with, of all people, her parents.

"Hi," said Robbie Brighton.

"Hi," said Bex.

Neither of them knew what to say next. They both looked at India, whose face did *Don't look at me* and *Wow, look at us* plus *You abducted my children*, all at once. You could see why she was such a good actor. Bex couldn't make her face do anything.

"Rebecca. Bex." Robbie's face was also doing a lot of different things at once, so maybe it wasn't acting. "Welcome. I'm glad you're here."

"Thanks," said Bex.

"Thank *you*," he said. "For coming. I know it must have been hard."

"It was." Bex felt glad someone had noticed and was giving her credit.

"And that you're going to be, uh, in trouble for a while."

Maybe understatement was hereditary.

"My mother doesn't like not knowing things," Bex said.

Robbie looked sympathetic, but India grimaced. "I mean, there's not knowing things, and then there's not knowing where your children are."

Which Bex had to admit was fair. She hadn't accidentally kidnapped Robbie Brighton's children. She also knew that any sixteen-year-old who snuck out of the house onto an airplane in the middle of the night to fly a thousand miles and then, four days later, snuck out of the house onto a bus in the middle of the night to ride a thousand more would be in trouble with her mom, no matter who her mom was.

But she did think it was going to be worse for her and that that wasn't her fault or even her mother's fault. It was India and Robbie's fault.

"You scared her," she told them.

"*You* scared her," India corrected. "And you scared me."

"Not yesterday. Back then." She got that India was trying not to be mad at her because it wasn't her place and because of extenuating circumstances, but was mad at her anyway because she'd absconded with her kids and also been kind of responsible for India's week and possibly life turning from a light drizzle into a Category 5 hurricane. But just like already being in trouble with her mother had made it a good time to sneak off to Oregon, India was already pissed and trying not to be, so Bex figured now was a good time to explain to her and Robbie this thing they'd apparently never thought of. "You both scared her. Or scarred her maybe. I'm like this living, breathing, walking-around-her-house reminder of what happens if you're too lenient with your teenager."

Robbie smiled. "You've got the cause and effect backward."

Which made no sense, so she was glad when India added, "That's why we picked her. We saw what happened when you were . . . less than vigilant. We thought a baby needed someone attentive and detail-oriented and in control. Your mom's not strict because you remind her of a pregnant teenager. Your mom's your mom because she's strict."

Except that was also a lie. Bex recognized it because her mother did it too. Maybe all mothers did it. Maybe part of being a mother was abusing the definition of "we." She wasn't going to bring it up, but here she was, here they both were, and she had come all this way. "It wasn't really *we*, though, was it?" They both looked blank, so she kept going. "When you decided. About me. You said *we* picked her, but it was you, right? Not him? He had nothing to do with it."

"I had everything to do with it." Robbie Brighton looked . . . confused? Surprised? Hurt? It was impossible to say. "We met your mom before you were born. I was there in the hospital with you, all of you."

"Yeah, but"—Bex couldn't look at him—"you wanted to keep me. You wanted to get married and have a baby."

"No," India and Robbie said together, but in completely different tones. Her *no* sounded like "Definitely not!" His *no* sounded like "It's complicated."

But Bex didn't believe either one. Her mother had told her, not when she was little but a couple of years ago when they sat down and really talked about it. She said India was positive but Robbie was conflicted maybe, torn, and though Bex's mom had asked if he was sure and he said he was, she'd wondered how much of him was going along with what India wanted just because India wanted it.

It wasn't that Bex thought her mom was telling the truth and India and Robbie were lying to her. It was that she worried her mother was right—she usually was—and India and Robbie were wrong because they were lying to themselves. And maybe it didn't matter anymore, but here they all were, so maybe it did.

"My mom said she knew *you* knew for sure." Bex pointed her chin at India without raising her eyes from the floor, then turned toward Robbie but without looking at him either. "But that you were maybe on the fence. And I figure India became Val Halla, so you could have had the love of your life *and* your baby *and* been famous and rich."

She made herself look up and saw that India was watching Robbie too. She had secret questions in her eyes, if that was even possible.

Robbie met India's gaze. Then he looked back at Bex. "I wasn't on the fence. I *was* the fence."

"You were the fence?" Bex and India said together in the same skeptical tone.

"One side of me in one world, one side in another, and the solid part, the part in between, was thin enough to scale."

No one said anything for a minute. Then India said, "That's not what makes a fence scalable."

"It's really not," Bex agreed.

"It doesn't matter how thick or thin a fence is." India demonstrated with her hands. "What matters is how tall."

"Or if there's, like, barbed wire on top," said Bex.

"Or footholds," India added.

"My point," said Robbie Brighton, "is I wanted to raise you and I also wanted you to have someone ready to be a parent. I wanted to be ready and I also wanted to be seventeen. The only thing I knew for sure I wanted without also wanting its opposite was I wanted to support India and want what she wanted."

"And anyway"—India sounded sad and happy together—"he couldn't have had all those things you listed, you and me and love and money and fame. And neither could I. And neither could you."

"Why not?" Bex said.

"Because I never would have been Val Halla if we had stayed together as teenagers and raised you ourselves."

Which was true.

Of course it was true.

Bex blinked. She blinked again. She felt like she'd been shuffling the cards of her brain and accidentally caught a thumb and sent them shooting off in all directions. She wasn't almost Val Halla's daughter because if she'd been India Allwood's daughter, India Allwood wouldn't be Val Halla. That life wasn't a *this close* fantasy that had slipped through her fingers. It wasn't a near miss on the hassles of the spotlight and the headache of the smears. She wasn't a phantom on Robbie's family wall or the missing egg from his half dozen. Whoever India would have been had she stayed Bex's mother, whoever Robbie would have been had he been her dad, was just as impossible to know or even imagine as who Bex herself would have been in that version of their lives. The only thing they did know was that their lives wouldn't be these lives: not a minor variation on them, not a giant divergence from them, nothing really at all to do with this or any aspect of this, their actual lives.

Since this was obviously true and had been obviously true all along, you wouldn't think Bex's brain would feel so wobbly, but it did.

India waited, and then she smiled. "I did use to think it was you, though."

Bex tried to remember what they had been talking about before she had to rethink everything she'd ever thought for practically her whole life so far. "What was me?"

"Both of you." India kept her eyes on Bex but turned her body toward Robbie. "When I got a callback, when I got the part I wanted, I thought you two were out there pulling the strings of the universe for me somehow."

"That's . . . weird," Bex said.

But Robbie laughed. "Me too!"

She watched them forget she was there for a second.

"I wasn't dead," she reminded them.

"Not like a ghost," Robbie said. "More like a really good politician."

"That's even weirder."

"It really is," India agreed.

"Like I knew you were out there making the world better," Robbie explained, "so when things were good I always thought, *No wonder, Rebecca's on the case.*"

Bex pointed at herself with both index fingers. "Not magic. Not dead. Not a politician." She could hear that her voice sounded shaky, and she felt a little shaky, but she also felt relieved. It had been sad all these years to think that her winking into existence had been so regrettable, so regretted. It had been sad to think she'd ruined their lives, even for a little while, even though it wasn't her fault, that she'd caused them so much pain, then and even still because they always had to carry around the absence of her.

Now, though, she was starting to realize that she was what made their lives—their current lives, their real lives—possible. If they hadn't given her up—but also, if they hadn't had her to begin with—they'd be completely different people now. Which meant India was Val Halla because of Bex. Which meant Robbie's five children, her five half-siblings, and Lewis too, and even Jack and Fig, also only existed because of Bex. India and Robbie were her parents, not in every way, but in some ways. But in some ways, she was also theirs. They had given her life, but she had given them lives, these lives, and not only them but a lot of other people too.

The adults split up to put their various kids to bed, even Camille, even though Bex protested that she was too old. Robbie gave the master bedroom over to Jack and Fig, and Fig did not complain that she didn't get to sleep with Bex or that Jack was smelly, and Jack did not complain about having to share a bed. India set up an air mattress on the floor for herself for later, kissed her goodnights, and turned off the light. They were asleep before she closed the door. On the other side of it, though, she found she could not leave them, not yet, and sank down to sit against the wall and weep.

Which was where Robbie found her.

"I came to check on you. You've been putting your kids to bed for a long time."

"Last time I tucked them in, it didn't take."

"Sure, but what about the two thousand times before that?"

She wiped her eyes. "You think you're an expert just because you had children in bulk?"

"Practice makes perfect." He slid down the wall across from her. "This is how it was the first time too, you know."

"What was?"

"When we met. You were sitting against the wall crying—"

"I wasn't crying."

"And I was telling you you deserved better."

"You were wrong, though. I didn't. You can't be in a musical if you can't sing."

"I stand by it. No one else in that show became a movie star."

"And I definitely don't deserve better now. There is no better. I got granted my heart's desire: my children, safe and sound."

"Yeah, but you deserved to skip the panicked-and-heartsick part."

"That's what parenting is," India said. "No avoiding that."

"Really? I've always found parenting relaxing and stress free." He smiled the smile that had made sixteen-year-old India—not to mention thirty-two-year-old India—glad she was sitting on the floor already so she wouldn't wobble on suddenly weak knees. The smile came with soft lines around his eyes and mouth now, which only made it more destabilizing.

"I'm glad you had so many children," she managed.

"Why?"

"Seems only fair somehow."

"Maybe. I always wanted a big family. And before you, I was always a little lonely."

"I remember."

"And since they've had this terrible thing happen to them," Robbie added, "I'm glad they have each other."

"Terrible thing?"

"Their parents got divorced."

"I'm a single parent," India said. "I was raised by a single parent. It's not so bad for kids. It's hard for you, but it's not so hard for them."

"It's not that." Robbie shook his head. "It's having to learn such a tough lesson at such a young age."

"What's that?"

"That love is not enough."

India considered this. "Enough to what?"

"Enough to sustain a relationship. Enough to hold people together. Enough reason to stay. We kept telling them all through the separation and the divorce and the move and custody arrangements that we still loved each other and we'd always love each other, like it was a comfort, but I think maybe it just taught them too young that love doesn't cut it. It doesn't protect you, and you can't protect it. And they're just kids. I mean, how old were you when you learned that?"

"I learned it from you." It was out of India's mouth before she realized it was true. "You loved me. I loved you. We made and gave up a whole person together because of that love and to protect that love, and it wasn't enough."

He let his head drop back against the wall behind him. "I'm sorry."

She wondered whether he was whispering so he didn't wake Fig and Jack or because he didn't trust his voice to be louder.

"Don't be sorry. It was the nicest thing anyone has ever done for me. It needed doing, and I would never have done it myself, and it was so hard and so sad, and you did it anyway. And you know what else?"

He shook his head, maybe because he didn't know what else, maybe because he disagreed with her.

"It's a valuable lesson. Not at the time, but once I could see it. It's good to know love, and it's good to know love is not enough. It's good to know love, and it's good to know love is not an obligation." She remembered when Jack and Fig first came home, her mother's point that it was never so simple as "Love makes a family," that it was only that easy on throw pillows and greeting cards. Love was a laudable goal, and you wouldn't want a family without it, though plenty of people had one, bio, adopted, or otherwise. But love did not preclude strife. It did not erase sorrows. It did not detangle complication. In the case of families, uncomplicated wasn't really the goal anyway.

"Maybe it's useful to learn that young," India said, "like how to cross streets or speak French. Maybe it's good to learn that sometimes people who love each other have different needs."

"Like she needs everything, and you love that she needs everything, but all you need is her?"

He was still whispering.

She was still meeting his eyes.

But she said, "That's maybe an advanced topic for a toddler. I was thinking more like you need a decent night's sleep and they need scrambled eggs at five a.m., so everyone has to take turns. It would be easier if humans learned that at three instead of thirty."

"In which case it's probably yours," he said.

"My what?"

"Turn. To get what you need. Lots of different motherhoods over lots of years have gotten in the way of your love life and your work life and your life life. Now you're not making any new babies for the moment, and the current ones are a little less fragile, and your whole life seems to have fallen apart anyway."

"Thanks, Robbie. This has been uplifting."

"So you have an opportunity you haven't had in a long time."

"Which is?"

"First love." His palms flipped up like they held the world. Maybe they did.

"First love?"

"Not first love. First, love." He nudged her foot with his. "We've been over this."

She laughed and felt sixteen again. "Half a lifetime ago."

"That's not so long."

"Didn't you just say love was not enough?"

"It's all about that comma." He drew it in the air with his hand, a motion like scooping water or cupping a child's head. "It's still first, the right place to start or start again. You get to choose. What do you want to do? Who do you want to do it with? Maybe love isn't enough to surmount the big problems— being pregnant at sixteen, getting divorced—but now your problems are rugged hills."

"Rugged hills?"

"Instead of towering peaks."

"I don't get it," she said.

"Easier to get over." He grinned. "They say you never forget your first love."

She smiled back. "This is true."

"Maybe it's so you can find your way back."

Then the door behind India opened and Fig came out, rubbing her eyes, hair tangled as tax code. She slid to the floor and put her head on India's shoulder.

"I can't sleep," she croaked.

"You were asleep."

"I was?"

"Before I even turned the light off."

"I can't sleep *now*. There's a weird noise."

"That's the ocean," said India.

"Can you turn it down?"

"I hope not," her mother said. "Want a lullaby?"

Now Fig was wide awake. She sat up and stared at her mother. "You'll sing to me?"

"Don't be ridiculous. But Robbie's a great singer."

Fig snuggled back into her mother, and they both looked at Robbie expectantly.

"No way," he said. "Too embarrassing."

"You're telling me you don't sing to your kids?" The Robbie she'd known would definitely sing to his kids.

"Every night they're here," he admitted. "And sometimes on the phone when they're not."

"Then why can't you sing to mine?"

He sang her Camille's song, Rebecca's—Bex's—song, from *Guys and Dolls*. "*I love you a bushel and a peck.*" He sang it low and slow, so it sounded like a lullaby. His voice was exactly as annoyingly perfect as it had been sixteen years before. "*A bushel and a peck and a hug around the neck.*" India hugged Fig around the neck. She unbent her knees and reached her feet out to press against Robbie's across his hallway, across time, a thing she had not done with any other human ever, a sensation the pads of her toes remembered at once, a feeling a lot like first love. His eyes never left hers, but when he finished his song, Robbie pulled his feet away so he could stand up. "I'll let you two talk. 'Night, Fig. See you downstairs, Fig's mom."

India felt she would have been happy to sit in Robbie Brighton's hallway with Fig's sleepy head on her shoulder for the next month until this whole mess went away. She would have been happy to sit there not saying a word until Fig had to leave for college. But Fig wanted to talk. Or really, India knew, Fig wanted to have the discussion she'd promised and get it over with already.

"I'm sorry, Mom."

Which was going to be hard because she was crying as soon as she opened her mouth.

"I know, baby."

"I was trying to help."

"I know you were."

"I didn't know what to do."

362 | LAURIE FRANKEL

"You didn't need to do anything."

"I heard you on the phone. You said our lives were being ruined, and our safety was being threatened, and your career was being on fire."

Ahh. So all of this was her fault.

"I am too loud sometimes"—India sighed—"but you shouldn't eavesdrop on people's phone calls anyway, and I was being hyperbolic. Exaggerating to Grandma."

"Lying?"

"To prove a point."

"What point?"

"That I was having a bad day. That's all. Nothing scarier than that."

"But you *could* lose your job. They said apologize, and you did it wrong. They said give an interview and show your family and home, and you said no."

"That's true," India allowed. "But none of that is a problem it's your responsibility to fix, and definitely not by sneaking out in the middle of the night and riding a bus to Oregon. You could have gotten lost or hurt or—" She cut herself off. She could list "or"s until dawn, but she only wanted to scare Fig enough to ensure she'd never do anything like this again, not scare her so much that she'd be retroactively traumatized by all she'd had the grace to avoid. If we had to worry about all our mothers' fears, who among us would ever leave the house?

Fig sniffled. "Bex wanted to meet him."

"I know, baby." India hugged her closer. "But that also isn't your responsibility to fix." She thought it might be hers, though. She considered the risks these kids, her kids, had undertaken to know one another. The lengths they'd gone to were foolhardy and misguided; they were impressive and ingenious; but more than any of that, they were on her head. Which probably meant they were also hers to account for.

Before she could figure out how, though, Fig added, "And we thought if we could bring everyone together, *everyone* everyone, the smears would see how fine we are and say sorry."

"We are fine. We're better than fine. But the smears never say sorry."

"And plus you don't want anyone to know anything about us."

"That's right. We're entitled to our privacy."

"But even when we're right, we can't tell anyone, and even when they're mean, we can't correct them, and if someone tries to talk about us, you say your kids are off-limits, and if I try to make a press conference to announce something important, you won't let me. It's like you want us to be loofs."

"Loofs?"

"Like you're a loof, so you want me and Jack to be loofs too."

Ahh. "Not so much aloof," India explained, "as protected."

"From what?"

From the answer to that question, she thought. She pressed her forehead to Fig's. "I'm making sure no one gets all up in your beeswax."

Fig giggled. "My bee's wax?"

"That's what Grandma used to call your own private business when she was your age."

"Why?"

"No idea."

"But not just the smears," Fig pressed. "You also tried to keep Bex and Lewis and Camille and the Andrews away from us."

"To protect their beeswaxes too. When I agreed to be on television, I also agreed to the smears. It was a package deal for me. But you and Jack never chose that. And neither did Bex or Lewis or their parents."

"Yeah, but"—Fig rubbed sleepy eyes—"probably there are more important things to the bees than their waxes anyway."

"Well, the wax is what keeps their home safe, I guess. So that's pretty important."

"But what about pollen and honey and your hive mates and flying around free to be a bee?"

India opened her mouth to say something placating to her daughter who was a child so could not be blamed for missing the point, when she realized the one missing the point was her. She was fuzzy on the details, but it did seem that the hive had to be waxed so the bees had somewhere to bring the pollen they harvested and store the honey they made, and this meant your foundation was important but your work was important too. Your own little family was important, but its borders were hard to define because there were your loves who came first but there were also your first loves. Safety was important, especially for little bees who had begun their life without enough of it, but so, unfortunately, was their freedom to fly—not across state lines and not without permission and not via middle-of-the-night buses and single-filing along the shoulders of highways. But still.

The smears, the dwebs, the tabloids, the industry rags, the studio execs, the pro-lifers, the adoptee advocates, *Val Halla*'s legions of fans, most idle scrollers on the internet, and very likely everyone in both her small and larger families would identify India as the queen bee. But India knew the queen was Fig—well, Jack and Fig. They were the ones around whose protection and well-being and rightful place in the world everything else was waxed and built and reinforced. Maybe she'd forgotten it over the past few years, or maybe just over the past few days, but the central fact of India Allwood's life had always been this: she was a worker bee to the tips of her wings.

And so she got to work.

TUESDAY

ndia called Evelyn Esponson before dawn the next morning. She did not feel bad about waking her up. "I need you to do me a favor," she said. "You owe me."

"I disagree."

"It will be a favor to you too."

"I'm more interested."

"Imagine my shock." But India told her what she had in mind anyway.

"Why me?"

"Good question."

"Asking good questions is my job."

"That's why," India said. "Also, you started this. Maybe you can end it as well."

Then she called Ajax. She felt a little worse about waking him.

"Over my own intense objections," she said when he answered the phone, "I'm going to do their goddamn interview."

"Hallelujah."

"Today."

"It's the right thing to do, India. I know it's hard, but it's time."

"In Oregon."

"Oregon, California, or Oregon, New York City?"

"Oregon the state."

"Never heard of it."

She ignored this. "I've gone ahead and set it up with Evelyn Esponson. She's got her own film crew. I'm using a friend's house."

"The execs wanted America to see your home."

"The execs can kiss my—"

"And what about me?"

"You want to kiss my ass?"

"I want to be there to support you. Though less so now than a moment ago."

"I appreciate that, truly, but I've got plenty of support here with me already. That's the point, actually. But Ajax . . ."

"What is it, India?"

"I need to tell you something. Before I do this. I don't want you to hear it on TV first."

"I already know," Ajax said.

"You do?"

"I've known all along."

"How?"

"How did I know you were really pregnant? By looking at you. I'm not an idiot. The Lenox costume department is good for a college shop, but it's not *that* good."

"Why would you . . ." India's brain spun, reordering the last decade and a half of her life. "Why did you lie?"

"I didn't lie! You lied."

"Why did you make me lie?"

"I wanted to see whether you could. As I keep trying to tell you, acting in a role is only part of the job. And I wanted to see how far you were willing to take a charade, how hard you were willing to work. Would you go to an audition half a week after giving birth? Would you come clean when a world-class powerhouse dream agent came courting, or did you want it badly enough to fake that you were faking?"

"What if I hadn't had the baby a month early?"

"Exactly. I wanted to see what would happen. Fun! But you know what else?"

"What?"

"You didn't need me. You didn't need a real fake pregnancy or a star turn as Lady M to get noticed. You didn't need the part of a lifetime to fall into your lap. If you'd had to do it the old-fashioned way, the hard way—open calls and running off headshots at the all-night copy shop and working the dawn shift at the diner to leave afternoons free for auditions—you'd have made it anyway. You have the talent and the drive. It had nothing to do with being pregnant."

"This whole time, Ajax, I thought—"

"I know."

"Why-y?"

"Keep you on your toes."

"It worked."

"As I believe I told you the first time we spoke," Ajax said, "I am very good at my job."

"This is true," India agreed. "And thank you. I'm glad to know you knew. It's a weight off my mind."

"You're welcome."

"But Ajax?"

"Yes, my dear?"

"That's not actually the something I need to tell you."

There wasn't much to get ready. She and Robbie dragged his sofa into the dining room, moved the coffee table against the wall, and pulled two chairs to face each other in front of the fireplace. Simple. There was no need to give a tour of her home because they weren't in her home, and Robbie's was so beach-casual she thought she might not even have to wear shoes. She hadn't packed—they'd left in such a hurry—so she borrowed sweats and a T-shirt to wear while she threw her own clothes in the wash and ran to the drugstore for civilian makeup and hair products.

Evelyn arrived amid a flurry of crew, cords, cameras, and complaints. "I thought you were kidding about Oregon."

"Why would I kid about Oregon?"

"It's like a snow globe here."

"It's eighty-three degrees."

"You know what I mean. It's all kitsch and sand and fudge shops." Evelyn ran her hands over her hair and suit. "I don't belong here."

"True," India agreed. "So let's see what we can do to get you elsewhere as soon as possible."

An hour later, India took a deep breath, held it, let it out slowly. Then she stepped onto the stage that was Robbie Brighton's rearranged living room and found her light. She was ready. She had only had the morning to prepare, but really she had had a lifetime to prepare. She looked at the assembly before her—Evelyn, the film crew, all the accoutrements required to make television—and at the one behind that, her family, fidgety and awkward and wide-ranging and there. She winked at Fig who winked back with her whole face.

India opened her mouth and delivered her opening line. "Thank you so much for being here, Evelyn, and for joining me for this conversation."

"It's my pleasure, India. Thank you for having me and for welcoming us"—Evelyn turned toward her camera—"welcoming *all* of us into your"—the smallest of pauses—"cozy vacation home this afternoon."

"It's just a friend's house," India demurred.

"We're thrilled you decided to sit down at last for a heart-to-heart," Evelyn rushed on. "I know everyone watching is eager to hear from you in your own words. Shall we start at the beginning?"

"Sure," India agreed amiably. "Let's talk eggs and sperm." Evelyn laughed, which India held for—she was a professional, after all—but she wasn't kidding. "Kids want to know how their families came to be. Kids want to know how they were made. This is what we tell them. Eggs and sperm. When mommies and daddies love each other. Et cetera."

Evelyn fake-clutched her fake pearls. "Are you saying that's not what we should be telling them?"

"I'm saying it's a story for children. We tell it because it simplifies something complicated, generalizes something diverse, sidesteps something complex." She paused for effect, then added, "Sanitizes something gross."

Evelyn laughed again and wrinkled her nose obligingly. "Surely that's appropriate for children."

"Of course. Unfortunately, you're an adult. I'm an adult. The real story is complex and contradictory and, yeah, sometimes messy. It doesn't fit into a post or a paragraph or a thirty-second clip."

"And what is that real story?"

"It's that families get formed in all sorts of ways, ways that sometimes have nothing to do with eggs and sperm, at least not the eggs and sperm you live with. It's that families also look all sorts of ways and are made up of all sorts of people and still count as family. It's more complicated than 'Mommy and Daddy fell in love and made a baby,' but that's okay. Life *is* complicated. And, if we're lucky, long. We have room and time to tell and to listen to complicated stories."

"Well that's why we're here, isn't it? To listen. Though I have to say, it's you who's been, shall we say, a little coy?" Evelyn chuckled to suggest this was all in good fun.

"Me? Coy?"

"Here you are, a woman who enters our living rooms every week, star of stage and screens large and small, who's graced the covers of a hundred magazines, whose every move generates hundreds of thousands of reactions on social media"—Evelyn paused, and India braced herself—"yet it turns out you've been keeping, frankly, shocking secrets."

"I do not enter your living room every week," India said. "That's Val. She's not me. She's got magic. I have to make do without it. She has superhuman strength, whereas I only have the regular kind and some mornings not even that, I'm afraid. Her story's make-believe but pretty straightforward. Mine's quite a bit harder to understand."

"You didn't tell us about the two babies you gave birth to as a single teenager then gave up for adoption because it was hard to understand?"

"Among other reasons, yes."

"What were the others? Perhaps regret? Even shame?"

India took a beat so that she didn't shout, *The other reasons were it's none of your goddamn business!* on television. "I am neither ashamed nor regretful. In fact, being pregnant was one of the best things—two of the best things—I ever did. By any measure."

"It wasn't terrible to give those babies up?"

"It was not," India said. "There were tears on all sides, certainly. There was sorrow and heartache and loss. But there was also joy and solace and wonder.

That was true with the babies I gave birth to and then placed for adoption. It was also true when I became a mother myself."

"Indeed," Evelyn drawled, "you are very pro-adoption, a process most of the people involved in one—and I'm including birth parents, adoptive parents, and children here—consider a last resort, an imperfect way out of worse circumstances that one therefore settles for."

"I think you're wrong about that, Evelyn. Either that or responsible for it."

"Me?" Evelyn's fingertips pawed her chest incredulously.

"It's true, adoption is sometimes a last resort. It's true it's sometimes settled for and worse. But to suggest—to insist—that this is always true, that it's true by definition, not only does a great disservice to all of those children and birth parents and adoptive parents you mentioned, it perpetuates that harm."

"How so?"

"Because constantly telling families they were settled for is one of the things that makes them undesirable. Plus, it's not true. For example, I did not settle for adoption. I chose it. In fact, I chose it three times. The media doesn't talk very much about those stories, but that doesn't mean they don't exist. Lots of people choose adoption for lots of reasons."

"Not the children."

"Not the children," India allowed, "although, as the most capable parent I know recently pointed out, that's true for children raised by their biological parents too. Most kids didn't choose the parents they got, and lots of them wouldn't have. Some adopted kids are misunderstood, unsupported, even maltreated, certainly enraged by their parents. But that's also true for some kids being raised by the parents they were born to. Unfortunately, some parents suck."

"Or perhaps are inexperienced," Evelyn hedged. Or maybe she just wanted the transition. "The first time you got pregnant you were only sixteen. A child yourself."

"Yes."

"You were so young. You must have been frightened and overwhelmed."

"I was."

"For many young women in that situation, the choice to terminate the pregnancy would be the obvious one."

"True." India imagined Ajax on his couch making frantic hand motions begging her to embellish a little bit, but Evelyn had stopped asking questions.

"Especially since it was a choice you were lucky enough to have when so many women do not."

"It wasn't luck," India said. "Abortion is a right. You have the right to rights. You don't get them because you're lucky. You get them because you're a human alive in the world."

"And yet you did not have one."

"Two, in fact," India corrected. "Abortion is the right choice for many people. I did not happen to be one of them. I'd point out this is true of adoption as well. It's not the right choice for everyone, but that doesn't mean it's not the right choice for anyone. It doesn't mean everyone involved in one has settled for it. Nor, for that matter, does choosing it negate all those tears I spoke of earlier."

"Some people would consider tears to be a sign of lamentation, proof that adoption is, at best, a mixed bag."

"I mean, sure." India waved her hand. "Isn't it always?"

"Adoption?"

"Family."

"My family"—Evelyn put her hand to her chest and looked away from India to the camera—"means the world to me. They're my everything."

"Of course," India agreed. "Everything. They're your most precious people. They tend your most precious people." She met Camille's eyes, then each of the Andrews'. "They're the ones who are there for you, even when they least expect it." She gave Davis the smile that was his alone. "They're the ones who sign up to help, happily, even after so many years." Robbie winked at her, and her breath caught. "On the other hand"—her eyes did not leave Robbie's—"family is a pain in the ass."

He grinned.

Evelyn looked like she'd stumbled off script, so India helped her out. "You know this, Evelyn." She turned to the camera again. "You all know this. We don't make a secret of it. Does anyone think of family and say, 'Now there's an easy and uncomplicated set of relationships'?"

"I suppose not," Evelyn admitted.

"This is true about children too, I'm afraid." India indicated hers with her chin and raised her eyebrows to Camille, who steered all four kids outside. India watched through Robbie's slider as Jack tried to fly off the deck using two empty pizza boxes as wings. It was only a couple feet off the ground, but the kids were all shrieking anyway while Camille and the Andrews waved at the throng of high-powered microphones in the living room and frantically shushed them. "I'm sure yours are innocent and lovely and wholly cherished, Evelyn. Mine too, of course." Jack was now using the boxes to whack Fig and Lewis. Bex appeared to be giving thanks she was an only child. "But kids are also exhausting, often frustrating, sometimes infuriating. Always time- and energy- and soul-consuming, all-consuming really. That's what's supposed to happen, but let's not pretend there aren't going to be tears."

"So just so we all understand," Evelyn leaned in, "you're pro-children, pro-family, pro-choice, pro-abortion, pro-adoption. You're even pro—*Flower Child*, concerns about which are what kicked off this whole mess. With all due respect, that feels a little too upbeat to believe."

India laughed out loud. "I'm pretty sure that's the first time I have ever been accused of being upbeat."

"It wasn't an accusation." Evelyn laughed too. "Just an invitation. This is a tell-all. You don't have to be pro-everything. It's okay to be embarrassed, chagrined, even distressed by some of the decisions you made when you were sixteen."

"Most of them, even," India allowed.

"Whereas it seems like you're trying to convince us all that you're perfectly happy with how everything turned out. Given limitless options, this is what you'd have chosen for yourself and all these people you call your family. The children you gave birth to are just as happy with their adoptive parents as they would be with you and their real fathers. Your adopted children are just as happy with you as they would have been with their real parents. You're just as happy—"

"Yes," India interrupted, because it seemed like Evelyn might unspool this thread forever and because if she used the word "real" one more time, India was going to say things she shouldn't on television. "That's right. I consider my family to be equal. I consider families formed by adoption to be equally strong and equally wonderful and equally worthy and, if you like, equally complicated and fraught as families formed exclusively by biology."

"But that's not always true, is it? AHAM's point, which you agreed was a good one, was that there's a lot of trauma associated with adoption for a lot of people."

"This is true," India said. "It's traumatic for some people to have babies. It's traumatic for some people to have abortions. It's traumatic for some people to be involved in adoption from any side of that equation you like. It's traumatic for some people to be with their families, biological or otherwise. I agree with all of that."

"But?"

"But I do not agree that adoptive families necessarily suffer any more trauma than any other kind. I do not agree that they are always settled for, or options of last resort, or, by definition, less than. I do not believe they are not 'real.'"

"So where does that leave us, India Allwood? It seems like you've admitted everything and nothing, and while I don't think anyone thinks you did anything wrong, per se, I also don't think those you've offended will be mollified. When you tried to apologize earlier this week, it did not go well. Now that you've had some more time, as well as everyone's attention, is there anything you'd maybe like to add?"

"Yes," India said. "Thank you for asking. One of the things family is famous for is giving unsolicited advice, telling you things you'd rather not hear but need to, providing the perspective only the people who've known you best and longest can. A member of mine offered words of wisdom yesterday that I think were all of the above: first love. He was right. And he's in a position to know. Therefore, effective immediately, with sorrow and heartache and with wonder and joy, I am heartbroken and delighted to announce my immediate retirement."

Like a sore loser, Evelyn Esponson gathered up her crew and her equipment and left, but India knew she was ecstatic. She had reason to be. That interview would live on the internet forever. India went upstairs to shower off the makeup, the hairspray, the interview, the whole week if she could. Then she pulled Robbie's T-shirt and sweatpants back on and emerged damp and new-made to talk to the only people whose opinions in all this actually mattered.

"So," Camille said, "what's the plan?"

"Mom." Bex rolled her eyes. "It's been thirty minutes. She doesn't know yet."

"Plans precede their declaration, Rebecca." It was the first time India had heard Camille call her daughter that in sixteen years. "It's been thirty minutes since she announced it. It hasn't been thirty minutes since she thought of it."

Not thirty, no, but not so many more. The heart wants what the heart wants, however. When you know, you know. Or maybe it's more that you recognize your loves when they come again. When you've had them and let them go and they return, you grab on for dear life.

Bex stopped looking smug at her mother and started looking smug at India and Robbie instead. "On the other hand, I guess you *have* had sixteen years."

"To what?" said Robbie.

"To realize you were still in love. That's what you meant, right?" she said to India. "First love? You two are getting back together?"

India's hair was still wet on the back of her neck. She looked at Robbie and smiled. "You were my first love," she agreed.

"And you were mine." Robbie laughed his Robbie laugh, and she was sixteen again. She felt the years roll away in her chest. "On the *other* other hand"—he smiled at Bex—"maybe it's you. First love, first born."

"I'm not returning her." Camille held a hand to her heart. "My baby."

"Eww, Mom." Bex rolled her eyes. "I'm not a baby."

"Actually," said Camille, "I might be willing to negotiate."

"Duh, it's us," said Jack, and India felt his confidence, the fact that he knew it for sure, spark joy in her toes that moved all the way through her. "Me and Fig. She loves us first."

But Fig said, "Temporarily." A body blow.

"Always," India corrected her at once. "Always and forever."

"No, like you meant first in time," Fig explained, "not rank."

Ahh. "Temporally," India said.

"Robbie and Bex are her first loves temporally," Fig informed her brother. "We're her first loves rankly."

India let that one go, never mind how apt it was.

"It could be Davis," Lewis piped up. "No offense," he said to Bex.

"It's not Battle of the Bio Dads." Bex rolled her eyes again. Maybe still. Bex rolled her eyes still.

"They look at each other the gross way my dads look at each other."

Andy made shushing motions with his hands. Drew pulled the mask part of Lewis's cape up over his mouth. India looked at Davis the way Andy looked at Drew. Davis looked at India the way Drew looked at Andy. It was several long moments before she could speak again, and she had once done the last three acts of *Macbeth* in tears, tears occasioned by this very love, these very loves.

When she could trust her voice to hold, she informed them, "You're all wrong. You're all right, but you're all wrong."

"Actually"—Camille cleared her throat—"when I asked what the plan was, I didn't mean India's retirement plan. I just meant dinner."

Robbie took Lewis and Bex into the garden to harvest vegetables. Fig and Jack found paper and colored pencils, all these years later still drawing comfort in homemade menus. Davis and the Andrews went to the store for bread and cheese and wine. Camille scouted the pasta situation and started sauce. India made dough and rolled it out. Being with Robbie Brighton gave her cravings for pie. The kids set the table, even folding napkins into blobs you might have called birds if you were feeling generous, even filling a mason jar with rosemary and lavender they picked by leaning over the side of the deck, even finding candlesticks and an electric lighter Robbie pretended was a wand and taking turns using it to light the candles. Even Fig.

"A toast." Robbie raised his glass when they were all assembled. His house was small but somehow had space for everyone, like Mary Poppins's carry-on bag. Through what could only be some similar sorcery, India looked around the table and found her family, nearly all of it, nearly all her loves, together. "To all of you," Robbie said. "Welcome."

"Us," India corrected. "And I think we can do better than that."

"I cede the stage to you." Robbie bowed and swept his arm toward India. His right sleeve caught one of the candlesticks and knocked it over, but he caught it with his other hand and flipped it back up without the flame even going out. Everyone burst into applause.

Almost everyone.

At the other end of the table, Fig leaped up. Her legs got tangled in her chair, which clattered to the tiles behind her with a crash that shook the room. She was ashen and wild-eyed, but mostly what she was was out of reach. India had felt only the slightest tug when Fig chose to sit next to Bex instead of her, but now the other side of the table seemed very far away. She considered all the people between her and her daughter and decided to crawl underneath.

But before she could, Bex righted Fig's chair and pulled her back down next to her. She put her arm around her. "I got you, girl."

India could see Fig shaking, chattering almost. The blood was gone from her lips. Her mouth was open but no sound came out, just too fast, too shallow breath.

India leaned over and blew out the candles.

Fig's eyes cut from her mother to Bex to the smoke curling slowly toward the ceiling to the overfull table and back again.

Bex tightened her arm around Fig. She waited till Fig's eyes found hers again and winked. She smiled at her.

And slowly, still panting a little, Fig smiled waveringly back.

India eyed her daughter across the table. "You okay?"

A deep breath, the deepest. "I'm okay."

"Sure?"

Fig nodded once and then some more. "Sure." Her color was slowly coming back. She snuggled closer to Bex under her arm and said quietly, "That was only like the fifth-scariest thing that happened this week."

Bex beamed at her. "And seriously, did you see those reflexes? Why do I suck so much at sports?"

And everyone laughed. Even Fig.

"Since you're standing . . ." Robbie prompted eventually. India's eyes found his, but she had no idea what the end of his sentence was. "You were going to improve on my toast?"

She'd forgotten about the toast. She cleared her throat and let that sharp, razored feeling that was the hallmark of motherhood ribbon up and away like the smoke. "Fig's right. It's been a scary week." An understatement and an inauspicious start for a toast.

"Hear, hear." Lewis banged on the table anyway.

"Not yet," Drew leaned over to whisper.

"But I've learned some things," India kept on, "and I'd like to offer you all an apology. Maybe more than one. I'd like to offer you all some apologies."

Lewis pulled down the mask part of his cape. "We forgive you. For what?"

"You"—Lewis was seated next to her, so she put a hand on his shoulder—"and you"—she nodded to Bex across the table—"so wanted to know me and Fig and Jack, to know your biological fathers, to know each other—"

"I didn't know he existed," Bex interrupted.

"So wanted or maybe didn't even know you so wanted," India continued, "that you, Bex, sneaked out of your house and onto an airplane all by yourself well before the crack of dawn, even though you knew you'd get in trouble."

"Not that much trouble." Bex shrugged.

"That much trouble," Camille corrected.

"That you flew across the country on the flimsiest of excuses," India said to Lewis and his fathers.

"Not that flimsy!" Fig insisted.

"Or climbed into the car of a stranger who used the term 'baby daddy.'" She raised her eyebrows into her hairline at Davis.

"That was pretty flimsy," he admitted.

"Or welcomed your high school girlfriend's college boyfriend into your home like . . ."

"Like family," Robbie supplied.

"Or walked through the night and made yourselves invisible to ride four buses for two days over a thousand miles fueled by nothing but faith."

"So we didn't have to use the bathroom on the bus," Jack explained.

"And I'm sorry. It shouldn't have been that hard. I wanted you to bond with your mom, with your dads. I wanted you to be theirs and them to be yours, one hundred percent. Two buts, though. But what I wanted wasn't the only important thing. But I didn't know what I was talking about."

"Sixteen-year-olds are dumbasses," Bex said.

"Thank you." India thought this was meant to be comforting. "It's true that I chose this family, this kind of family, but I was lucky already when I did. I was lucky that I could. Not everyone would, but more than that, not everyone can, not even all of you. I'm sorry I thought you'd want space and privacy over answers and connection. I'm sorry I didn't know how to tell the whole world how lucky and grateful and proud I am."

"If you'd let us on social media—" Jack began.

"I'm sorry you ever thought I was ashamed. I was the opposite. But I'm a mother. Protecting you—all of you—is my first job. I'm glad to know you both." She looked from Lewis to Bex and back again. "I'm glad to have you know us, all of us, and to have the world know about you. But mostly, Fig is right. More is more. Family doesn't take away from family. Family begets family. That's how family works."

"What's 'begets'?" Jack leaned over to ask Andy.

Andy bent and whispered in his ear.

"Gross," said Jack.

"I thought we were special"—India opened her arms, her hands—"but I was wrong about that."

"I'm damn special," Jack said.

"You are damn special, baby." She kissed the top of his head. "But that's not what I meant. Before this week, I knew we were family even though we were a different kind of family, not just knew it, insisted on it, that families come in all kinds, varied as leaves. What I learned this week, though, is we aren't just a different kind of family. We're also the same kind of family."

"Cheesy?" said Bex.

"Among other things, yes"—India nodded—"which makes it hard to talk about. It's too trite. It's too timeworn. Family is age-old, but so is adoption. And our family is beyond explanation."

"'Baby daddy' is a pretty clear explanation," Bex said.

"Not 'beyond explanation' like it's unclear." India was undeterred. "'Beyond explanation' like the explanation is just the beginning. We are beyond explanation, well beyond, out in the open ocean, out among the stars."

Her voice broke, but that was fine. She'd said what she needed to say. She'd said it to all of them together, all at once, a luxury. She knew too, though, that she didn't need to say everything tonight. There would be other nights. There would be other dinner tables with these people gathered around. They were entangled, not like extension cords you'd thrown in a pile in the garage and when you needed one you had to spend forty-five minutes unknotting it from the others first. They were entangled like fibers woven into threads spun into yarn knit into patches bound into quilts worn into heirlooms, something to pass down, to pass on, to inherit.

Davis met her too-bright eyes and swollen smile. "To being beyond explanation," he said, and everyone raised their glasses to that, and India's weren't the only eyes that were wet.

She took one of the extra menus her kids had made—her own, she'd save for the rest of her life—and tore it into tiny pieces, which she cupped in both hands for a moment before flinging skyward. Her family watched the pieces flutter down and settle, more like snow than confetti, and considered all there was to celebrate, not least that India had extinguished the candles before showering the table with paper.

"Now what?" said Camille.

"God, Mom, stop asking that." Bex rolled her eyes so hard India worried they wouldn't come down.

"Rebecca India Eaney, you are in enough trouble already without adding rude, insolent, and uncommonly irritating to the list of infractions."

Everyone hushed.

"You named her after your grandmother," India whispered.

"My grandmother and you." Camille smiled. "And when I said, 'Now what?' I only meant dessert."

"Oh." India remembered, and wiped her eyes. "I made pie."

She got a standing ovation, not her first, but also not her last. Or maybe her family was just getting up to clear the table.

FOR IMMEDIATE RELEASE

Two Sarahs Productions, the new venture of Broadway veteran India Allwood and newcomer Dakota Day, is proud to announce the transfer of its inaugural show, *Family Family*, following a sold-out run at the SoHo Playhouse, to Broadway's Lyceum Theatre. The play, in which the two co-producers and onetime college roommates also costar, is written and directed by Ms. Allwood and loosely based on her own family's stories surrounding adoption. Of her triumphant return to the New York stage and the much anticipated transfer to Broadway, Ms. Allwood said, "There is something about your first love you never forget or let go of. I am lucky to have found my way home."

Tickets now on sale.

AUTHOR'S NOTE

About three years into our marriage, my husband and I decided, as people often do, that we wanted to be parents. We had no reason to believe I wouldn't get pregnant if we tried the usual way. Nonetheless, we didn't. Instead, we decided to adopt. There were lots of reasons for this, a few of which I can even articulate: We thought there were a lot of children in the world already. We knew some of them needed parents. We looked into our hearts in that way you do when making big decisions and saw no barrier to loving a child to whom we weren't biologically related. We read and researched and talked to people and considered all the challenges put to us by various experienced professionals, and we believed those challenges were ones we could successfully navigate and help a child successfully navigate as well.

Other reasons are harder to explain. Like most reproductive choices, ours were entirely personal. Telling about them always feels like something of an overshare, TMI, like if I asked how much sex you had in your third trimester or what position you used the time you conceived.

What I can most simply and honestly say is it was not a decision at which we arrived lightly, but after much research and groundwork and soul-searching, one summer day late in the aughts, my husband and I started the paperwork that would lead—exactly nine months later, as it happened—to our daughter becoming our daughter. In between, we undertook all the usual parent-to-be projects—assembling a crib, installing a car seat, turning my office into a nursery—and some that were more unusual.

I am a white woman. My husband is a white man. Our daughter is Korean.

In addition to all the board-book buying and onesie procuring, we learned the Korean alphabet and some basic conversation and vocabulary. We learned Korean customs, religious and cultural traditions, etiquette, and history. We bought Korean cookbooks and practiced making dishes, sought out Korean music and literature for children and adults, sampled Korean restaurants in our city, made lists of Korean classes offered in our area, noted the dates of Korean festivals and holidays on our calendar, joined playgroups where our daughter would be able to meet other Korean children and other adopted children as well. We wrote pages and pages about what we'd do when our child asked why she didn't look like us, why we'd taken her from her homeland, why she was a different race than her parents, what about her ancestors, whether she was an immigrant, why her birth mother had given her up, what about the rest of her birth family, could she ever meet them, did they ever miss her, why wasn't she adopted in Korea, what would her life have been like there, why was she treated differently when she was with us than without us, why was she treated differently from her classmates. We armed ourselves with books, toys, outfits, artifacts, discussion approaches, philosophies, answers, comforts, solutions, strategies, and supplemental activities. We prepared for the questions she would ask out loud and the ones she might have but be unable or unwilling to voice. We prepared for these questions and the ones they would beget and the ones after that and the ones after that.

She asked none of them. Instead her question (as loyal readers, bless you, will recall) was why we kept saying she was a boy when in fact she was a girl.

As I have been at pains to point out elsewhere, this was surprising at first, but in fact I think is just the way it is when you're someone's parent, no matter how that relationship came to be. If you're lucky, if you can, you prepare for what you think will come up. What actually does is almost guaranteed to be something else entirely. Parenting turns out not to be something you can research in advance like hotels for an upcoming vacation, but because we want, more than anything, to do all we can for our children and soon-to-be-children, we do it anyway.

This is one of many reasons representation matters. As Bex points out, however, the problem with adoption is not lack of representation but bullshit representation. Literature is lousy with orphans. In fact, there are loads of adoptive families in books for all audiences and indeed in all media. Adoptive families are used so often as both topic and plot point, I didn't even notice until I became a member of one myself. But that representation almost always falls into two categories: the tragic or the tragic-then-miraculous.

In the former category, we get adopted children who are alone, abused, neglected, or violently misunderstood by their adoptive families. We get birth mothers who begin their stories in ruin then fall further because they've been forced to give up their children. We find adoptive parents who cannot love children who aren't really theirs.

In the latter category, the miraculous one, we get stories where families are threatened with but ultimately saved from the horrors of adoption. So: orphans or adopted children who overcome endless adversity to find their way back home to biological families who were waiting for them all along, birth mothers who magically recognize and joyfully reunite with babies they placed for adoption three decades before, troubled adoptive parents and troubled adopted children who at first do not but eventually, against terrible odds, learn to love each other.

Invariably, the stories include tremendous hardship, overcome in the case of the miraculous stories, succumbed to in the tragedies. That depiction of hardship, the challenges faced by members of adoptive families, is good and necessary. It's important to talk about the many reasons a person might have a baby they are unable or unwilling to raise, and about just how hard and terrible are the limited options that come next. It's important to talk about the heartbreak of people who want to be parents but cannot, again for any number of reasons, get (or stay) pregnant. It's important to talk about the ways love is *not* all an adopted child needs, what those other needs are, how they can best be met. It's important to talk about the challenges many adopted kids face beyond the challenges all kids face.

These are important stories. But they are not the only stories. Representation matters not just because it matters that you see yourself in the world but because it matters that you see yourself *positively* in the world. Representation matters because it matters that you see not-yourself—people who are unlike you, families that are unlike yours, possibilities you hadn't thought of yet—and it matters that you see not-yourself positively too.

In fiction and nonfiction, books and television, movies and plays, even in musicals, the people in adoptive families resort to adoption because they have no other choice. Lacking any other option, they settle for it and, at best, make do with inferior circumstances, the lesser of some number of evils. But my family is not an evil. It is not inferior or settled for. And I think adoption wouldn't be so many people's last resort if we stopped insisting that it was one. The choices I made—joyfully, ardently—are rarely considered a possibility. They are rarely even considered choices.

Adoptive families aren't always loving, nurturing, healthy, harmonious, or able to meet the needs of all of their members. This is because they are families. I don't know you. I don't know anything about your life. But I still know this: your family is complicated. That's not falling short of the standard. That *is* the standard. The argument I am forever trying to put into words and build stories around is that wider ranges of "normal" make the world a better place for everyone. Which is to say, your strange family isn't strange. It's just a family. Some days I feel staggering awe and gratitude at being part of an adoptive one. Some days instead I feel frazzled by math homework and flute practice and carpool and extracurricular activities scheduled five minutes and fifteen miles apart during which we must stop for pizza or risk starvation. In other words: harried and hectic, sublime and exalted, entangled and blessed. And remarkably—though also entirely unremarkably—normal.

This story is fiction (I am not a movie star; I *love* musical theater) because I am a novelist. My job is to make things up in order to tell the truth. It is to use old stories to tell new ones. It is to uncover what we share across great divides and ferret out where difference is cast as shameful or deficient, where custom masquerades as natural and normal. I did not write this book to deny the trauma, sadness, challenges, or systemic failures surrounding some adoptions. I wrote it to add another note to the cacophony, another entry to the manifest, another family to the canon. Another way to be—and be normal—in this life. We need more stories (and all their complexities), more voices (and all their contradictions). I wrote this one to say: Us too. We're family too. And we wouldn't do it differently for anything.

ACKNOWLEDGMENTS

In matters of bookmaking, it is hard to make "thank you" mean all it must. But I will try.

Thank you to Molly Friedrich. Your own book about your own adoptive family is what led me to you in the first place. I will always be grateful to you for that and roughly eighty billion other things.

Thank you to Amy Einhorn. You are better at your job than anyone I know. I am lucky to have you as my editor, but also I am lucky to count you as my friend.

Thank you to Lucy Carson for doing all you do and doing it so well and so warmly and with such admirable power and good humor.

Thank you to a truly all-star publishing/cheerleading team: Lori Kusatzky, Micaela Carr, Caitlin O'Shaughnessy, Clarissa Long, Laura Flavin, Sonja Flancher, Chris O'Connell, Jason Reigal, Christopher Sergio, Steven Seighman, Janel Brown, Emily Walters, Flora Esterly, Bonnie Simcock, Scottie Bowditch, and Conor Mintzer, and extra well-punctuated thanks to Jolanta Benal for copyediting that was always excellent and occasionally mind-blowing. I learned a lot.

Thank you to Marin Takikawa, Heather Carr, Dana Spector, Stephen Susco, Bridget Foley, and Kelsey Day.

I started this book at Ragdale artists' residency, which means thanks are due to Ragdale and especially to Hannah Judy Gretz, whose incredible generosity and out-of-the-blue kindness brought me there. Alas, one week into a scheduled three-week retreat, that residency, this book, and the whole entire rest of the world were derailed by global pandemic, and so that week and the people I met during it held me up through all that came next.

Thank you to my own family family and early readers: Sue and Dave Frankel, Erin Trendler, and Lisa Corr. Thank you as always, but special thanks this time, to Dani. Myself, I won the family lottery.

And, also always and forever, thank you to Paul Mariz. You are all of the above: early reader (and late and everything in between), editor, cheerleader, consultant, best friend, best family, and favorite one.

ABOUT THE AUTHOR

Laurie Frankel is the *New York Times* bestselling, award-winning author of novels such as *The Atlas of Love, Goodbye for Now, One Two Three*, and the Reese's Book Club x Hello Sunshine Book Pick *This Is How It Always Is*. Frankel lives in Seattle with her husband, daughter, and border collie. She makes good soup.